Praise for *The Golems of Gotham*

"[An] inventive and electrifying epic. . . . [Rosenbaum] adds art to ambition and intellect in this dazzling novel, writing in language so lively it practically bubbles off the page like an ancient potion." —*Boston Globe*

"Appealing. . . . *The Golems of Gotham* is also a complex novel. Rosenbaum has a fluent style that can pivot and change direction on a single word, and the novel is rich in detail and vignette." —*New York Times Book Review*

"A vivid sense of how the Holocaust, far from being a discrete and completed event, is an open wound in the Jewish psyche. . . . Rosenbaum writes something strong and true." —*Washington Post*

"A book at once magical and natural. . . . Rosenbaum's novel is at once chilling and warm, rigorous and fanciful, savagely witty and profoundly reasoned. *The Golems of Gotham* charms as it frightens and moves us, and shows a novelist moving into the fullness of his imaginative capacity." —*San Francisco Chronicle*

"Hilarious. . . . More touching than tragic, more absurd than abject. . . . Very funny and a joy to read. . . . Comparisons to Michael Chabon's brilliant *The Amazing Adventures of Kavalier and Clay* are unavoidable. . . . Written in an offhand, approachable prose that's full of lyrical pyrotechnics. . . . With compelling characters, both dead and alive, prose that captures your attention but keeps you rooted in the story, [and] serious issues addressed amid humor and fantasy, *The Golems of Gotham* is eminently readable, deeply personal, and surprisingly satisfying." —*Denver Post*

"The humor of the novel is balanced against a constant sense of outrage." —*New York* magazine

"Stunning." —*Miami Herald*

"Intriguing. . . . Entertaining." —*Publishers Weekly*

"A wonderful fantasy. . . . Demonstrates a brilliant imagination blended with justified rage." —*South Florida Sun-Sentinel*

"Mr. Rosenbaum's novel is filled with wonderful comic invention . . . but there is a much more serious point hiding behind Mr. Rosenbaum's high jinks. . . . If the novel is filled with the fantastical, it is also just as full of the prophetic, and it is the latter that resonates long after the leaps of a very playful imagination have receded. No review can do justice to the richness packed into the 367 pages of *The Golems of Gotham*. I found myself rereading whole sections for the shape and ring of their paragraphs, as well as the sheer emotional power packed into every catalogue, every observation of the world."

—*Forward*

"*The Golems of Gotham* is a big, risk-taking work of Jewish imagination. . . . The golems, post-Holocaust Peter Pans, bring a kind of *Miracle on 34th Street* paradisaic ambience to New York. . . . Rosenbaum enchantingly harnesses some of this dream magic to create a haunting and disturbing ghost drama, exploring themes that thoughtful people continually confront."

—*Moment* magazine

"Rosenbaum's most ambitious work yet."

—*Jewish Bulletin of Northern California*

"A miraculous, cautionary new tale about the twentieth century's defining event. . . . Astonishing, one of the best novels of the year."　　　　　　　　　　　　　　—AnnistonStar.com

"Writing with trouble in mind and sulfur in his pen, *[The Golems of Gotham]* seems a riotous marriage of bitter wisdom and urgent magic. . . . What you look for is the kind of poetry, the music a writer can make of his nightmares. . . . Rosenbaum shows that he can reach into the primal, wordless core of an emotion—into the lava of disaster—and raise the hair on the back of our necks."

—*Buffalo News*

"A mesmerizing novel of imagination, philosophy, tragedy, and humor. . . . It is difficult to exaggerate the impact of this original and courageous book. . . . With his popular language and imagery, [Rosenbaum] tackles seriously weighty themes: cynicism, retribution, healing, Jewish tradition, cultural memory, and rage. Everyone should read this important book."

—*Emunah* magazine

"*The Golems of Gotham* . . . embodies the hopeless longing of contemporary Jews to resurrect a past annihilated by the Holocaust. . . . Rosenbaum has fun putting these ghosts through their paces and inflicting them, poltergeist fashion, on contemporary New York City." —*Slate* magazine

"Thane Rosenbaum has broken new ground in *The Golems of Gotham*. It is, like Jewish experience itself, both heartrending and ecstatic, a work of magic realism that descends into the pit of Holocaust memory while still casting its gaze upward toward a vision of beauty and redemption. *The Golems of Gotham* represents a significant advance not only in Rosenbaum's development as an artist, but in the entire genre of post-Holocaust fiction."
—Rebecca Goldstein, author of *Properties of Light*

"A brilliant novel of ideas. A great romp. A work that plumbs the nature of loss and suffering like no other. An unavoidable and unforgettable book." —Daniel Jonah Goldhagen, author of *Hitler's Willing Executioners*

"Thane Rosenbaum gives the idea of ghost writer a whole new meaning. Funny and fearless, he has conjured the departed masters of Holocaust memory, marched them down Broadway, and turned all of Manhattan into the haunted head of a tormented Jewish writer." —Jonathan Rosen, author of *Eve's Apple* and *The Talmud and the Internet: A Journey Between Worlds*

"From the darkest and most complex source, Thane Rosenbaum has fashioned a surprisingly entertaining novel."
—John Turturro

"In the face of unfathomable loss and abandonment, Rosenbaum conjures plural golems as a rescue team for a self-absorbed and lost world, and gives us a profound, humorous, irreverent book of life—made all the more affecting by recent events in Gotham. What Job may have written if he had a wry sense of humor." —Chaim Potok

"A darkly comic ghost story that invokes the full horror of the Holocaust—only to liberate us from it. Rosenbaum's *The Golems of Gotham* is ingenious, fast-paced, and—most surprisingly—fun."
—John Sedgwick, author of *The Dark House*

Keni Fine

About the Author

THANE ROSENBAUM is the author of *Second Hand Smoke* and *Elijah Visible*, which received the Edward Lewis Wallant Book Award in 1996 for the best book of Jewish-American fiction. His articles, reviews, and essays appear frequently in the *New York Times*, the *Los Angeles Times*, and the *Wall Street Journal*. He teaches human rights, legal humanities, and law and literature at Fordham Law School. Rosenbaum lives in New York City with his daughter, Basia Tess.

ALSO BY THANE ROSENBAUM

Second Hand Smoke

Elijah Visible

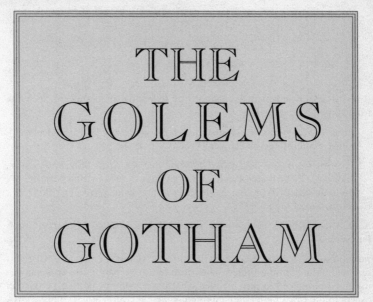

THE
GOLEMS
OF
GOTHAM

THANE
ROSENBAUM

Perennial

An Imprint of HarperCollins*Publishers*

FOR BASIA TESS

Grateful acknowledgment is made to the following for permission to quote from copyrighted material:

From "Indoor Fireworks" by Elvis Costello. Copyright © 1985 by Sideways Songs, administered by Plangent Visions Music, Inc.

Excerpts from *The Little Red Lighthouse and the Great Gray Bridge* by Hildegarde H. Swift and Lynd Ward, copyright © 1942 by Harcourt, Inc., and renewed 1970 by Hildegarde H. Swift and Lynd Ward, reprinted by permission of the publisher.

A hardcover edition of this book was published in 2002 by HarperCollins Publishers.

HarperCollins books may be purchased for educational, business, or sales promotional use. For information please write: Special Markets Department, HarperCollins Publishers Inc., 10 East 53rd Street, New York, NY 10022.

First Perennial edition published 2003.

Designed by Phil Mazzone

Illustrations by Judd Palmer

The Library of Congress has catalogued the hardcover edition as follows:
Rosenbaum, Thane.
    The Golems of Gotham / by Thane Rosenbaum.—1st ed.
      p.   cm.
    ISBN 0-06-018490-6
    1. Jews—New York (State)—New York—Fiction. 2. Manhattan (New York, NY)—Fiction. 3. Holocaust survivors—Fiction. 4. Jewish families—Fiction. 5. Writer's block—Fiction. 6. Authors—Fiction. I. Title.

PS3568.O782 G6 2002
813'.54—dc21   2001039439

ISBN 0-06-095945-2 (pbk.)

03 04 05 06 07 ❖/RRD 10 9 8 7 6 5 4 3 2 1

ACKNOWLEDGMENTS

≈

WITH THE DEEPEST GRATITUDE TO SO MANY PEOPLE WHO MADE IT possible, and necessary, for me to live, and write and love, who were so generous in so many unending ways, who gave me more than a second thought even when my own thoughts went elsewhere, who watched over me when I neglected myself, and whom I can never repay, not with these words or with anything else, because the spiritual currency they keep is superior to the company I offer.

My editor, Julia Serebrinsky, and my agent, Ellen Levine.

And the extended family.

Paul and Judy Berkman, Sandee Brawarsky, Marcelo Bronstein, Janet Burstein, Heather Case, Sam Dubbin, Joe Feshbach, Keni Fine, Eva Fogelman, Cristina Garcia, Danny Goldhagen, Thomas Hameline, Vered Hankin, Andrew Hartzell, Tracey Hughes, Marcie Hershman, Annette Insdorf, Carolyn Jackson, Myrna Kirkpatrick, Andy Kovler, Barbara Nuddle, Ellen Pall, Brett Paul, Paula Rackoff, Carol and Seymour Sarnoff, Brenda Segel, Nina Solomon, Irene Speiser, David Stern, Aryeh Lev Stollman, Ivan Strausz, John Thomas, Robert Weil, Paul Martin Weltz, and Susan Wolfson.

Much appreciation to Jane Beirn, for her passion in the promotion of this book; Carolyn Philips, for her editorial assistance; and Susan Llewellyn, for showing great soul and heart in copyediting this novel.

Many thanks to Don Walker and Eileen Bernstein of the Harry Walker Agency.

And special gratitude to Menachem Rosensaft, for his extraordinary commitment to the early drafts of this novel, and to Alicia Svigals, who provided the model and music for the violin sequences throughout this book.

A warning to all readers: Please take the labeling of this book as a novel seriously. It is indeed a work of fiction.

While it is true that the writers Primo Levi, Jean Améry, Paul Celan, Piotr Rawicz, Jerzy Kosinski, and Tadeusz Borowski were all Holocaust survivors who ultimately committed suicide, many of the events described in this novel that relate to the pre-suicide lives of the authors, as well as the circumstances of the suicides themselves, did not in fact take place. Similarly, all the writers in this novel are resurrected as ghosts, and it is in this form that they haunt its pages. To the best of my knowledge, this supernatural phenomenon never happened to any of these men, although I wouldn't put it past them—particularly Jerzy.

The effort here is to recruit the imagination into the service of answering the unanswerable, to find some logic in numbers that simply don't add up, to find an acceptable way to respond to so much collective longing, to seek hope and reconciliation in a world that provides so little reason to do so—but yet we must try. The reason is simple: There is no choice other than the one that these writers ultimately settled on, which brought about a loss that was unimaginable, and irreplaceable, for their families and readers. We stand before their suffering with respect and humility, and contemplate the way their loss has compounded our own.

Indoor fireworks
Can still burn your fingers
Indoor fireworks
We swore we were safe as houses
They're not so spectacular
They don't burn up in the sky
But they can dazzle or delight
Or bring a tear
When the smoke gets in your eyes

—Elvis Costello

THE
GOLEMS
OF
GOTHAM

1

 HE WAS CALLED TO THE TORAH, AND BEFORE reciting the blessing he reached into his *tallis* bag, removed the silencer, aimed it at his temple, and pulled the trigger. A Jewish brain shot out from his head and splattered all over the unscrolled sheepskin as though the synagogue had just hosted its first animal sacrifice.

"Lothar!" Rabbi Vered screamed.

Too late. The bullet traveled through the skull at a speed much faster than sound, then lodged itself inside the cantor's pulpit. Within an hour a Miami police detective would dig into the pierced mahogany, retrieve the shell, dust for prints, and search for clues. But there were none. Lothar Levin gave no prior warning that he would take his life in this way. He left no note; the bullet wasn't talking either.

"Huh," the cop, perplexed, said, long after everything had settled down. He held the bullet in the air, picking up the light from a lantern that was poised in front of the Ark. "Never seen this kind of caliber before." The detective squinted. "Who's got the piece?"

Cantor Feldman, still shaken by what had nearly been a ricochet assassination, pinched the gun at the bottom of its handle, making the barrel go limp as it pointed down toward the floor. He then walked it over stiff-arm and handed it to the detective. No one in the synagogue that day, other than the detective, ever wanted to see that gun again.

It wasn't just the sight of the suicide that had unnerved them all. The sound was equally horrible. This experience taught them that the acoustics in the synagogue, which had long been known for elevating the talents of their amateur choir, also had the effect of amplifying a muzzled gunshot. Instead of silence the congregants heard a wail of agony that sounded like a shofar still attached to the ram's head. There was unmuted outrage in the air. And the smoke, which should have vaporized within seconds of leaving the barrel, instead lingered over the *bima* like dark clouds refusing to downpour.

But there was more to it than that; Lothar was only half the story. The fallout from the murder died down just when another commotion was beginning to take shape elsewhere. Shouts and stuttering gasps swelled throughout the sanctuary in the way crowds settle into shock. Everyone seemed to be moving in yawning slow motion as the horror of what they had all just witnessed started to sink in: Murder in a synagogue. But not just murder. It was self-murder, an unritualized, bloody suicide, a cardinal sin for Jews, even among the non-Orthodox. And there wasn't only one casualty, either.

Slowly all eyes shifted to the middle row of the sanctuary, the aisle seat, where Lothar Levin's wife, Rose, usually sat. Her husband had just blown his brains out, in front of the Ark, with the Torah open and God presumably watching. And there she was, dead too, slumped over her lap, eyes closed, the cyanide tablet having already dissolved under her tongue. The coroner would later estimate the time of her death to have coincided roughly with Lothar's more extreme, and violent, end. A dead tie between husband and wife.

A *Shabbos* suicide pact is not exactly what God had in mind for his day of rest. But Lothar and Rose were Holocaust survivors; God would have no say in this matter. He had become irrelevant, a lame-duck divinity, a sham for a savior, a mere caricature of a god who cared. That's the price you pay for arriving late at Auschwitz, or in his case, not at all; you forfeit all future rights to an opinion. Yes, it's true: The taking of a human life is a sin in the eyes of God. But this was a God who had already blinded himself. It mattered little to the Levins whether he approved of what they had done under his watch, and that's why they showed no fear in taking the liberty of poking God's eyes out one last time.

And what about sin? Well, nobody took that seriously anymore either. Another house speciality of Auschwitz. The Nazis had given new meaning to sin, raising the ante on atrocity, showing the world the deluxe model. Original sin seemed puny, and frankly unoriginal, by comparison. Zyklon B was now the ultimate forbidden fruit. Faster-acting, easier on the stomach. All Eve would have had to do was get Adam to inhale, then say Kaddish.

Survivors had the right to do whatever they wanted with their lives. They had earned at least that much. They could live with abandon, or they could simply choose to abandon. The old rules didn't apply, as much as they didn't apply to anyone anymore. That's because the Third Reich had killed off all the old biblical commandments, wiped the tablets clean; the Golden Calf had been the right religion all along. Mankind was left to finish out the century without any moral landmarks and signposts, forced to thrash and stumble about in a new world empty of faith, kindness, and love. And yet, when it all became too much, there were still places of worship that one could turn to—if not for spiritual salvation, then at least as an ideal location for a mercy killing.

Who knows if that's what Lothar and Rose Levin were thinking on that sultry Saturday morning back in October 1980. They had silenced themselves with a riddle that no one was qualified to answer. Why survive the camps only to later commit suicide—together, in concert, without any explanation? Paradoxically they had turned their survival skills—the very life source that had defeated the Nazis— against themselves.

The *Miami Herald* placed the story on the front page of the Sunday paper: HOLOCAUST SURVIVORS SUCCEED IN SHUL SUICIDE. Newspapers across the country carried the story as well. For a brief time the mystery became a spellbinding national obsession. Television cameras traveled down to Miami Beach to record anything that approximated a clue. The *New York Times Magazine* and *The New Yorker* sent their best writers to do think pieces that defied rational thought. So too did *Civilization* and *Psychology Today*. There was no shortage of analysts—from both the media and the kind that charge by an hour that is measured in fifty minutes.

All those who had happened to be in Temple Beth Am, initially as congregants, and finally as mourners, naturally had something to say on the matter. America's long love affair with the eyewitness. But in Miami or elsewhere, no one had an intelligent answer or a plausible theory. The Levin double suicide would fall into that bottomless pit of similarly inscrutable phenomena: Was there a second gunman in the Kennedy assassination, or had Oswald acted alone? Did the Rosenbergs possess actual secrets that they passed onto the Russians? Was Raoul Wallenberg still alive, rotting away in the Soviet gulag? Now there was a new imponderable: What about those two Holocaust survivors in Miami Beach; why did they do it, you know, off themselves after Auschwitz? The Levins had become tragic figures in a world long ago inured to tragedy.

Everyone was stumped. And that perhaps was how it should have been. In the absence of a suicide note, there was no way ever to know. Despair, if nothing else, is a private matter. The mind isn't required to share such information. That's because the soul is the master of its own short-circuitry, the system shutdown, the fading pulse that monitors the brokenness of both spirit and heart. When a state of mind sinks to a point where life itself—the day-to-day engagements, the nightly slumber and silences—becomes unbearable, who are we to second-guess or armchair analyze? There was no way to properly insert oneself inside the minds of the Levins and follow the logic of survivors who would one day choose a synagogue as the setting to turn off their own life-support systems.

And yet the one who had the most immediate difficulty accepting the tragedy was Rabbi Vered. It wasn't just that his congregation had been diminished by two, or the fact that the Levins had survived the concentration camps of Europe only to call it quits one day on his own turf. The arc of their lives had traversed one unspeakable tragedy after another, making it hard for a rabbi not to confess his own cynicism. How much happy-faced spin-doctoring would it take before the congregation saw right through the facade? What possible lessons could be drawn from their deaths? Rabbi Vered couldn't think of any. But then again, after Auschwitz, such were the problems of those in the God business. Making sense of the senseless; accounting for God in all his absence. Perhaps that's why Jewish clergy in the postwar era so often chose to keep God out of their synagogues. Instead they focused on other, more concrete matters for the secular minded: assimilation and intermarriage, divorce, female rabbis and cantors, building funds, Israel Bonds, and, in Rabbi Vered's case, tennis.

But the situation here was even more improbable and complex. For one thing, statistically, Holocaust survivors, as a group, didn't kill themselves; indeed, there had been a remarkably low incidence of suicide among them. That's not to say that there wasn't damage. All sorts of pathologies settled into the psyches of survivors after the camps were liberated—depression and fear, nightmares and repressed grief—but virtually never suicide. The Levins' postsurvival strategy was unusual largely because it was so final, and also because it may have hinted at no strategy at all. Their deaths echoed loudly inside a hole left in the world after Auschwitz. This was not an ordinary death wish, this spousal copycat suicide. The message here was more ambiguously poignant. Surely they were trying to say something. But what? When it comes to impassioned shouts into the void, no one has the credentials to do a simultaneous translation.

Rabbi Vered had his own history, which had mostly been unknown to his congregation and explained perhaps why the Levins' suicide was impossible for him to accept. He had been outdone by two of his own flock. Here was a man who had devoted his entire rabbinate to one nonliturgical, nonhalachic endeavor: sticking it to God, breaking ranks and all the rituals. He ate rye bread during Passover and shellfish from Joe's Stone Crabs on Yom Kippur. After Saturday services, he hustled tennis matches from younger opponents, faking a bum hip, pretending not to know which end of the racquet was up. He drove around Miami Beach in a red Cadillac convertible with rock music blasting from the radio. He played high-stakes poker with the synagogue's building fund, and was known to bang strippers—and preferably not even Jewish ones—in his office at the synagogue.

Despite this stunning example of degenerate Jewish faith, he had now been fully upstaged.

"Fucking Levins," he was heard saying for years after their deaths. "Where the hell do they get off pulling that stunt? That's the kind of thing everyone expects of me. How am I going to outdo that and come up with something more original? God will never notice me again."

Yet the odd thing was, for all the attention they were about to receive—soon to become Miami legends and national enigmas—at the time, Lothar and Rose didn't give any hint that this Shabbos was going to be different from all others. There was nothing unusual or out of the ordinary in the way they entered the synagogue. Nothing about the way they dressed—a light blue suit for Lothar and a gray skirt and maroon blouse for Rose—implied an apparent wardrobe for human sacrifice. They were neither noticeably depressed nor anxious nor avoidant nor desperate, nor did their behavior in any way betray that the sanctuary of Temple Beth Am was about to be used for such an unholy purpose.

"After kiddush we should drive down and go for a walk on Ocean Avenue. What do you say?" Lothar slyly asked a number of his survivor friends. His back was slightly bent on what was already a short frame. His face was wrinkled, liver spotted, and tanned, making it hard to read, like a Rorschach test. His eyes were ocean blue but concealed within a permanent squint—eyelash seaweed that made eye contact impossible. Both of his hands were clamped behind his back—one hand holding the other wrist—a familiar incarcerated position for him. He seemed cheerful, undistracted, not the disposition of a man packing a pistol in his *tallis* bag and with his own murder on his mind. Also in the bag, a full bottle of nitroglycerin pills, the medication that had for so many years served the purpose of quelling the palpitations, steadying the blood flow to the heart. Now they were there to make sure that his heart would cooperate just long enough until its final beat.

Rose was seemingly at peace as well. Her face was round and powdered white, as if taunting the sun with a bull's-eye. There were prison-bar spaces between her teeth and stocking-stuffer flesh under her chin. She sat down next to Betty, one of her closest friends. They worked at the local Hadassah chapter together and were now discussing a special brunch that they had planned, with Abba Eban as an honored guest.

When that conversation was over, and before services began, Betty asked, "So, how is Oliver doing?" And that was perhaps the first and only sign of a hairline fracture in Rose's facade. She stiffened and looked downward. For an instant it looked as though she were about to cry, but nothing came of it.

She and Lothar had discussed the plan in advance. They had agreed to keep it a secret, and not to think of Oliver, otherwise they might lose their will and abort their journey. Their ways and motives would forever be unknowable as they passed on, if not quite to the other side, then at least to somewhere in between.

Let them all—Oliver included—keep guessing. Force them to search for some symbolic, false closure. Surely there was deep meaning in this unprimal act—if not to be gleaned now, then perhaps sometime in the future. But Lothar and Rose knew better. Those looking for answers were simply wasting their time.

The plain fact was: The Levins had simply had enough.

2

THERE'S A ONE-TRACK MIND THAT GUIDES THE traffic along Broadway outside Zabar's: the consumption of smoked fish. To be sure, there are other distractions as well, things that make observing the rules of the road a real challenge on the Upper West Side. But these too are epicurean in nature. So much of the real estate on Broadway is devoted to New York's love affair with food. All those discerning palates refusing to discriminate among cuisines, from pizza to sushi, *sag paneer* to *pommes frites*. And in this particular neighborhood, the variety is endless and the appetites equally without bottom.

But all that changed one day with the opening of a violin case. That's all it took to alter the atmosphere on the Upper West Side. The girl lifted the instrument to her shoulder, placed its rounded stern under her chin, and began to play. And then suddenly, inexplicably, pedestrians on Broadway behaved as though they were no better than savage beasts—not because of their usual aggressions, but rather because they had surrendered to something more soothing. Their pursuits stopped, and their instincts alternated. No longer spineless captives of their noses and salivary glands; the balance of power had now shifted to their ears.

Music. It was the music. Escapist and disarming. Transporting and quiescent. And once that happened, the aromas inside Zabar's no longer stood a chance.

Her hair was the color of late afternoon sand, and her eyes, large and round, were the kind of ambivalent blue that turns gray in the backlit sun. She had an immobilizing smile, proven to brighten any mood. Her nose was slender and her lips thin. She was tall for her age, with long arms, sloping shoulders, and the awkwardness of body that came from growth spurts that couldn't quite keep pace with the rest of her development.

The girl positioned herself defiantly with her back against the window, bread machines and cutting boards on the other side of the glass, while she ticklishly sawed the fretless strings of her violin. With each note, each slide that stretched a mournful phrase, each vibration that soared as if it were a newly invented sound, quarters and dollars dropped into her open violin case.

"Beautiful, child, simply beautiful," said a woman dressed elegantly in a pink Prada suit and Manolo Blahnik shoes—an apparent refugee from Park Avenue traveling courageously without a passport on the Upper West Side. "Wherever did you learn to play like that? And what do you call that music?"

The girl didn't reply, she just continued sliding the bow, dipping her shoulders, knees, and head whenever the music and her own mechanics allowed for such impish improvisation. The sounds stuttered, with quick starts and stops—the trill created in the empty space of a strategic pause.

Others joined the growing audience. A tall, trim yuppie on Rollerblades was receiving stock quotes from his wireless. Everything on him, except the wheels and the phone, designed by Tommy Hilfiger. A homeless man, unshaven, his posture without vertical dignity, wedged a coffee cup against his hip—empty of handouts and coffee. Two elderly Hungarian sisters from Great Neck, clinging to bags loaded with whitefish salad and Russian coffee cakes, swayed as though summoned by the Transylvanian sounds of their youth. And there were children—gap-toothed, Gap-clothed—standing around, admiring the gumption of the teenager with the bouncy fiddle. An NYPD patrolman, pale faced and freckled, his arms folded and night-stick dangling from his belt like a standby percussion instrument, tapped a lazy, rhythmless foot.

Appropriately this street performance was being held just a few blocks uptown from Lincoln Center, a place where violins still mattered, where unplugged music resounded without a jolt from Con Edison. No need to synthesize what has already been deemed classical, or surround with drum machines and artificially sampled sounds. This instrument of high-pitched melancholy may have lost its prominence in this new musical age in which strings are pulled and strummed all for the sake of making a racket, but the appreciative audience standing outside Zabar's still knew a violin when they saw one.

And yet, somehow, what the young soloist was playing didn't much favor the smooth lines and sparkling wood finish of those other violins that filled the friendly acoustical spaces of Avery Fisher or Alice Tully Hall. Neither a Stradivarius nor a Guarneri was making this street music on Broadway. Far from it. This violin looked more like a bastard piece of wood that had been sent out to sea and had returned waterlogged. The horsehair strings resembled copper wire, and the fingerboard was no straighter or sturdier than a rotting gangplank. And in addition to its misshape, its color was coarsely rough hued—a weird, bruised blue—as if it had been dragged from behind for miles. A mongrel violin of folk origins that looked as though it had been rescued from a band of musical gypsies, which it probably had.

But it wasn't just its appearance that seemed so tuneless; the sound it produced was equally jarring—foreign, even to many of these listeners, who, being Jews, should have known better.

It was, after all, their mother music, but they didn't realize it, or perhaps, as so often happens with communities flung out so far in their own progress, they had become deaf to the ancestral melodies that had once sustained them. The Jewish lullaby no longer had the power to put them to sleep.

Maybe that's because for so many years their eardrums had been snared by other sounds: Benny Goodman swing, Bob Dylan anthems, Beastie Boys Jewish rap. Like everything else, the pop music of the shtetl had been drowned out, as well.

Klezmer had once supplied the hip jazz sounds of Eastern and Central Europe. This was long before Broadway put a fiddler on a roof and called it musical theater. But in the post-Holocaust era, klezmer had all too often become no better than kitsch, cosmetic music that filled in that awkward gap between the serving of the fruit cup and the main course at Jewish weddings and bar mitzvahs. It was now a halfhearted national anthem played at 78 rpms—chipmunk music to lead the guests through the obligatory hora before making way for the electric slide.

Yet the teardrop notes that spilled from the child's violin seemed to recall to the listeners another time that couldn't actually be recalled at all—just simply felt. With each assured stroke, and those arranged skips and hesitant hops, also came the slicing of their souls. The echoes were faint but, even from that distance, unmistakably sad. Is there any doubt why air violins are often played in imaginary accompaniment to any story of sympathy and woe?

Old traffic was replaced by a new audience, the invisible velvet rope behind which people lined up for an unexpected dose of melancholy. But there was one woman poised along the arc that had formed around the young soloist who wouldn't surrender her spot.

She couldn't get enough of what the child was giving away. The woman was slightly built, a brunette with willful curls that dressed up a high forehead, and a large smile that for now was hidden behind a tight-lipped mouth. As the child played, the woman noted the familiar tunes. She knew each one, her own private Top 40, the uncharted *Billboard* of unrecorded vinyl. The bullets here had registered not riches, but death. She recognized the *dobridens*, *zogekhts*, *freylakhs*, *kaleh bazetsns*, *khusidls*, and of course, the most mournful melody of them all—"Invitation to the Dead"—the one that the girl was playing over and over, like a needle that cheerfully awaits the scratch in the broken record.

Tanya Green knew this music better than most. She had been teaching European klezmer music for violin and *tsimbl* to students for years. In fact, for a long time now she had been one of the leading klezmer violinists in the world—not that the world was paying much attention anymore. Her talent, after all, was focused on playing a dead music—Sanskrit, Aramaic, and Latin you can dance to. Klezmer was the musical analog of Yiddish, the spoken language of the shtetl, which, like the music itself, had gone silent, as well. Yiddish without the words and yet a musical clone of all those sobbing sounds made by cantors, grandmothers, and mourners trapped in that intense zone of emotion between ecstasy and anguish.

But here on Broadway it wasn't just the music that captivated Tanya Green. It was the child's posture as well. She played like Paganini, with the scroll of the violin pointed downward, as though aimed at the earth, or whatever might be buried underneath. Paganini was not a klezmer violinist, but this child prodigy on Broadway certainly was. Tanya Green saw something in her musical body language that was trying to speak, not just about the music but perhaps the place where it came from.

The child was finished with her serenade. She restored the violin to its case, where it now shared room with an extra cushion of dollar bills and some jingling coins. The crowd splintered like molecules along Broadway. Some, their appetites renewed, returned to Zabar's for yet another fix of smoked fish and fatty French cheese. Tanya hesitated, then approached the young prodigy.

"Excuse me, but . . . how do you know this music?" she asked.

Ariel Levin grabbed the handle of her violin case and was about to head back the several blocks to the brownstone where she and her father lived, but she stopped to answer the woman. A seasoned New York City kid, Ariel knew not to talk to strangers. An even more emblazoned lesson of the New York playground is knowing how to root out the strangers from those whom you have simply not met yet—the unknown who happen also to be undangerous. Ariel was able to size Tanya up as just a mere stranger, otherwise harmless.

"Why do you want to know?" Ariel replied.

"I'm sorry to be so rude, but how could I not want to know? You are an unusual young girl. You don't normally hear this type of music played by someone your age. I would know that," Tanya continued, her voice straining. The girl's performance had left her feeling both nervous and exhilarated. "This music has been a large part of my life; I've been listening and playing it for nearly thirty years now. I started when I was about your age. I had good teachers, and my parents came from Poland and spoke Yiddish. We played this music all the time, and my parents had friends who came to our apartment and brought instruments and played along. We had concerts in our house. But that was a long time ago, and there are no homes like that anymore. That's why I want to know how you learned. I mean, I was never as talented as you when I was your age, even with all the exposure I had to klezmer music. Who are you studying with?"

"No one."

"No lessons? Nobody is teaching you?"

"No."

Tanya flattened her lips and furrowed her brow; her nose crinkled as well. Her entire face was battening itself down as the news grew even more improbable.

"What about your parents?" Tanya wondered. "They must play, then."

"I live with my father. He doesn't listen to much music, and he doesn't play any instruments."

"And your mother?"

"She left us when I was two. Haven't seen her since; I don't even remember her."

"Was she a musician?"

"She left us when I was two," Ariel repeated in a tersely clipped voice, as if nothing more about her mother ever needed to be said again. Ariel knew what the stranger seemingly didn't: that abandonment is the worst crime of all. It beats all other hands—the full house that creates an empty house in that collapsing house of cards. A mother who walks out on a family will never overcome that awful item on her parental résumé.

"But these songs . . . they . . . they don't just come to a person like that; you can't just pick them out of the air. There has to be some immersion. The way your fingers move; the way you play *krekhz*. I saw it all," Tanya Green said, as her fingers and sliding arm air-danced on an imaginary violin. "And the way you bend the long notes as taut as a stretched rubber band. And how you pull sobs out of the violin with a flick of your little finger and nudge of your bow arm. The way you move from levity to sobriety in a single phrase. The ease with which you improvise on the melodies, ornamenting them differently each time. You know all the secrets to making those sounds and notes. You have all the modes down perfect in every key: *freygish, misheberekh, adonai maloch*. It's simply unfathomable to do that without lessons, endless years of practice, and playing along with old records. And even with all that, the musical language is too rare and difficult to master. You play like you were born in Lublin or Budapest or Bukovina."

"I'm not from any of those places. I'm from right here, around the corner on Edgar Allan Poe Street."

Tanya Green wasn't listening. "And even the way you stand. It's a strange position. It doesn't look very comfortable, and yet you make it look like it is. I've never seen a klezmer violinist play from such an angle. You're playing the music right into the ground. Who taught you to stand this way?"

"No one. I already told you that."

"I'm sorry," Tanya said, exasperated in her search for an explanation. "May I ask how old you are?"

"Just turned fourteen."

"It's truly fantastic. A musical miracle. . . . I just don't understand."

"It's pretty spooky, I guess."

"Where did you get that violin? It looks like it came from a junkyard, or a graveyard."

"I found it in the attic a couple of months ago. I took it out, put it under my chin, and it just fit. I could feel the music even without hearing it."

"But the repertoire. How did you teach yourself the music without hearing it somewhere first?"

Ariel shrugged. Even that gesture was performed with unusual grace.

"No recordings, no sheet music? It's simply not possible to become a master of a particular musical style without learning the actual melodies. It's like speaking with a Yiddish accent and not knowing Yiddish at all, or never having heard it spoken before. It simply can't be done! Did you know that klezmer musicians in Europe once had their own secret language?"

"No."

"They called it *klezmerloshen*. Don't tell me you can speak it, too."

"I don't know. Say something in *klezmerloshen*."

"I don't know the language, but this whole thing makes me think you do, that you can speak the secret language of the *klezmorim*. I heard you play 'Invitation to the Dead' several times. Why did you play it more often than the rest?"

"Which song was that?"

"Of course you don't even know the names of the tunes," Tanya said, her face now flushed with a new shade. "You probably don't even know that they have names."

Ariel blinked and began to sidestep away from the now certifiable stranger. "You're scaring me," Ariel said and turned.

"I'm sorry, but do you know you were playing a song meant only for orphans? Listen to me for a second and try to understand. That song you kept repeating, the one that everyone on Broadway loved so much, was written to be played at the graveside of parents whose child was getting married. It is a song that invites the dead parents to the wedding ceremony of their orphaned child. The child is alive, a living adult who is about to get married and wants his parents to be at the wedding. And since they are dead, the song invites their ghosts to attend instead. That's what the song is about. It was played at Jewish cemeteries all throughout Eastern and Central Europe. But you brought those strange weeping sounds, and that incredible depth of feeling, to shoppers on Broadway. You slowed down the music, and we all entered a different world."

"I gotta go," Ariel announced. "I'm late for dinner. My dad is waiting for me."

"Please, can I come with you? I want to speak with your father."

"No. Why?"

"He must know what's going on here. Does he realize how extraordinary this all is?"

"You can't follow me home."

"Then please promise to come to my studio. Play for me. I'll teach you some music that even you may not know. I have records. But I fear you'll end up playing music for me that I have not heard before. So, will you come?"

Ariel started to walk away. "I don't know. I like playing here—in front of Zabar's. I've been coming here since October. I guess about a month ago. It feels right, like this is where I'm supposed to play."

Glancing at the violin case, Tanya Green said, "I saw that the tips are good here. You should probably also try the Seventy-second Street subway station."

"You think the tips would be better?"

"Not necessarily, but some of your music was intended for people who live underground. Maybe that's why you're pointing the violin down like that."

"See ya," Ariel said, and then darted away down the block.

Tanya Green made a megaphone out of her palms and yelled out, her voice caught in the humbling commotion of Manhattan's static crossfire, "Wait! I'll come back tomorrow and listen to you play. Are you here every afternoon?"

The girl and her violin soon disappeared into the twilight of Broadway like stardust. Later that evening, when the streets were less crowded and the terribly peculiar merited less than even a second look, a curious phenomenon appeared that soon became no more than another rite of passage on the Upper West Side.

A baby carriage of sturdy Swedish design, with large rubber wheels and a blue canvas hood, strolled up and down Broadway. An empty basket of crisscrossed metal lay flat underneath, clamped between the wheels. What was so strange was not that a child was out so late at night past its bedtime. New York, overrun with insomniacs and predators of the evening, has long been known as a town with little regard for curfews—even for its children. No one would have registered even the slightest disapproval. But what could not have been ignored that night was that the stroller itself was empty.

The only reason anyone bothered to peek inside to check was that the carriage was missing not just a passenger, but even more chimerical than that, a driver, as well. No parent or nanny was anywhere in sight; no one was pushing at the helm. Just the stroller itself, freely traversing the avenue, parading along Broadway, observing the traffic lights and the common courtesies of the road. It was moving neither too fast nor too slow, not dawdling or jostling. But it was surely distracting to all those who charted its undeterred, otherwordly movements.

Night watch, sentry duty—for all the orphans, and the dead.

3

ALL I WANTED WAS TO FIX MY FATHER, AND that's why I did it.

It felt so weird when Ms. Kennedy told us we were taking a class trip to the lighthouse, me and all the other kids from our ninth-grade history class at Stuyvesant.

"The lighthouse is a special place," she said, her bright red hair always looking like it had caught on fire, like it was radiating its own light. "It's up in Washington Heights, underneath the George Washington Bridge, right up against the rocks on the shore of the Hudson River."

I knew all that. I remembered when I was younger, how Oliver used to read me a children's story about that same lighthouse, and the bridge, and what it's like to feel proud even when you're small, and how sometimes even if you're not really a brave person or cut out to rescue someone, you still feel like that's what you're supposed to do, like it's a job that you can't get out of. That's what happened with the lighthouse, at least the one in the story. And that's what I'm feeling now, about Oliver.

I loved the way he used to read to me. And not just because he was my father. I mean, he was great at reading out loud. Maybe that's because he's a writer, and writers do that sometimes: read their books into the open air, not for themselves, but for people who come to hear them. It's different, sometimes harder, to listen to a story read out loud than just reading it for yourself. Maybe that's because listening is tough for most people. It's much easier making your own noise.

Writers live in their own made-up, quiet worlds, inventing stories and writing them down. But if writers don't come out sometimes, they can get stuck in silence, and go crazy or something. I guess when they read out loud, it reminds them that words don't have to be quiet; you can take them off the page and let them live in your ears.

I think Oliver is better at it than most writers. Both the silence, and the reading out loud. He has a great voice, like an actor's. And he knows how to play all the parts, changing his voice for each of the characters. He can do funny accents, or talk like a baby or an old person. He can do African American voices and Spanish ones, too, and people from Europe. He can make silly sounds, and imitate the noises you hear on the street. And he knows how to use props. Like for the lighthouse story, he used to rattle the sheets on my bed, and that would be the sound of crashing waves. And he would move the pillows around, each one standing for a different kind of boat on the Hudson River. And when the story needed fog, he would snap the bedcover and let it float back down, and that would be our fog. He would use flashlights underneath the sheets, and ring bells when we needed one. With other stories a shoe in the darkness became a mouse, a hanging plant a nearby forest, bookshelves the side of a mountain.

I wish he could have kept reading me that same story every night of my life. But one day he stopped reading out loud in our home. That was it. No more. He still did it at bookstores or at places where they invited him to come read. But never again where we lived, and never again for me.

He didn't stop because I got too old or anything like that. He stopped a lot of things when she left us. Not reading the lighthouse story wasn't such a big deal when you think of everything else he wasn't ever going to do again.

Before I tell you what I did, and why I did it, maybe I should first tell you the story about the lighthouse. It's not just the place where I got the mud. Lots more happened there, a long time ago, before I was even born. I didn't know any of this until they came and explained it all to me—told me about my father, and the way things were before he changed so much. Maybe that's why Oliver used to read that story to me, because he wanted to remember who he was back then, and what he was running from before it had all been taken away. But it must have also reminded him of everything that had gone wrong, and maybe that's why he stopped reading out loud. It was like throwing it all back in his face, and torturing his ears.

The other day I started to realize that I'm a lot like the lighthouse. All kids are, really—tiny lighthouses trying to rescue their parents. Children know that mothers and fathers are sometimes like boats sailing in the dark. When the storms are dangerous, with the wind thrashing and the fog making it too hard to see, no matter how many flashing lights and loud bells we send out, telling our parents to watch out, keep away, the rocks are getting too close, there's nothing we can do to save them.

The story goes something like this. There's this Little Red Lighthouse way up near the northern tip of Manhattan. Every day it guided all the steamers, canoes, and tugboats that traveled on the Hudson River. It would say, "Flash, flash, flash," whenever it sent off its beam of light. It also had a bell, and it would scream, "Warning!" when the fog was so thick that the boats couldn't see the beacon of its light. The lighthouse was small, but because of the way it saved all the boats from crashing against the rocks on the shore, it felt big and important—"the Master of the River" I think is what it called itself.

But one day the lighthouse noticed that men were putting up these great big steel crossbars and girders. This worried the light-house. Day after day passed, and soon, stretching across the Hudson River, with the Little Red Lighthouse underneath, was the Great Gray Bridge. It too had a beam of light, and so the Little Red Lighthouse, seeing the size of the bridge and the reach of its light, didn't feel so important anymore. At about the same time, the man with the key to the lighthouse who used to turn on the gas, which made the light go on, and sound the bell, stopped coming. The light-house was sure that everyone had forgotten about it. Now only the Great Gray Bridge would rescue the ships and boats that sailed the Hudson.

But all children's stories have happy endings, and this one did too. One day there was a big storm, with lots of wind, big waves, and fog. The bridge called down to the lighthouse and asked why it wasn't shining its light. The lighthouse replied with sadness in its voice that it didn't think it was needed anymore. The bridge explained that *its* light was for airplanes—the ships of the air—but that the Little Red Lighthouse was still the Master of the River. The man, who had actually only lost his keys, finally came to turn the lighthouse back on. After that the lighthouse and the bridge each had their own jobs to do, and they lived together happily ever after.

That's the story, anyway. And it is a kid's story. I know real stories don't end that way—at least most don't. Adults don't have to go to sleep with a happy ending in their heads. I don't even think that Oliver's books make you smile after you finish them. Actually, happy endings are not how the stories of our family turned out. Even though I don't know much, that much I know. Why would Oliver believe in a story—his or someone else's—ending any other way?

I pretty much forgot about the lighthouse story until Ms. Kennedy told us where we were going for the class trip. Most of the other kids didn't know about the lighthouse and had never heard the children's story before, either.

Ms. Kennedy didn't plan the trip because of the lighthouse or the bridge. We were learning about the history of New York City, and how Washington Heights was an important part of the Revolutionary War. Long before the lighthouse and the bridge, George Washington and his men fought battles all around this part of New York and New Jersey—in Fort Lee, and Fort Tryon, and other forts I don't know the names of. Ms. Kennedy thought that a trip to Washington Heights, and a picnic down at the lighthouse, would make us feel like the American Colonists who fought for our independence. But I had another kind of battle in mind—the one to fix my father.

Because Washington Heights is so high up, you have to walk down a few hills to get to the lighthouse. Up on top there are old brick buildings with neat gargoyles poking their laughing, spooky heads out from doorways and ledges. Oliver would love to see those gargoyles; he has a real thing for them. And there are also stacks of fire escapes that didn't seem very safe if there ever was a fire, not just because they're rusted all over, but because they're crowded with houseplants and beach chairs. It's so hilly up in Washington Heights that there are steep drops when you least expect them, as if every block is like a trapdoor. Most of the people who live there now are Dominicans, and some Russians and artists over on Dyckman Street. There are bodegas on every corner, and Spanish restaurants, and during the summers, people blast Latin music from their windows, and the street sounds like a salsa disco. In the old days mostly German Jews lived in Washington Heights. That's when Oliver and his parents lived there, but I didn't know that either until they came back and told me.

Mr. Walker, the bus driver, parked the school bus near one of the hills, along Cabrini Boulevard and 181st Street. He was a heavy African American who slumped in the driver's seat like a jiggling Buddha. His large teeth were visible behind thin lips, but his mouth was nearly always plugged with a cigar that he never lit up.

"I'll meet you all back up here in two hours," he called out to Ms. Kennedy, "and you all mind your teacher, you hear me?"

"Thank you, Mr. Walker," Ms. Kennedy replied. She was nervous while counting our heads, but she waved back at Mr. Walker anyway.

It was the middle of October, when trees break out from the green boredom of the year and shine with their bright autumn colors. Soon the fall show would be over, and the leaves would turn from shiny to crisp, then drop to the ground only to get trampled on. But then it all begins again; nature's way of allowing for second chances, the fall that will eventually become spring. That doesn't happen with human beings. But sometimes . . .

Down at the riverbank there are picnic tables near the lighthouse. The Hudson flows right up against the Manhattan shoreline, teasing, tickling. There's really no other place like it in Manhattan, because you're right at the water's edge, without fences or seawalls or train tracks or raised marshes or highways keeping you from getting wet.

So before we took the trip, I had this great idea. The lighthouse, the Hudson, the rocks—this is where I should get the mud. If I was going to be able to bring them back, it would have to come from this clay. Not like the story I heard in Hebrew school, about the rabbi who went off in the middle of the night to dig up mud from some river in Prague—that's in Czechoslovakia, actually in the part now called the Czech Republic. I couldn't go all the way to Prague, no matter how magical the mud might be there. No way Oliver would understand that, even though I was doing it for him.

"Where are you really going?" he would ask in a suspicious way.

"Some faraway place."

"Why are you going?"

"To save you."

"And how are you going to do that?"

"By making a golem."

"How will a golem help me?"

"Because it's our family's grail."

"A golem? What does a golem have to do with us?"

"It's not just any golem. I have a special one in mind."

"Ariel, I'm your father, and I don't want you messing around with golems. They're not for children—very dangerous stuff, worse than smoking. Besides, they only show up every five hundred years or so, and even if you can figure out the recipe, they always go too far, and then you can't stop them."

That's what he'd probably say, which is why I didn't tell him. Sometimes it's best to leave your parents out of whatever plans you have to save them.

So even though it wouldn't be as magical as the mud from Prague, and probably no one had ever made a monster out of Hudson River mud before, I decided I should at least give it a try, because it was my best shot. For this golem Hudson River mud would have to do.

"Ariel, come!" Ms. Kennedy called out. "It's time to go! Pack up your things."

"I'll be right there!"

We had finished our picnic lunch, and some kids were running around the rocks, trying to climb onto the lighthouse, which you couldn't get to anyway because it was surrounded by a gate. Each iron bar was like a spear with an arrowhead on top, all sticking out from the ground.

Everybody was now heading up to Mr. Walker and the school bus. From where I was standing, way back at the edge of the river, my class looked like a big ant colony trying to climb a steep hill, one ant at a time.

I had to work fast because I wasn't finished when Ms. Kennedy called out my name. While everyone else was eating or checking out the lighthouse or staring up and down the river, throwing rocks, trying to give New Jersey a black eye, I wandered off to a lumpy carpet of lopsided rocks that took me right up to the water. That's when I started to fill my Backstreet Boys backpack. The night before I was getting ready, and I lined the backpack with a whole bunch of large Glad bags, each one stuffed inside the other. I had to make it waterproof, or actually mudproof. I couldn't have the mud leak out of my backpack, spilling into the bus, and leaving a trail that followed me back to school.

Thank God I had that shovel with me. It made it easier to get all the mud I needed. I borrowed the shovel from Alejandro; he's the man who takes care of some of the brownstones on Edgar Allan Poe Street, where Oliver and I live. Alejandro is short and stocky, with dark hair and big ears. One of his eyes doesn't open up all the way. When he walks, his left leg looks like he's dragging it around, and he's a little bent over with a hump on his back. Even with all those problems, he still gets the work done. He speaks with an accent, but I'm not sure from where. In a way he's like family, because Oliver and I don't have any other relatives. Sometimes Alejandro comes over to eat with us, or he watches TV in our living room when Oliver is out for the day. Our neighbors think it's weird that we're so close with our building superintendent. But it's Alejandro's job to watch over the building, so we don't mind if he also watches over us.

Alejandro makes sure that the garbage is all ready to be taken away when the sanitation men pull up to Edgar Allan Poe Street, which is West Eighty-fourth. He binds the newspapers for recycling and separates the bottles from the large black bags. He's also a maintenance man, fixing things when they get broken. Oliver wouldn't even know where to find the fuse box if Alejandro wasn't around to help out.

I told Alejandro I needed the shovel for a school project and I would bring it back later.

"What kind of project, Ari?" That's what he calls me.

"Ahh . . . I don't know, just some planting and digging . . . nothing special."

I couldn't tell Alejandro the truth either. It had to be a secret. What if he told Oliver? My dad might take away the violin, and that would only make things worse.

I opened the Glad bags real wide and started to dig into the wet sand. The cold stream from the Hudson River lapped over my hand each time I plunged into it. My yellow parka was getting wet. My boots, even though I was standing on the rocks of a small jetty, were drowning in the foamy whitecaps of the river, while the kneecaps of my jeans turned almost white from sliding back and forth against the rocks.

Just before I finished stuffing my backpack with as much mud as I could carry, before it started oozing out through the zipper, I cut my hand on something in the water. I thought it might be a sharp rock, but my finger was bleeding too much for that. I wondered whether it was some glass, and not a rock at all. Manhattan is an island of litter. Garbage cans are always overflowing. Everything that people want to get rid of seems to just pile up. That happens on the street, and maybe also in the river. Maybe there were drunk teenagers who hung out at the lighthouse at night, drinking beer and chucking the bottles against the rocks, shattering them into the Hudson. Maybe that's what I cut my finger on—a broken beer bottle—but I didn't have time to see what it really was.

Instead I put my finger inside my mouth to make it stop bleeding. With my left arm I swung my smudged backpack over my right shoulder and carried the wet, chocolate brown clay up the hill. As I walked I rehearsed in my mind how I was going to turn this mud into something alive. I had been preparing for a long time, making plans, excited but also scared, not that it would work but that it wouldn't. Because without their help, how would I be able to rescue Oliver?

WHEN A WRITER IS SUDDENLY LEFT WITHOUT words, it forces him to seriously consider his options. Not about a change of careers, but about that far more delicate, unmentionable choice: the "to be or not to be" dilemma, which no matter what anyone tells you is not the exclusive province of Danish princes or earless Dutch painters or the mere moody, lovelorn, or incurably despaired.

Artists have always had the inside track on the early exit. Perhaps that's because for the artist, the outtakes of a life loaded down with disappointment inevitably get reimagined as art. The artist has no other alternative. Repression is not an option. Neither is forgetting nor denial. The artist becomes the warden of his own prison, a jailer without mercy.

There is a tragic human paradox at work here: The more painful the life, the more profound the art. The artist experiences the affairs of life too harshly, or at least lives it as though he does—without moderation, filters, or even hindsight. These are not the kind of people who bother with sunscreen, retirement plans, Pap smears, blood tests, seatbelts, abstinence, safe sex, speed limits, or a good night's rest. They don't learn from their mistakes. They simply recycle them until inspiration takes over and all the amassed misery and anguish gets refashioned into something that can be read into the night, hung on a wall, or popped into a VCR.

Now, none of this really applies to me. I mean . . . I *am* a writer, but I'm no artist. Far from it. I write gothic mysteries; courtroom legal thrillers. My aesthetic never qualifies as emotionally complex or intellectually challenging. I provide no insight into life, no glimpse of the human condition, no window into the inner workings of a troubled soul. My work is all a mindless, connect-the-dots formula—pablum that leaves you hungry. I drop clues like bread crumbs; my detours are actually decoys awaiting an ambush. I misdirect. I like my mirrors cracked and my smoke to linger. My characters are flawed but easy to figure out.

I start with New York City as the obvious setting for mayhem and murder, with all its downtown havoc and fast-forward incivility, the immoral trappings of Wall Street, the dank streets sterilized with homegrown despair. The Big Apple, neurotic to the core. A rich husband gets whacked, a corporation poisons consumers, a whole bunch of fat cats engage in a coverup. Now enter the down-on-his-luck, go-it-alone lawyer who at the tale's end, after a long, redemptive struggle, triumphs despite all that has been aligned against him since chapter 1. Throw in a few brain-dead but willing fashion models, a gum-chewing, Ivy-League-educated female detective, maybe a slasher sequence, and a sinister, dark-haired foreigner from a country seeking self-determination, and you have a crockpot boiling over with suspense. Well, at least that's how I do it.

But a real artist doesn't care about facts, details, adventure,

intrigue, or even plot—just truth. When art is pumping on all emotional cylinders, when it shakes itself loose from what the mind will
believe, when it aspires not to copy but to reinvent, not to please but
to disturb—to rub everyone the wrong way—the result can split your
veins, crush your heart like a piece of fruit, make you gasp and
breathe backwards. And if you can make someone feel all that, could
anything else be more important, or frightening? Perhaps that singular, terrifying, runaway power is what drives some artists either to
madness or to the obituaries.

Fortunately I have avoided this problem—at least until now. This
book in your hands, the words inverted in your eyes, is a new beginning for me. Or is it an end? I thought I had been spared, that I had
figured out how to stay clear of those pathetic destinies that make
the artist's life so tragic. I self-medicated myself, but without any
medicine. It was pure avoidance. Flawless hiding. Grief masking. My
inner demons would have to come looking for me, and even if I gave
them a head start, I would always remain one step ahead. A battle of
wits and wills that never resulted in an actual confrontation. That
was my secret: the refusal to emotionally confront all that had gone
wrong, and all that had walked away.

I had a life tailor-made for hemmed-in emotions. A strategy to
protect myself from myself. But somewhere along the way I lost
these initial advantages, the early warning systems went unnoticed,
eventually leading me to this point, exposing me to these visions,
and the compulsion to write these words.

My parents were Holocaust survivors. Need I say more, or should
I just go ahead and ruin your day? They had been in the camps,
breathing without gas masks, but still breathing. They outlived the
shootings, the typhus, and the death marches. All their relatives were
dead, even the no-good distant cousins who all of a sudden were
longingly missed.

Adult orphans everywhere. They found each other after the war,
like matching lottery numbers in a special sweepstakes for the
damned. Life, after that, comes across as pretty dull and uneventful.

Starting over is total fantasy. You come to expect the worst, because you know better. The Nazis gave you the gift of a lively imagination. Once you've seen a death factory up close, no future horror can ever again be thought of as mere fiction.

Except my parents took it all one step further. They killed themselves. I was away at college, and one Saturday morning, while I was playing in a freshman football game, my parents, in one simultaneous stroke of showmanship, turned themselves into a poster boy and pin-up girl for Holocaust martyrdom—forever overshadowing their survival by taking their lives—in a synagogue of all places. I returned to my dorm and learned not only that my parents were dead, but by their own hands, without saying good-bye or offering me any advice on how to live my life given all that I would have from now on to play down.

Years later my wife abandoned me and my two-year-old daughter, Ariel. I still don't know where she went, or why she left, or whether she's still even alive. I'm not even divorced, yet; no official papers, just a missing wife. But isn't that also a death? When someone you love disappears, the feeling of absence plays no favorites between death and a body that may actually still be alive. She might as well be buried in the ground. The loss lives that deep, and knows no difference.

And that's why for as long as I can remember, I've been haunted by loss. Everywhere that I've lived has been haunted this way. It is my private ghost. My private companion, always with me. The loved ones are long gone, but the loss never leaves my side.

There were the ghosts of the Holocaust and the vanished family of Levins I never knew. The damaged parents for whom a bullet and cyanide were somehow more appealing than a life of reliving murderous memories in old age. A wife who forced me into being a bachelor and a single parent. Even though it has already been twelve years since she left, it's still hard for me to be in this brownstone. Every day is a reminder of what it was once like, and what is no longer there. You can't just remove one member of a family and still call it a family. The loss must be noted in some special way. It's not like bean counting, where one less is hardly noticed. A family that has been depleted, robbed, and reconfigured needs its own name, something that describes the fact that it will always be something less than whole, a permanent deficit, an immutable minus. Compromised and forever imperfect, a family only because there is nothing else to call it.

Self-preservation works best for those who don't dwell. But then something happens, and dwelling becomes not an afterthought, but an implacable obsession. And sometimes dwelling has no place to go other than inside a book, and when that happens, self-preservation is all gone.

It all started with writer's block. Then the voices and visions. Years ago, back when I was a Wall Street lawyer, I used to work late into the night on behalf of Fortune 500 companies, servicing the faceless ones, those hiding behind corporate veils, soulless suits, bottom-line fishers nibbling at balance sheets, puking up like insatiable bulimics, and then ready to do it all over again.

The numbingness of it all began to wear on me. Late into the night, I would ride down elevator shafts and hear voices that I attributed to a mind that had gone far too long without sleep. Now I'm no longer so sure that sleep deprivation was the problem.

I eventually quit the firm and went off to concoct gothic legal thrillers. I found an agent, then a book deal. Not long thereafter I purchased an entire brownstone for myself. The building is on Edgar Allan Poe Street in Manhattan; I know . . . but I couldn't resist.

One day, a short time ago, I discovered that I was suddenly unable to think up a plot, or a story line, or even a passable name for a new character. Words wouldn't come, as if all along they had only been on loan, and now the debt was being called in. Each one became just a synonym for another, a syntax without rhyme or reason.

Blockage did have its rewards. During root canal, Dr. Rothstein said, "Oliver, I really should give you an anesthetic. I'm going into the third canal today, very deep, and with this fat instrument. You're going to be very uncomfortable," and he would hold up some peg with an attached long needle, waving it around my face as if he were about to ask, "Is it safe?" and I of course already knew the answer to that, and so I replied, "Go in. I'm not really feeling anything."

Which was true. All my nerves, not just the ones in my teeth, had lost sensation. He's digging and rubbing and pushing and getting readings from some torture device that was hanging from my mouth like a meat hook, and I'm staring up at the ceiling, hoping that some original sentence will pass before me like a subtitle, and I'll be cured of my blockage even if the canals inside my gum still need widening.

There were times when I crossed the street just as the Walk sign was turning green. Cars hadn't quite come to a full stop, and I was passing in front of them, casting out my arm, thinking somehow that I was able to hold them back, but fearing nothing if I failed. I was acting as though the cars would simply drive right through me as I made it safely to the other side.

I had the same feeling about big winds. How little it would have taken to turn me into a long flapping kite, the spool letting out way too much line as I backed away from trees and birds and clouds and airplanes, wondering whether the world would even miss me as I orbited some other planet entirely.

A few months into the block, not being able to write anymore was only half of my trouble. It got even worse. I started to hear noises. Different ones, I think, from those that had once shared that Wall Street elevator with me years earlier. Tiny, indistinct rattlings, stirring almost everywhere in my home. Clatterings in the kitchen and bathroom. Scratches inside the walls. Squeaks coming from faucets as if someone were trying to turn on the water without success. Pattering footsteps like dropped coins on a wood floor. The brownstone that my daughter and I occupy is a large one—four stories, with an attic on top. So usually by the time I heard something and raced over to check it out, the noise had already moved on to somewhere else. I was out of breath, the room went silent, but I knew better—whatever it was was still there.

At night I heard voices that I assumed were part of a dream. But then I realized that I wasn't asleep, that I was lying awake, eavesdropping on conversations that were taking place in my own home, carried on by squatters I couldn't see. And there were also heartbeats, but they were not mine. I could hear them: slow, fading, but regular—coming from the walls, thumping under my bed, echoing in the bathtub, from inside my computer terminal.

What the hell is going on here? I asked myself frantically. Maybe I should get a baseball bat and swing at something. But what?

My eyes circled the room, surveying, sensing, on the lookout for whatever was lurking. I wasn't alone, and I could feel it. All those years that I had been writing, the house had always remained deafeningly still. Except for my tappings at the keyboard, there were never any strange, unaccounted-for sounds. It was always in fact too quiet for my taste. I could have used the company back then, a moment of noisy inspiration to startle the silence. But the brownstone had been an impenetrable fortress. There was never a break-in nor unexplained broken glass. I wound up buying a white-noise machine from the Sharper Image, to darken the contrast. But now I no longer needed the artificial sounds, because suddenly I was being treated to a symphony of unnatural ones. Noises filled the brownstone. Howling. Laughing. Mocking. Slamming my household appliances. Always one room ahead of me.

When I asked Ariel whether she had heard anything, she replied, "It's all in your head, Oliver. You're not writing, so your head is playing tricks on you, trying to get you back to work."

My head had never worked this way before. Such tricks I would normally reserve for my books, not my life. So I asked Alejandro, who lives in the neighborhood and works as a superintendent for me and some of the other building owners, if he would mind coming over to take a look around. Maybe it was the plumbing. Or something to do with Con Edison. A radiator leak; a busted exhaust hose?

Infestation, perhaps? Alejandro told me he had once moonlighted as an exterminator in the Bronx. Surely whatever was crawling around my brownstone was the kind of thing that could be exterminated.

"I'm either imagining things or I've got a vermin problem, Alejandro."

"Mice? Rats? Which?"

Alejandro was stocky and ruddy faced. His dragging, gimp leg, hunched back, and one eye at half mast would no doubt be frightening to vermin.

"I don't know what exactly," I replied, "but there is definitely something in this place. You'll be able to find the solution, right?"

Alejandro didn't want to make any promises.

"Maybe Ariel is doing a science project and she's not telling you that there's a white mouse running around in here," he said with a thick Cuban accent. "She's been acting strange lately, Mr. Levin."

"You noticed it too?"

"She borrowed some gardening tools from me, and when I asked her what it was for, she made up some excuse that I didn't buy for a minute. Also, that violin she keeps playing. What kind of music is that? It is fast, but you can't mambo to it."

Alejandro then squared his shoulders and took a few determined, intrepid steps into the basement to face whatever was down there waiting for him. Fifteen minutes later he returned, shut off his flashlight, and slipped it back inside its holster like a lawman after a gunfight. Alejandro's utility belt was also weighted down with a rubber hammer and a cube of retractable measuring tape. Finally, he confirmed what I had feared: Despite the heartbeats in the walls, there were no telltale signs of rodent droppings, or anything else, anywhere to be found.

"Whatever you got down in there, Mr. Levin, it's not mice," Alejandro said, filing his report with assurance. "I can throw some more poison around and plant some sticky traps, but in my opinion no vermin is going to turn up. There may be something in your house, but it's not pests."

Whatever it was, it wasn't content with just making noise. Household items started to disappear. A pair of clogs and some toothbrushes; a few bowls from the kitchen. Blankets. A razor and a comb. A Yankee pinstripe uniform and cap. One of Ariel's old train sets. Leftover bread, which I used to leave outside for the homeless, vanished before I even had a chance to throw it out. The sound of stale bread being devoured in the middle of the night was the only noise I could identify among the choir of squeaks, moans, and sundry crashes that I couldn't.

Oddly enough Ariel's old baby carriage was gone, too. It was an old Swedish one with big rubber wheels that had once functioned like four-wheel drive through inches of piled-up Broadway snow. Even when Ariel got older, I couldn't get myself to part with it. So I parked the carriage on the top floor of the brownstone, barricading a bedroom that we hadn't used in years. One day I went up there to poke around, searching for a book inside a closet full of shelves, and I noticed that the carriage was no longer on the floor. Later I asked Ariel about it.

"I haven't taken it for a ride in years, Oliver. I can walk on my own now," she said dryly.

"Well, it had to go someplace!" I demanded. "The thing just didn't roll out of here on its own. Will someone please explain what's going on?"

5

 IT WAS ALL IN THE NUMBERS; THAT'S WHAT I finally figured out. The mud from the river wasn't going to do it all by itself. I needed to learn the magic math, the secret to those numbers. They were burned there for a reason and remained on their forearms, never to be washed away. Those tattoos weren't just decorations, like blue body paint. The numbers must have been a combination to something, the key to some kind of lock. Numbers that once kept them in prison maybe now could set them free.

But a lump of clay can't come to life without some sorcery. I had to start thinking like a witch, but not just any witch. A Jewish witch. My magic wand and broomsticks, the potions and the spells, came from the kabbalah. I was playing God, even though I was only in the ninth grade.

Later that night, after dinner, Oliver went off to work in his study—staring at his computer without hitting any of the keys because he couldn't think of anything to say—and I snuck up into the attic and worked on my project, like some mad scientist with wild hair and a scary laugh. I saw an old black-and-white Frankenstein movie on the SciFi Channel about a year ago. Some Halloween special, a marathon of Draculas and wolfmen and Transylvanian sickos who now wear hockey masks before they slash you to death. I practiced saying: "It's alive; it's alive!"

I'm not really that good with my hands, and I wasn't sure what the monster was supposed to look like. But I did remember that in the story I heard in Hebrew school, Rabbi Loew's creature wasn't pretty. It was alive and dangerous, a giant without a soul, the image of a man with the table manners of a monster. You don't have to dress up a golem. He's not a double agent; he's not supposed to look like a friend who fits in. He doesn't infiltrate the enemy, just destroys it. And he can't be stopped. The golem was an early-model Terminator, without all the cyborg nuts and bolts.

"Ariel, where are you?" Ms. Kennedy shouted again. I couldn't see her through the dappled red, yellow, and orange leaves. Everyone was already on top of the hill, at the Henry Hudson Parkway, ready to make one more climb up to Cabrini Boulevard. By now Mr. Walker had probably gotten up from his nap, slipped the cigar, like a pacifier, back inside his mouth, cracked his neck, and swerved the door handle to let us all back in.

"Coming," I answered weakly, because I was so out of breath from lugging the mud, and myself, up the hill. Ms. Kennedy didn't hear me, which is why she came down part of the way herself.

"What on earth were you doing down there?" she scolded. "It's dangerous for a girl all alone."

Could I tell her that I was down at the river getting the ingredients for a golem? Surely a girl and her golem have nothing to fear from anyone. Better than a rabbit's foot or a lucky charm or a guardian angel or a bodyguard.

"I'm fine," I replied. "The Master of the River was watching over me."

"Cute, Ariel, real cute." She obviously knew the children's story. "But the lighthouse has been shut down for years, and there are drug dealers and derelicts all over this place. You should know better than that. Now hurry up and let's go. We have to get back to Stuyvesant. Let me help you with your backpack."

"No thanks, I got it."

I was staring out the window as the bus rumbled down Broadway. Eventually it made a right turn and got on Riverside Drive. All the other kids were talking loudly. Somebody mentioned Sugar Ray and Smash Mouth. Tess said she was going to rent *Titanic* again over the weekend. I think she's seen it at least ten times by now. Rachel invited some of us over to her house after school. I didn't answer. I just sat alone, acting real quiet, guarding my golem kit on my lap.

First I had to get the numbers right—but what numbers? I thought about it for weeks, and then I had an idea. I had the numbers all along. Numbers are what makes my family special; our secret arithmetic.

I never knew my grandparents. Never saw their arms. Never touched those blue marks. They didn't die when the Nazis wanted them to, so they got to keep their numbers as souvenirs, mementos of not getting killed. But then comes the crazy part. Get this: They survived the concentration camps, and then one day, years later, they killed themselves. That all happened long before I was born.

My grandparents were buried in Miami, and their arms were buried with them. But I was sure that the numbers weren't dead, that they still had another life, some other purpose. The flesh turned to dust, then the numbers moved over to the bone and stayed there until they found something else to cling onto.

I wondered whether the numbers could bring them back and make my grandparents alive all over again, so I could know them, so they could help me rescue their son.

But it wasn't just finding the numbers. I had to use them in the right order. And not only that, there were words I would have to say, too. Each Hebrew word added up to a number. Like the letter *A* is a 1, and *B* is a 2, and *C* is a 3, and so on and so on. They call this *gematria*. Different words can add up to the same numbers, depending on the letters in the word. And because I had the numbers, I had this feeling that I probably had the right words, too, even though I wasn't sure what those words were yet. It was all supposed to be done in Hebrew, but I didn't know enough Hebrew. Could an American golem made out of Hudson River mud come alive from an alphabet that George Washington couldn't understand?

Some family histories are so big, the future can't overshadow the past. The climax and crescendo has already happened, and nothing will ever rate as large again. The Holocaust is that way with us. It's not in the past. For my family the Holocaust is always present and real, even though it happened a long time ago, even though we never speak about it.

How many generations will it take before we start having our own dreams? Time stopped while the rest of the world went forward. But not everyone could follow. The Levins didn't; we're still back there, even though me and Oliver were never there to begin with.

He was their only son, but he hardly mentions them, as if he didn't have parents. And he never talks about the Holocaust, or what it was like to grow up in a house where your mom and dad were almost gassed to death. Oliver is a writer, but he doesn't write about any of this; and he's a storyteller, but these are not the stories he tells. I wish he could tell me, but maybe he doesn't know himself. And if he did, I might be too scared to listen, like a horror movie where it doesn't matter if you're past PG-13 because it's all too scary anyway.

The only special powers all kids have are the ones they hold over their parents. You just look behind the faces of the people you come from, and you can spot the pain they're trying to hide. All parents are lousy liars. We know when they're faking a good mood, when laughter is just a smokescreen—the kind of smoke that fools only strangers. Kids can see right through it, even if they can't just blow it away.

"Have a great time at school, Ariel babes," he usually says when I leave in the morning. We go our own separate ways. He takes a walk up Broadway to buy a newspaper; I go in the other direction, catching the subway downtown. He bends, kisses me, then squeezes real hard. I hold my breath and feel him pressing his chest against mine. He doesn't want to let go; he's afraid to let go, but he has to. That's what parents do—they let go. But most don't worry that their kids aren't coming back at the end of the day.

"Bye, Oliver, see you after school."

He's not so sure. He smiles and pulls away with that long, moonwalk stride, and I watch him, so tall, his back straight, his hands cuffed together from behind. I don't move; I don't rush. I just hang around, watching him walk uptown. Sometimes he turns and waves, but not always, even though I think he's figured out by now that I'm always there waiting for him to turn around. Usually he forgets and keeps walking, cuts the corner, and I'm there wondering where his head is at, what's going through it. Doesn't he know that I'm back there, watching over him?

A few seconds later he's gone. So I wave anyway, as though my hand is bigger than it is, a blow-up palm that can be seen from any distance, a catcher's mitt scooping up my father, holding his hand. Do you have to see someone wave at you for it to actually count?

If I don't rescue him, who will? And then who will rescue me? Sometimes the things that happened before you were born, stuff you had nothing to do with, can stunt your growth, keep you in diapers no matter how old you get.

My grandparents killed themselves, and Oliver never found out why. And my mother left him, and he never found out why, either. When the people you love leave you, when they just disappear and you never hear from them again, something inside you goes away as well. It's a form of violence, as bad as any bruise. It's not right to call it a broken heart. The heart works just fine; it just doesn't want to.

You become less of what you were. Not because of the pain, but because of what you have to do to protect yourself from it. You learn to cover up. You have to decide whether you should love anymore, whether it makes sense to feel all over again—the love, and the loss. Because maybe feelings of loss are stronger than feelings of love, even at their best. I suppose some people are better off without love because they wouldn't survive if they had it and then suddenly it was taken away. I don't know. I can just read my father out loud, and he is definitely wearing a mask, hiding back a face that is afraid to love.

Oliver doesn't wave back at me because he doesn't trust it. For him it's just a hand in the air. One day it might let go even though it was never really holding on to begin with. And then where would he be?

So back to the numbers. In one of the rooms, on the top shelf of a closet, Oliver had a large box filled with pictures that he had never put away inside albums. Or maybe they used to be in albums, and he took them out and scattered them like he was shuffling a deck of printed memories. Like the life he was leading, the pictures should also be out of order, scrambled, out of focus. There were lots of pictures of my mother inside the box, but there were also old pictures of my grandparents.

I sat on my bedroom floor and spread all the pictures out in front of me. I was looking for a close-up of their forearms. The parquet floor was the background for a big jigsaw puzzle of my broken family. It was my job to move the pictures around, reuniting images that hadn't seen each other in years. But they didn't fit very well; the photos were mismatched and, when brought together, fuzzy. I wound up starting all over. I lined up the ones of my parents, over-lapping them as if I was trying to get the pictures to kiss, or at least hold hands like Kodak's answer to Ken and Barbie.

After a while I gave up on playing house. I've played this game before, many different times and many different ways. And I always end up feeling more sad. Some homes exist only in your head. It's all a fantasy, but the kind you can really imagine, the one you want the most. My parents and me are together only in those pictures. That's how we live as a family—inside a box, unshuffled and unframed photos, up on the top shelf of a locked closet in a room that we don't even use anymore.

But there were also many pictures of my grandparents, and that's what I came to look at this time. There they were, smiling in one picture, serious in another—but always together. I was staring at their pictures, not to see what they looked liked, but to peek underneath their sleeves, trying to read the arithmetic, those magic numbers that might bring them back and make everything right again.

In most of the pictures they were all dressed up: Rose in long-sleeved dresses; Lothar in jackets and ties. But in some they were on the beach, in Miami Beach, because that's where they lived after they left Washington Heights. Oliver was in some of the pictures, too, a little boy caked in zinc oxide, a diving mask strapped to the side of his head like a tumor, standing in front of sand castles, holding his blue canvas raft as if it was a surfboard. A sad face, like he was afraid of the ocean, or maybe it was something else.

I couldn't find a good picture of my grandparents with their arms naked. The camera never got close enough to take a snapshot of the blue numbers. Probably nobody was pointing the camera in that direction. You don't take portraits of that kind of thing. And they were probably hoping to keep their tattoos out of the picture. That's why they moved to Florida: The Sunshine State was the one place where they hoped they could burn those numbers right off, make the blue dye go away like peeled skin. And if that didn't work, they could just tan right over it. They never imagined that their granddaughter would one day need a picture not of them, but just the numbers, the digits they were trying to get rid of all along.

I used a magnifying glass, focusing on their arms, trying to bring the numbers closer. Then I had a better idea. I would take the pictures to one of those fancy photo-developing shops down in the Flatiron District. That's where all the fashion models and professional photographers go.

"You see the numbers over here?" I said, turning the picture side-ways, the tip of my tongue touching the corner of my mouth. I do that when I get nervous.

"I don't see any numbers," the man working at the counter replied. He was nice and patient. His oily black hair was long and seemed to stick to the back of his motorcycle jacket, which he was wearing even though we were inside the store and the heat was on. In one of his ears were two gold-studded skull-and-bone earrings. I don't think he took a bath that day or even the day before that.

"It's hard to see it, but it's there, I'm telling you," I tried to convince him. "You see these marks . . . ?"

We laid the pictures under a strong light and took turns squinting into a magnifying loupe. We were like astronomers trying to bring one distant star into focus.

"Yeah, there it is," he said, pointing. "I see it, right there. Wow . . . they really are numbers!"

The guy working the counter settled down and asked, "Why would these people have numbers on their arms? Were they in some kind of college fraternity or something? They must have been really cool for their time."

"Yeah, cool," I said, and then felt sad for all of us. "Is there a way to blow this picture up so I can actually read those numbers?"

The next day there was a larger version of the same picture. The two left arms—each with a row of blue numbers—were much easier to read, but the blown-up picture made my grandparents look like giants.

I still needed one more item to complete the potion. Candles. Special ones—the Jewish kind. *Yortzeit* candles remember the dead. If they can do that, maybe they can also work to resurrect them. So I went to the Korean grocer on Broadway and Eighty-fifth Street, headed straight to the back of the store, found the bottom shelf, right next to the Keebler cookies and the cat food, and grabbed eight *yortzeit* candles, which I juggled against my chest and finally dropped into a basket.

I never saw Oliver light a *yortzeit* candle in our house, even though, in our family, we would never run out of reasons for lighting them. So many dead people. And for Oliver, a dead marriage, too. I wondered whether you could, or should, light a *yortzeit* for that.

A young Asian woman was behind the cash register. She gave me a funny look. Probably no one ever came in here before and bought so many of these candles at one time. It wasn't like the store was having a sale on *yortzeit* candles, trying to get Jews to stock up for later.

"Special occasion?" she asked, then smiled.

"Family reunion," I answered.

Right by the cash register, stacked in two neat rows, were packages of Drake's Funny Bones. I picked one up and added it to my order, for variety, to break up the monotony of my grocery basket.

Finally it was time to start my séance. That's when I realized that there wasn't all that much mud in my backpack, after all. I couldn't return to the lighthouse, so I had to make do with what I had. I shaped my monster the best I could, added more water and even some leftover matzo meal from a Passover seder a very long time ago. But my golem looked puny, less like a monster than a Star Wars toy. A Jewish Buddha, or Jabba the Hutt. Not very threatening or alive. It didn't look like it could ever rescue this family, or any other.

The eight *yortzeit* candles flashed their beams on my golem like the Little Red Lighthouse washing the river with its light, searching for lost ships. I took out my violin and began to play. An uncalled-for ingredient in the golem recipe, but I felt like I had to improvise with my own formula, which included Hudson River mud, an empty attic filled with *yortzeit* candles, klezmer violin solos, and numbers that once belonged only to Lothar and Rose Levin.

I played all the songs that were already in my head, freeing them to wander inside the attic, letting them run around, bounce off the walls, and whisper into the ear of my golem. The lady on Broadway told me that one of the songs was meant to be played only for the dead parents of orphans. So I kept repeating that song, "Invitation to the Dead," over and over, because my grandparents were dead, and their son was an orphan, and I was inviting them—if not to a wedding, then to an unburial.

My face was drenched in sweat, which was seeping into the tailpiece of my violin.

Finally I called out: "Two, zero, one, six, seven, one, four, eight, two, two . . ." I chanted the numbers, using the blown-up pictures as a crib sheet, repeating them, making sure they were in the right order. And when I was finished, I improvised some more: "Auschwitz, Birkenau, Majdanek, Treblinka, Bergen-Belsen . . ."

The *yortzeit* beamed brighter, dancing all over my golem like a sunrise. The music from my violin, which I had stopped playing, still echoed in the attic, like the drone inside a seashell. It even got louder. My head was filled with numbers and the names of concentration camps and the music I was no longer playing. I started to feel dizzy. But then I looked at the golem, and he looked dizzy too, as if his head was filling up with the same things that were in mine.

A FEW DAYS LATER, ON AN EARLY-WINTER NIGHT with snow falling lightly and Christmas trees for sale at opposite corners of Broadway, I left the brownstone, yanking up my coat collar, checking the gargoyles that watched over my building, and walked downtown to Lincoln Center. Evelyn Eisenberg, my agent, had called earlier in the week and invited me to have dinner with her at Tavern on the Green.

"Come on, I want to see you," she said over the phone. "We have business to discuss."

Evelyn is slightly built, with commanding hair, a large, disarming smile that often turns into an effusive laugh, and calipers for a handshake. Always impeccably dressed, she wears feminine power suits, bright silk scarves, and eyeglasses the size of storefront windows.

It had been more than a year since I last showed her the manuscript I had been working on—the book before the one that I had
abandoned because of the block. I hadn't yet told her what the problem was. The book she was looking for me to finish was under contract; the block was not. My delivery date was now like a missed
birthday; I couldn't get it back. I would just have to wait for the next
one. But Evelyn wasn't interested in another book. I knew why she
wanted to take me out to dinner. A face-to-face dressing-down was
what she had in mind.

A white Manhattan sky consumed the evening darkness. Large
snowflakes were beginning to fall harder and fast, but disappeared
when hitting the ground, like darts with collapsible needles. The
urban lights from buildings, cars, and windows careened off the
clouds and reflected back onto the street. The pedestrian traffic was
typical for a Saturday night: manic and musical. Three men shared
one umbrella, stutter-stepping as though part of a Bob Fosse chorus
line. A blind man tapped his stick, somehow managing to sort out
the various noises that surrounded him. Another man blew his nose
without a Kleenex, clearing one nostril at a time, mucus projectiles
that found friends on the pavement. A large woman wearing hoop
earrings the size of handcuffs was applying makeup and lipstick
while she walked. She was way off on precision; her face becoming
an expressionistic painting, something out of de Kooning—one of
his Women series, not on a bicycle, but on Broadway. A homeless
man with baggy pants and an open fly muttered loudly about some
injustice, but to no one in particular. Then came a sudden change of
temperament, and he demurely began asking for help—some
money, loose change, leftover food? Two young lovers paused at a
flower shop, examining the prepackaged bunches of lilacs, roses,
daffodils, and tulips that leaned like javelins against one another
inside oval buckets. The young man smelled the back of his girlfriend's hair while she sniffed the petals in front of her, proving once
again that the thing about falling in love is not about the love, but
the falling.

Before turning east toward the park, I wandered into Lincoln Center and sat by the plaza fountain. It sprayed water like fireworks, gripping the edge without overflowing, teasing the opera buffs who never got wet.

I passed a few horse-drawn carriages parked right outside Tavern on the Green. Next to them were yellow cabs and some blue stretch limos. The dark brown horses were anxiously tugging away at their reins, rebelling as if they knew this to be an unevenly matched race. I entered the restaurant, checked my coat at the counter and my face in the mirror, and asked the maître d' whether there was a reservation for two under the name of Eisenberg.

Evelyn was already there, prepunctual as always. She rose while I made my way over to our table, one that was set against the window, overlooking the brightly lit patio and garden—the bare trees decorated with seasonal Christmas lights. We kissed the way the French actually do, not on the mouth but on both cheeks. Neither of us was French.

"Oliver, you look pale," Evelyn observed. "You're all right, aren't you?"

"I'm fine, just having some trouble sleeping lately," I replied, sitting down, unfolding my stiffly creased napkin and setting it on my lap.

"I haven't seen you in so long, and you always seem so rushed and nervous on the phone. Look at your complexion." She held my chin and turned it toward the window, which reflected my face back at me, surrounded by melancholy Christmas lights. "I'm a little concerned," she said, staring. "Do you see what I mean?"

"Have you eaten here before?" I changed the subject.

"I occasionally take some foreign scouts and coagents here. Why?"

"It's so funny," I began, surveying the room. "All these people look like tourists and foreigners to me. Strangers to the city. First-timers. Everyone's got a camera right beside their bread basket."

"That's why I thought it would be nice. Something far away from those trendy, literary places down in the Flatiron area. I guarantee there won't be any other writers here tonight. Just you."

I looked over the menu, eyeing appetizers while Evelyn started in with her entrée for why she had suggested this meeting.

"How's the book?"

I froze inside the oversized menu as though it were a bunker.

"Just as I thought. Oliver, your novel is now obscenely late. Do you realize that? You need to finish the book already—"

I stopped her in midreproach. "Listen, Evelyn, I've been meaning to tell you, but I was afraid to hear your reaction, afraid to even admit it to myself, but here goes: I'm blocked. Haven't written a word in nearly a year. Even grocery lists are hard for me to compose nowadays."

"Not good, Oliver," Evelyn mused. "I never had a bestselling author with writer's block before. It's usually the serious, literary types who wind up with this kind of problem. My better writers."

"Thanks so much."

"Oh, come on, Oliver." She snickered. "Okay, have it your way. We both know who pays the bills around here. But at least let's give the artists their due."

"It would be nice to join their ranks, just once, maybe," I bemoaned, then adding, "I do have some good news. I think I figured out how to cure the block."

"Terrific. Let me hear."

A waiter arrived at our table bearing inside information on the specials for the evening. Evelyn shooed him away as if he were at the wrong restaurant.

"Well? I'm waiting," she said impatiently.

"Okay, don't laugh, but how about if I write something else entirely, something I've never done before? A literary novel, perhaps. Maybe something with a Jewish theme. How's that?"

Evelyn blinked behind those large glasses, which magnified both her eyes and her disbelief. Otherwise she was silent. Finally, she said, "Oliver, I don't know. You've been on Larry King. I don't think you have another genre in you."

"Evelyn, I can't do the old stuff anymore. I'm done with it. I have no more of those books in me. I feel like there's some other story out there somewhere. Maybe I'm blocked for a reason; maybe I'm going through a literary midlife crisis."

"Yeah, and you'll wind up a midlist writer, if that." Evelyn paused, then continued, "Let me think about this for a second." She pressed her lips together and looked up at the ceiling. The fingers on her right hand galloped like a racehorse on the white tablecloth. "Oliver Levin's first literary effort. Hmm . . . So tell me, what do you have so far? Any ideas?"

"No."

"Written any pages?"

"No."

"Taken any notes?"

"No."

"Done any work at all on anything?"

"No."

"Maybe you should pay for dinner. At least it will give you something to do."

The waiter had by then returned with his pad and his memorized script of unmenued items. Evelyn negotiated with him, the waiter not realizing that she drove hard bargains for a living. I was staring out the window into the garden, admiring the clinging procession of tiny lightbulbs and sculpted hedges. Guarding one flank of the patio was a King Kong made of black straw. Two bushes were landscaped into the shape of horses rearing in place.

The waiter left, and I couldn't remember what I had ordered or whether Evelyn had actually ordered for me without asking my opinion. Then she asked, "So how's Ariel?"

"She worries about me too much. And now she's getting into Judaism, way too deep for my blood. There are all sorts of books about the kabbalah in her room. That stuff is dangerous. And did I tell you she's been playing the violin?"

"I didn't know she could. When did she start taking lessons?"

"She hasn't taken any, as far as I know."

"What is she playing? I hope it's something classical like Mendelssohn."

"I don't think it's him she's been playing. I can't hear it so well. She mostly plays in the attic."

It was at that moment, looking up at the trees, that I saw them. It was their first appearance—barely distinct, hazy and disembodied, empty visions, there and yet somehow not there at all. I was able to see right through them, and yet they were real, more lifelike than the scarecrow Kong that otherwise dominated the garden. Before then they had been just hide-and-seek noises. Now, haunting outside my house for the first time, they had taken on shape, and body, and expression.

"What's the matter?" Evelyn asked, then turned toward the window, following my visual path. "Pretty trees, don't you think? I love how they do this every year. I wonder if it hurts the branches?"

Whatever was out there was becoming clearer, the focus sharpening, tuning into my frequency, crystallizing the reception—both the vertical and horizontal hold. The visions had faces, and they brought friends with them—six in all. All men, each perched on a separate branch, scattered on different trees, each blinking at me, dead eyes sending out private messages.

Their faces seemed hollow, with sunken cheeks, even though the rest of their bodies appeared well fed. Their eyes were enormous, dilated by fright, their souls lighting up the sockets.

And there was something more. They were wearing uniforms. The colors were fading in and out. I squinted, and seconds later, the uniforms appeared to look more and more like threadbare gray pajamas. And the colors were not colors at all, but rather black stripes on white.

Those who had once lived with demons had now joined the other side.

I stood up from my chair and headed for the side entrance. My napkin fell off my lap and floated like an enchanted bedsheet down to the ground.

"Where are you going?"

Evelyn followed me out, but first she went to the coat-check room and retrieved our coats.

"Here, put this on," she said, while we stood outside. "We'll freeze to death. What are we looking at?"

I peered into the naked trees as if I had lost a kite. The visions had each dropped down a branch or two. Friendly, inviting creatures. Obviously they wanted to make it easier for me to take a closer look. Music was being pumped out in stereo onto the patio; the lilting rhapsody of "Strangers in the Night" lifted into the darkness. I could hear the horses parked out front pulling wildly on their reins, neighing as if anticipating danger. Animals are sensitive to high-pitched warnings. It's in their nature. But what about me? While everyone dined in oblivion inside, the horses and I seemed to be the only ones aware that we weren't alone.

"What's going on? Do you hear those horses?"

I didn't answer, nor did I hear Evelyn say, "Oh, Oliver, it's so beautiful. Dance with me, Oliver. Dance with me."

Ever the determined agent, Evelyn strapped her arm around my waist and reached out to straighten my left arm. Soon she whirled me into a spin, which resulted in a near whiplash moment since my eyes weren't quite finished gazing into the trees. Evelyn obliged by dipping me into a position from which the phantoms of Tavern on the Green now stared back at me upside down.

"What a wonderful night," Evelyn remarked joyously. "The cool night air, the winter garden, the lights on the trees, the beautiful waltz music—"

"The ghosts in the trees."

"What?"

Then the music changed, abruptly but seamlessly, as though a DJ had just been handed a new request. It was the music from *Mary Poppins*, the movie that Ariel had loved so much as a child. The song "Chim Chim Cheree"—the one about the chimney sweeps of old London. But this time, while Evelyn and I twirled around the patio, with dining tourists watching us from within the warm belly of the restaurant, I realized that we were no longer dancing alone. The visions had floated down from the trees. They picked partners and began to dance as well. Now at eye level, their uniforms became even clearer, or was it simply that they had made yet another quick change of costume? What had earlier looked like soiled, striped pajamas now resembled black tuxedos and tails, with top hats, no less.

Evelyn danced blithely, unaware that we were waltzing on a suddenly crowded dance floor.

"This is the most fun I've had in years," she said. "What a great idea to come out here. You'd think other people would step out and join us. What's with them? No spirit whatsoever. I wonder if the waiter will tell us when our dinners arrive? What do you think, Oliver?"

By then I had already fainted, completely collapsed into Evelyn's arms. An ambulance, a loud siren blaring as if we were in the middle of an air raid, a red beam flashing like that of a bloodied lighthouse, was taking me to Roosevelt Hospital, with Evelyn sitting beside me worriedly.

I don't remember what happened after that. All I recall is feeling groggy, as if I had been drugged. But it was an unusual sensation, not like the buzz from an anesthetic. It was more like an altered dream state, slipping in and out of REM—but not even my own—an uncanny awareness that there were other pockets of the universe, and that I had just exited out of one.

"What happened to him?" I heard a young ER attendant ask urgently.

"He was acting a little strange, we were dancing, and then he just fainted," Evelyn reported with a quickened, anxious voice. "It was really like he saw a ghost or something. He turned white, and the next thing I knew, he fell into my arms."

"A ghost?" I heard Ariel ask. She must have made it to the hospital as well. Yet she didn't sound alarmed, but rather relieved, reassured in some knowing way.

I started coming to just as Evelyn felt the need to clarify: "Well, . . . I mean . . . not a real ghost, certainly, but . . ."

THE MATZO HAD ARRIVED, WHICH WAS A GOOD thing, because this wasn't Brooklyn, but Turin, and matzo makers weren't exactly sweating away on every street corner. Here in Italy you can get all the cheese and macaroni you want; and white, long, crusty breads; and the richest of olive oils; but not the yeastless, semiburned wafers of Jewish affliction.

Primo had called the Jewish Center and was pleased to hear that the Passover tables of Turin would once again have their matzo. So he went for a walk. Through the town square and around its ancient and ornate Florentine fountain, past the local shops and playground. Children were laughing on rocking swings, and he stopped to observe. He was well known throughout Italy and had become a national treasure, but in Turin he was more like a beloved grandfather.

While watching, Primo remembered many other children whose play had been interrupted, who never got another chance to rock but instead had burned. And he thought about his life, here in Turin, as manager of a chemical factory, the days spent with his family, all his writings and public appearances, and most of all, his testimony.

When he was young he had dreamed of nothing but the sciences, and hiking through mountains, and his love of nature and Dante. But the world had changed positions—the moral axis bent, the gravitational pulls and continental shifts crisscrossing in opposing directions—and his position in it had changed too. Suddenly this shy man, intimidated by women and spiders, was called upon to be one of the world's foremost witnesses. He never asked for this responsibility, but it had become necessary and inevitable. He had been selected for this purpose. He was morally bound to tell the story because he had seen the fire, and such revelation could not remain a secret. It had to be shared. How could it be otherwise?

During the past few years his depression had deepened, and fewer people seemed interested in what he had to say. And he really didn't have anything new to describe because, for the first time, he was suffering from writer's block. After all these years he had finally been silenced, not by those who wouldn't listen but by himself. His art had betrayed him. The steel trap of his memory was now snapping shut on itself. He had been sabotaged by a mind that had for too long reflected much too deeply on the losses and the pain of his people. Perhaps now the memories that had been burned into him had finally burned themselves out. And there was nothing he could do about it. Just wait, and perhaps one day the synapses, the nerve endings, and the inspiration would return.

But what to do in the meantime? As much as he tried to shut his eyes while watching the evening news, or while reading the national papers, he could not block out what had obscenely, and unconscionably, returned. Neo-Nazis were marching all over Europe. Their numbers were small, but so had Hitler's storm troopers been fifty years earlier. There is no comfort in knowing that fascism begins at the margins, because Primo knew that such ideas often have a tendency to creep their way into the center of human life—when the conditions are right, when morality is on hiatus, when the conscience is forever clear, when guilt loses its meaning, and when all that matters is the deaf drum of indifference. The Nazis had come back. They were once again young, towering, blond, and monstrous, and at the same time, in denial of what their forebears had done.

Primo walked home, retrieved his mail from the concierge in his building—whom he addressed politely and without any hint of despair—and walked up the four flights of circular stairs to his apartment. A few hours later he emerged, closing the door to his home, and stood silently, tentatively, and deliberatively at the banister. Where was he to go? What was waiting for him down there? It was going to be Passover soon, and the matzo had arrived. Maybe he would be able to write again. Maybe the new Nazis would stop marching. Maybe his years of witness would soon result in a better world, one that was listening and finally understood. But he had lived long enough, and had seen enough, to place more trust in his doubts than in his hopes. Cynics are made, not born—the consequence of ongoing double-cross and disappointment. The world saw him as a life-affirming optimist, but that perhaps was itself too optimistic. What is a man who has survived the darkest, red-hot abyss that even Dante himself could never have envisioned?

His muscles were frail, but they were strong enough to propel him. Down the stairs he tumbled, turning over and over like an infant in a poisoned womb.

∽∘∾

[*Following a commercial announcement.*]
"We're back with Jerzy. So tell me, I heard this story about you, and I'm not sure I should believe it."

"If it's about me, I'm afraid that it is probably true."

[*The audience laughs.*]

"I heard you said somewhere that you are a professional hider—that you know how to hide in any spot, no matter how small, no matter where it is."

"Yes, Dave, that's true."

"Come on . . . what does that mean?"

[*The host then produces his own goofy laugh.*]

"It's no joke."

"Are you saying that I could pick a spot, any spot, and you would be able to hide there?"

"And nobody would be able to find me."

[*The audience laughs once again.*]

"How long could you stay there?"

"As long as I'd have to."

"What about food?"

"I'd eventually find some, and then go back into my hole."

[*The audience and the host laugh even louder.*]

"That's really hard to believe."

"Well, I could prove it to you if you'd like. For instance, I could find a small place right underneath your desk, right by your feet, and I could stay there for the rest of the show and you wouldn't know it. You would never feel me or hear me breathe. Time would pass. You would bring out more guests, you'd shuffle your feet around, and you'd never notice I was there."

[*Much greater laughter this time.*]

"Right under my feet, right there?"

"Yes. I would make a home for myself, and you would go about your business, not noticing me."

[*The room goes silent. TelePrompTers lose their effect on everyone.*]

"Jerzy, you are an amazing and always entertaining guest. Thanks for visiting us again. Please come back real soon."

"Of course, Dave, always. . . ."

∽○∾

Oh, the ironies that go unnoticed by a popular culture oblivious to history. Let them laugh; the joke was on them all along.

This was how people knew him. Raconteur, bon vivant, celebrity guest, party animal, sexual deviant, pathological liar. Controversial prizewinning novelist, accused of having relied on ghostwriters. But why expect anything else? Ghosts and writers. This is what Jerzy knew best. He spent most of his lifetime communicating with ghosts—whether they were writers or not. And isn't it true that all writers of atrocity are essentially ghostwriters?

Jerzy was the life of the party; no, he *was*, in fact, the party. Wherever he went people were charmed by him, laughed with him, were hypnotized by his stories, his wit, his intellect, his deceit. He made up fantastical stories, adventures that he could never have lived, and then convinced himself and others that he in fact did live them, just as he had said. That's all they saw, and what he showed them. He prowled the city's sex clubs and engaged in carnal acts that gave his personal life the allure of a carnival. He climbed over and around New York's toniest social circles. He appeared in movies and continued to write despite the dark cloud that hovered over the authenticity of his authorship.

One day he composed a note to his wife, informing her that he was about to take a very long sleep. He then swallowed the recommended number of barbiturates required to end one's life. He slipped a bag over his head and dipped himself into his bathtub. A short while later, the eccentric clown who had made everyone laugh, the painted bird who was always in hiding, was finally dead himself.

❧

He was one of the men of Canada—not the country but the barracks. They worked the transports; the cattle cars pulled in, the choking doors slid open, the mobs and the feces and the dead piled out, half-living eyes squinted in the new light while Tadeusz and his fellow ramp workers stripped the arriving inmates of all they had brought with them.

"What will happen to us?"

"They said we were going to be resettled."

"Is this a work camp?"

"What do you call this place?"

"Has anyone seen my daughter?"

"Please help me, my husband is sick!"

"Why are you taking my belongings from me?"

This was the daily foreground music that surrounded him as he performed his work. The same questions asked over and over in different languages. All throughout the day the transports arrived, and when the whistle stopped blowing and the doors swung open, Tadeusz heard the same questions, asked again and again, spoken by the most desperate, clinging, and paralyzed people on earth.

He wasn't Jewish, but rather a political; that's what it said on his patch. And that designation, combined with his privileged position as a man of Canada, made his situation less ominous than almost everyone else's. And he was far better fed than the Jews who were marked for a death sentence that had virtually no chance of ever being commuted or reprieved. If he didn't screw up, he would survive. But then to do what? The music in his head would never stop; in a broken world it would play on like a broken record. Over and over again he would hear it, long after the last transport had arrived, when the smoke over Auschwitz had cleared, when the Russians had finally come to liberate all who had been there—the more privileged and the completely damned. But these Russian comrades had the power to liberate only his body; they couldn't do anything to free him from his memory.

The music took on many atonal melodies, none sweet. Each one lacerating of the soul, puncturing of the eyes, murdering of the mind.

There was a mother running away from her own child, and about this he wrote:

She is young, healthy, good-looking, she wants to live.

But the child runs after her, wailing loudly: "Mamma, mamma, don't leave me!"

"It's not mine, not mine, no!"

Tadeusz turned on the gas to an oven that was wedged into the corner of a small flat that he occupied in postwar Poland. He made sure that all the windows were closed and then plunged his head inside the open door of the oven. He could think of no other way to silence the music, to take the needle off the record, to finally put a stop to the crucifying coda that played mercilessly without end.

∽∘∼

We shovel a grave in the air, he wrote.

Could anything be more true, and indicting, and yes, even poetic?

He had become Germany's greatest postwar poet, a Jew, a survivor, writing in the language of the murderers. *The Death Fugue* was virtually a national anthem, performed on radio, mandatory reading in all German schools.

The philosopher Theodor Adorno had warned that it was barbarous to make poetry after Auschwitz. And yet that's what Paul did; he wrote poems, in complicated, thick, elliptical Germanic verse. Some accusing, some not. Often biblical. Nearly always inaccessible. But it was through verse and lyric and meter that he demanded from Germany's mother tongue the acknowledgment of the atrocity, an aesthetic reversal of that other murderous poetry—the Final Solution to the Jewish Question.

In this way, in this improbable form, his poetry haunted the very land that had given birth to all those ghosts—most of whom he had never met, and those whom he would only later come to know.

But while living in Paris, after years of suffering through long periods of despair, and outraged by the return of neo-Nazis, Paul jumped from a bridge into the Seine and drowned. Although he had once been a good swimmer, on that day he allowed himself to sink like a stone, to close his eyes and surrender to the stream, thinking of nothing else other than the golden hair of Margarethe, and the ashen hair of Shulamith.

∽ல்∾

He who has been tortured remains tortured.

Jean not only wrote those words, but lived them, as well. For him there was no recovery from the torture. No way to heal, and no real interest in healing, either.

So his writings and private dealings always had a caustic edge; his sword raised high, bitterness his natural suit of armor. He refused to forgive and mocked anyone, particularly those who had survived, who appeared to soften or showed insufficient rage. He called them "forgivers," and for him that was the worst insult of all.

Was it all cathartic—the more intense the hate, the stronger the internal life force, the better one is able to vanquish the memories? Or was the opposite true? Perhaps hate was a sure-fire way to self-sabotage, to choke on the unvapored poison of the Nazis—not the gas, but the hate itself. An even cleaner death; so much more lethal and pure than Zyklon B. Hate is the chemical reaction that works from within. It is an organic toxin that poisons heart and hope. It may not bring on the most immediate death, but it is without question a long-lasting cancer—the slow burn of the soul.

He said that faith in humanity could never again be recaptured. But he still had to live among men, in a world so prone to human error, where the lessons go unlearned, the crimes unpunished, and the madness repeated.

And so, how does one find a reason to live? The answer is simple: One doesn't. At best a person just exists, leaving the quality-of-life concerns to others.

One day, with nothing troubling him other than his usual obsessions, Jean decided to torture himself with those pills, his "last path to freedom," as he would say. And in doing so, he choked, for the first time, on something else—a finality that silenced the hate but still brought no peace.

∽ல்∾

When the Russians arrived to liberate the camp, Piotr, like his fellow prisoners, didn't have much energy to applaud or show much gratitude. It wasn't because they weren't grateful. It's just that they had been left for dead, and in their minds (their bodies hardly existed at all) it was difficult to know whether they had yet passed over to the other side. Perhaps this new vision of soldiers who came to rescue rather than exterminate was all a mirage. Piotr and his wretched companions had been living for so long inside their own nightmares. Real life was not yet, if ever again, to be trusted or believed. That's why they were cautious in accepting what was before their eyes.

The Russians, on the other hand, were shocked to discover a camp that was a ghost town—from hell, of all places. Under the circumstances they didn't expect much pomp and ceremony from the ghosts who lived there. Dancing, overly appreciative skeletons, all exposed with their gross anatomies, was not what they would even have wanted to see. The gates to the camp were open, and credit properly belonged to the Bolsheviks. But the Russians were disgusted and simply wanted to leave. Throughout the war they were notoriously fearless. Yet here in the camp, the Russians were spooked by something they hadn't seen even in the Battle of Stalingrad.

That's because the camp was actually a cemetery, a way station for those who hadn't quite been finished off yet. But that didn't mean that the prisoners were alive, either.

How does one come to accept liberation when the central metaphor is death? The survivors were now free, but to do what? When Piotr had arrived at the camp less than two years earlier, he hadn't come alone. There were a young redheaded woman and two small children with him in that cattle car. A boy and a girl—Nathan and Malka. They barely made it alive in the airless, overcrowded coffins that brought them there.

During the first few months Piotr worked hard in the rock piles, and in his head. He had to convince himself that the smoke that billowed above the camp and lingered in everyone's lungs was not his family. He knew what everyone else knew: Thousands were being killed each day, gassed and then burned with such a frequency that Poland no longer had a sky, just a black firmament of death that insulated the sun from a world that deserved no natural light. The senses rarely encountered smells other than incinerated flesh. Could he smell the children, could he make out their faces in the clouds? He would look up, shudder, close his eyes, and return to the rocks.

He peered through the surrounding barbed wire each day, looking for the redheaded woman of his memory, and for Nathan and Malka. When the Russians finally arrived, he knew they couldn't liberate his family from a fate the Nazis had already sealed for them before they left. Only he was alive to walk away.

So much for liberation.

Piotr clung to the camp, not wanting to leave. This is where his family was. Without his family, there could be no liberation, no freedom. Parents are never expected to outlive their children. But in the underworld of Auschwitz, parents made radical adjustments to what they from now on would come to expect. Parenting had undergone a major paradigm shift. The little ones could die first; the little ones would die first.

Back in the day of the shtetls and villages, the big cities and quaint towns—before Auschwitz—no one knew from such things. There was no way to prepare for the nightmare, and no way to live with it either.

Piotr wrote and remembered, but remained anchored in Poland, as close to the camp as he could be—in case the old smells returned or the skies blackened in a nostalgically familiar way. He often stared at the sky, dreaming that the Polish clouds would rearrange themselves for a family photo—a new kind of photosynthesis, for the children, who could never sit still for a portrait.

One day he realized how much he wanted to become liberated all over again. But this time without the Russians. He simply had to summon the courage to liberate himself. With an early-evening checkerboard frost blanketing the tracks, he jumped in front of a train and was killed instantly. There was no human sound, not even any noises of the night, just a chugging undertaker of a locomotive charitably ending the misery of a former freight-car passenger.

Yet another leap toward liberation. He wanted a second chance to get it right. Perhaps this time liberation would bring him closer to his family, so far away from Poland, and even farther away from the camp.

8

THE NEXT DAY, AFTER I WAS DISCHARGED FROM the hospital, Ariel and I took a cab home. There was slurpy snow on the cratered roads of New York City, turned black from radial tires and vagabond grime. The sun was shining; Ariel was holding my hand in the backseat.

"Don't worry, Oliver," she said gently. "I think what happened last night was a good thing for you."

"You think seeing ghosts is good?"

"I think the ones you saw are good."

The cab pulled up and double-parked near the curb outside the brownstone. I slipped a few bills out from my wallet without paying enough attention to whose patriotic face was framed on the currency. For all I knew I had just paid a year's worth of tuition for the

Pakistani driver's kid at City College. After the taxi peeled off, its loose muffler sending up sparks from behind, we made our way to the curb and headed up the stoop.

I scaled the stairs and glanced at the gargoyles that watched over my home, the very same menacing ones that I relied on to protect us against evil. I have always had a special fondness for gargoyles, and these were particularly good at their job. Carved into the main entranceway, above the doorframe that led into the parlor floor, these Gothic images swelled from the stone with hanging tongues and mordant scowls. Confronted by watchdogs of such granite expression and constitution, who would dare violate my space, trespass on my homestead?

Yet on that day I noticed that my gargoyles, without my knowledge, had undergone a facelift. They were no longer nasty and fearsome looking. Their masks were now smiling, clownish almost, like unthreatening welcome mats.

"What the hell . . . ," I said. "Ariel, look at the gargoyles! Do you see anything different about them?"

"No."

"What do you mean, no? Somebody put a smile on our gargoyles. They weren't like that before. Don't you ever notice anything?"

"How could their faces change? There are no plastic surgeons for gargoyles on brownstones. Come on, Oliver, get real. Let's go inside."

My expression remained stone faced, somewhere between guarded and curious. My gargoyles, unaccountably, were able to display a much wider range of emotions. I hesitated before unlocking the door.

"What are you waiting for?" Ariel asked. "You forgot your keys?"

"No, my keys I have; it's my mind I think I've lost. Is there a surprise party waiting for me inside?" I looked at Ariel suspiciously. "Did you send out invitations?"

"Yes, but not for a party."

"What for, then?"

"A homecoming."

"Who's coming home?"

"Open the door and let's see."

I did as my daughter suggested and then tentatively turned the lock and opened the door. I entered and immediately noticed that the alarm system had been disengaged. There was no sound. I heard nothing at all.

"Did you forget to put the alarm on?" I asked.

"I guess. I ran out of here pretty fast after Evelyn called. I took a cab over to the hospital. I must have forgotten the alarm. Sorry, Oliver."

"I just don't want any break-ins, that's all."

"It's okay. The house is safe."

"How do you know that?"

"No one is coming to get you, Oliver. At least not in a regular break-in kind of way. If anyone is here, they're not robbers."

I was showing little curiosity in my daughter's insights. She was already late for school. I gave her money and watched her flag down a cab on her way to Stuyvesant.

"Have fun today, Oliver," she said before ducking inside. "Maybe what happened last night will get you back to writing."

"I don't see how insanity will help."

Soon after she left I entered the master bathroom, closed the door, and dropped my jeans. It was then that I saw the shower curtain jolt, then quiver.

"Who's there?!" I shouted.

I would have run straight through the apartment and out the front door, but for my pants, which had collapsed around my ankles and would have cuffed me and made me fall. I was too terrified to reach down and pull them back up. With the alarm left off and with no one here overnight, I feared that a prowler had heard me come in while he was up to no good. Now he was hiding in my bathroom, not having had time to make his getaway.

"Come out!" I demanded. "I'll let you go. I won't report you to the police. Just don't hurt me." This was a fairly typical negotiating strategy between the solid citizens and common criminals of New York.

Absolute silence; even the toilet, which was usually backed up, made no noise. All I could hear was the sound of my own breathing, which only heightened the standoff between me and whoever was in my shower.

I could no longer tolerate the suspense. A sudden impulse of courage, or perhaps more likely, fear, led my arm to sweep back the shower curtain. And it was then, with my jeans gathered at my ankles and my heart throbbing through my chest, that I came face to ghostly face with my parents.

Even though they were in the shower, they were fully clothed, but incorporeally so, like invisible shadows of themselves. And they weren't alone. The standing-room capacity of that small space had now reached its maximum. It looked like an uncaged lava lamp, with shapes stretching and narrowing, elbows flailing like boomerangs, a body grafting along the tile like soap film, an ethereal but swaying head staring down at me from the ceiling like a nervy cloud, other figures crouched in the tub like snow globes. My shower had become an overcrowded fire hazard—filled not with water, but with the reincarnated dead.

"Put your pants back on, Oliver," my mother said. "This is how you come to see us?"

"Rose, we're in his home," my father defended me. This happened quite frequently when he was alive, too.

"Actually, we're in his bathroom, not his home," clarified a ghost with deep black eyes, wild black hair, and pixelated stubble that covered his face like war paint.

"More precisely, we're in his shower," said a balding, bent-over ghost with a stub of a neck and a squat nose that was as formless as dried-out Play-Doh.

"So appropriate, don't you think?" a tall ghost with an angular face and unruly gray eyebrows added.

"It was my idea," boasted a thin, curly-brown-haired ghost whose eyes disappeared into slits whenever his mouth smiled or laughed, which he did often. "Where better for us to hide? Who knows more about showers than we do? I, personally, turned a bathtub into a coffin."

"This whole idea still sickens me," my mother said, finding it hard to maneuver inside the cramped space of the pearly porcelain bathtub. "This is no way to drop in after all these years."

"I don't remember you having a better idea," the one with the curly hair defended his birthday-cake surprise. "We've been tiptoeing around for many days, making noise, moving things around, and he still didn't notice us."

"And then we went dancing with him last night, and he fainted on us," said a portly ghost with a long thin nose, narrow-set eyes, brown hair, and a formal, professorial demeanor.

"Yes, perhaps there was no other way to introduce ourselves," said yet another ghost, this one of slight stature, white spiky hair, thick-lensed black-framed glasses, and prominent owl-like ears.

Stunned, gutted of all reason, stripped of all sensation other than a jackhammer for a heartbeat, I would have pinched myself, but I had lost that power, too.

"This isn't really happening . . . right? Nobody's actually in my shower. This is just a nightmare. Okay, Ariel, joke's over."

Now I was talking to myself, too. I spat out a nervous half laugh.

"I know you must be surprised and upset, son," my father added dryly. "You couldn't have expected us. But we're here."

"You're right," I said, suddenly carrying on a conversation that for a second seemed perfectly ordinary. "I certainly wasn't expecting this. I kind of figured that if I ever saw my parents again, it wouldn't happen before I was dead. Wait a minute—am I dead?"

"Of course not," Rose reassured me.

"I assumed our reunion would be in heaven or in hell, but never on West Eighty-fourth Street. How . . . ? What . . . ?" I asked hopelessly, and to no one.

I counted eight in all—including my parents. I had never seen Rose and Lothar as ghosts, but the others I had. I recognized the remaining occupants of my shower as the very same visions I had seen in the trees at Tavern on the Green the night before. Now they smiled at me, shyly, these invisible creatures, projecting the kind of embarrassed expression that comes from having all once shared a one-night stand—in the form of a dance, and a spell, of the fainting kind.

"*Everyone out of my bathroom!*" I screamed, for the first time exerting authority over my home and bathroom.

"Go ahead, nature calls," said the one with deep black eyes, whose wild black hair was matted against the tile wall of the bathroom like bats' wings. "I really can't breathe in here anyway. You have us packed in like it's a cattle car, Jerzy."

"A fine way to come to the rescue, don't you think?" Jerzy, the mischievous curly-haired one, boasted. "And there's no gas in this thing, just water."

"Oliver, you should go and splash water on your face; then do something with the pants," my father suggested. "We'll meet you in the other room."

As I hoisted up my jeans, the ghosts, one by one, exited my shower, passing me as if I were taking roll call. They walked through my bedroom and out into the living room.

Gathering again, they seemed to be levitating as though they hadn't quite yet reacclimated to the altitude of Earth. But maybe they had been here all along, and it was I who needed to get used to the suddenly new, unsteady ground. Two of them sat on the sofa, doing so weightlessly, without sagging the upholstery. Others streaked through the air like projected light—jumpy, colorful images, moving as though they had just escaped from a kaleidoscope. They were curiously drawn to the bookshelves, examining the spine of every volume as though looking for something in particular.

My father then began, "We should all have something to eat."

"I vote that we send out," Jerzy suggested. "There's no real food in this place. What do you and the kid ever eat?"

"Oliver, what about you?" my father asked. "Have you eaten?"

A few of them started to bicker over whose turn it was to come up with a lunch plan.

"Chinese food," the tall one with the copper-wire eyebrows suggested.

"No, we had that yesterday," said the dapper portly one.

"Anything but kosher," insisted the unshaven black-haired ghost. "We should only eat *trayf*."

"How about Middle Eastern?" said the balding squat-nosed one.

"I would prefer pasta," said the one with the black-rimmed glasses, white-bristled hair, and conch-shell ears.

"Okay, cut it out!" I refereed the dispute.

What I really wanted was answers, which was a common theme in my family, even when my parents were alive. The questions were always mine, always open-ended and without resolution. But this time, with these visions docked so securely into my consciousness, I began to sense that answers were finally forthcoming—not right now, perhaps—eventually delivered in some new language, one that I didn't believe I spoke.

The eight of them started arguing all over again in my living room.

As a dream, no matter how unsettling or prolonged it was, it would soon have to come to an end—as all dreams do. I would wake up with a drenched sheet, heaving breath, and a resting pulse way over the speed limit. But even as a dream, there was no consolation. I was very much present in its unfolding. I was not a mere spectator. This nightmare was making demands on me, forcing me to participate, to not get too comfortable. It had no interest in me having a good night's rest. I couldn't wait it out by simply waking up.

This was no dream. This was a much lower depth of subconscious, the crucible where all riddles are revealed. This was a strange, unguided knowledge. Existing outside of books, and yet somehow finding their way back in, buried deep inside my brain, mocking my imagination.

"Enough!" I yelled out. "Stop it!"

The shrieks of ghosts deadlocked in debate came to an end. They screamed as if I had just scared them. Then each of their heads turned sideways to face me.

"Somebody better explain what's going on here!" I trembled. "This is my home. And this is my head you're all messing with!"

"What, he's going to call the police now?" the black-eyed, raven-haired ghost remarked jokingly. "They'll think he's crazy and lock him up."

Two others cackled, hiding their smiles behind invisible hands.

My father put his forefinger to his lips, quieting his cohorts. He then stepped toward me. I doubled back for obvious reasons. I wasn't quite ready to accept that my dead parents had returned—regardless of what brought them here, or for what purpose they had come. The haunted were now haunting, but why?

Despite his present wispy, ethereal silhouette, this apparition was so clearly my father. In death he had grown a short white beard. And while his final act in life was to blow his brains out, his spectral head was surprisingly still on straight. There was no sign of blood anywhere. A quick inventory of his X-ray anatomy revealed that for a dead man, his vital signs were excellent. Sure, what had once been a proud Florida tan hadn't quite held up so well in the next world. But I couldn't imagine that it mattered so much to him anymore. When he was alive Lothar walked with his back tilted a bit forward and his hands locked behind him. But now, as he skimmed toward me as a ghost, I noticed that he couldn't have been standing any straighter, and his hands were free to do whatever they wished. Wherever he had gone after committing suicide, the climate obviously agreed with him more.

"Oliver, we are all sorry," my father said, while my mother and their fellow underworld travelers nodded in sympathy. "This must be very difficult for you to understand."

"Yes, Oliver," my mother acknowledged. "This kind of thing doesn't happen every day."

"To say the least," the ghost with jet black hair and three-day facial growth added.

"Some of us have children, too, and they also would have been stunned by such a surprise visit," acknowledged the slight one with dark-rimmed glasses.

"Not all of us have children," the slouching, balding ghost with the squat nose said in a solemn voice.

"What is going on?" My voice sank and I started to tear. "What are you all doing in my house? Are you all real? Please, tell me. . . ."

"We're golems," the curly-haired ghost spoke up smugly.

"Well, not real golems," corrected the tall one with the thin sundial for a face and wiry gray eyebrows. "More like ghosts brought back to life because of a golem experiment gone haywire. The girl had the right idea; it's just that one never knows what can happen when you improvise with the kabbalah."

"Let's just say that your daughter overdid it just a little," said the chubby brown-haired ghost with the pompous air about him.

"A *little*?" the ghost with the curly hair and seemingly perpetual laugh added. "You call all of us a little? She's a mad scientist, that's what she is. She should stay away from experiments from now on."

"My daughter? Ariel?"

"Yes, your kid," the one with the brown Brillo pad coils for hair snapped again. "She's cute, but she's no kabbalist."

"Watch it, Jerzy," my mother defended. "She's the best kabbalist in her school."

Spoken like a true Jewish grandmother—dead or alive.

"She played too many numbers, you see," said the hairless, stubby-necked, but amiable ghost.

And then all of them, including my parents, in one flashy, choreographed move, each rolled up their sleeves and proved their membership in a singularly fated group, an unsecret society of once condemned men and women. There were the numbers, aniline blue, pulsing like tropical neon on invisible flesh. The ghosts stared at me as if they expected me to do something to fix the injustice, to somehow address the outrage. But I had never done anything like that before. So instead they remained still like accusing mannequins: fists clenched, arms straightened, blue numbers fuzzy in the miasmal glare of suspended death.

"I don't understand," I said.

There was magic in the air, but there was nothing under their sleeves other than those numbers.

"What's to understand?" my father explained. "It's the black magic of Birkenau."

"She was trying to make a golem, a creature of rescue," my mother explained. "But what she really wanted was to bring us back to life—your father and me. The poor child lost her mother, never had grandparents, never knew us. By bringing us back, she hoped we could fix things—for the both of you."

"A terrific child," the balding, squat-nosed, bent-over ghost with the round Slavic face said. He then spilled some tears of his own, which brought the other ghosts over to his side for comfort.

My mother continued, "She used these numbers—the ones on our arms—but she played too many combinations. That's why we didn't come alone. Ariel didn't realize what she had done, but she allowed us to bring along some reserves. It is an accident that these men are with us, but maybe it wasn't an accident at all. You have things in common with them, and that's why they are here."

"What, am I a ghost?"

"No, you are still mortal," Lothar reassured me. "But they are all writers, like yourself."

"Mystery writers?"

"No, atrocity writers," the ghost with black-rimmed glasses and white hair said.

"We should introduce you," my father apologized. Pointing at the ghost with the black-rimmed glasses, slight build, and distinctive, cable-dish ears, my father said, "This is Primo." The man nodded politely. "Over there is Jerzy," he continued, pointing to the one with the deviant smile and curly brown ringlets. "Right beside me is Tadeusz." He was the tall, thin one with the angular face and overgrown eyebrows. "And there is Piotr." He was the short, balding one with the bent posture. "Sitting on the couch is Jean." Jean hadn't spoken very much; he was the one with the shoe-polish-black hair, severe, unshaven face, and preternaturally angry, sullen expression—a levitating ghost obviously weighted down with despair. A cigarette was attached to a flashlight beam for a hand. Although unlit, the cigarette entered and exited his mouth with the controlled proficiency of a military salute. "And this is Paul," my father concluded, gesturing over to the portly brown-haired ghost with the thin nose, beady eyes, and professorial manner.

There was silence. I looked at my parents, who had nothing to say, and neither did I. After all these years what should any of us have expected? The way they came upon me, and surrounded by so many dead strangers. Surely I could not embrace them. And was there anything to grasp other than air?

"You don't know who these men are, do you?" Rose wondered, interrupting the impasse.

"No, should I?"

My mother, the ghost, began to cry.

"Yes, you should," Lothar said. "They are writers, all Holocaust survivors, and like us, each took his own life."

Paul glided over to console my mother. He was joined by Tadeusz, his face so thin and the light of his spirit so blurry that it looked as if my mother was standing beside the tripod reeds of a halogen lamp.

"I'm sorry . . . ," I began haltingly. "But what have you all written?"

"How can he not know of us?" Jerzy snapped, very much offended. "He's a child of Holocaust survivors, and a writer himself."

"He has a right to ask in your case," Jean scoffed, still sitting on the sofa. This was the way he normally blew smoke.

Primo approached me and gently said, "Like your parents, we lived through the unimaginable, but as writers we spent our lives trying to actually imagine it, to give it an image, to make it more real, as we had remembered it, even though the task itself was impossible, because we never could succeed in describing it. We wanted to make sure we wouldn't live our lives believing that it was all a dream, that it didn't really happen that way, that it was all in our heads. But the tragedy for us was that the more we wrote, the more it remained in our heads, and that itself may have been too much."

"Oliver, these men here," my father said, "they have written some of the most important books and poetry about the Holocaust. They have made art out of death; they have defied the limitations of language and used words to describe a scream and the sound of agony. You should be proud to have them in your home. We will all be living here for a while."

"Living? But you're all dead."

"This is true, but not completely," Primo, who had been a chemist, and so the life and death of organisms was of concern to him, said. "How to explain? Yes, well, normally when the body dies, all vital functions cease to work, and the spirit goes to a place in the universe that accepts its final journey. But sometimes there is the matter of unfinished business and unanswered questions. In our case, when we killed ourselves, we thought we were finished with this world—that's why we did it! But your daughter called us back. We had been discovered; our departure was premature—we weren't entitled to leave after all. We were reenlisting in life, but as dead people. And maybe that is as it should be."

My face channel-surfed through a variety of expressions without settling on a final one.

Primo continued, "The crimes of the Nazis were so great. Whenever one of the witnesses is no longer alive to testify, there is such universal outrage and revulsion. And because we all committed suicide, and because we were all artists, maybe we had no right to exit before we explain the meaning behind our final acts—even though we are not so sure ourselves. We owe this to the world, and to our fellow survivors. Do you understand?"

Jean and Jerzy both scowled at Primo and shrugged weightless, dissenting shoulders at each other.

"How long are you staying?" I asked. "And why here?"

"Until we're finished," Rose added.

"Finished with what?"

"You will soon see," Primo said. "As writers we relied on words, but as golems we know that sometimes words are not enough."

"More forceful, drastic actions might be necessary," Jean said, with ballast and bloated fists.

"Our deaths have taught us much," Paul added. "The suicides were not without purpose or lessons."

"We tried to warn the world while we were alive," Primo said, sitting on the windowsill, levitating, a sage in repose. "Perhaps we can do more this time, this way. The bloodiest century is ending, and a new one is beginning. Who knows how much more blood will be lost. The world must learn how to live with the Holocaust as it steps into the future, otherwise there will be no future. We know that man has a faulty memory, and a continuous need for new stimuli. In the next fifty years it is inevitable that the Holocaust will be deemed less important than it was in the last. New historical events will eventually overshadow this dark cloud; other stories will become more newsworthy."

"Like the O.J. trial," Jerzy said, "or that Jewish girl who gave the president a blow job."

"Jerzy!" Rose yelled.

"Well, it's true!" Jerzy replied. "A Jewish girl gave the president a blow job. Good for her, and also good for him."

Primo tried to ignore his friend. "The fact that the Holocaust will one day become marginal, maybe even irrelevant, was too difficult for us to bear. We could see it coming."

"Now we want to leave something that the world will remember," Tadeusz said. "Something different from what we wrote in our books, and even more lasting. Out of death can also come renewal."

"And maybe there is something we can do for you," Piotr said.

"What do I need?"

"You are a writer," Tadeusz said, "but you are not writing."

"But I'm not a Holocaust writer," I said.

They all flashed incandescent, ironic smiles.

"The writer's block is not what we are here to fix," Piotr said. "It is the other block that should be more important to you."

"What other block?"

"In science, it's always good to ask the right questions," Primo said. "Better even than having the answers."

"Yes, and a good mystery is best when it solves itself slowly," Paul said. "We have time for everything that we are planning to accomplish here."

"Yes, yes, we have plenty of time," Jerzy said, impatiently, then clasped his hands together, which made no sound at all. "This is our first night. What do you say, I'm back in New York, let me take us all to a club? What's the hip spot nowadays, Oliver?"

"What is a club?" Tadeusz asked.

"Dancing, drinking, models, drugs . . . ," Jerzy explained.

"No clubs," Primo said.

"All I want is to take a walk down Columbus with my baby carriage," Piotr announced.

"The carousel, the carousel," Paul chimed in. "That's what I suggest."

"No merry-go-round, but dancing again at Tavern on the Green," Tadeusz voted. "I love the music they play there. The old standards, the torch songs."

"What's playing on Broadway?" Rose asked. "I would like to see a nice show, a drama maybe."

The room began to spin, or maybe the room wasn't moving at all, but it was just me who had lost all balance. This time, however, there was no fainting. I was getting used to this new sensation—a stability that arises from vertigo itself. Whatever paranormal roller derby was playing itself out in my home, I had an obligation to stay alert, to take notes. I had all this proximity, and artistic curiosity. I am a writer, after all. Yes, blocked, but not brain dead. The gravity of their apparent visit was not lost on me. Nor were the narrative possibilities, even though these skills had seemingly abandoned me just when I needed them most.

"Oliver, go lie down and take a nap," my father suggested, and placed a floating hand on my shoulder. "You'll need your rest. We all need to rest."

9

THE VERY NEXT TIME THAT ARIEL WENT TO Zabar's—not for deli but to play her fiddle—she wasn't alone. She brought her grandparents with her. But before beginning her regular streetside concert, they all took a detour through Riverside Park.

Empty park benches overlooked the Hudson River. The glinting sunshine moonwalked on the water's surface. A large flower garden empty of flowers was planted right beside a sunken playground carved into the valley. Inside the playground were large, soft sculptures of hippos that children loved to climb on. Modern jungle gyms featuring animals that actually came from the jungle, rather than abstract, geometrical monkey bars. In the summer the hippos spouted water like the fire hydrants hijacked by

Dominican children uptown in Washington Heights. A hot-dog vendor stood underneath his umbrella stand and, curiously, sold more ice cream pops and soft, salted pretzels than Sabretts on a bun.

Ariel, Lothar, and Rose walked east toward Broadway. The young girl, flanked by her ghostly grandparents and toting a violin case, all of a sudden felt more protected, and parented, than ever before. At one point she lifted her arms and grabbed hold of the luminous, light-shaft limbs of her grandparents. It had been so long since she had last walked arm-in-arm between two adults. Ariel had little memory of being a child shielded by two parents—familial siding, the only coated protection there is outside the womb.

Yes, these were her grandparents, but they were dead relatives no matter what phantasmal phenomenon had resulted from her beginner's luck as a Jewish mystic. Her mind was now open to all possibilities, but her fists were closed tight around her grandparents' feathery, invisible hands. As her father had already wondered in his own reunion with his parents, no matter how desperately Ariel craved this very moment, she may have been grasping at nothing more kindred than air.

The grandparents spoke, and she answered, out loud, to what appeared to be no one in particular. Those who passed by her, walking their dogs or strolling alone, assumed that the young girl was either memorizing her lines for a school play, or still had not outgrown the occasional conversation with an imaginary friend. But Ariel wasn't concerned with appearances. Her grandparents had returned, all because she had summoned them. Her broken family had called in reinforcements, circled the wagons, brought in the reserves. Desperate measures had been necessary. Ariel's homespun experiment in mysticism and music had worked. And that's all that really mattered.

Perhaps it was all beginner's luck. Maybe it would have happened anyway. But what couldn't have been denied was that this family had been sorely in need of more hands—even invisible ones. Ariel's mother had abandoned her by leaving; so did her father, with silence. What was left was a single-parent home and an inversion of responsibilities. A shift in the parental paradigm. The kid was in charge. The father paid the bills; the daughter handled all the emotional deposits and withdrawals.

Samantha left, and Oliver became a broken man. Children need at least one parent who is in one piece, but her father was like a complicated model kit.

She began by asking all the right questions.

"What was Oliver like as a boy?"

"Was he happy?"

"Did he feel safe there?"

"Were you good parents?"

"Is the Holocaust responsible for everything?"

All loaded questions, and the grandparents were happy triggers. The girl wanted answers, but also feared them. Maybe she already knew what they would be. The test was fixed; her life was its own crib sheet. Her father's childhood was her childhood—only one generation removed. She knew what he felt because she had inherited those same feelings. This self-awareness painfully proved how unfinished her experiment had been, how much further she had to go. There was no quick fix in righting the twisted, tangled grief that kept her father bottled up with a curse far more crippling than mere writer's block.

The usual audience members had assembled outside Zabar's. Ariel's performances had achieved great word-of-mouth, having become a hot neighborhood free ticket. She was now playing three afternoons a week—from 4 P.M. to 5 P.M.—and again on Sundays, from 2 P.M. to 3 P.M. Loyal listeners stayed for the entire hour. This itself was uncommon for street performances in New York, where pedestrian traffic is always on the run. The best a performer can hope for is to break someone's stride just long enough to entice a hand to reach inside a pocket for a throwaway gratuity.

By contrast, Ariel's audience was more likely to plan their days around her concerts, finding any excuse to visit Zabar's, H & H

Bagels, Westside Kids, or even Barnes & Noble just in time to catch the afternoon klezmer show. This community, caught in a spell, was being summoned by a stringed musical instrument that had all the primal urgencies of a tom-tom or shofar.

Ariel removed the violin from her case, tapped the soundboard for good luck, then tuned the strings, beginning with the G, then D, then E, then A, a warmup exercise she had become fond of even though her intuition about tune and pitch was entirely instinctive and untutored.

As Ariel was getting herself ready, a dog, a scruffy white bichon with small, black eyes, barked at a homeless man who was wheeling a shopping cart filled with recyclable soda bottles. The homeless man managed to flee the scene, and then the self-satisfied dog waddled over to Lothar and Rose, sniffing at them as though he had picked up their scent, as if he had had prior dealings with golems. Lothar and Rose crouched down to pet and calm the dog, whose ears had instinctively perked up. From that position they noticed a stream of black soot that sailed out of a chimney on Columbus Avenue, breaking up into the sky.

Ariel looked into the crowd and saw Tanya Green, who waved at her shyly. Ariel then began to play, starting off with some of the lighter, bouncier, faster-paced pieces that always managed to whip people up into a wild klezmer mood swing.

"Keep this arm straighter, and loosen the one holding the bow," Rose said.

Ariel didn't know that her grandmother was a musician.

"So nicely you play," Lothar said encouragingly. "I wish we were alive to hear this."

"She is good, but I would like to see her playing the Bach Double Concerto," Rose said in a severe tone. "That would be a nice piece of music to hear. Let me tell you, *Kind*, this is not real violin music. Even when I was a child in Poland, klezmer was already considered too Jewish. I leaned toward classical tastes."

The violin case was once again beginning to fill up with greenbacks, puffing out of the box like unquilted, goose-down feathers.

"My God!" Rose exclaimed. "A person could make a decent living playing on the street like this."

"And it's all cash," Lothar noted.

"America is such a strange country," Rose remarked. "Klezmer music on the street, and all these people come. Are they even Jews?"

"I can't tell." Lothar squinted through eyes doubled up in laugh lines.

Ariel didn't stop. Music rose from within her, but so too did the sounds of her grandparents.

"What was he like as a boy?" Lothar resumed the conversation. "This is a good question. But the truth is, he never was a boy."

"That is true," Rose acknowledged. "We didn't give him a chance for such things."

"He was alone in the house, even though we were there with him all the time," Lothar said. "And he grew up afraid to be in his own home. We were too scared, and scarred. We probably should not have been parents."

"Lothar!"

"It is true, Rose. We had no right—we were arrogant and narcissistic—to think we were entitled, capable of raising a child in a normal home. We lost all sense of what it meant to have a home, to feel safe in one, and that is the most important thing that a parent can do for a child."

"Yes, a child must feel safe," Rose conceded, while a stranger placed a lost, broken doll, ripped at the leg and leaking its stuffing, on top of a corner mailbox.

"And how could we give him what we didn't feel ourselves? We couldn't feel it, and we were incapable of showing it because we didn't believe that safe was possible anymore."

"And so he was afraid," Rose said.

"Of everything."

A loud car alarm echoed with nerve-jarring, sense-numbing repetition. Ariel concentrated and continued her strokes, but felt the presence of panic beside her, as if a dog whistle had just battered her grandparents' eardrums. Lothar and Rose jumped out of their non-existent skins.

"What was that?" Rose screamed.

"Nothing, just a noise from a car," Ariel whispered without missing a note.

"The streets of New York are not noisy enough? Why should a car make such a noise?" Rose wondered. "Where was I?"

"We were telling Ariel about Oliver," Lothar regrouped his wife.

"Of course, yes, I remember, . . . and he would run to other homes."

"Because there, or anywhere away from us, was better for him."

"Unforgivable of us."

"Yes, unforgivable."

"And he excelled at all things," Lothar said, "because he felt that he had to be all things, to compensate for and replace everything we had lost."

"But what we lost could never be replaced."

"Nobody could do all that."

"He tried to rescue us, to fix his parents."

"But we couldn't be fixed or rescued." Rose pitied herself. "I'm not sure we even wanted to be rescued. Children can never do that for their parents, no matter how hard they try—even if there is no Holocaust in the family history. Do you hear what I am saying, Ariel?"

The ghosts of her grandparents shook their heads from side to side like metronomes to Ariel's music, but klezmer was now no longer in the foreground. The answers to the girl's questions had become the real performance sounds of the street, although no one on the street, other than the main attraction, could hear them. The audience had fallen under the spell of Ariel's klezmer violin, while the virtuoso herself had succumbed to an entirely different kind of magic—the same snake-charming sorcery responsible for the music and for turning her home into a haunted house.

"But he tried, and children don't like to fail their parents," Lothar said. "And we made him feel like a failure, because we were never anything other than damaged. That was our legacy to your father."

"Did you know what a tremendous student he was? And an athlete?"

Ariel answered her grandmother not with words, but with overly gestured and silky strokes of the bow. Some came with rapid-fire stabs, others were gentler and more delicately paced. And there were other movements, ones that had nothing to do with the violin at all. Welled-up tears threatened to soak the violin, but for the sake of the music, waited out the concert.

"And what he could play on the piano and guitar!" Rose boasted.

"What couldn't he play," Lothar said.

A boy about Ariel's age, with blond hair cut finely against the back of his scalp and a monstrous crush on the klezmer sensation of Upper Broadway, sidled over to get a better look. He tried to make eye contact before floating a mangled dollar bill into the crammed bed of cash that was now begging to be relocated to a cello case. This adolescent mating ritual, however, for the moment at least, was lost on Ariel.

"Our son doesn't know how to trust," Lothar said.

"And your mother didn't help him, with what she did."

"And neither did we."

"He is still very scared, with no sense of the future, or that there will even be a future."

"How in the world did he look after you?" Rose asked.

"We broke all the rules for good parenting. Then we killed ourselves, because however much we tried, we could never figure out how to be good parents. We were robbed of the essential qualifications for the job—faith in life, and humanity, at least as it applied to us. But by ending our lives, what hope did we leave him with? All he knows is loss."

"And how to write a good mystery story, because for him, his whole life was a mystery."

And Lothar finally answered Ariel's last question. "And no, we didn't talk about the Holocaust much in our home, because we didn't have to. You don't speak about it with your father either, because you realize, just like Oliver did at your age, that it lives inside you. And you already know that the Holocaust is responsible for everything."

Confessions accompanied by music. The dollars kept coming. More passersby joined the gathering crowd. Tanya Green's head swayed while she took mental notes on Ariel's technique. And all the while the grandparents continued to spill their saga, uncarting their laments, exhuming their contritions, filling the air with yet more unseen music that only their grandchild could actually hear.

And later that night, preparing for sleep, with the violin tucked away, the golem doll poised on her dresser, and her grandparents sitting on either side of her bed, Ariel asked, "Please read me a story. The one about the lighthouse."

"Aren't you by now too old for us to do that?" Rose wondered.

"Nonsense," Lothar scoffed. "One can never be too old to be read to at night. In fact, everyone should have a bedtime story read to them before they go to sleep—the young, the old, and the in-between."

The teenager had gone far too long without her father reading to her at night. She had not outgrown it at all, but understandably longed for it even more.

"And, ah yes, the lighthouse story," Lothar said while pulling the book closer to his reading glasses. "We know this one well."

"We have another story to tell you about this lighthouse, a surprise." Rose smiled knowingly. "But for now, this will have to do."

10

PRETTY SOON JUST ABOUT EVERYONE ON THE Upper West Side got used to the fact that their neighborhood was haunted. The confirmations were evident and everywhere.

"Oh my God, what happened to my anklet alligator tattoo?!" a purple-haired, nose-ringed Barnard coed shouted on awakening one morning. "It's gone! Erased, like it came off in the shower."

Speaking of showers, elsewhere, in some hedge fund manager's penthouse apartment on West End Avenue, the shower was turned off for good. The lever was spinning around like a scene out of *The Exorcist*, but there was no water coming out of the spigot. The angry resident yelled at the super as if shouting out bids on the Chicago Mercantile Exchange, but to no avail. "I'm paying a shitload of maintenance for this apartment. And is it too much to ask for water to come out of the showerhead?!"

A tourist from France with a serious, unfiltered nicotine habit scrambled around the neighborhood scrounging for a cigarette, but there was none to be found. Korean markets and lotto shops no longer sold them, and nobody, except for this tourist, seemed to mind.

"What is it with this stupid country?" the Frenchman snarled and flipped his hand and nose in the air. "You cannot get good wine or cheese, and now you cannot find cigarettes—even American ones. What is the explanation for this?"

The Yankees were playing in the World Series again, but they were not wearing their standard-issue Bronx pinstripes. The uniform was regulation, except for the missing stripes.

"Hey, man, I liked the way we looked in our old unis," shortstop Derek Jeter complained to the equipment manager.

"It's not my fault, Derek," the Dominican from Washington Heights, fearing for his job, replied to the All-Star. "The uniforms came back from the cleaner's this way. I guess the stripes got washed out."

There was nothing left for anyone—including the young short-stop—to do other than think ghostly thoughts. Either these people had to embrace the enigmas head-on and accept that not everything in life was meant to be fully understood, or they had to surrender unconditionally to madness. Their unsheltered world had suddenly become overrun with something from a more audacious other.

These New Yorkers were not so good at leaving it at that. This was a community comprised, for the most part, of the sound and rational mind. They prided themselves on a certain refinement, an awareness of both self and surroundings, and a commitment to keeping their aspirations focused on worldly, practical things. For this reason, horoscopes, tarot cards, psychics, tea leaves, the I-Ching, Ouija boards, and the like had little influence, historically, in guiding the conduct of those who inhabited the Upper West Side. These were not the sort of people who walked the streets with their heads in the clouds and eyes on the stars. The neighborhood was overly muscled with Ph.D.'s and assorted others who possessed advanced and professional degrees. Customarily a tough crowd when it came to unsupportable facts. They liked to see their data hard and their statistics free from sampling errors. Upper West Siders were people of the world—but most assuredly *this* world. It was difficult for them to accept the New York Jewish equivalents of Sasquatch and the Loch Ness monster. With no shortage of cynics among them, how were they to explain this invasion of mysterious phenomena, and its tampering with their rational lives?

They simply couldn't. Yet the improbable facts were hard to dispute, and sometimes even harder to see. Special effects more commonly seen in feature films repeatedly dazzled and bewildered the neighborhood. Strange vapors were swirling like spells. Miracles came quickly, then left without explanation before the next ones arrived. This was no mere Halloween parade in Greenwich Village, or David Copperfield's Statue of Liberty disappearing act, or Christo's pop art stunts, familiar parlor tricks that long ago ceased to impress New Yorkers. What was happening on the Upper West Side was not the enchantment of mere mortals play-acting as wizards. The sleight of hands came not from human limbs. What was happening here was a much more sophisticated sorcery, a hocus-pocus not imported from Hollywood or any known corner of the Magic Kingdom.

And it wasn't just limited to Piotr's ritual of taking to the streets with Ariel's old baby carriage, although that in itself was not easily ignored. The stroller would get wheeled up and down Broadway—unpushed and unoccupied—as though operated by remote control. Those out on the streets on their way to a corner market for a pint of Chunky Monkey, or an all-night drugstore for condoms, or simply having just gotten off their shifts from bars and restaurants, would gaze bleary eyed and recall that others had tentatively, and bashfully, reported the same sightings. A highly domesticated, identifiable moving object was making its rounds on the Upper West Side. But who—or what—was responsible for making it move?

Naturally the police and the mayor's office had been asked to investigate.

"There's a haunted baby carriage rolling down Broadway! Come quickly!" someone would yell into a pay phone after nervously punching in the numbers 9-1-1, while a frail, old woman dropped anchor on her foot with a bag of groceries. "No, I'm not on drugs! No, I haven't been drinking! Listen to me! I'm telling you to send a patrol car over here before it gets away!"

The stroller had committed no crime, nor was it in any way life threatening. It didn't impact negatively on the quality of everyone's life, like loud boomboxes, car alarms, drug deals, or urination on the public sidewalk. And by New York standards, although it was very much haunted, in all other respects the autopiloted baby carriage didn't stand out as either an eyesore or an extreme oddity. After all, freakier scenes have been observed in Gotham, and in great abundance: men dancing with dummies in the subway; college students walking and talking with parrots; hippies wearing live snakes as turbans; drag queens receiving Communion while still in costume; stockbrokers posting trades in the buff, power yellow ties still wrapped around their necks.

Granted, initially it was a shock to see. But in time, people became inured to its appearance. They even came to welcome it, as though it had become the unofficial mascot of the neighborhood. Some stopped to have pictures taken alongside of it. Most simply shrugged it off, convincing themselves that the baby carriage wasn't haunted at all; the four-wheeler was nothing more than another indulgent child-care curiosity on the Upper West Side.

With people accepting his nightly patrol, Piotr decided to venture out in the daytime, as well. But while the sight of the stroller became less creepy, the sound it made was another matter entirely. Those who heard the wheels venting a running commentary with each turn never managed to get those sounds out of their minds. It was the noise of grief. As the carriage strolled, Piotr, from behind, wept. He pushed the carriage as though it were a Sisyphean rock, all the while recalling why it was empty.

The closer one got to the carriage, the easier it was to pick up that unmistakable moan, that wrenching exhale of sorrow, that stuttered sob, those most pitiful of hyperventilated breaths. Piotr missed the children. He couldn't get over that loss while he was alive; now that he was dead, his ghost suffered from the same affliction.

"Malka and Nathan never had the chance to live as children," Piotr would say, in between the more familiar wordless laments. "And I never had the chance to be there for them."

"I think the carriage is crying again, Mommy," a toddler on the Upper West Side would exclaim.

"Yes, dear," her mother would reply, "you're right, but we have to hurry—we're late for your gymnastics class at Chelsea Piers."

"Can't we do something to make it feel better? Maybe I should put one of my dolls inside."

Kind sentiments, but truthfully nothing could be done. In fact, the overly diapered ambience on the Upper West Side made it all even worse. There were simply too many young, taunting families for Piotr to bear. Everywhere he looked he saw strollers—parked or in transit—and smiling families loping right beside them. Platoons of the prekindergarten. The offspring of all manner of insemination. Twins. Triplets. The adopted Chinese. Queen Esthers all dressed up for Purim. Such a torturous landscape for the childless, like throwing overeaters into a chocolate factory, or alcoholics into a distillery.

Not long after Piotr had been recalled to a half-life hovering around the Upper West Side, he realized that in order to coexist in this fertility-friendly neighborhood, he would need a crutch, a prop, some piece of emotional armor that would protect him against the very thing that eventually killed him: the murderous memories of what could never be replaced, the absence that was always present. Malka and Nathan were dead. And he was now the dead, unrequited parent—bereft and deprived in life, and now tormented in death, surrounded by the children everyone else seemed to have. He was a phantom in desperate need of self-deception. Dickensian ghosts rattled chains, but the Golems required more nuanced imagery.

Piotr wheeled the ultimate symbol of parental status on the Upper West Side—a luxury baby carriage—the hood partially drawn and the blanket bunched up as if a child were actually sleeping inside.

Yet the whimpering carriage was only a small part of the otherworldly encounters that everyone was steadily getting used to. Throughout New York City strange changes were taking place. It started with the tattoos. They disappeared—from everyone, and everywhere. All the tattoo shops in all five boroughs, almost simultaneously, closed down. They went out of business; the entire industry vanished, as though the blue ink had suddenly become scarce and invisible. Sailors and punks began to feel even more embattled than usual. There was nowhere to go to get a freshly painted anchor, or a simple rose, a blue butterfly, an ominous eye-patched pirate, a black-crested insignia for poison, or a Nazi swastika. Banned. Outlawed. Yet there was no official sanction, no legislative mandate, no act of executive or judicial decree. It was simply that the tattoo artists would have no more of it; they surrendered their stippling needles, packed up, and left.

Perhaps they realized that all this time they had collaborated in a sin. Body painting, after all, had always been a sin for Jews, a desecration that was lost on the Nazis, who were far too busy numbering arms to appreciate the irony.

"No more writing numbers on the arms!" Jean said emphatically at one of their early meetings. "I have an even better idea: no more *anything* on the arms. Arms were not meant to be written on. Now, all in favor, raise their hands."

"But wait," Rose interrupted. "The same should go with ankles, backs, and other parts of the body."

"Agreed!" they all shouted.

The Golems cast a unanimous vote. And just like that the tattoo business came to an abrupt, and seemingly unprotested, end. But not only had the existing supply run out. What had once been thought to be indelible suddenly became perishable. Lifetime tattoos that had settled in like second skins disappeared. They were forever erased from the epidermis, leaving neither an outline nor a pale shadow of their former design.

"They can live without it," Primo said firmly. "It's a silly pagan practice anyway."

Paul had an even better idea. "But for Holocaust survivors who are still alive, the brand should stay—just like ours. The only tattoos that survive will be the numbers, as a black reminder of what was once done with ink on flesh."

Now here Jerzy squirmed, but only slightly, because unlike the others, his brand had been self-inflicted: He had signed off on his own arm. He had never been in a camp, although he had survived in the forest and countryside. Without an actual, authentic tattoo, Jerzy would suffer from survivor envy, particularly among this cadre of distinguished ghosts, all of whom possessed the genuine articles for left arms. Of course with Jerzy there was so much pretense, untruth, and transparent fakery that this small deceit hardly raised any objection from the other Golems, except from Jean, who once shouted, though no one took him seriously, "Kick him out already with that bum limb!"

So the numbers stayed; all other aniline images vanished. When it came to dye on skin, the Nazi tattoos were the longest-lasting of all.

But the Golems also had a thing about crewcuts and shaved heads. Barbers found the task impossible to fulfill—the minute the cut was complete, the hair grew back, longer than before. Soon they stopped giving them altogether. It was as though all the shearing machines in New York had suddenly broken down, gone on strike, or refused to cross the most radical of picket lines. Voluntary bald heads would never again be in fashion.

And then the zebras from the Bronx Zoo woke up one morning to find that, like liberated ex-cons, they had mysteriously lost their stripes. Painted freshly white, they were now no more distinct than Shetland ponies.

All the showerheads in Manhattan stopped raining water. The only option from now on was to take a bath.

"You can never be too sure what will come out of those heads," Tadeusz said. "It's better not to take any chances."

All the tooth fillings and crowns went from porcelain to gold.

"The Nazis wouldn't have made us cough up ceramic," Jean said. "That's for sure."

The practice of smoking outside of office buildings ended as well. The Golems didn't like the congestion it created.

"You shouldn't have to walk through a cloud of smoke when coming in and out of a building," Lothar said.

They didn't stop there; they had an even more extreme solution to the problem. Smoking itself stopped. What all those warnings from the surgeon general and the American Cancer Society—and all those antismoking campaigns, nicotine patches, behavior modifications, and frightful images of iron lungs—had failed to accomplish, the Golems pulled off in one lucky strike. It took ghosts to teach everyone how to quit, without having to scare it out of them. The impulse and addiction simply disappeared like smoke.

Their motives, of course, were not guided by public health concerns. They had other, far more selfish agendas in mind: the complete eradication of smoke itself. Burning carbon. Visible gas. Clouds that had nothing to do with the weather. More than anything, the Golems despised smoke. It was for them the ultimate eyesore. The emissary of fire that blackened the sky and the lungs, and then followed up with all that interminable choking.

And for this reason, not surprisingly, the Golems weren't that hot on chimney smokers. And they didn't care too much for the sight of chimneys, either. Over the next few winter months, all the household chimneys of New York became detached from working fireplaces. The flues were permanently shut down; Santa Claus would have to ride the elevator or find the back door.

"How can a Jew look at smoke and not see the faces of other Jews?" Primo said, as a tear surfaced on his cheek. "The Nazis polluted the air with dead Jews, and for that reason, the smoke that we remember is holy and can't be confused with firewood or a pack of Marlboros."

And then came the business with the subways. Always such a sluggish fixture of New York City, the main canvas for graffiti artists, the preferred receptacle for litterbugs. But for those who regularly swiped their MetroCards, rotated turnstiles, and hung from metal straphandles, the underground adventures of the subway system changed soon after the Golems arrived.

All throughout Manhattan, no matter whether these subterranean transports were running during rush hour or off-peak, the doors automatically closed once all the available seats were taken. No more unbreathing, rumpled commuters. If there were any standing passengers, the cars refused to run. The conductors were seemingly powerless against such insubordination; the trains now had minds of their own. Homebound and late-arriving travelers, and sabotaged city transportation officials, were furious. They had long grown accustomed to the turbulence and mechanical arrogance of these locomotives, and they liked it that way. But this was different. This was civilized, purposeful anarchy, an attack against the Nazis and their obsession with keeping trains on tight schedules.

"What the fuck is going on here!" a pink-skinned brute wearing high-top Timberland boots and toting a lunch pail filled with leftover barbecued chicken and macaroni salad bellowed. His swollen beer-sloshed stomach, arriving before he did, clapped and then jiggled against the closed doors. "I gotta get to woik!"

"How curious, indeed," a professor dressed in tweed and loafers followed with his own commentary, then opened up *Paradise Lost* until a more compliant car arrived.

Whoever was tampering with these underground transports of New York life had some explaining to do. Eventually the mayor himself was forced into the fray.

"Until we decide how to address this problem," he issued a statement at a press conference from Gracie Mansion, "I urge all citizens of New York to remain calm and to rely on above-ground transportation until we're back to normal."

"But, Your Honor," one member of the press raised a pen and asked. "What kind of criminal minds are behind all this? They have taken our trains hostage. Are they international terrorists? What kind of demands are they making?"

"Yes, Mayor," another anxious member of the press corps stood up and wondered. "Are we all in some sort of danger? What's next: buses, taxis, elevators?"

"There is no need to panic," the mayor said nervously, clutching a tooth-bitten pencil. "There is, at this time, no emergency. As far as we know this may all turn out to be a coincidence, some kind of malfunction we simply can't explain at this juncture. But I pledge my assurance to the citizens of this city that there will be a reasonable explanation for everything, and a day of reckoning." The mayor then offered his constituents and the press a hopeful political face. "I think it's best that we simply try to relax until we learn who or what is behind all this."

But the Golems of Gotham struck again; they weren't satisfied with just hijacking the subways. These were ghosts with grotesque memories of jam-packed trains. And they also had little interest in seeing them run on time—not that that ever happened in New York anyway.

"We should do the same thing with MetroNorth," Tadeusz said, recalling his days as one of the men of Canada, those who worked the transports, clearing incoming prisoners off the trains at Auschwitz. "And Amtrak, and New Jersey Transit, too."

Soon, commuters of all types gave up on trains as a reliable way to travel. Tracks that used to shuttle large numbers of passengers began to carry lighter loads. Grand Central and Penn Stations became the setting for more peaceful surroundings, no longer symbols for urban Armageddon. Even during rush hours they felt more like open-air piazzas—so peaceful at twilight and dawn. The hustle and bustle gave way to more casual movements, not unlike the pacing of Piotr's baby carriage.

As New York City continued to immerse itself in the supernatural, the Golems proved that their best magic resided in the spiritual.

It started with a change in scenery. Jewish life that had once existed on the Lower East Side of Manhattan reemerged, oddly transplanted to the Upper West Side. A switch in time zones, a flip in geography, and yet the scent of the shtetl was all the same.

All along Broadway, Amsterdam, and Columbus Avenues sprang kosher butchers, Judaica shops and even Chinese and Mexican restaurants operating under strict rabbinic supervision and catering to those who wanted their chopsticks *flayshadik* and their margaritas no less holy than Manischewitz. On any given Saturday morning, before or after services, the Upper West Side featured a parade of Jewish families all dressed up for their day of rest. Synagogues had been resurrected, and some were built from scratch. Renegade *minyanim* broke off from more established ones and yet, as a sign of solidarity, amicably still shared space in the same sanctuaries.

They greeted one another as if they had all socialized just the night before, which they probably had. And when they approached, it was always on a first-name basis, because they knew one another's business. This one knew that one, or wanted to and soon would. Nobody was anonymous, or godless, anymore. The city that once felt crowded but lonely was suddenly overrun with yentas, but was also suffused with warmth and connection.

This renewed spiritual community built *sukkah*s and took over part of West End Avenue to dance with Torahs, and on Friday nights they welcomed the Sabbath by linking arms and dancing the hora. Following that, they would gather in apartments all over the Upper West Side to light candles, recite blessings over the wine and the challah, and sanctify this moment in their lives. During Rosh Hashanah they tossed bread crumbs into the Hudson River to symbolize the casting away of their sins.

This was all taking place in an updated ghetto without walls—an unofficial *eruv*—and yet it was more inclusive than ever before. In some synagogues women occupied a larger role in the services.

Uncloseted gays and lesbians opened the Ark. Single parents looked for new mates among the *minyanim*. African Americans wore white yarmulkas and recited the *Shema*. And there were many Jews by choice, those who had converted from some other religion—answering the call of either coercion, compromise, or spiritual connection—and now entered the tribe with all the privileges of membership and burdens of a Jew. The inhabitants of this reconstituted shtetl all prayed with their eyes closed, not unlike the grandfathers of old, and swayed to the liturgical melodies of ancient Hebraic hymns—the rapturous outpouring of a people who were once again fully invested in their faith.

Was this all the mischievous handiwork of medieval monsters right before the new millennium? The rantings of prophetic banshees? Perhaps. The original Golem was a creature of rescue and retribution, but the latest models came outfitted with shrewd minds, big souls, and a flair for restoration.

And they also had a quirky sense of humor. Con Edison switched from gas and went entirely electric.

11

WITH MY PARENTS IN TOWN AND THEIR DEAD friends in tow, the brownstone was beginning to look more and more like a haunted house. For one thing my guests, invisible to everyone but me and my daughter, were leaving ghost droppings all over the place—proof, albeit supernatural in substance, that they existed in some fashion other than solely in my head.

The ground rules for cohabitation still needed to be worked out. These spirits had been resurrected—by my daughter, or by millennial reckonings, or historical imperatives, or natural selections of Darwinian rather than Nazi origins—but regardless of how they got here, they had somehow settled on my home as their place of business, whatever that business might eventually turn out to be. For the time being they still hadn't announced what it was they wanted, why they had come, how I fit in their plans, and what was to become of us all. Apparently they weren't in such a hurry to explain. So for now, with anticipation measured and intentions unproclaimed—with everything about their visit basically on hold—they just simply were. It was as if their specific aims and assignments were still being worked out, while I waited patiently for further notice.

Living not quite among us, they were still very much present in my brownstone, a place where they could be their most paranormal selves. Animated, but only for the benefit of a spooked father and daughter. R and R for the dead. But for survivors who had once been so good at hiding, they proved to be much sloppier in covering up their ghostly tracks. Souvenirs of their unbodied state were left around everywhere: metal soup bowls, toothless gold fillings, rotten turnips and potatoes, noiseless clogs, flesh-toned lampshades and foul-smelling soup, zebra uniforms streaked with the stool samples of dried-out dysentery. And worst, and most prevalent of all, stains of crusty, lacquered red blood appeared throughout my home as if it had been the scene of a gangland massacre.

"Mr. Levin, my God! What happened here? Are you and Ariel still all right?" Gloria, my cleaning lady, screamed. "Who died? There's blood everywhere!"

"Nobody died," I said feebly.

"I'll never get these out. It doesn't even look like real blood. Are we getting ready for Halloween?"

She was right. The new paint in my house was neither oil, latex, nor ordinary hemoglobin. It was much darker and coarser, like unrefined crude oil, the kind of fluid that didn't look capable of giving life. More likely to choke veins than run through them.

Sometimes the Golems simply left behind pebbles, as if my house was a tombstone.

I immediately gave Gloria four weeks' pay and told her not to return until the end of the month, at which time I presented her with an even larger bonus and asked her not to return until spring. It was all I could do to stop her from heading off to Gristede's to explain the sanitation problem she was having over on Edgar Allan Poe Street.

I also told Alejandro not to enter the brownstone on his own anymore. I didn't want to frighten him, and I feared what he might find.

"Sure, Mr. Levin," he said with a resigned, dejected voice. "Whatever you say. I guess you and the kid have some things to work out."

Since Samantha left, Alejandro had fallen into that tragically common postmodern category of surrogate family, a collection of well-meaning, haphazardly recruited strangers who functioned as necessary bindings in a world patched together from the torn fabric of family separation.

But I had no choice. I had to limit the circle of intimates. Whatever was taking place inside my home had to be subject to the strictest of confidence. So hot was the nature of this invasion, that for all I knew it could have been a matter of national security. My large brownstone had been converted into a Pandora's box. Open it up to the outside world, turn it inside out, search every crevice, and perhaps all the riddles of modern times will be solved. These shrewd former survivors may actually possess the antidotes we all crave, the magic elixirs, the Hebrew brew, the exotic formulas that could set us all free from the madness of the past and the amnesia of the present. Unlocking mysteries of both the mundane and the simply unknowable.

I imagined the pop-cultural possibilities for the *National Enquirer*, *E!*, an episode of the *X-Files*. I would have become a conversation piece in every chat room. Golems had landed in Gotham. Better than even an Elvis sighting. Survivors who had inexplicably taken the nonsurvival route were now, shockingly, back. Surely that meant something—for all of us. A divine sign, perhaps. The universe finally speaking, but in Greek.

Their stories, not the ones they had written but the ones they had never started, needed to come out. Their continuing journeys depended on it. And now they were trapped in a place where time was neither suspended nor warped. They had been shut out from all the important doors, the black holes and seams in the universe that allowed entry into the otherworld. Unwelcome until there was closure on Earth, until they explained what they had done, because we needed to know and they had to tell.

The century and millennium were ending, but we had focused so little on the time that had just passed, the one we had lived through, squandered, and violated. Rushing. Always rushing. We had an appointment with the next century, and we didn't want to be late. What would the future think if we hesitated and reflected? How rude it would be for us to pause and pay our respects to those who hadn't lived long enough to brave the next leap forward.

We had gassed and tortured, and dropped many different kinds of bombs—some atomic, others simply smart—but right now there was no time to consider payloads and death tolls. A new millennium called. We were being summoned. To what, we did not yet know. But it didn't matter, because our strength has always been in our strivings for the future, no matter how we get there. Looking back and lamenting has always been perceived as a weakness, but one that so few of us share.

My houseguests had traveled back and forth, taken the round trip, seen the most gruesome sights, logged the most grisly, exotic, and extreme of passenger miles—Auschwitz, America, Paris and Milan, heaven and hell, and who knows what hubs in between. Surely they possessed valuable information. What if it got into the wrong hands, in a modern world so overpopulated with wrong hands?

So I huddled my daughter and myself inside until I figured out how much of this was really in my head and how much was actually in my apartment. A plague on my house or merely madness in my head?

It was just about then that she first knocked on my door, when I was most reluctant to let anyone in.

I peered through the opaque glass that was positioned at eye level on my heavy wooden front door, and I noticed her kissing the mezuzah. Her hand reached up to the doorframe, touched the tube, and then traveled to her lips. It was a fairly passionate kiss. She took her Judaism seriously, which was more than you could ever say about me.

In all the years that I had lived here, I had never once shown such affection for either the scroll or my religion. I attended no synagogues. I was a Jew living on Edgar Allan Poe Street in New York. So much I knew. My parents had been Holocaust survivors who killed themselves. That was enough of a recital to constitute my name, rank, and serial number in case of capture. The enemy wouldn't have been able to get anything else out of me, because frankly, I didn't know anything else, nor was I sure that there even was an enemy. I didn't recall putting the mezuzah up on the doorpost in the first place. Ariel may have been the one who did so, or perhaps it had been Alejandro.

In kissing the encased scroll, the woman was not only affirming her faith, she was also making an assumption that the light was on, that someone was home, and would let her in, which wasn't the case at all. I had no intention of opening the door. I didn't want her in anyway, and certainly not at the risk of anything that was already inside flying out.

Even through the fuzzy distortions of a window designed to keep things private, I could see that my visitor was attractive, but in an awkward sort of way. And it wasn't merely the funhouse quality of the glass that made me think so. Her chestnut hair was curly and undisciplined, as if it answered only to its own split ends, scorning all other fashion advice. Her eyes were blue but small, and seemed lost within a net of long lashes. She had lips that were full for an otherwise small face, and a smile that was stacked with tiny, yet luminous, teeth.

She buzzed the doorbell again.

"Who is it?"

"Mr. Levin?"

"Yes," I replied, still safely behind the door. "What do you want?"

"My name is Tanya Green. I am a violinist and a music teacher. May I come in?"

"Now is not a good time."

"I'm sorry to bother you, but your phone number is unlisted, and I followed your daughter to this address last week."

"Why were you following my daughter?"

Of course she knew that this would get my attention. Yet true stalkers and kidnappers rarely announce themselves ahead of time, and they don't make house calls. The woman at the door didn't look very threatening. So while I didn't think I had anything to fear, a responsible parent would have wanted to know more, and so did I.

"May I come in?"

She entered hastily and without hesitation, as if she had pushed others aside in order to be the first one in, as if the doors to my home had opened to mark the beginning of some Memorial Day sale. What's more, she seemed to know what she was looking for, like a professional shopper who had memorized the layout of the merchandise beforehand.

I wanted to be polite and to ask if she wished to sit down, but that would only prolong her visit. Besides, I feared whom she might sit on, and whether trampled light might make an offended noise. I so hoped that everyone in the house was either asleep or off wandering the Upper West Side.

"I'm sorry to come in here this way, Mr. Levin. As I already said, my name is Tanya Green."

"And you teach music, and you've been following my daughter around."

"Yes, so you heard all that. It's not as bad as it sounds. You see, I've been attending Ariel's concerts."

"What concerts?"

"The ones outside Zabar's, of course."

I blinked and said nothing, which apparently told Tanya a lot.

"Surely you know that she plays there nearly every afternoon."

"Plays what? Is she in some kind of after-school lox program?"

"No, the violin."

I must have had the expression of someone who had just been smacked in the face with the backside of a violin, and after the blow came numbing elevator music. Tanya Green sensed that she was carrying on a conversation with an insensibly blithering man. So she continued, and assumed that eventually I would come to and catch up. "She performs . . . with her violin"—gesturing freely with her hands—"outside of Zabar's. She plays the most extraordinary klezmer music."

"A street performer?"

"Yes, precisely."

"Like a juggler or a flame eater or one of those people who play the blues with only a few strings on their guitars and a couple of teeth in their mouths?"

"Let me assure you that your daughter is a very special street musician. In fact, she shouldn't be on the street at all, and that's why I am here."

"She's playing klezmer music outside of Zabar's? For money?"

Obviously I was having trouble wrapping my mind around this idea and taking the conversation on to the next level.

"Yes, she plays beautifully," my mother said from behind me, as usual arriving on the scene at the most opportune moment for criticism. "You're her father. How come you don't know what she does after school?"

"Wonderful strokes, Oliver," my own father joined in. "And the unusual way she stands, playing right into the ground, so confident for a little thing, and the sounds that come out of her. An angel from the old shtetl. You should be very proud. You've done well."

"Done what?" I whispered. "*You* must have done something! There's no music in me."

"What?" Tanya asked.

"Nothing."

"Don't be rude, Oliver," Rose said. "Pay attention to your guest."

My guest and I made our way into the parlor while my parents followed us in, hovering from behind, unseen by Tanya, who was otherwise looking right at them. But instead of noticing that we weren't alone, she was examining the appointments in the room: the nonworking fireplace (a recent occurrence); the large, gilded mirror hanging above it with baroque moldings; the long, black leather sofa; the Indian rugs and ottoman chairs; the built-in mahogany bookshelves.

I wanted to tell my parents to go away, to stretch their legs even more than the limbering calisthenics of their death already allowed, but I was coming across as a distracted, apathetic parent, and I didn't want to add deranged man to that already unfavorable first impression.

"And so, as I was saying, she's quite a special musician," Tanya repeated.

"From my side of the family," Rose said. "Before the war, there was always music in our home in Warsaw."

"We loved music, too," Lothar said. "I had a brother, Haskell, who, if I remember correctly, also played the violin. But after Auschwitz, the only symphony for our ears came from barking German shepherds."

"Have you heard her play?" Tanya asked.

"Not really," I replied, trying to mediate the multiple conversations piping through my ears. "She usually goes up into the attic. I didn't realize she was learning how to play klezmer music. I can't believe she's that good. Who's been teaching her?"

"That's what I wanted to know. You see, I'm a klezmer violinist myself. I've spent most of my life playing and teaching klezmer, so when I heard your daughter, who is so exceptional, I assumed she had been studying for years. And I was dying to find out with whom. But when I spoke with her, she said she had just recently picked up the instrument and started to play without any lessons at all."

"Just like that? In my attic?"

"That's what she said."

"Is that possible?"

"I wouldn't have thought so, but what else could it be?"

I already had my suspicions.

"She told me that you don't play any instruments."

"That's true. Well, I used to, but she doesn't know anything about that."

"And your wife didn't play either."

"Oh, she told you about her?"

"Just that she left when Ariel was still very young."

"Samantha wasn't musical."

My face must have turned sour or gone stale, because Tanya stiffened in my presence, and then began to stammer.

"I'm sorry. . . . I didn't mean to bring up a painful subject?"

"The fact that she couldn't play any instruments is not the painful part."

"She's a lovely girl, Oliver," Rose said. "And Jewish, too."

"And she plays the violin, just like Ariel," Lothar added.

"She would make a nice mother," Rose said.

"Stop that!" I shouted.

"Stop what?" Tanya wanted to know.

"Don't yell at the girl, Oliver," Rose said. "How will she like you if you're yelling at her so soon into the relationship?"

"I'm not yelling at her! I'm yelling at you! And there *is* no relationship."

I spun around so that my back was now to Tanya's face.

"Who are you yelling at?" Tanya asked.

My parents were no longer behind me. They must have levitated to another part of the room, throwing their voices around from elsewhere—but for my ears only. Ghosts have a way with light feet and deft exits. I made yet another full turn like some rotating toy and faced Tanya once again.

"Strange times," I said somberly. "Sorry for my behavior. Very hard to explain, so I won't. You come here, and I find out that I have a violin prodigy for a daughter and I didn't know it. It's just . . . I don't know. Something strange is happening out there," I said, knowing full well that the outside was innocent. It was my brownstone that was the true culprit.

"I know. It feels different lately." Tanya hugged herself. "Even the air seems thicker. And the clouds are brighter, like they've been polished. Black-and-white images look sepia. And you can now see the stars, which was almost impossible before. New York City feels like it's been placed in a snow globe and the rest of the world is watching."

The brownstone started to feel damp. I glanced over at the mirror that rose above the fireplace and saw two streaks of dried blood curving sideways like a runaway train.

"Have you seen the baby carriage?" she continued.

"What baby carriage?"

"You know, the big blue Swedish one that strolls by itself—with no baby in it and no parent standing behind it."

"No, I haven't," I said as my tone sank, finally realizing where Ariel's childhood chariot had gone. "I've been distracted lately."

"Well, either someone is playing a joke on all of us, or a baby carriage is haunting our neighborhood."

I looked around the parlor for a Golem—any Golem—who was willing to take this opportunity and confess.

"And all the other things that have happened lately, too."

I was afraid both to ask and to admit my ignorance. There was so much of the peculiar in my home—things I was trying to explain to myself rationally, and others that I was merely trying to cover up from the outside world—that I hadn't paid any attention to the possible spillover onto Upper Broadway. Obviously my guests had been keeping themselves busy without telling me what they had been up to. I wasn't the only one they had chosen to torment.

"Well, the reason I'm here, Mr. Levin, is because I was wondering if you would allow Ariel to study with me. I wouldn't charge you anything. I just couldn't in this case. For this kind of privilege, I probably should be paying you. I just want to find out how far your daughter can go with her music."

Given the unmusical influences that were conducting this metaphysical enterprise, I had this terrible parental feeling that Tanya was underestimating the distance my daughter's talent was capable of traveling. I assumed Tanya was thinking something in the nature of Carnegie Hall, but lately, under these supernatural circumstances, other worlds were possible, too.

"The violin!" I said.

"What? Yes, I want to teach her the violin."

"No, no, no, . . . I mean the violin! Where did she get it?"

"I don't know." Tanya paused. "Oh, wait a minute, I think I remember. She told me she found it in the attic, right here in this house. Actually, it's an amazing-looking instrument. Not beautiful at all, but shabby and broken, like it had been through a war or something."

"The attic?"

"Why, what are you thinking?"

"I don't know," I said, reflecting, pondering. "Why don't you come with me for a look?"

"Inside your attic?"

"Yes," I said. "I'm not about to go up there alone."

"Okay, I'll go." She shrugged puckishly. "Why not."

We took to the stairs, each step carpeted thickly like a sponge, sliding our palms against the smooth wood banister. After we scaled one flight, I could see that Tanya noticed that one step was caked in red and didn't offer any cushion at all.

"Sorry, I'll clean that up later," I said dryly, as if every Upper West Side apartment was booby-trapped with such unusual, out-of-control liquid. Odorless, with the texture of red canvas, these bloodstains had made a patchwork quilt out of my carpet. But Tanya, amazingly, was not alarmed.

Four flights later, and without any further incident, we reached the top floor. The attic was housed between two gables that poked out like Vulcan ears from the front of my brownstone. Outside was a parapet of stone, on which several small, once-menacing gargoyles nested. There was a drop ladder that extended down from a trapdoor in the ceiling. I had never been inside the attic before. Alejandro had many times. So too had Samantha, no doubt. And Ariel, of course. But never me. I usually stayed out of such dark, confining places— even in my own home.

"Would you like me to go first?" I offered.

"It's your house."

"I'm not so sure anymore."

She followed me up as my head lifted the trapdoor, which toppled over like an unsecured hat. Some light from the floor below us now spilled into the attic. But it was still too dark for anyone but a vampire. I held out my hand and pulled Tanya up so that now, like me, she was standing in the cramped crown of my home.

"Light a match?" she asked.

"No, there must be a light somewhere."

"Very spooky. I'm in an attic on Edgar Allan Poe Street. Is a raven going to come flying out of here? Will I hear a heartbeat in the wall?" Tanya giggled nervously. "Now I see where you get your inspiration for those novels you write."

"Have you read me?" I asked as I searched for the light switch, feeling emboldened.

"No, I usually go for the more serious books."

Deflated and fearful once again.

The light went on, but it was more like a half light, the lowest of wattage, a slight improvement on a lantern.

"Still too dark," I conceded.

"What are we looking for?"

"I don't know. Haven't been up here before, but maybe this place will give us some clue about the violin."

The space was small and tight, and there wasn't really that much to see, except that the room did not resemble a garret at all. There was accumulated dust but no lack of charm. The compressed, inward-leaning walls were lined with red velvet. The ceiling, although low, was rich in ornate fixtures and moldings, and there were several Roman columns, which in that setting looked more like dwarfed, decorated stumps. A few old, wooden, high-backed chairs, cushioned in red like a poor man's throne, sat in the middle. Crumbling Hebrew books—holy only because of the holes—tattered *tallisim* and moth-eaten yarmulkas were spread out all over. And set against a wall in my attic was an Ark with the curtain drawn and what I assumed to be an ancient, but tranquil, Torah inside.

"Wow, very cool place," Tanya observed. "It's like an old synagogue in here. Was this brownstone once a *shul*?"

"Not according to the title search," I said. "This is definitely news to me."

The curtain to the Ark fluttered, and Tanya jumped back and fell into my arms, grabbing tightly around my neck.

"Are there ghosts in here?"

"In 1999, in this city, on the Upper West Side?" I said mockingly, as I searched the room for my parents. "Come on, give me a break."

"Maybe you're trying to play tricks on me. I'm not going to wind up in one of your books, am I?"

"No, just in the Rue Morgue."

Taking Tanya's hand, I inched us both toward the Ark, which now seemed to be making noises in concert with the hyperactive curtain.

We stood before it. The noises and the rippling finally stopped. Tanya and I glanced at each other. I remembered what had happened in my shower when they first appeared. I bravely readied myself for yet another curtain call. I slipped my hand behind the velvet and searched for a drawstring. Meanwhile, while I fumbled, Tanya found something more interesting. Carved into the crest of the Ark, in a language we could read, was the following: ALTNEUSCHUL, PRAGUE, 1583.

I tugged at the string, and the curtain slid open. There was no Torah, but there were two Hebrew letters—alphabet toys—made out of wood, about the size of flash cards, leaning up against the back of the Ark. One was an *aleph*, the other a *shin*. They glistened in the faint, jagged light that came from the lower depths of my home, the part that gave no hint that I was housing a synagogue. The letters were like adjusting eyes that hadn't seen anything other than darkness in some time. An Ark empty of Torah but yet not entirely empty. Tanya and I didn't speak. And we didn't get any help from my parents, either.

There was silence and strangeness throughout the brownstone, although the gargoyles, guarding outside, continued with their improbable smiles.

12

"WHAT HAPPENED TO THIS PLACE?" THE MAN in the motorcycle jacket asked his friends, although he realized that they couldn't possibly know. "It was never like this when I was alive."

As a writer living in New York, Jerzy had always been in hiding—from his past and what had happened to him there. The lies and deceits of survival. The shame and the stain. As a child he had escaped the Nazis by pretending to be a gentile, and as a refugee in America he continued to perfect this particular skill of living underground in an otherwise uncovered world. In fact in America too he was a gentile, no more a Holocaust survivor than a Hell's Kitchen priest.

He built a solid and often dizzying life around avoidance. His psyche and self-image were always on alert for an immediate reversal.

One minute L.L. Bean, the next LL Cool J. Perhaps that's why when he was finally discovered—as either a charlatan or a Jew—the raw nature of his exposure, the way it detonated the core of his existence, made it impossible for him to live any other way. Survival spelled camouflage; circumvention was his oxygen. Without the anonymity of the mask, the unprotected face couldn't bear being seen. And so he took the pills and ended the internal bleeding that had come with his unmasking.

But old habits die harder than bodies. Now, even as a ghost, he still cultivated a persona founded on disguise. Death gave him the curious freedom to try on new masks.

"What's with the motorcycle jacket?" Jean asked. For his own costume Jean was wearing brown slacks with a white shirt and a collar fanned wide open in the style of Israeli politicians. "We're the only ones who can see you, for God's sake."

"You can't hide from us," Paul, outfitted in a gray business suit, reminded him. "And there is nothing to hide. We all know what is underneath your masks. We're wearing them, too."

"Except we didn't have to appear on David Letterman to make that point," Primo said. He, too, was wearing a white shirt, with round mother-of-pearl buttons that were queued up to the top like runway lights. His black pants were loose and baggy. "Jerzy, we all come from the same place. So why the black leather jacket and those silly sunglasses? You look like a bank robber. I can't even see your eyes."

Jerzy didn't answer. His cohorts had been pestering him about his revolving wardrobe from the very first moment they had all arrived. One day Jerzy was a gay fashion photographer, the next a fireman, then a British dandy, a Sandinista rebel, a Domino's Pizza delivery boy, a Venetian gondola skipper, a masked beekeeper, a Russian limo driver, a swinger in a green zoot suit, a black Muslim. He was, without the hustle music, a one-man Village People.

Finally he spoke. "When I was alive, these islands were filled with Jews talking about politics and books, poetry and theater. Where are all the people?"

Jerzy and friends were in the very center of the avenue at Broadway and Eighty-seventh Street. Some were sitting, others standing. What Jerzy referred to as islands were actually landscaped meridians that split the street, with park benches at either end. As cars, buses, and trucks barreled up- and downtown, and as commuters waited for traffic lights to change, one could have a seat on these benches and take in the paradox of nature in New York—not the bucolic but the boisterous, not the vernal but the city at its most kinetic.

But the Golems were not necessarily castaways on this island, because they weren't entirely alone. There was a foul-smelling man with a toothless jack-o'-lantern mouth stretched out on a bench beside them. His shoes were too big for his feet, the laces curled up and out in formless loops. A rope was tied around his waist to hold up his pants, and all of his possessions were in a shopping cart that he guarded as faithfully as a Brink's security officer.

The homeless man wasn't exactly the company Jerzy had in mind. What he was referring to were the old Jewish men who used to argue about socialism, wives by their side, whispering about the scandalous sex scenes in Isaac Bashevis Singer's latest novel. Jerzy recalled the days when serious, thoughtful words mattered, when there was integrity in the simple act of having something original to say. Jerzy longed nostalgically for those moments, believing that people were at their best when ideas occupied even life's idle time. Intellectuals were not simply those with doctorates. The freedom of a restless, searching mind was entirely egalitarian and democratic. Nearly everyone read several newspapers each day, or read certain books, or weighed in on heavy political or moral issues. Before cable and computers, before machines became our only emotional and life support, there was the compulsion to be part of a community, and to know what was going on.

But that was no longer the case, and Jerzy wondered whether he and his friends could bring any of those moments back to a people who no longer allowed themselves time to sit patiently and discuss anything other than summer shares and stock portfolios.

The subway—the number 1 or the 9—rumbled underground as the Golems bounced on air above the rusted grille that gave pedestrians a peek at the tracks. It was the middle of the day, but the sky was dark, an early twilight. The air was chilled but without wind. Pigeons took crumbs from a mumbling old woman. Children abandoned neighborhood parks to the creatures of the urban night.

A fire engine with screaming sirens raced by. The Golems all winced and covered their ears. There were certain sounds they had never gotten quite used to, nor would they ever: air raids, barking dogs, commands in German, the unexpected knock on a door. A red, double-decker tourist bus caused the Golems to perform a unified double-take as it navigated noisily down Broadway. Jerzy and Tadeusz waved at some tourists who were snapping pictures with throwaway Fuji cameras. But the tourists focused around and behind the ghosts, who remained unframed within the lens. The bus driver, amplified like a school principal, pointed out the relevant sights of interest.

"Over there is where Isaac Bashevis Singer used to live. He won a Nobel Prize, you know. And over there, a few blocks on your right, is Zabar's. . . ."

A garland of black smoke spewed from the top of a fashionable Central Park West address, curling around its Gothic crown. The Golems stood at attention, as though paying homage. Ghosts and smoke. Yet another unphotographed group portrait, so loaded with symbolism it couldn't possibly be spontaneous. When they recovered, the Golems made a note to take this matter up with that building's superintendent.

But first there were other issues to attend to. Another strategy session, held out of sight and earshot of Oliver and Ariel.

"How will we know when we are finished here?" Tadeusz, wearing casual all black, asked.

"We can't stay forever," Piotr said, standing by his baby carriage, which was parked right beside the homeless man's shopping cart. Yet, it wasn't at all clear whether Piotr actually minded staying on the Upper West Side. As he spoke, he spied lovingly, and also jealously, at a caravan of young families bounding with their own strollers, off to area parks, local playdates, or family functions that Piotr would never experience.

"There is still much to do," Primo advised.

"Yes, we haven't yet decided what is to become of Oliver," Paul reminded them, his hands resting on his belly as if awaiting a fetal kick.

Rose and Lothar remained silent, sitting close together on one of the benches. They were grateful for the intervention of their friends on behalf of their son, and didn't want to seem too demanding on what the ultimate manner of rescue should be. At the same time, an irrevocable, unyielding license of tough love wasn't what they had in mind either.

"There is nothing we can do—for him or any of these people," Jean snarled.

"Always so angry," Primo said. "We are here to teach how to move on, how not to live in the past."

"Like us, like we did?" Jean said scornfully. "The past is your prison. For me it is my home."

"We should have moved on." Tadeusz wondered.

"I don't want to move on—dead or alive," Jean snapped back. "Unlike the rest of you, I didn't come back to atone for my suicide. It still makes perfect sense to me. It was the only logical choice. I swallowed the pills and choked myself. And I am not here to explain why I did it, or to apologize. You all came to rescue, but I am here only to watch."

"We owe humanity some answers," Primo said. "We are one of its great mysteries."

"I owe nothing to anyone," Jean snapped.

"What about to yourself? What do you owe yourself?" Paul asked. "You are still in chains. Didn't you want to free yourself, isn't that why you swallowed all those pills—your 'last path to freedom,' as you have said? All of us, we wanted to purge ourselves of the black milk, to exorcize the demons—to make them finally go away. We couldn't do it in life, but maybe in death such freedom was possible. We were all so haunted when we were alive."

"Spare me the piety, please," Jean said, his eyes closed, throwing up his hand at Paul, a gesture of utter dismissal.

"Yes, we all wanted the ghosts to go away," Paul said.

"But now we are the ghosts," Piotr noted.

"In coming back," Primo reminded them all, "we now have a responsibility to help others, to help Oliver before it's too late. We don't want Ariel to become an orphan."

Rose bit right through her invisible lip.

"We need to show the world how to finally come to terms with the inhumanity of the twentieth century," Paul continued.

Jean, not being much of a cheek turner, always refusing to let things pass, scoffed, "'Come to terms.' Such fancy words of modern psychology. It's good we didn't invite Bruno to join us."

"There is no need for such anger," Primo said.

"Why are you so afraid of anger?" Jean asked. "And how can you be so sure that the smiling people are the happy ones? Anger is a far more honest emotion than all of your words of healing. And you are completely wrong about me. I am not angry at all. In fact, I see things more clearly than the rest of you—without anger or bitterness. I don't waste my time trying to fix what is broken. Only a fool would live on hope alone. It didn't work in the camps, and it won't work here, either. I was tortured once, and I remain tortured, even in death, not because I wish to be, but because it will forever be a part of me. And for this reason, I am not interested in coming to terms with anything. I'm not going to reconcile myself, to learn to cope, to make peace with the past. I don't want to heal, to find redemption, acceptance, or tranquility. I have no reason to do so. What's more, I refuse to. Acceptance is the first step toward forgetting, which I cannot, and will not, do."

"The world needs to heal, otherwise another kind of poison will spill out from the untreated wounds of the past," Primo, ever the chemist, said. "The best among us died in those camps. There is nothing we can do about that. But the rest have to move forward. That's what humanity requires, even in times when humanity fails. And in order to do that, the pain, and yes, even the anger, has to go somewhere. It has to resolve itself, run its course. Otherwise, someday it will be discharged as violence and pathology."

"Primo," Piotr said distractedly, cautiously turning to his friend, "do you think it is possible . . . you know, to heal?"

"Maybe easier for others than ourselves," Paul said softly.

"Why is that?" Tadeusz asked, much taller than the others, looking down on his poet friend.

"Because we, as artists, were trained at Auschwitz," Paul replied. "And because of that we have no filters, just photographic memories. We know of no way to block out the pain. We didn't allow ourselves the luxury of repression. The brokenness stayed with us at all times."

An intuitively understood answer. Each nodded in silence.

What does it mean to die of a natural cause? Is there really such a thing? Sure, death certificates often blame nature. But those are merely medical forms and formalities. They don't capture the full story, the tale underneath the flat line and unplugged life support. Life is always rebelling against one inevitable end or another. The Golems didn't die from suicide. The true cause of death was too much reflection; casualties of a life lived in furious remembrance. The closer they looked, the easier it became to self-kill. Those who examined too close inevitably saw too much. Each one an Icarus, flying too near the sun, and then, for the sake of finality, stared intrepidly, and fatally, into the hypnotic face of a Medusa head cut off from the corpses of Auschwitz.

The true survivors, those free from the camps and the compulsion to make art, were the ones who opened themselves up to the possibility of distraction: new families, new careers, and lives. But the Golems had been unconditionally, and fatally, undistracted. They lived, but due to the imperatives of their profession, they did not survive. They never left the Europe of the Nazis—psychically, at least—

never found anything to replace it with, never *wanted* anything to replace it with. And so they became martyrs to an art that owed little to beauty and everything to atrocity. And not just any atrocity, either. The crowning achievement of evil had been let out of the cage. The internal had suddenly become poetic, and literal.

"We made art out of madness," Jean said.

"And we used words, inadequate ones, to describe what we had seen," Primo said.

"And some of us used the language of the murderers to express what they had done," Paul said, "even though all languages, most particularly German, had been debased and corrupted."

"We were failures as artists," Jerzy said. "Our words never could speak to the Holocaust. We couldn't make any sense of that lost world."

"But even without adequate words," Piotr said, crouching forward as if wishing to arrive sooner than his message, "there will still be lessons to teach—if not as artists, then now, at least as rescuers."

"There are no lessons!" Jean insisted. "The Holocaust taught us nothing other than that human beings are quite capable of mass murder. What else did we learn? What more can we teach? Here are the messages of the Holocaust, and believe me, they are not mixed. The world has few rescuers. Most people enjoy watching others in pain. You want more lessons? Let's see, some survivors were ruthless, and still are. How about something more abstract? There is no God. And if there is, let me just say he's nobody I would wish to pray to."

Several yeshiva boys were walking home from school, their yarmulkas secure but their *tzitzis* flapping. Jean tried to slap them on their heads as if to knock some sense into them, but his hand passed right through their skulls without causing even a slight migraine. Walking behind were cackling yeshiva girls, their heads covered, too, their hair braided in pigtails.

Jean chuckled and continued, "We are arrogant if we believe we can achieve something through our deaths that we couldn't with our pens while we were alive. We couldn't understand then, and we can't understand now why morality fails, why indifference is the most universal of all languages. To think we can suddenly figure it all out, to inject everyone with the magic-bullet cure and set them all on the right course is the most pathetic of wishful thinking."

"We have already helped in some way here," Primo said, removing his black-rimmed glasses and wiping them on his white sleeve. "Just look at this neighborhood. It is much different than it was before."

"Why, because more people dance at *shul* and eat kosher foods?" Jean laughed, his black eyes taking on the intensity of simmering coals. "Why, because they can see the empty stroller that carries Piotr's dead children?"

"No, because we are showing them how to care about life," Paul said. "The preciousness of each moment."

"Who are we to teach them how precious life is?" Jean asked.

"He's right." An otherwise silent Jerzy reentered the conversation, holding back his laughter and mockery, at least for the time being. "You just watch, soon enough the people of the Upper West Side will ignore our lessons and turn against our teachings."

"Why do you take his side?" Paul asked Jerzy.

"Because there is a limit to what we can do. We should prepare ourselves for failure. We can bring back some of the sounds of the shtetl, but the soul will have to come from them alone. The world has gone too long without soul. Who knows if it can be revived."

"They can do it," Primo said confidently, his prominent ears enjoying wonderful reception of the voices around him.

"Yes," Tadeusz said. "Look at all they have done by themselves, even before we arrived. They have museums and memorials, and they take trips to Auschwitz, and they send their children on the March of the Living. They make movies, and they film survivor testimonies."

"Concentration camps are no places for children," Jean sneered, "even just as tourists. Let the dead march there alone, in peace. And let the children instead go to Disney World. I hear the carousels are best there."

"Yes, yes," Jerzy said, supporting Jean once more. "I know, and they chase after Nazis and force the Swiss to give back looted gold from Jewish teeth. But there was also an American president who traveled to Bitburg. And remember, the Austrians elected a Nazi as their president. And of course there are so many people who have learned to forgive the Germans."

Jean now looked truly nauseated. "And you have forgotten the biggest gift of all," he said. "The world has learned how to recite the best slogan ever written." His voice dropped, and the others could barely hear him when he chanted: "Never Again."

"What?" Paul asked.

"The anthem, of course." Jean's voice was rising. "Never Again! Never Again! How quaint. All revolutionary movements need a good song. But what good has it done them? Jews are all chasing their tails. No matter how much they sing, it is very likely to happen again. There is nothing they can do to stop it, and surely the slogan won't help. All the banners and songs in the world can't prevent a good pogrom. Hasn't anyone learned anything from history? The Jews are destined for another Holocaust. The slogan Never Again is not a gas mask; the words will choke inside the lungs of the victims whether they say it or not."

"He's right," Piotr said defeatedly. "What has that slogan really accomplished? All it did was make Jews more angry, self-righteous, and defensive. It justifies the way Israelis have dealt with the Palestinians. Never Again has made the Jews crazy with vengeance and paranoia, and has made it impossible for them to connect to the more soulful aspects of their existence. We were once shepherds, poets, and rabbis. And now look at what the Jews have become. That slogan has done more than anything else to justify Jewish rage, and it has made Jean the way he is today."

"No, wrong, my friend," Jean said, his index finger pointed sky-ward. "I am immune to slogans; the Nazis can take all the credit for that. I never believed that work would set me free, and I'm not a sucker for Never Again either."

"Words are important, and slogans are necessary," Paul said. "Poetry can and must change the world. The Nazis taught us to take all threats seriously, that a Final Solution may not just be idle words. Sometimes madmen are not kidding around."

"I hear you, brothers," the homeless man said.

The Golems spun around slowly, as if the tables had now been turned on who was doing the haunting around here.

"That's right, I'm talking to you guys." The homeless gentleman rose. A pungent gamey smell followed his voice and his movements. "You, the Jewish spooks in front of me. You don't think I can see you, but I can. I didn't understand everything you all said, and I sure's hell don't know where you all come from, but it sounds to me like you're talking truth. I can sure hear that. The world just ain't right. It never was, and it's getting worse, man. There's no respect out there. Did you know that the mayor doesn't like me sitting here like this? They say I'm loitering. Some of the brothers and me used to come out here and chill out in the afternoon, but the cops drove us away. You hear what I'm saying?"

Piotr and Tadeusz smiled. Primo nodded. Jerzy coveted the man's army camouflage coat. The homeless man continued on, eloquently, grievously, about his own experience with injustice and suffering, knowing somehow that the Golems were a particularly susceptible, sympathetic audience.

Later that night, when Oliver and Ariel and even the homeless man were all asleep, the Golems made a pilgrimage to a place they had visited many times before since their return to half-life—the carousel at Central Park. The Golems hovered from above, like twisting wind currents, fireflies sparkling in the dead of winter, before finally setting themselves down. And there they found the handsome horses frozen in semitrot. Streaking chariots. Laughing clowns gawking from a beige, umbrella-shaped ceiling. The horses painted in magical, lacquered colors of red, orange, white, black, and brown.

The looping music of waltzes and polkas.

Children monopolized the horses by day. That's because the carousel is never open in the dead of night. But here, in the black silence of a ghostly park, the horses had become corralled for another purpose—a merry-go-round for the dead.

The carousel itself, surrounded by birch and oak trees, sweeping pastoral walkways, neoclassical overpasses, and small, algae-plagued ponds, reminded the Golems of Old Vienna, even though so few of them had actually been there. But it was at least a memory of Europe—the Europe that existed before and after Auschwitz. If not Vienna, then Crakow, or Paris or Milan.

Jerzy, dressed like a carnival barker with a sackcloth change purse tied around his waist, pulled the switch, the lights went on, the music swelled around them like atoms, and the horses began their up-and-down prance that would lead them back to where they had all started. The Golems each claimed a pole, slid their translucent feet through the solid stirrups, and readied themselves for the ride.

Some Golems were more daring than others. Tadeusz stood up on his saddle, clasping the pole and waving his arms like a circus performer. Jerzy's feet left his black horse altogether and angled out, wishbone style, on both sides of the steed. Rose leaned back on her white horse, one hand gripping the pole and one leg wrapped over and around the horse's mane. Lothar rode backwards, facing the other direction, gripping the horse's tail like a leash. Piotr brought his baby carriage with him and strapped one of the horse's reins onto the handlebar as if he planned to take the children for a ride but didn't wish to wake them. Primo and Paul held on to their animals tightly, hands clutching both pole and rein, thighs and abductors pushing against muscled pasterns and flanks. Jean sat solemnly, scissoring an unlit cigarette, stewing by himself inside a chariot, looking bored, as if he wished that someone would be kind enough to hand him a newspaper.

The contraption picked up speed, so that the image of haunted horses was nothing but a fluorescent blur. The waltzing music soared, and the wooden horses trotted as if responding to animal instincts. The Golems giggled as they circled around. But then their laughter hastily turned to something else. A spontaneous, unrehearsed chant grew louder with each whirl. The rising sound traveled outside the park, cresting through the canyons of Fifth Avenue and Central Park West and rousing the sleep of those nestled inside climate-controlled, doorman-protected buildings. And as the evening passed, the Golems continued to howl: "Never Again! Never Again! Never Again! . . ."

13

"SLOW DOWN! DON'T FIGHT WITH THE VIOLIN. IT was meant to be played, not ravaged."

Ariel lowered the violin and bow to her sides as though raising the white flag of surrender.

"The mode needs more exploration in the beginning," Tanya continued in an exaggerated, urgent voice, "and then you should really dig into the new tempo." To demonstrate this point, she sliced the air with a limb disarmed of a musical instrument. "We need more legato bow work."

"Did I do anything right?" Ariel wondered.

"The octave passages on that last piece were quite fine."

"Anything else?"

"Let's hear it again."

It all sounded harsher than it actually was. The teacher was merely establishing her authority over an ambivalent student. Ariel didn't want to be there at all, which Tanya realized, so she decided to go light on the fawning. This was a prodigy unseduced by the lavish, insincere compliment. Sycophants made her sick. And she had infused the entire Upper West Side with the spiritual life force of a dead poets' society. Obviously, Tanya sensed, she didn't need lessons in self-awareness and maturity. As a student she would have to be handled differently.

Ariel was hard on herself, and she liked it when others were even harder. She didn't fear criticism or those who easily find fault. Perhaps her ease with overachievement was a response to her father's silence. Or maybe it had to do with being bound by an altered DNA, the restricted autonomy of the Holocaust, where all future ambitions and life cycles had already been decided for her.

Tanya could have swooned and marveled—indeed, Ariel was very much deserving of that—but it wasn't clear whether that's what Ariel was looking for in coming to Tanya's studio in the first place. The audiences that gathered outside of Zabar's showered her with such affection regularly and uncritically. Tanya believed that she had to offer something more. What Tanya didn't understand was how little the violin had to do with Ariel's commitment to each lesson. Klezmer was beside the point: It was the certainty, even for an hour, of a woman's presence in Ariel's life that beguiled her more than the music.

And then there was the father. Tanya could only speculate on why Oliver Levin had consented to his daughter receiving private tutoring from Tanya. Perhaps it had to do with the discovery of a medieval Czech synagogue housed within the attic of his own brownstone. Or maybe he simply realized that he had no choice. Oliver was powerless to banish his parents and their literary friends back to wherever it was that they had come from. And wherever that was, Oliver imagined that their resurrection in Manhattan had something to do with Ariel's music, which he wasn't ready to turn off yet.

Perhaps it was all a strategic surrender. There were now incentives to making music. Oliver's world was no longer as self-contained as a courtroom mystery. The Golems had forever inverted the old formulas so that the pen was now pointed inward—sharp, leaky, and undrainable.

Oliver's life had suddenly taken on the nightmare noir of a thriller. And no one would have believed it if it weren't unfolding right there in his own neighborhood, in front of everyone. Yes, the plot lines were invisible, and the characters were all essentially dead, but they were also somehow breathing outside his imagination, forcing him to collaborate on a ghostwritten story. They were writers who had lost their bodies but somehow had retained their imaginations. And his parents were there, too. Strange signals were calling out to him—radarless and undetectable. An SOS from the survivors of the SS. And unlike the accessible, intellectually undemanding stories he had famously penned in the past, the tale that had now overtaken his life was metaphysically writing itself.

Larger literary forces had taken over. And whether they were indeed writing a book or merely toying with his head he did not yet know. It was a mystery, one that not even his own practiced mind for such things could disentangle. And so for now at least, while living in this spangled, electrified climate of shtetl revivalism, it didn't hurt to have a daughter who was a maestro on the klezmer violin. If for no other reason, there was value in being able to produce funeral music for such a wide array of associates who were, in actuality, dead.

"I want to take a break," Ariel requested.

"No, let me hear the last few bars again."

"This is child abuse," Ariel said. "I'm a street performer, on the street outside of a Jewish deli. I don't need to practice this hard to make it to Broadway; I'm already *on* Broadway—just not in the theater district. I'm never going to play at Carnegie Hall or Lincoln Center. That's not where you hear klezmer."

"Why not bring the music of the Hungarian forests to Avery Fisher Hall? Don't sell yourself short, Ariel. With you it might be different. Your audience might grow beyond the smoked-fish crowd. There is another world that wants to hear you play."

"I know," Ariel muttered. "The underworld."

And so, with each day, Ariel continued to practice and Tanya listened, but not without the occasional criticism. Tanya, of course, wanted to be more than a mere audience, but sometimes all an artist needs is an audience. The creative process often goes unassisted. All that is required is that it be witnessed. There is nothing to be done but tune in.

The source of those sounds was more primal than musical, the pitch allied with unregistered frequencies, the airwaves a traffic jam of voices from elsewhere. What was happening on the Upper West Side was a merger of the mystical with the musical—a static charge magnetized by bow and string. And while in the presence of such wonderment, teachers are essentially irrelevant and obsolete, less than a sideshow, not even worthy of being a warm-up act.

Despite a lifetime of immersion inside klezmer's jazzy sanctum of Jewish dreams, Tanya Green was tone deaf when it came to appraising her latest student. Everything about Ariel's mastery of the violin was unnatural, freakish, metaprodigious—monstrous, even. Lacking a more sensible explanation, Tanya began to wonder whether this child of Manhattan was actually descended from somewhere else. That was a good deduction. But how could Tanya ever imagine that the music before her was, in actuality, a mutation of Auschwitz.

Classically trained Jewish musicians who had played in the finest orchestras throughout Europe had been forced by the Nazis to trade in their tuxedos for the striped pajama uniforms of concentration camp inmates. And, while decomposing in places like Majdanek, Treblinka, and Theresienstadt, they serenaded the condemned who were on their way to the gas with the sweet, death-march music of Mozart, Brahms, and Chopin. And on other occasions, the music was a mere misdirection—a musical charade to fool the Red Cross, prefabricated proof that prisoners were being well cared for, that high culture could somehow coexist even in places that practiced lowbrow cannibalism. Ersatz for the ears.

Once the Nazis were bored with the pretense, when there was no further reason to dress up these ignoble enterprises of death, the human bonfire simply sizzled, sparkled, and moaned without any musical accompaniment. The musicians, no longer necessary, were soon transformed into treble clefs of wispy smoke. Perhaps Ariel—untrained, untutored, undisciplined, and playing an entirely different musical idiom—was their way of still making music, taking discordant revenge. The music that nobody wanted, and that the Nazis had tried to silence by murdering all the musicians, was back, and exhilaratingly so.

"That last note is an E, not a G. And the tempo should be adagio, not presto. Play it like I showed you before."

Ariel thought about the absurdity of bringing order to what was essentially the music of Jewish gypsies. What difference did it make what note she played, or how fast or slow she played it? She couldn't read the music anyway—those lined and barred sheets were like encrypted code—and her pitch was far from naturally perfect. Yes, she was making the music, but only in the same way that a phonograph makes music. The sounds were already there and prerecorded; all she had to do was put the bow to the strings like a needle on a record.

This was so untrue of her teacher, however, who had spent her formative years classically trained at Juilliard. Tanya Green worshiped the importance of precise notes, pure tones, carefully chosen tempi, liquid octaves, scale filigree passages, left-hand pizzicati, and clean trills. But for Ariel a G-string was no more exotic than erotic underwear. The fact that she could ever play a note was an accidental shriek of history—a kabbalah experiment gone haywire. One thing was for sure: Ariel's music had nothing at all to do with Tanya's tutelage.

The bow and violin once more rested against her legs like weapons that had run out of ammo. Ariel's breath was rapid, not sprinting, more like trotting; her chest took in small gulps of air as if she were a binge eater with a tiny stomach. Her blond hair was tied in a ponytail and slipped through the back opening of a green, teamless baseball cap.

Her eyes glanced across Tanya's spacious West End Avenue apartment like a burglar casing a job. Individual pieces of sheet music clung to the carpet like patchwork lily pads in a swamp. Scratched vinyl LPs of cantorial and klezmer music, along with a couple of anomalous Led Zeppelin albums, were scattered throughout the room like warped Frisbees. There was a Steinway baby grand anchoring one end of the living room, with almost every other piece of furniture balancing out the other. The furniture was part Bauhaus and some art nouveau, along with accumulated dust piles and other domestic debris, all of which looked as though it had been there for as long as the furniture itself. Ancient, amateur paintings depicting various languid stages of shetl life fought for space on walls busy with original moldings. One of the paintings was of a frenetic marketplace, overrun with hagglers and *handler*s. There was an obligatory barnyard scene with cows neither flying nor upside down, but simply in various poses of dairy-making activity. Another was of a Jewish wedding, huppah raised high, the bride and groom showcasing the nervous expressions of a shotgun courtship. And of course the walls were covered with various watercolor and oil canvases of *klezmorim* making music—fiddlers, *tsimblist*s, clarinet players, all engaged in the music for the masses of *Mitteleuropa*.

There were books by the great masters of Yiddish literature—Peretz, Shalom Aleichem, the Singer brothers, Grade, Leivick, and Mendele Mocher S'forim—crammed onto shelves like a body into a tight-fitting girdle. And some of the Russians were there too, although they didn't write in Yiddish but deserved to be included because of a shared annihilation. There were towering volumes of Babel, their hardcover jackets frayed and withered like coats that had been exposed to far too many Siberian winters. And a few cookbooks specializing in Eastern European cuisine—borscht, blintzes, and the exponential ways in which to prepare herring, the tofu of shtetl Jews.

Tanya Green's apartment was a shrine to a lost culture, as if the apartment itself had just come off the boat, covered in smocks and babushkas, tested for TB, reeking from steerage, and painted in the darkest seasickness shade of green imaginable—an apartment that didn't quite yet know the lay of the land.

The building was old, prewar, the way New Yorkers define their architectural landmarks. In San Francisco they measure such moments of demarcation as prequake and postquake. In Miami hurricanes provide the memory-serving signposts. Disasters are seemingly the best way for civilizations to mark their history—whether it be Pompeii, Jerusalem, Hiroshima, Beirut, or the Upper West Side.

The outside bricks and stone appeared as though they had been assembled by a toddler—uneven, unappointed, and soon to collapse. Years of pollution and neglect had given the building the complexion of soot. Wraparound gargoyles were stationed at various points, scattered along ledges and on top of gables as if guarding a maximum-security Gothic facility. Chipped paint of various unmatched colors flaked from the interior walls. The elevator rattled from rust and moved as slowly as a dumbwaiter. The lobby mirror was on loan from a funhouse. A napping doorman, who was older than the building and as alert as a wooden Indian, greeted visitors.

"Look, Ms. Green, I appreciate what you're trying to do for me, but I'm not some shtetl monkey with you as my organ grinder," Ariel complained, still holding on to the violin but making eye contact with the piano, as if trying to provoke a jealous reaction. "And I have to tell you the truth: I don't know what any of these musical notes are; they're just letters of the alphabet to me, except I can't tell the difference between them. I haven't understood a word you've said in weeks."

Tanya dipped her chin toward her shoulder, an act that concealed a knowing smile.

"You're giving me too much credit," Ariel continued. "You think I know stuff, but I don't. And you're assuming I want to get better at playing this thing, which I don't either. I could care less."

"So then quit," Tanya challenged her pupil. "Stop playing."

"I can't."

"Why not?"

"Because I'm not the one who's playing."

"What are you saying?" Although Tanya already knew. "You think you're the front person for someone else, nothing but a pretty face, the Milli Vanilli of klezmer?"

"You know what I mean, Ms. Green."

"Okay, suppose I do. Then answer my question: Why are you here?"

"Huh?"

"Why are you here? Why are you showing up for these lessons if you don't want to play or have any control over your playing?"

"How can you ask me that? You practically begged me to come. You nearly chased me down Broadway, remember? I was afraid you were some kind of stalker."

"Yes, I know, I remember. But now that you're here and you've been coming so regularly, you know me better. And you also know that despite all of my chastising and coaching, I'm having absolutely no effect on you. My teaching is useless; everything I promised you and your father has turned out to be false. I've oversold myself. I can't improve you at all; I can't teach you anything. I'm out of my league, and we both know it. You should be teaching me."

"I've learned some things," Ariel said sympathetically.

"Come on, Ariel, my ego can take it; it's okay. I've done some wonderful things for some marvelously talented students over the years, but . . . ," Tanya hesitated, shaking her head, "with you . . . it's different. What's coming out of you is something else entirely. It goes way beyond talent or technique. It's a divine possession, an act of God, a revelation with a klezmer soundtrack."

Ariel's closed fingers gripped the scroll of the violin as though she were squeezing someone's hand.

"You woke up one day and discovered that you could play the klezmer violin better than anyone in the world—probably better than anyone has ever played it. And you found a violin that was buried in your attic, one that your father didn't even know he had, one that looks as though it was a violin for the ages—the same kind that the old *klezmorim* used to play, those who made music in the valleys and forests of Hungary, Romania, and Poland, the ones who never lived to survive the war, for whom the music stopped at the gas chambers and open grave ditches. No, this isn't even God speaking; it's something else altogether," Tanya added quietly.

"You're starting to scare me again," Ariel said. "It's much better if I just play without thinking about it too much."

But now the teacher no longer wanted her student to play. "So tell me finally, why are you here? You don't need me to get to Carnegie Hall."

"You asked me to come! I already told you that."

"Is my apartment just some hangout for you where you can taunt me like I'm Salieri to your Mozart?"

Ariel missed that reference entirely. "I think I'm going to leave now," she said, and reached down to shove some of her things, like sheet music, lip gloss, and a purple hairband, into her backpack. "Should I come again tomorrow?"

"Ariel, stay, . . . talk to me. What is it? What's going on inside you?"

Ariel hesitated, then said, "There's so much sadness in my house."

"You're sad?"

"No, . . . well, yes, . . . but . . . it's really my father. It's hard to be there every day, and so I show up here. I've been trying to fix him, like he's some broken person, which he is. This music has something to do with it." Ariel's eyes got caught up with tears, which then interrupted what she had to say. "Sorry. I can't tell you what's going on. You wouldn't believe it anyway."

"The synagogue in the attic?" Tanya blurted.

"You know about that?"

"I went up there with your father. I came over to ask him to let you study the violin with me. He showed me where that violin came from. I don't think he had ever been up there before."

"It wasn't always like that."

"What do you mean?"

"The attic—it used to look just like a regular attic."

"When did it change?"

"When everything else did. You know, the haunted baby carriage, the screwed-up subways, the Yankees losing their stripes. I can't say any more about it; I can't, it just wouldn't be right."

"So you, . . . and that violin have something to do with what's going on outside?" Tanya pondered quietly, eyes darting, her voice trailing away, only to return seconds later with renewed vitality and volume. "But what about your father? Does he know about all this?"

"No."

"Why not tell him? He seems capable and generally fine to me. Well, . . . perhaps a bit scrambled and distracted, but okay otherwise for a neurotic Jewish Upper West Sider."

"Do you know what it's like not to have a mother?"

"I thought this was about your father."

"It is. It's totally about him, but it's about me, too."

"You told me the first time I met you, outside of Zabar's, that you didn't have a mother."

"I know. I remember you asking me."

"It's all still raw for you. She left you guys, didn't she? Is that what's wrong?"

"No. That happens to other people. What's wrong is being born into a Holocaust family."

"Your grandparents were . . . ?"

"Yes."

"That's not all. They killed themselves when my father was in college."

"Oh my God!" Tanya gasped, wanting to reach out for something but not knowing what. "How horrible."

"And my mom left us a long time ago. I was too young to

remember her. I have no memory of my family being together. She just left, never said where she was going, and we haven't heard from her since. I've been living in a house without a mother, and with a broken father, and so many ghosts."

"A house haunted by abandonment," Tanya concluded, but in a barely audible voice.

"A haunted Holocaust house," Ariel corrected her.

"Yes, I see." But Tanya couldn't possibly conceive all that Ariel had seen lately.

"Kids aren't supposed to be responsible for taking care of their parents," Ariel lamented. "It's supposed to be the other way around. I made a big mistake messing with the mystical world."

"You mean musical."

"No, mystical. I don't know what I was thinking. I wasn't qualified. I'm way over my head. I'm only in ninth grade; I haven't even had physics yet. And besides, who's taking care of me? Who's trying to fix me?"

"Tragedies always change the accepted rules," Tanya said gravely. "I'm so sorry. You are the third generation of the Shoah. It is quite extraordinary, the way this legacy gets passed down. It's a curse, really. Relief can only come by way of exorcism. Or maybe a kabbalist has to be brought in. I suppose you and your father never considered that option."

"No, never."

"I would have hoped that by the third generation, the damage would be less present in your life, that it would wind itself down and exhaust itself."

"Not when a mother leaves you. That doesn't help things. This shouldn't have happened to Oliver or me, and there is nothing I can do to fix it. I know that now, because I brought help with me this time, and I don't think it's going to do much good."

"What kind of help? Does it have something to do with the violin?"

"I can't say."

"Maybe I can help you."

"You can't. I miss my mother, and I don't want the job of fixing my father. And I want someone to take care of me."

"You both deserve that," Tanya said, then wrapped herself around her pupil.

"Ms. Green, now can I ask you something?"

"Sure. What would you like to know?"

"Why did you want me to come here if you already knew you couldn't help me with my music?"

"Easy question. How could I resist wanting to be so close to genius, watching it evolve even though it isn't even aware of itself? How often does something like this happen? And with you it's even more astonishing, because you have put magic in the air. The whole neighborhood seems to have been transformed. The music is only part of it, but it all seems to be connected somehow, as if that violin is some kind of channeler of the spiritual world. That's what you're not telling me, and frankly that's why I'm not asking, because maybe I'm afraid to know. What I do know is that I love that vanished European world," she said longingly as she scanned her own apartment, glancing at the artifacts she had managed to preserve. "But it somehow feels like it's all coming back and being reclaimed. And if it started with you and that violin, then all the better. But I also feel like we've been invaded by visitors who have the power to make things right again, if that's even possible. Do you know what I mean?"

And with that Ariel shuddered and squirmed as if possessed, not by a dybbuk but by her own resentment. The responsibility was too great. Her childhood had not been taken by the Nazis, but the effect was not so different. And her parents had been complicit, too. No child should have to begin meeting the demands of adulthood so soon.

She once more lifted the violin, which now all of a sudden seemed heavier. But this time she elevated it way above her shoulder and jawline to a point over her head. This was a position not for making music but destroying it. With both hands wrapped around the fingerboard she plunged the curved bridge of the instrument down like a nightstick on a resident of Harlem. The violin was aimed at the baby grand, a target Ariel could not miss. Two classical instruments not in concert but in collision, filling the air not with harmonizing vibrations, but with the sound of wood crashing on impact.

And as the soundboard of the violin came within a solitary inch of shattering against the smooth black body of the piano, Ariel's wrist was intercepted and detained by an invisible handcuff. Tanya was stunned, not so much by Ariel's rebellious technique of playing the violin, but by the suddenness and dexterity with which she managed to reverse it. What Tanya still did not realize was that Ariel was not acting alone—neither as a klezmer violinist nor as a demolitionist. Someone else had entered Tanya's apartment that afternoon, someone who was also interested in the preservation of music and didn't want to see it interrupted. That had happened to him once before, with tragic results.

With tearful, pleading eyes, Tadeusz held Ariel's wrist as if it were broken. The pulse faced up as Ariel released the violin from her hands, laying it safely on the piano. The violin had survived yet another ritual murder.

14

THE HOUSE ALWAYS FEELS SO EMPTY. THAT'S true of every home I have ever lived in, even before ghosts started arriving as stand-ins for dead relatives. Sometimes physical space is best filled with furniture alone. You hang pictures on the wall, throw rugs on the floor, interrupt the stillness with music, rearrange lifeless but massive sofas—all decorative clutter that makes the surrounding emptiness less noticeable. The spartan apartment as modern-day Greek tragedy.

Breathing bodies are another matter entirely. They are harder to come by; surely they are less faithful and accommodating than asskissing sofas. That's because fixtures don't pick up and leave on their own. They are fixed by nature with built-in stability—anchored to the ground or hammered to the wall—that makes them so unlike people, who are mostly portable and about as conscience-stricken as a sofa.

It is not true that those who presumably love you the most are also the ones who will stay around the longest. That's just a fairy tale of wide appeal, a bedtime story that makes soothing, reassuring sleep possible. We all long to live in a moral universe that has no sinister parallel. But that's not where we live, is it? Our galaxy comes without any guarantees. All that is certain is the vastness, and the silence of an empty home.

The problem as I see it is that love is negotiable. It can be bought and sold. It has its own values and valuation. And emotions have their own momentum. They ignite quickly and can fizzle just as fast. And like any impulse that is aligned with the heart, it is always subject to swinging moods, rashness, and volatility. How could it be otherwise? Love, after all, is not an exact science. In fact, it is antiscience; it doesn't want to have anything to do with formulas and proofs, theories and equations, vaccines and placebos, potions and serums.

This is why matchmakers were always dismissive and aloof when it came to the subject of love. All along they knew that marriage is not about the mating of souls but rather the continuity of communities. Reading between the lines of a marriage contract reveals no clauses on love. But written in bold, block, boilerplate letters there is much said about investment, sacrifice, honor, and the planned future. In the family business, a marriage founded on love alone is a money-losing, nongoing concern. Love is undisciplined and disloyal, frivolous and irresponsible, cunning and coy, self-sabotaging and easily bored.

The heart aspires to beat to the music of virtue and honor, but it is simply too capricious an organ for that. Or maybe it's because the heart, no matter how well conditioned, actually lacks stamina. It is an impulse buyer. A starry-eyed, one-stop shopper. An addict of immediate gratification. It wants what it wants when it wants it, and then wants something else, operating entirely on the selfish assumption that no matter what promises were exchanged, love can always be taken back for a full refund—no questions asked, without hassle.

And it doesn't end with marriages. Families have equally perishable shelf lives. It's all part of the new social bargain: the ephemeral family, the ancestral homestead empty of ancestors.

Among the various lessons of the Holocaust—lessons, I might add, that came to me late in life even though the course materials were right in front of me all along—is that there is no point counting on families staying together. They are more likely to be snatched or missing or absent than intact. Poor Otto Frank learned this all too well. You can't hide in an attic to save your own skin, or the skins of the people you love the most. Attics are for preserving the unsightly, the forgotten, the irrelevant, and the obsolete. It's where you keep your monsters, not where you hide from them. And in the end, there is nowhere to hide.

In the modern world the family cannot be sheltered, cannot save itself from itself, from dissolution and divorce and, in the extreme cases, annihilation. The family is a highly vulnerable entity, always in a perpetual state of code blue, too listless to fight back, and too fragile to resuscitate.

So if you're not safe in your own home, if people will leave you and ghosts will return in their place, then where is there true sanctuary from loss and abandonment? Are there such places anymore? Did they ever exist? Perhaps not. You can't buy that kind of protection, can't will it to happen, can't pray for it suddenly to appear. Shutting the door of your own home won't make it safe. But maybe you can shut the door on yourself. Hide in one of those rooms, maybe even in the attic. Crawl inside and take cover from all the hurt. After a while, with any luck, no one will even notice that you've been gone. That's how Jerzy said it's done, anyway. All that's left to decide is when, if ever, to reemerge. It's the only hard-won, time-tested, scientifically proven place of refuge that I know.

But is it enough?

Parents are required to care for their children. That is their duty, their job. But what if they can't perform? What if they have been disqualified even before they start? Paralyzed when it comes to parenting. Incapable of carrying out the essential tasks. Too cynical for caretaking. They can procreate, because that's the easy part, merely a mechanical act of nature. Fucking does not require arm-twisting. The difficulty lies in the day-to-day assignments after the progeny comes. This is where the central nervous system comes into play. But what if the parents are too nervous to activate it, or what if the systems themselves have already been systematically destroyed? They have lost their nerve, or their nerves have already been shot. Whichever way, the parents can't parent.

Now, you'd think I'm speaking about my own parents here. Those two Holocaust survivors who wound up killing themselves, leaving no paper trail or answers to explain why they had done it. But it's not them I'm referring to, but me—Ariel's father.

My parents had an excuse, after all. They simply couldn't do it, and finally they just gave up. The responsibility of parenting was too much. They had no faith in a trouble-free, postliberated life. Or faith in anything, for that matter. Raising a child requires a leap into the unknown, but the jump is pointless if there is no wide net of faith below to break the fall.

Lothar and Rose were incapable of explaining this all back then— either to me or to themselves. When they eventually spoke, it was in the language of suicide. Now that they have returned, perhaps they will finally say more.

But what is *my* excuse, exactly? The one who now claims to live in the empty house. Yet that's not true. My daughter lives here, as well, right alongside me. I am not alone. And yet Ariel's presence has brought me no comfort. In fact she doesn't realize it, because I can't tell her—because it is too horrifying to admit—but she has made it even worse for me. Because of her there is someone breathing in my home whom I fear I might lose. Such things are possible, you know. And I can't help thinking about it because I have learned the toughest, most humbling lessons of all: Loss, like love, has its own will—it cares little for what it leaves behind.

I have parented as if I had been preparing the entire time for an empty nest, as if Ariel were about to go off to college before she even took her first steps. I've hardened myself to early departures, developed an emotional nonstick surface, resisted growing too attached to anything with legs.

"It's time for hide-and-go-seek," she once announced, many years before what she was hiding was not herself but her secret experiments. Those were the days before there was a Manhattan Project upstairs in my attic, the European séance that wasn't satisfied with mere voices.

"I don't like that game."

"Why not, Oliver? You're good at it, as good a hider as anyone in my school."

"Ariel, I'd rather not have to come find you. And I don't like hiding from you either."

"It's just a game, Oliver."

"Games sometimes make you think about what if, . . . you know, the game came true."

"I'm not going anywhere, Daddy," she reassured me.

I hesitated, taking in her words, looking into that small, unfolding face. "You called me Daddy."

"That's who you are, right? I have to remind you sometimes . . . you know, that you're my daddy."

But I didn't want to be called "Daddy." It is the most personal of nouns, the one word that signals complete umbilical, parental responsibility, that you belong to someone else. First names are easier—informal, without attachments.

My perspective on parenting has been focused almost exclusively on the avoidance of tragedy. That's how I have done it, but I've missed so much doing it in this way. I've been unable to see, haven't allowed myself to see. That's probably why this golem redux experiment was able to take place inside my attic without me even knowing about it.

Thankfully, fate has so far shielded Ariel from this cursed family. But I wait for all sorts of other shoes to drop. Yet even my most practiced, paranoidal nightmares can't change this unchallengeable fact: My daughter is essentially very safe. She has never spent a night or an hour in a hospital or an emergency room. She has no broken bones. Her tonsils still belong to her. She is overinoculated and underprotected. And yet in that foreign, dirtless cemetery that once was the attic of my house and now seems to be a two-way portal for suicidal spirits and ghosts, I know she has been trying to cast an ancient mystical spell that will free us all. She wants better for herself; she wants better for me.

This legacy of the Levins runs deep. People leave. Sometimes with violence, sometimes with simple silence. You return home and they are gone. They cut the rope, but it is not a clean break. The cord is shredded, as though snapped by a wild, unleashed animal. The kind of break that aspires not only to freedom but also to expression. Abandonment is both an act and a statement. What remains is a crime scene of manufactured emptiness. The chalk outline of the body is no longer there, not because the person who departed is dead, but because she has never been more alive.

When Ariel was little, we would sit on the sofa together and watch *Sesame Street*. "Mommy, she always comes back, . . . Mommy always comes back," some fuzzy, button-eyed puppet would sing. Ariel glanced up at me, the look of an astute child who knows when it's time to switch the channel. Elmo, let me tell you something: Spare the kids. Mommy doesn't always come back.

The abrupt, smokeless violence. These heart vandals and soul killers. They steal shared memories and keep them for themselves. And they are never heard from again. They are, indeed, missing persons, but no one is looking for them. Their pictures do not go up in post offices and on cereal boxes. Abandonment is not a crime. It is a celebrated, self-liberating choice.

Such was the case with the Levins. You can't stop someone from blowing out his brains, or downing a poison pill, or simply packing a bag and closing the door for the very last time.

What will it take for the Levins to be reassured that the world won't go away, that there are antidotes for emptiness, that the past doesn't always have to swallow the future, that faith and trust are not toxic, lethal impulses, that demons can be undone or even reformed into friends, that the way to fill a home is not with furniture alone?

15

SHE CLOSED THE DOOR ON HER OWN HOME AND never opened it again. All that existed for her back inside was emptiness and furniture—so stationary and predictable. The family and the fixtures weren't moving out; only she was leaving. Unannounced. But perhaps not totally unexpected. Her husband and young daughter would return later and discover her gone.

No one wants to wreck a home, especially when that home is their own. The enduring versatility of the scarlet letter, that first symbol of the alphabet that can spell a variety of transgressions and can also, imprinted on a forehead, give life to a golem. When a mother leaves both a child and a husband, what it spells is abandonment. Perhaps a greater moral sin than adultery. But sometimes it must be done even if it's the last thing someone would want to do.

She had changed but nothing else had, as though the people around her were like furniture, as if they were required to keep pace with the randomly blinking switchboard of her inner world. She had made discoveries about herself. She wasn't who she had thought she was, and yet who she was now was equally unknown to her. She was trying to catch up to her new identity, which was elusive, always a step ahead. She had to find herself all over again. But not here. Not with him.

He had felt her withdrawal—all that was being untouched and ignored—but he was also unable to imagine where it would lead. What eventually happened was inconceivable, and so he blindly chose not to consider it. Distance doesn't have to lead to a disaster. Simply because a wife moves away emotionally doesn't mean that one day she'll pick up and actually move away. Feelings can return, find their way back, restart, and revive.

The baby was still young, after all. Just turned two. Families don't break up so soon. Such severe, radical, and final solutions take time to evolve. Even the Nazis took years to eliminate what they had decided they no longer wanted around.

But from a position of withdrawal, everything looks and feels different, because withdrawal is the enemy of intimacy. The freedom that Samantha sensed was incompatible with relationship—at least one with him. Yet, given his family history, given where he came from, where his parents had been, and what they had done to numb themselves at his expense, she knew she could not experiment too liberally with her wishes, if they clashed too much with his. Leaving him was not tough love but self-love. A harsh remedy. But staying with him might prove worse. Reclaiming the self requires a radical plan: The most important thing is to do away with those who had an investment in, and a memory of, the person you used to be.

But Oliver's circumstances were special. Samantha would have wanted to take Ariel with her, but how could she, given whom she had married?

"The future of the family is in my arms, Sam," she recalled him saying the day she gave birth to Ariel. He was crying unstoppably and shaking joyously, as if he never imagined becoming a father, as if the prior nine months had all been a hoax. The Levins had much more of an affinity with death than birth, so perhaps Oliver's skepticism was understandable. What should he have expected, a miracle? "She's a miracle. So amazing looking, don't you think? And she belongs to us."

And on days when Ariel would be crying, longing for her father while Oliver was away on a book tour, Samantha recalled herself saying, "Shush now, Ariel, it's okay. Daddy will be back soon. He always comes back. . . ."

To have taken Ariel away from her father would have been a criminal act—morally, if not legally. And moral crimes carry their own punishments—the last of all judgments—like ticking, internal bombs, forever terrorizing the conscience.

Oliver seemed oblivious to his family's origins. He never openly gave them a second thought, nor did it keep him awake at night. But Samantha knew better. She understood that such a legacy need not be discussed in order to be active. A legacy is like a volcano, one minute dormant, the next explosive. It can't pretend to be just another mountain. Even when it is unspoken it nonetheless lurks in the background, looming like an overextended shadow. A past that is very much present but ignored. Samantha knew that it was Oliver's attic to open, like a safe-deposit box whose contents were extremely unsafe and where there was no shared power of attorney to make the opening easier. The key was his alone.

The good news was that there was no rush, no particular timetable. The crimes committed against his family, and then against him, could never be forgotten or forgiven. There was no statute of limitations on spiritual murder. His legacy would simply linger like the noiseless wind, an unexamined inkblot, an anonymous tombstone. When Oliver was finally ready, it would be there waiting for him. His own private echo, unheard by others and yet delivered in his own voice.

Samantha knew this all to be true even if he didn't. The time would come, she was certain, when he would tire of all those years of avoidance and denial, of being able to lose himself successfully inside murder mysteries that sprang from his imagination rather than his memory. His actual life was being underutilized in his art. He had the moral authority to write from personal experience, but he refused to do so. He could have been like those dead men who had recently come alive in his home. The ghosts who were now redirecting his sanity, disturbing his peace of mind, and turning it into an all-out war. Was it even possible to write about the Shoah without eventually ending up like them?

After all, he had the perfect pedigree for becoming an artist of such heavyweight material. His artistic license could never expire. His family had been in the death business. They were neither undertakers nor morticians, just simple statistics. This gave him a deeper intimacy with loss than he had let on to his readers and, most of all, himself. And yet despite such a mother lode of emotional resources at his disposal—unguarded access into the intestines of atrocity—he denied himself these privileges under the pretense of saving himself.

Instead he chose to write about pedestrian murders and ordinary crimes. The kinds of homicides that are easily investigated and eventually solved, where there is justice and closure and endings—often thrilling, even if unsatisfying. For him to have written about the evil that he actually knew, the one that was in his bones even if not in his head, would have demanded much more than an active imagination. It would have taken guts, real guts—untwisted and uncoiled. Not metaphorical agents of courage but actual organs. Because that's where the story lies, in the stomach, where everything, not just the food, goes after it gets ingested, and before becoming buried.

But that's not where Oliver wanted to focus—either his eyesight or his energies. It was all too terrifying and, frankly, revolting. As a writer he wasn't going to draw any inspiration from it either. Just blanks. The true art of his life was artifice; the real profit in those courtroom thrillers came entirely by way of personal camouflage. The brownstone that had been paid for by those lightweight novels had now, ironically, unleashed the most unnatural of high-literary forces on his slumbering spirit, exacting poetic justice from the man who had buried himself inside books—unfortunately, the wrong ones.

Samantha believed that one day Oliver would have the courage to confront his bunkered, impacted, calcified self. Or maybe he would be forced into it against his will. She just didn't know when that would happen or, more precisely, how. All she knew was that she wouldn't be there to witness it. She also realized that she couldn't allow him to do it completely on his own. He needed company, some family even among the depleted ruins. If not her then the next best thing—the only other thing that mattered—their daughter. One day he would encounter his ghosts, and who better to witness it with him than the child who would bring them on.

But not without cost. There was going to be yet another abandonment in the family. The only question was: How severe? Samantha would have to abandon two in order to save one. As much as she wanted to, she could not take Ariel with her. To leave her husband with nothing other than his haunted history seemed even more cruel and unforgivable than abandoning them both. She couldn't live with him anymore, but she also couldn't take from him the only family his family had managed to produce in the aftermath of all that death.

Ariel, who had barely had time to know her mother, remained with her father and grew to understand the various ways in which he had been scarred, even though he never said a word in his own defense about the offenses committed against him. Over time Ariel would take drastic measures to relieve him of his demons by animating them, giving them refracted shape, piercing voice, and a syringe shot of soul. She conjured antidotes from another world. Samantha would have been proud of her daughter. Instinctively, at such a young age, she sought to repair the parent who had suffered such double damage. A child of many musical and mystical talents; the heroic pied-piper kabbalist of the Upper West Side, ghosts trailing behind, klezmer music wafting in the chimed wind.

But Samantha would not leave without the piñata. She had to

cut the final cord. This one, however, was not umbilical, but rather ceremonial. Together Samantha and Oliver, using papier-mâché, had constructed a green Chinese dragon with a flaming red tongue and a flamingo pink heart. It was an arts-and-crafts project in anticipation of the birth of their daughter, something they once did for laughs at the 92nd Street Y that later became the family's talismanic mascot. It wasn't stuffed but hollow, hanging from the ceiling fan that ventilated the parlor floor of their brownstone on Edgar Allan Poe Street.

Samantha lifted her suitcase and shuffled over to the center of the living room, right underneath the ceiling fan with the dragon hanging overhead, a string around its neck as if the dragon had been lynched rather than slain. Holding a small pair of scissors from her purse, she raised her arm and cut the string. The dragon dropped to the parquet floor, still intact and unbroken, no candies spilling from its insides. Kneeling down, she lifted the piñata and placed it inside her bag.

Still in a squat, Samantha turned her head and scanned the room one last time, but from a low vantage point, the one that her daughter saw. Tears flowed as her eyes regarded Ariel's favorite dolls flopping over one another in pint-size white wicker chairs. And there was a bucket of toys brimming with Legos, building blocks, and Play-Doh compressors. A scuffed Frisbee that Samantha and Oliver used to toss in Central Park now rested on a sofa as if pooped from dancing in between all those tricky wind currents. Samantha rose to her feet and dabbed her eyes with the sleeves of her sweater. It was all becoming too much to take in. She couldn't have a nostalgic revisit ruin this most reckless of good-byes. Oliver and Ariel would be home soon. Samantha took one final look, turned off the lights, and was gone, leaving everything in the dark.

Well, at least that's how Oliver imagined it, anyway.

∾∘∾

"I know this must be a rough time for you, Mr. Levin, but I have some questions I'm afraid I'm going to have to ask."

Lieutenant Costello was the detective from the Twentieth Precinct of the NYPD assigned to investigate the disappearance of Samantha Wexler Levin. He was a large man with an obvious appetite for fast food, which rendered him slow and listless, like a senior citizen in a retirement village immediately after lunch. His face was blank and without expression, as though drawn with white crayon. His hair was brown; his sleepy, half-mast eyelids rested above folds of wrinkled flesh. His teeth were sharp, dark, and uneven, like the rusty grille of an old Buick.

"It's been two days, and we're going to need to fill out a missing persons report," the police detective said.

Oliver was still very much shaken from the past forty-eight hours. That was understandable but, in his mind, surprising. Such is the hold our emotions have on our actions and reactions. Oliver's parents had killed themselves while he was away at college. Surely with that kind of tragedy behind him, bad news was something he should have been prepared to hear at any time. The manner of their deaths had been so grisly, so senseless. From now on he would forever be invincible to emotional fallout. His composure had been battle tested—hardened to hardship, resistant to any type of collapse.

But when it comes to loss, practice does not make perfect. In the area of catastrophe, we are all novices and low-rank amateurs—the strong ones and the weak, the seasoned and the unsuspecting. Oliver was no better prepared than anyone else; in fact the lessons had been wasted on him. There is no readiness for disaster, no auto-piloting, no safe landings.

To Lieutenant Costello, Oliver looked the part of a bereft husband who had resigned himself to accepting that his wife wasn't coming home anytime soon. He hadn't shaved. He had taken perhaps only one shower since she'd left. The few meals he had eaten didn't travel well in his system. He held Ariel close, confining the two of them to only a few rooms in the brownstone. Space suddenly frightened him.

He tried to comport himself, for Ariel's sake. He focused on being a father, but the part of him that was still a husband needed its own reassurance. But there was no one to give it to him. With Samantha gone, what should he tell his daughter?

"Mommy had to go away for a while," he explained without emotion.

Ariel nodded and then cried quietly. For many years she didn't speak about it—an early manifestation of the Levin instincts for survival. She would search rooms, as well as inside chests and underneath beds. Sometimes, when she was somewhat older, she climbed up into the attic, a little Anne Frank, not hiding, but yearning for her mother.

"Mommy, she always comes back . . . ," Ariel sang, the lying lyric all choked up in a child's tears.

Oliver asked Detective Costello to arrive at the brownstone during Ariel's nap time, while she was upstairs, dreaming her own dreams.

"Would you like something to eat?" Oliver offered his guest, a man not of blue but of rumpled civilian charcoal gray.

"No, thanks, this coffee will do just fine."

The detective was staring at the pictures angled like tepees above the fireplace. One at a time he removed a few frames from the mantelpiece, examining them closely, his eyes squinting as though he were looking at rare stamps. What interested him most were the photos of Samantha: one at Big Sur, the rocky Pacific coastline placidly behind her; another in East Hampton, the beach suntanned and level, except for one lonely dune off to the side; and with Ariel as an infant, a mother-daughter moment surrounded by fall foliage in Manchester, Vermont. In each of these seasonal pictures, Samantha's smile was large and her body language loose and unaffected. Most of the photographs seemed to have been taken recently, which made Lieutenant Costello suspicious.

If the camera never lies, he mused, then these were not the portraits of a woman soon to take flight. Of course he was experienced enough to know that cameras never get a good peek at what's held close to the vest. The secrets of the soul are coy, camera shy, and decidedly unphotogenic. Sadness lies deeper than what the F-stop can capture. The detective returned the photographs to where he found them, and then cautiously walked toward Oliver.

"Maybe I should start off by telling you that me and the missus are big fans of your books. I think this runs against department rules by me saying this, and I hope I'm not embarrassing you, but you're my favorite writer. Wait till I tell her who I bumped into today! I'm only sorry it had to be under these terrible circumstances."

Oliver wasn't sure whether he was supposed to thank the detective, so he said nothing.

"Oh, yeah, we love all of them," the detective continued. "Not that we're such big readers, but this much I do know: You sure can tell a good story. You're terrific with death, and I'm saying this as a guy who used to work in homicide."

"Thank you, I think," Oliver said awkwardly, barely looking up from his seat on the sofa. The Frisbee was right beside him. It hadn't been moved in days, as if he were trying to maintain a grounded, undisturbed crime scene.

"So, let's get back to where we were, Mr. Levin." The detective flipped over a few pages in his small spiral notebook. "I got you down as saying that you and your wife weren't having any arguments or anything like that on the day you last saw her."

"That's right."

"And she wasn't acting strange or unusual in any way."

"No, not really."

"And she left no note?"

"No, she left no note," Oliver conceded. He recalled having said this before, back when he was in college.

"Did she have any enemies or anyone who might want to harm her?"

"No, none that I know of."

Detective Costello sighed while continuing to take notes and fill in blanks. Oliver's instincts as a mystery writer made him realize that he had not given the detective any of the answers he had hoped for.

"Well, Mr. Levin, I've been a police officer for a long time. I've seen it all, believe me. Most of the time the situations are never as suspenseful as the ones you write about in your books. Of course, that's the difference between what's real and what's made up. So let me explain something: There's always a good reason why people are missing or run away. There has to be. People just don't disappear for nothing—poof, gone, just like a ghost!" The detective motioned as if he were waving a magic wand. "People don't just vanish; they aren't taken away from their families without a trace. That kind of thing doesn't go on anymore. Maybe it does in the movies, but not in real life. Law enforcement is too sophisticated, and people too pre-dictable."

"So what are you saying, Detective?"

"Nothing yet. If you don't mind, I'd like to search for some clues and call in a forensic examiner. I'm also going to contact the FBI."

While the detective spoke, Oliver chuckled at how unoriginal these routine procedures were. Almost all of his novels included a salty and telegenic character who'd mouth these very same words.

"But don't worry, Mr. Levin, your wife will turn up. I got a feel-ing about this one. Besides, it would be too weird for a guy like you—you know, murder mystery writer and all—to lose a loved one this way."

"Not weird at all, Detective, not weird at all."

16

BY NOW OLIVER'S HAIR HAD TURNED COMPLETELY white. It was as though he had been to Mount Sinai and back, having carried on a conversation with a florist's choice for the personification of God—a ventriloquist's dummy in the form of a burning bush. God's entry into Exodus is surely a strange one. Why a bush, after all? It's no less absurd than a talking camel? And if it had to be plant life, why did God need to set it on fire—even an unconsuming one—as a way of moving its mouth? The voice of the Almighty could simply have been piped in from the heavens, like the way they do it in the movies or in kosher hot dog commercials.

There was in fact biblical precedent for what was going on in Oliver's brownstone. For, like Moses thousands of years earlier,

Oliver's once-thick brown hair had suddenly turned wavy white, sparing none of the strands. Revelation has that kind of effect on people, on lawgivers and writers of courtroom thrillers alike.

That wasn't all of it. Oliver was also now beginning to have nightmares, which was no small miracle, because before the Golems arrived, he hadn't been much of a nighttime dreamer. During the day he invented suspenseful stories from scratch; at night his dream life was unsensational and unmemorable.

But now, like his hair, his dreams were coming in, but without color. They were vividly cast in black-and-white. He was dreaming the dreams of ghosts whose lives had been lived out in the most somber of grays. The sounds of terrified, abandoned, screaming children, the soundtrack for cattle cars snaking along train tracks. A sky blackened in smoke, no blue horizon or white clouds anywhere in sight. Guns fired at ranges too close to be anything other than an execution. Gas pellets dropped into hissing showerheads, turning concrete chambers into heavenly white tombs. These nightmares were now his for the taking, because the dead no longer dreamed for themselves. The task was taken up by well-chosen surrogates, uncomplaining proxies.

Oliver had unwittingly opened his home to the unliving. In doing so, he also shared with them access to the nighttime endeavors of his head. And the result was such descriptive, even if unrecognizable, dreams. The wire was barbed, the train cars boxed, and the gas wasn't for cooking. Each frame advanced smoothly, although not without an occasional freeze-frame, no matter how deep the sleep.

And the dreams had changed him. He was becoming a different writer, and a different person. There was turning, and opening—an up-ended cube, an orbiting, rotating sun. He was confronting a new and strange coherence. What had made sense before no longer suited him. A good part of his day was now unlike the way it had been. Because when he was not dreaming or nightmaring, the rest of his time was spent sleeplessly and fitfully. He was busy tapping into his family's past, and then tapping on rows of alphabetical boxes, the

building blocks of words and sentences that broug
the darkness and the dormant. Once he had been frozen
write, looking for something else to do—the gym, movies, m
mysteries—his own and others'. Now no distraction was compelling
enough to divert him. The keyboard would lock and jam, the collision not of too many letters but of vulnerability put into words. The
path of light that shines from pain, breaking through the eyelashes of
night. He would have to stop and pause and sit with all the sadness,
realizing that after the flood, nothing is ever the same. Everything
gets washed away and looks different. But rebuilding is not necessarily a bad thing.

∽o∾

Oliver's outlook was now drawn inward. The external world was of
no interest to him. It wasn't just what he was seeing; it was more
about how he was choosing to see and the manner in which he was
keeping his time. He began to write again, slowly moving along a
predetermined, detourless path that was being laid out for him and
his own emotional undoing. It could lead only in one direction.
Those responsible for provoking him in this way were not unmindful
of the risks ahead. Oliver may have been new at this, but they had
taken their lives on account of it. And while they feared for him,
they also remembered that this was one of the reasons why they had
come.

"The new work is impressive, don't you agree?" Primo said.
"Much passion, and pain."

"Yes, but compared to what? The old writings were junk," Paul
replied dismissively. "No poetry. No nothing."

"I don't know about that," Jerzy said defensively. He was dressed
in a long, leather Terminator coat with black Jean-Paul Gaultier sunglasses, the temples adorned with vents. "Writing for a popular audience is not necessarily a crime. I hear that some of his books were
made into very fine movies."

Tadeusz asked.

"___y?" Jean snarled.

"___ed," Primo said. "That should have mean-
___what that can do to a writer."

Piotr rebounded the question. "He could be
___n even more pain. Unblocking could lead to a
terri___.

"Yes, Pio___ght. What is it you want my son to do?" Lothar
wondered respectfully. "I don't want him harmed."

"We don't want him to fight wars we could not win ourselves,"
Primo explained. "He needs to confront his past, but without going
too far."

"What happens when you go too far?" Lothar wondered, though
in the end he already knew.

"Head in the oven," Tadeusz said.

"Pills in the mouth," Jean said.

"Bag over the head and suffocate in the tub," Jerzy said.

"Drown in the Seine," Paul said.

"Jump in front of a train," Piotr said.

"Plunge down three flights of stairs," Primo said.

"Poison under the tongue," Rose said.

"Bullet to the head," Lothar said.

The Golems stood there and faced one another, saying nothing.
They had just recited their secret passwords, their sloppy final sign-
offs and shrieking swan songs. An exclusive club of suicidal survivors, even more inscrutable than their concentration camp tattoos.

"How much is too much?" Piotr asked, but with trepidation.

"I fear for my son," Lothar said.

"You should," Jean said.

"Maybe we should set him free," Tadeusz said.

"We came for a reason. Don't forget that," Paul reminded them
all. "He must enter our world in the same way that we have entered
his."

"But must he leave in the same way?" Piotr asked.

"God forbid!" Lothar shrieked.

"This is what Ariel wanted," Paul said, "and what we want for him, too. This is the only way for him to fix himself and heal. He must write about it. There is no safe place in our universe. What we witnessed is what separates us from everyone else—dead or alive. It was our duty, and curse, and now it is his."

"But why, to what end?" Piotr wondered, sipping a Yoo-Hoo. "How will this benefit him or, for that matter, how does it help us? Why did we return if all we will bring about is more death? This isn't the way to cure him."

"Why do we even care what he chooses to write about?" Jerzy said. "Why is it so important to us? Let him write comic books for all we care!"

"Because the world didn't listen the first time," Primo said.

"That was not our fault," Tadeusz said. "The world wants to kill its messengers. And we complied with assisted suicides."

"Why would they listen to Oliver anyway?" Lothar asked. "He wasn't there. He didn't witness anything, other than me and Rose, the way we were after Auschwitz. What moral authority does he have to the story?"

"Stories live forever only when they get repeated," Primo said, "and not necessarily by the same person."

"We are turning over the burden to him," Paul said. "We could have left him alone as he was, but that was not alive, either. He needs the challenge. It is only in the extremes, on the margins of existence, where life is worth living, where we learn what's possible for ourselves and for the rest of humanity. The middle of the road leads nowhere, it reveals nothing about man other than ambivalence and fear."

All of this was being said underground—much deeper than six feet. The conversation was taking place below where the dead normally rest—whether in peace or otherwise. Here everyone was alive, although languidly, in the dark. The Golems had surrounded themselves with urban commuters in various rush-hour poses—all riding on the IRT number 9 local. The destination was downtown, although the Golems weren't going anywhere in particular. Perhaps to the main branch of the Public Library at Forty-second Street. Or to the museum on Ellis Island. Maybe even to scour the bargain tables on the Lower East Side. Not that they needed the raucous services of New York City Transit to shuttle them anywhere. These ghosts could get around the city with much more alacrity and quickness simply by taking to the air.

But you miss everything when you travel that way, which is why they decided on underground transportation, where they could be among the living, and do so without a MetroCard or a senior citizen's pass. The Golems lived in a perpetual state of the what-might-have-been. In aborting their lives they had given up so much. And they knew it, but suicide was, for them, necessary. They needed to end the private pain, and they wanted to send a collective message.

But now their new existence was inevitably, and inseparably, linked to the way in which they had chosen to cancel their prior lives. They couldn't experience one without a nudge from the other, always mindful of how this new lease on life depended on an earlier lease broken by death. So this time they had to do it differently. Yes, they were back, but their return was not going to be one just of rescue. There were also selfish motives. This was a haunting that mixed business with pleasure.

The sounds of the subway, however, could have awakened the dead. All that shaking, rattling, and clattering—the strange ecosystem of underground tracks and tunnels, undisposed waste and overfed rats, misplaced nerves and constantly revolving turnstiles of impatience. The cars snaked and queued like arthritic joints.

Many sat there with ears connected to Sony Walkmen, half-hearing the outside racket. A proud expectant father announced to a complete stranger, "We're having a baby. It's going to be a girl. The doctor asked us if we wanted to know the sex," he continued jabbering, "and at first we said no, but then we decided, why not? It makes it easier to figure out what toys to buy." The Golems listened intently while a pregnant woman in a very advanced, delicate condition took a seat at the other end of the car. Piotr left his baby carriage, which had been at his side, and walked over to the pregnant woman. He leaned over and placed his open palm on her distended belly as though blessing the life inside.

In another corner of the car a Hispanic teenager in a faded blue denim jacket was pressing his slightly built girlfriend up against the wall, kissing her so forcefully that she nearly slipped through the rubber crease that joined the sliding doors. An exhausted house-painter, blotches smeared all over his face, hands, and body as if he were using himself as a palette, was dozing off with each blackout blink of interior light. Elsewhere several elderly New Yorkers were discussing the weather, raising the importance of their conversation to a level that such talk never deserves.

"They predict rain tomorrow," a woman in a fake-fur coat said.

"What are you talking about! They know nothing about the weather!" a senile man shouted, although he imagined himself as being quite calm. No one is ever too loud, or ubiquitous, in the sub-way, so his rantings went largely unnoticed.

"It's chilly outside today." A courtly African American gentleman offered an opinion.

"I didn't dress warm enough," a German-Jewish widow said sternly.

"But at least you have your umbrella," said the woman in the fake-fur coat.

"True, true . . . , but."

Primo was curiously interested in all this banter. He approached them guardedly, as though he were an invisible anthropologist. Is such frivolous talk a function of advanced age, he wondered? Or is he talking about the weather necessary to sustain life, even more so than the weather itself? It may have nothing at all to do with dress-ing sensibly or knowing when not to leave the house without an umbrella. What is important is the talk, even if you wind up under-dressed or soaking wet. Talk can be cheap, but it's also essential, regardless of what's being said. Social animals depend on banalities; the need to make conversation and to be heard while doing so. And the lighter the fare—the lower the maintenance on the mind and memory—the better.

The Golems had never learned this lesson when they were alive. Had they known, or done it differently, it could possibly have saved them. But of course they were given no other choice. There was no luxury of mindless distraction in their lives. The Nazis had prescribed their postwar professions, as though cattle-prodded into the family business. Recruited into the service of harvesting horror through the written word. Unfortunately, and inexorably, the Golems, when they were alive, had simply spent too little time talking about the weather.

On the platform at the Columbus Circle station a crooning sub-way singer was being drowned out by the uptown express. His competitors on the other side were three African Americans, one playing an acoustic guitar plugged into a lunch box of an amplifier, another with a snare drum and cymbal, and the third a Motown musical stylist. The trio alternated between Smokey Robinson (*sans* Miracles), Marvin Gaye, and the Temptations.

The Golems began to feel claustrophobic in the subway, so they went outside to experience life on the tracks. Commuters gathered in one of the cars to examine the crisscrossed blood specks that had settled on one of the hard, molded, uncomfortable seats. Before going upstairs, the Golems raced against the car while it was still in motion, legs stretching out like well-cast fishing lines, riding between the rails, competing, seemingly, with subway traffic. Piotr was cautious on the tracks, remembering that this was how he had chosen to meet his fate. The Golems were on a test run for the senior survivor circuit, invisible parallel trains outpacing the express, baby carriage trailing from behind.

As they bounded up the stairs, leaving the subway station and returning to the street, a backdraft fueled by a departing B train escaped from the stairwell like a creeping tailwind and lifted the weightless Golems upstairs and outside. The gust carried over onto

Forty-second Street and raised the toupee of a hot dog vendor a few inches above his head, registering a look of unpressurized anger in blowing his top.

The Golems spent a few minutes seated like pigeons on the book-end stone lions that guarded the main branch of the New York Public Library. A fire engine was responding to a four-alarm fire somewhere on Fifth Avenue. All manner of professional rescuers went to work. Sirens cried above the bedlam of Manhattan with their spinning, blinding lights that swept over the darkening streets. The fire trucks roared past the Golems. There were once fires that could not be appeased with water alone. The Golems looked skyward as a gas truck from Con Edison streaked after the hook-and-ladder, each sniffing out the direction of the smoke.

Finally the Golems entered the revolving doors of the library and roamed the main reading room, admiring the celestial ceiling and the long wooden reading tables with their built-in computer sockets complete with surge protectors and Internet access. As authors they couldn't resist floating into the stacks like *Luftmenschen*, bathing themselves in books and also, for reasons having as much to do with ego as general interest, making sure that their own written words were available for borrowing. They wanted to be read, to be remembered not for how they had departed but for what they had written while they were still here. Unfortunately, while their books were in fact represented on the shelves, they looked as though they had rarely if ever left them. Their bound words appeared new, without stamped due dates or dog-eared pages.

So the Golems took to the streets in their own signature style—marching uptown, passing right through all those tourists carrying cameras, looking out for celebrities and skyscrapers. The Empire State and Chrysler Buildings, with their dagger antennas, were fencing with the heavens above. But on this chilly day there were even more unusual things to see. Some tourists with the presence of mind to keep their eyesight at street level took out their cameras in time to snap pictures of Piotr's self-propelled baby carriage.

"Hey, get a load of this," a sagging-jowled man from Milwaukee observed to his bored, long-suffering wife. "I told you. You see! They got everything in the Big Apple. I bet they sell one of those babies at Hammacher Schlemmer."

Other tourists were flaunting high-fashion shopping bags from Madison Avenue. The Golems invaded their souls, trying to instill better values. Taxis, buses, and cars skidded near the curb, splattering crescent streams of soiled snow. There were all sorts of dogs—poodles and terriers, labradors and shepherds—barking loudly, as if sensing that the streets, on this day, were unusually congested with both the feverishly living and purposefully undead.

The Golems wandered into Central Park. They felt especially at home there, more so than in Oliver's brownstone, which they haunted but in other respects did not inhabit. The park offered more alluring pleasures. And it wasn't just the carousel that aroused them. What they enjoyed most were the trees. These were men with a deep appreciation of the density of nature. Forests were places of both beauty and camouflage. And for survivors, cover was as crucial as good luck.

Unlike the rest of the island, Central Park managed to keep its snow white and intact. It was still on the ground rather than in the sewers, still in sheets rather than plowed into blackened ramparts. The Golems raced into the Sheep Meadow, across the road from Tavern on the Green, the restaurant where they had first revealed themselves to Oliver. The Sheep Meadow was surrounded by a chain-link fence, which in another time the Golems would immediately have associated with barbed wire—curling and spiked at the crown—and the silent buzz of electric currents. But this was yet another time for the Golems. What they saw before them now was merely a gate, and a fence, and a sign that announced that the Sheep Meadow was officially closed for the winter.

Unfortunately for the Parks Department, these were ghosts who had a bitter distaste for rules posted on signs and attached to gates. *Arbeit Macht Frei* had been a lie all along, a wicked, false incentive that rendered all future signs suspicious and reviled as symbols of false advertising. From now on, all lesser signs were equally tainted and to be flouted—from speed limits to trespass warnings.

Most people, however, take their signs seriously. On this late winter afternoon with the edict in full view, the Sheep Meadow was barren except for the invisible presence of seven apparitions, all that snow, frosted skeletal trees, and a baby carriage stationed at the side like a getaway car. And while they didn't leave footprints, the Golems did produce other, irrefutable evidence that they had actually been there.

Snowballs took to the air, flying back and forth, tossed around as though set in motion by backstage jugglers. These friends were engaging in an old-fashioned snowball fight. The balls were perfectly round, white, and hard, lofted into the cold air with alternating arcs, varying speeds, and straight lines. The Golems were adept at mixing up their pitches. There was laughter. A great deal of it, in fact. Jerzy blindsided Piotr, pummeling him with a mound of snow. Paul simply threw his snowballs up in the air and waited for them to come crashing down on his bald head. Primo, the scientist, formed the snow in his palms and examined its chemical properties. His extreme focus did not deter the others from raining their snow down upon him. Jean's pitches melted in his hands. Tadeusz flung his snowballs so hard that the other Golems were forced to dodge and weave before reassembling to pack their reprisals. George Steinbrenner would have shown great interest in Tadeusz if these had been different times, if he weren't already dead, if he hadn't already worn a striped uniform—zebra, instead of pin—during his youth. Lothar ran around the group and never threw even a single snowball—just jogging, circling, enjoying the frolic.

The late, sparse lunchtime crowd at Tavern on the Green huddled up against the scenic window. They peered out past the trail of Christmas lights in the garden, over toward the Sheep Meadow, blinking googly eyes fiercely and incredulously. Based on all that had been going on in Manhattan as of late, the audience should have been prepared for anything, and yet no one would have given this particular vision a snowball's chance in hell of ever materializing. Tavern on the Green was now a dinner theater, except that the food was completely subverted by the show. The cuisine and the dessert cart went unnoticed. The attention was directed entirely outside the restaurant, and while no one could see even the inorganic outline of ghosts, all who were there that day finally understood what Oliver had felt the last time he had eaten at this restaurant.

The hard-packed white snow bounded back and forth like horizontal rain. But that wasn't all. Jerzy, Lothar, Tadeusz, and Paul had somehow borrowed two tandem bicycles, which they were using to cruise Central Park. Now others would notice what the diners at Tavern on the Green had just seen. The circle of eyewitnesses was expanding. It was moving beyond the Upper West Side. Other neighborhoods were progressively getting caught up in this demonstration of Jewish witchcraft. With such fast-moving pedals unattached to invisible feet, there was the real threat of cardiac arrest for those who caught sight of this spectacle. A young boy swollen with a blue, down-feathered coat raced after the two tandem bicycles on a motorized skateboard. Piotr had his arms wrapped around the boy, the wind hissing and swirling as he nuzzled his face against the child's ear.

Further up, near the carousel, there was a playground of assorted swings, slides, a climbing catwalk apparatus and a boarded-up sandbox. In one corner a child and her helpless father solemnly stared up into the sky, spying a red-ribboned Mylar helium balloon that had lost its way when the girl accidentally let it slip from her hand. She watched, red faced, as it got itself tangled up in the naked branches of a Central Park sycamore. Unable to coax the balloon down or reason with his daughter about simply getting a new one, the father merely resigned himself to praying for a miracle. Just about then, Piotr levitated to the rescue like an Off-Broadway Peter Pan and returned the balloon back into the hands of the young girl. She smiled at her relieved father, who didn't want to look a gift ghost in the mouth. He hastily concluded that either his prayers had been answered or that the balloon had fortuitously had some of its air taken out of it.

"What's that baby carriage doing here?" the young girl asked her father as they strolled out of the playground, the balloon held fast in his hand, bucking from behind.

"I know," the father noted. "And it's such a nice one to be sitting here empty and alone. What a tragedy."

The father and daughter left, but even in the afterglow of an otherwise noiseless dusk, they couldn't hear the music of Piotr's whimpering tears, serenading them as they paraded away.

The Golems left the park, as well, walking east along Fifty-ninth Street. Somewhere on the edge of York Avenue, they stopped abruptly, as if this time it was they who had seen a ghost. There was a man standing there whom all of the Golems had recognized. A slight man with a sad angular face and mournful eyes, wispy, grayish black hair changing direction with each gust of wind. In fact they all knew him well. He was one of them in almost every way possible, although, unlike them, he was still alive.

In the suddenness of the moment, the Golems were unable to speak. The strange thing was that the man who stood before them was silent and frozen, as well, and not because of a red light. He was staring at air, and apparently that was fine by him. Nothing seemed to be preventing him from moving other than a sober feeling that it was better that he stay.

The standoff continued. By now all sorts of pedestrians had passed on either side of the gentleman, as well as time itself. He had become a streetside nuisance, blocking traffic, but he didn't much care. And yet he still had no idea what was detaining him; paralyzed, and yet free to go.

Finally the Golems marshaled the courage to speak.

"Elie," they all said in different, circulating accents, in various but familiar tongues. If he could have heard them he would have recognized their voices.

"Elie," they each said again, taking turns, throwing their voices around some more. They were experimenting with pitch and tone, phrasing and emphasis, but their vocal cords were stripped of sound. All they wanted was to somehow make contact, send their survivor friend a message, a wink, a sign. His eardrum was picking up none of their vibrations.

"It is us," Primo pleaded. "We are here. We are still with you."

That he probably always knew. But to communicate with the dead was no easy task. The survivors of the Holocaust had more reason than most to experiment with séances and other long-distance calling plans. Yet so few tried. They were either too rational or had assumed that the place where the Nazis had sent their families and friends was ultimately unreachable. Elie would never have imagined one day conversing with some of the very people who had troubled him the most—not because they had died, but because of the way in which they had done it. Dishonoring their survival and leaving him all alone.

Elie hadn't succumbed to the temptations of a final, expedited rest. He knew there was an escape hatch from the burden of memory, a gateway through which there was relief, the only known cure for their condition. But for him this was not an option. Was his pain threshold that much higher? Or were his extraliterary activities more eventful, more fulfilling, obliging him to live on? The spirits around him had once led a life of Yiddish and Hebrew, while he somehow straddled the secular and the liturgical, tethering himself to the world of Ariel's violin, as well as to all the irreverence and anarchy that is oxygen for the artist. Could that have been the reason? Perhaps was it simply that his life somehow managed to buffer just enough psychological space between his demons and their denouement. Elie did not know the answer.

"We are sorry," Primo began. "None of us wanted to be the last living survivor. That would be too difficult a responsibility, worse than the one we already had. I wouldn't want to wish that on anyone."

"Whoever is the last one should remember on his way out to flip the world the finger," Jerzy said.

"Who knows what the world will even be saying about the

Holocaust by then," Paul added. "Who would want to be a symbol by yourself, to argue all alone, especially in old age when you're too weak to fight back?"

"It already became that way for us," Piotr said.

"They doubted what we had seen," Jean said bitterly.

"As if the passage of a few decades made our stories incredible, which they were, but for different reasons," Paul said.

"It is so simple to question rather than to just listen," Primo said. "So many didn't want to accept that we were special, that we had anything important to say, and that what we were saying, and shouting, was true. We were not madmen, but we had reason to be because we had seen madmen and their ways. And because we had come back from the dead, where no one else had been, it was easy to dismiss, to say that our testimony was tainted, that it could not be trusted."

"That's what happens in a world without moral standards, where everything is deconstructed and relativized," Jean said. "All crimes are now the same, no different from the ones committed by the Nazis. Truths are subjective. Absolutes don't even exist."

"Wasn't Paul de Man a Nazi?" Jerzy laughingly asked. "That makes sense."

"We would have wanted to stay longer," Tadeusz said, "but the noises in our head were too much for us."

"And there were new Nazis to replace old ones," Paul said.

"Maybe silence is the loudest language after all," Primo wondered.

"We will continue to pray for you, Elie," Piotr said.

"We just don't know who to pray to." Jean smirked, the kind of deviant expression that would never graduate to even a half smile.

In this atmosphere rich with metaphysics and madness, Elie realized that he was not alone. He somehow felt their presence and yet, looking right at them, saw nothing. They crowded around him— groping, lunging, hugging, like the wretched, the starved, those consumed by longing. Without grabbing on to anything, they somehow touched him. Elie felt something familiar. Or maybe it was just the empty baby carriage that he had recognized.

But in the presence of so much unseen, unspoken fire, Elie had the urge to open his mouth and speak, even though he didn't know what to say, or to whom. He was about to utter a familiar whisper when, to his surprise, nothing left his lips. All he could manage on that day was a single gesture of eloquent silence—one that he himself couldn't control, even though in other ways it had already made him famous. And when he returned home, he noticed that his once-black hair was now a spooky shade of biblical white.

17

THE GOLEMS WERE NOT CONTENT JUST BEING ghosts. The encounter with Elie made them realize that a metaphysical existence, which may have had some advantages, was, in all other respects, not a great way to engage with the world. They had transformed a lost neighborhood into a shtetl, reviving the religion and music of a people who had all too often approximated their spiritual identity with bagels and lox. And they were in the process of rescuing a numb pop novelist at his daughter's request. Each was a virtuous, although in many ways unsatisfying, deed. An endless procession of mitzvahs and miracles can only end in resentment for those always on the receiving end.

The truth is, the Golems had selfish aspirations as well. They wanted to participate in the world of the living—not only in saving souls, but also by putting flesh back onto their own invisible skins. Experiencing the world rather than merely haunting it.

Put simply, the ghosts wanted to live. Their greatest striving was to have a second chance, which they had once been given, but which they had squandered, frittered away like a political connection. Now they wanted to do it all over again. Not the death camps or the death marches. Once was enough, thank you. No, what they wanted was to take back their post-Holocaust, presuicide days. Another stab to finally make it right, if that was at all feasible.

On this drive-by visit to Manhattan—courtesy of a kabbalah misfire—they were tasting life once again. And this time around they did so in ways that were far superior to how they had done it before. This was, however, an unfair comparison, because the full, unreserved, pedal-to-the-metal enjoyment of life after the camps was, for the most part, impossible. The Nazis had stripped their prisoners of their hair, which eventually grew back. And they had taken away their names, which the survivors managed to remember and reclaim. But the taste for life, well . . . that was another matter. In so many ways taste, like life itself, had died. Buds that once flowered with the sensations for life had been squelched, never to bloom, as if by a winter that lingered too long into spring. The anatomy for tasting life was a casualty of Mengele's medical experiments on the salivary glands.

Time never healed. The world would have to invent new wives' tales and folk wisdoms to explain away this one. Old remedies on how to survive a failed romance, or sustain oneself in the aftermath of bad news, were useless and insulting in the extreme case of mass murder. Not all trauma can end in a recovery, nor perhaps should it. Atrocity has a way of fitting the eyes of the living with new lenses. The vision that ensues is not corrected, but distorted. There is no way to repair how survivors see. Their outlooks are fundamentally and tragically unalterable. The best one can hope for is not a cure but an accommodation, a determination to go on even when there is no reason to do so.

Of course the Golems had been failures in this regard. The artist doesn't embrace life so much as clings to it. The other survivors were able to take on the trappings and vestments of conventional life. They assumed mortgages and built businesses, paid their bills, attended PTA meetings, gained weight, voted in elections. While these routine signs of life all happened around them, the Golems merely assumed more suffering, took on memories that weren't even their own, altogether lived with too much. That's what made them writers. They weren't born artists. Without Auschwitz as a finishing school, they would have likely settled on more earthly, practical pursuits—the safely mundane, the reflexively unimaginative.

The Nazis would forever change their vocations. After the war, survivors possessed Ivy League credentials from the finest concentration camps Europe had to offer. That made them unqualified to drive a rig or drill for oil, but the aesthetics of death had now become their domain. And there was great irony in this, because the Nazis were unabashedly self-righteous, cold-blooded killers. They never envisioned themselves as career counselors—job placement specialists—providing inspiration from their own handiwork. What they wanted most of all was dead Jews. And in this they mostly succeeded. But along the way, some survivors had no choice but to respond to their near-death experience by producing art. Whether it was for themselves, their lost families, or the world did not matter, just that it had to be done. The Nazis demanded it, even if inadvertently so.

This time around would be different for the Golems, if there was to be another chance. They had learned many lessons in life, and in death, and frankly, they preferred the former. They wanted to do it all over again, starting right now, with the advantages of hindsight and unhealable regrets behind them. The Golems liked the world the way it looked right now, on the fringes of millennial anticipation, with its technological wonders and medical miracles. They wanted to surf the Net and the Pacific, to sample sushi, tiramisù, and oysters on the half shell—in no particular order, and without kosher compunctions. Having already liberated themselves by death, the Golems now had eyes to hip-hop like inner-city homeboys and bungee-jump like flannel-wearing slackers, to pump themselves so full of Viagra they would forever roam the earth like vagina-seeking missiles.

But how to do that? They were still dead, after all, and that was a not insignificant obstacle to the goal the Golems had in mind.

"What about reincarnation?" Tadeusz proposed.

"You mean the milk?" Jerzy quipped, dressed up as a soda jerk, right down to the wedge-shaped cap.

"That's Carnation," Lothar said humorlessly.

"I don't want to return as someone else," Jean insisted. "I want another chance in my own skin."

"Besides, Jews don't believe in reincarnation," Piotr said.

"Oh, but golems they believe in," Jean mocked.

"After this," Tadeusz reasoned, "anything is possible."

"Would we even be writers and poets if we could do it all again?" Paul wondered.

"What if I hadn't been a chemist all my life?" Primo fantasized.

"There must be some way to find out," Piotr said eagerly and breathlessly, imagining himself a father, the baby carriage and the diapers full, strolling along Broadway, no longer as a ghost but as a shamelessly proud, cooing parent.

Finally Rose, who had been sitting there quietly watching the men overheat with longing, volunteered a suggestion. "Maybe we should talk to Ariel about this. Maybe there is something in the kabbalah that could give us life, real life, just like it brought us back as ghosts. This time we wouldn't be the living dead, but the real thing, the fully realized living."

"You mean an improved potion?" Jerzy said. "Like Golems 4.0?"

"Do you think such a thing is possible, Rose?" Lothar said, ignoring Jerzy.

"Brilliant idea," Tadeusz said.

"Sounds like more witchcraft to me," Jean mumbled.

18

THE TASTY PASTY, A STRIP CLUB ON THE WESTERN fringes of Midtown, featured the best in exotic dancing. Some of the women were garden variety go-go dancers, out of the cage and stripped of their bunny suits, lifting their legs, swinging their arms and hips, seducing a pole, and spinning around like frustrated refugees from Alvin Ailey. But there were also lap dancers who descended from the runway, bumping and grinding their G-strings right up against zippers that rumbled with aroused but shut-in members. Nearby bouncers, men named Tony and Gus, were paid to ensure that the dancers themselves went ungroped by the clientele.

On some nights the catwalk was teeming with flash dancers. Here the artistry was in the dance and not in the burlesque. The

women never revealed anything more risqué than an exposed cleav-
age or a half-mooned tush. Some wore sequins and glitter, others
feathers; some stuck reflexively with S & M imagery—whips, chains,
leather, an occasional Nazi prop of physical domination. Nevertheless, the main selling point was always uncopulated sex. That's
what the audience wanted and what everyone came to see.

The Tasty Pasty fancied itself as an upscale provider of sexual illusion and fulfillment. The establishment was not an inviting hangout
for beer slugs, Teamster organizers, forklift operators, or Mafia
underlings. Not the sort of place where patrons knocked off the night
by downloading images into their brains, only to whack off later by.
Yes, discharged seed was fully expected each night. And it was more
likely to be found in the men's room than anyplace else. But at least
this semen originated from high-end members: Wall Street brokers
who had sweated through the day making margin calls, now looking
to generate a different kind of heat; dot-com entrepreneurs who
looked too young to have lost their virginity and too busy to find a
date; Upper East Side aristocrats satisfying a gentleman's fetish; and a
surprising number of women, placing themselves on a market
primed more for ejaculation than mating.

Jerzy was equally comfortable cruising both men and women.
He went both ways. Not surprising for someone so capable of camouflage. Learning to adapt easily and experiment liberally were
trademarks of those who lived life in increasingly smaller spaces of
physical freedom—whether real or imagined.

"I would like to buy you a drink," Jerzy announced, always the
dignified European, at least on first impression. Jerzy possessed a
boyish appearance, and his august yet clumsy mannerisms often
added to the paradox, because he had in fact lived long and hard. It
was only his accent that aged him and gave him away, which was so
true of immigrants in general. Adults with accents seem older to us,
older than they actually are. The command of a native language can
be perfect, but an accent always exposes an alien as an asylum
seeker. For Jerzy, his disguises often detracted from his accent, mak-

ing him hard to place. On this evening he was outfitted in yet
another inventive costume, even by his own clownish standards: a
white suit, lavender shirt, white tie, and a red rose sticking out from
the jacket's lapel like a serpent. "Would you be so kind as to accept?"

"Maybe," the woman answered, shifting her body on the bar
stool in a way that ended the mystery of whether she was going to
play hard to get. "It all depends."

"On what?" Jerzy wondered.

"Whether we were meant to drink together, the only way to
know if we're a good fit—for drinking, and for other things, too.
What's your sign?"

Her eye contact momentarily went from Jerzy to the shine on
her shoes, then returned, renewed with fluttering eyelashes and
pouting lips.

"My sign?"

"Yes, what is it?"

The woman was young and dressed alluringly in tight black
Calvins and a mesh halter from Donna Karan. Her brown hair was
streaked with blond highlights. A strand fell across her face, dividing
her forehead like a frozen windshield wiper. Her skin was unmarked;
her neck long and bowed like that of a Modigliani portrait. She had a
smile that radiated warmth but also insecurity. Her hand gestures
were untamed, and she used them to speak far too quickly, particularly given the inconsequence of what she had to say.

"I'm still not sure I understand," Jerzy said.

"You know, . . . your horoscope."

"Ah, yes." Jerzy gathered himself, recalling this modern dating
ritual in which sex on Earth depends on how well the stars and
moons cooperate in their celestial alignments.

"Don't tell me," she then interrupted. "Let me guess. Okay, I
would say . . . you . . . look . . . like . . . a . . . Capricorn. Yeah,
Capricorn, that's it. Am I right?"

Jerzy shook his head in a way that suggested she guess again.

"Oh, shit, I'm usually never wrong about these things. That's a bad sign," she said, then snorted out a laugh at the inadvertent pun. "Okay, okay," she said, her hands motoring like unlicensed karate chops, "let me try one more time. How about Aquarius?"

Jerzy once again signaled a buzzerless denial.

"Not an Aquarius either? Well, I give up. What is it?"

He hesitated before plunging, as if a parking space had just opened up, then lied, "I'm an Auschwitz."

"An Auschwitz! What sign is that?"

"A very special one," Jerzy said emphatically.

"I've never heard of it before. Is it some New Agey kind of thing?" she jabbered on.

"Look here, I'll show you."

Jerzy removed his white jacket, laid it down on the bar without crushing the decorative rose, and began to roll up his left shirtsleeve.

"Wow, what's that?" She examined the arm as he rotated its underside. "Someone read your astrological chart and wrote it down for you, right there, on your arm, in blue ink, like a tattoo? Huh, it's all in the numbers. How interesting. . . . Does it come off?"

"No, never, and I wouldn't want it to, either."

"Why, what does it say?"

"It predicts my future."

"No kidding! The person who read your chart could do all that in just a few numbers? He must be good."

"Better than good. The best. We're talking master race here." Jerzy downed a shot glass of Chivas, pleased at his calligraphy, since the penmanship was all his own, even if the inspiration came from elsewhere.

"Well, tell me. I can't wait. What does it say?"

"That I'm destined for greatness." A beat later. "And for great sex."

An exotic dancer with long legs, stiletto heels, and small breasts was humping a fire pole, then made her way over to Jerzy who, showing timely, coordinated moves of his own, slipped a few dollars inside her G-string. She blushed as though he had located her G-spot,

or maybe Jerzy's aura was simply overwhelming, like the G-force of a tornado. He smiled and then returned to his date.

"Oh, stop it! You're putting me on, aren't you?" she giggled slyly, her sexual confidence suddenly building up.

"Not at all, my dear. I speak the truth. It is exactly what these numbers mean. That's the future right there," he said, laying his forearm on the table like priceless jewelry on a velvet mat. "That's what it holds." Jerzy stared fiercely at his disfigured limb, the always reliable conversation piece that rendered all other pickup lines or foreplay unnecessary.

∽o∾

Each of the Golems was experiencing this new lease on life without giving any thought to the possibility of eviction. They made decisions and acted swiftly, not knowing how long this was going to last. They only knew that Ariel had given them yet another gift, and they were not going to wait around to one day discover their time was up once again. Jerzy returned to his blade days with an audaciousness that made a mockery of safe sex. But the others were equally active.

Lothar's last job before he retired to Miami Beach had been as a manufacturer of textile equipment in New York. With that particularly unemotional line of work, it is surprising that his real interest was actually in psychotherapy. Not that he had ever pursued formal training in the mental health profession. In fact, given his own exit from this world, it seemed unlikely that he possessed a natural gift for assisting others with their emotional problems. Yet Lothar decided to spend his newly bought time as a Manhattan-based psychotherapist.

His very first patient was an anorexic fashion model with a billboard on Times Square whose self-image had no greater density than an editorial page out of French *Vogue*. She soon became his most afflicted patient, the one he wanted to rescue the most. The irony of having a Holocaust survivor—a former inmate of a death camp, no less—trying to cure an anorexic was not lost on Lothar. How do you explain to someone who lives in a time of abundance that food was meant to be eaten, that it shouldn't wind up as a weapon in a fight with oneself? It is absurdly sinful, wasteful, and paradoxically self-indulgent to deprive the body of what it needs to live.

The modern world luxuriates in trendy emotional problems—the convoluted interplay of external excess and internal privation. The underlying pain is real, but the self-help remedy is overtly sabotaging. Only in a land of plenty is it possible, and acceptable, to send messages of distress by way of a hunger strike. The only thing that enters or exits the mouth is the primal scream—and an occasional bulimic barf.

"You choose not to eat, and in doing so, you exert the only power you think you have," Lothar counseled her calmly, delicately.

His office was on West Eighty-fifth; his manners more Jungian than quintessential Freud. He sat in a sloping black leather recliner—metal frame, postmodern design—a chair with a sofa complex. There was a notepad in his hand, but he hadn't written anything on it yet. His white beard was rough and tangled, like the growth in an untraveled forest. There were unframed diplomas and medical certificates Scotch-taped to the wall, the parchments curling at each corner. His name was penciled in fancy calligraphy. A vagrant setup perhaps suggesting a new practice, or a mere apprenticeship. At any moment he might get called back to the other side, leaving his needy patients hanging—but hopefully not from a noose.

"It is the only power you think you have, but you are turning it against yourself. It is your own punishment, and it comes from self-hatred. You can control what's inside you by what you put into your body, because you fear that you have no control outside in the world. But starvation is not the way to show your strength. There are better ways to speak to the world, even one that you think is not listening."

She was tall, with a straight back and an awkward walk, her knees and feet pivoted so far inward that even pigeons mocked the positioning of her toes. Suddenly she had become famous, not for her walk but her face, which was no longer her own but belonged to other, faceless entities: cosmetic and skin-care companies, corn chip and soda pop makers, automobiles in need of a gorgeous hood ornament. Her body was a mannequin for designer jeans, swimsuits, and Wonderbras, but her insides were completely naked, the kind of double exposure that no makeover can fix.

"I've been having these dreams lately," she said.

"Tell me about them."

"I'm in the camps."

"What camps are you in?"

"The ones in Poland," she said, sounding annoyed, as if there were only one answer, as if summer camps, yoga retreats, and fat farms no longer existed after Auschwitz. "The concentration camps, of course."

"And what are you doing there?" Lothar said, working his fingers through his beard, making a clearing.

"I am trying to survive," she said, her eyes closed, her voice stammering, ". . . to make it through another day. I'm very thin, even thinner than I am now."

"Why are you there, in the camp?" Lothar asked.

"What do you mean?"

"Well, you're not Jewish, are you?"

"No."

"Gypsy? Homosexual? Handicapped? Subhuman supermodel?"

"No," she replied, defensively.

"And you were born long after the camps were liberated. Is that right?"

"Yes."

"So why do you suppose you are having dreams in which you are imprisoned in a death camp?"

"I don't know," she said, her eyes now open, welling but not releasing a thin film of suspended contact water. "That's why I'm telling you! I want to know why this is in my head!"

"I can only tell you this: you have no business being in a concentration camp—even in your dreams. You may feel like a victim in life, but your subconscious is playing a terrible trick on you. The camp was a nightmare, a real one that took place during the day, and without sleep. What you have is an eating disorder. You are not eating food, but you are consuming images that don't belong to you. Your dreams are making your problems worse. Anorexia is painful and real, but it has nothing in common with a death camp. Believe me, I know. You have your own nightmares, having to do with your childhood and the silence in your home that was so present there, and the sexual abuse. There is plenty of material for nightmares from your own life without having to borrow from the camps."

She began to cry.

"Now, now, there, there," he hummed softly, handing her a tissue, then stroking her hand. "It is not your fault. It is all too common nowadays. We live in a world that has internalized the phrases and images of atrocity. There is survivor envy everywhere around us. I have a secret to tell you," Lothar said, then edged closer to the couch on which she was sitting. "If you were in a concentration camp, you would be considered one of the fat and well-fed ones."

She smiled, which halted, only for an instant, the downstream rush of tears.

"I am not telling you this so you will starve yourself even more. The point is that you can't and shouldn't even try to become thinner, because it was much more than just calories that we . . . I mean . . . these people, were lacking."

Lothar stared out the window, onto the street, and contemplated how dark so many lives are, even without a sadistic nudge from the Nazis.

"Today we call policemen storm troopers, but even the worst cops are not that. The leaders we disagree with are referred to as Hitlers, but there too the comparison is insulting to those who were gassed by a monster with a moustache. AIDS and abortion are compared to Auschwitz. Overcrowded subways are cattle cars. And yes, anorexics are no heavier than Auschwitz inmates. We have taken the horror and adapted it for our modern times, and trivialized and diluted it by comparing it to completely the wrong situations. It is as if we insist on having the right to analogize. But there is no analogy here. Your problem, my dear, we can fix. You must trust me. But the people in the camps were not so fortunate; no one could save or fix them just by giving them back their confidence—only a righteous army could have helped, or a God, but neither was interested, or worthy."

∽∾∾

She told them to place their bets, then gave a good yank on the chrome knob of the roulette wheel. After a number of hypnotic spins, the wheel came to a stop, the white ball exhausted from all its centrifugal movements. It landed on a prime double-digit number. There were chips stacked everywhere, on soft matted settings, and right beside lucky winners. Yet most of the chips were held by the dealer herself. The house always wins in the casino game. This is true all over the world, and it's certainly no different in Las Vegas.

When she was alive and a housewife in South Florida, Rose dreamed of having a job in a Vegas casino. She had outgrown the card rooms on Miami Beach where she had suckered many a guileless tourist out of his or her discretionary vacation allowance. But these were all small-stakes establishments, breeding farms for pigeons. The hotels and condominiums didn't have the glamour of the floor shows, the addictions of the high rollers, the dreams that disappear into cascading neon. She was stuck in Miami, where decks of cards also suffered from humidity and tropical boredom. It was only through a bizarre experiment in the Jewish occult, conducted by her own granddaughter, that she wound up in the city of her dreams, employed at one of its most storied casinos.

"Place your bets!" she yelled before initiating yet another spin.

The captains had her running both the roulette and the craps tables, alternating as if she were a plate spinner. She was cunning

with wheels and sly with dice. The big bettors and high rollers somehow lost some of their steam at her tables. She was a disarming,
elderly Jewish woman. Her hair was still dark auburn. A wide space
glinted between her front teeth as if she could bring it to shine even
in darkness. She was overweight but happily so. Her natural laugh
made its entrance before she did. As a winning croupier, she didn't
appear to be the sort who was a candidate for suicide. But then
again, that had been a long time ago, and the act itself was freakish
and unnatural, not unlike the reasons that brought it on.

More so than any other place on the planet, the casino made
sense to her. It called out to her like a natural habitat. She didn't
need daylight, just the twinkling, hypnotic bulbs, the pulsing sounds,
the feverish stares of those who had also experienced the rush of
risking everything. Her own survival, and death, had depended on
such impulses. More than anything else, she understood the risk and
reward of playing the odds, and then chancing them.

"Twenty! We have another winner!" she announced in concert
with the cheers around the rectangular table.

The raw, indivisible interplay of luck. So familiar to these people.
But which people? The Golems or the gamblers? For one group it is a
game, entertainment that slides into an addiction. The gambler lands
himself in the basement of a church reciting a twelve-step mantra, a
member of some anonymous organization that collects dues and
shares stories of loss and inner collapse. The other group traded on
wits and luck in order to sustain life, then, paradoxically, succeeded
in suicide only to resurface later, as ghosts in the attic of a brownstone.

Which group understands the gambler's game better?

"Spin again!" she said, followed by a cackling, carnival laugh.

Of course it was not just the extreme awareness of risk, the flirta-
tion with odds, that made Rose so adept at any line of work where
chance separated winners from losers. It was also the numbers. They
were on her arm and in her head. The Nazis installed them permanently in both places. She was not going to be able to remove the tat-

too or the newly programmed math skills. They were a part of her; it
made her both thin skinned and hard headed when it came to the
importance of numbers, the faith in luck, the reverence for the dangerous and the grotesque, and the imperative of a good yank at the
crank—of both life and the wheels of chance.

"Yes . . . sixteen . . . over there . . . we have another winner!"

∽o∾

The story made headlines everywhere. The Swiss banking system,
the envy of the world, known for its vaulted secrecy and discretion,
brought to its knees, its reputation destroyed, its coffers emptied.

This all took place several years after the scandal had come to an
end—the one about the hidden numbered accounts and the pilfered
gold bullion. By then all the outrage and recriminations had settled
down. The Swiss government and its banking system agreed to create
a restitution fund to compensate Holocaust survivors and their families for the misdeeds of a presumptively neutral nation that showed
bias only when it came to money and its own greed. The payments
were made grudgingly, the remorse counterfeit. The world once
again forgot, all in the service of moving forward. It always does that.
After all, the debt had been repaid, although with pennies on the
dollar. The Swiss said they were sorry, although there was no official
apology—nor would there ever be. They never even sent a box of
Swiss chocolates. It was time to finally put it behind us, because
that's what an advanced society always does with its miseries and
injustices.

The international banking system, and its monetary funds,
depended on the Swiss to stand as a symbol of integrity and honesty in
the handling of other people's money. They had brokered this role so
ably in the past. Like churches and governments, banks are institutions
that depend on trust. The Swiss ultimately understood all this and
obliged—making things right and whole again. They resumed their
banking, because that's what they always did best—even more so than

manufacturing wristwatches and cuckoo clocks. Everything returned to normal. Accounts opened even though they were unsettled, but confidence was restored nonetheless. The scandal was erased in everyone's mind with the same heedlessness of, if not embezzlement, how those assets had been taken away from Jews in the first place.

But then one day, the most intricate, inexplicable, undetectable wire-to-invisible-wire transfer of vast sums of bank-deposited wealth mysteriously disappeared. In an age when banks are controlled by microchip computers and large servers, a massive glitch of cyberepic proportions, or perhaps it was the work of a planned hacker blitzkrieg, resulted in billions of dollars leaving the ledgers of banks all throughout Switzerland at the mere push of a button. Untraceable. Unthinkable. A devastating financial catastrophe that sent international banks and markets into a nosedive without any sight of land below.

So sweeping and ruinous was this reverse cyberswindle that a number of bank presidents and scions of venerable Swiss banking families climbed simultaneously on the ledges of their office towers and plunged to their deaths. A mass Swiss suicide, all because of money, and pride, and justice. An eye for an eye. A leap for a leap.

The money was never recovered. And no one ever discovered the source of the scandal. But shortly before the job (and the penniless bankers themselves) went down, three men, dressed appropriately for this line of work and suited with all the right credentials, found executive positions in three of the largest and most morally tainted banks in Switzerland. And when the heist was all over and the wealth had been redeposited where it rightly belonged, these men, who went by the first names Jean, Paul, and Tadeusz, were never seen or heard from again.

∽◦∽

Days before Christmas and all along Broadway, the spirits were alive with the sound of bells, the sight of curbside Douglas firs and balsams waiting to be taken home and trimmed, and angel ornaments hanging from high wires that crisscrossed Broadway from one street lamp to another. There was even snow. And of course, a Santa.

Primo had never dressed up as a Santa before. Why would he have? In Turin he was a cherished Holocaust survivor, almost a messianic Jew. The Italian Christians would never have expected him to put on a costume in celebration of their holiday, even as a spokesman for peace on earth and goodwill toward all of God's creatures. But here in America, in New York, on the Upper West Side, years after his death, he was finally liberated to try new things.

"Merry Christmas!" he shouted above the urban clamor, seasoned by the competing noises of the season. A small man in an oversized red suit without the regulation belly, Primo was standing beside a makeshift Salvation Army wishing well. A survivor with the charitable impulse to save. "Won't you please give to the less fortunate!" he chanted in tune with his chiming bell. "There are needy children all throughout New York! Thank you, miss. It's wonderful to be alive! Isn't it just terrific? Life is such a gift. We should all embrace and share our good fortune."

A few cynical New Yorkers regarded this new Santa as insane—yet another loud, costumed kook, a Nick who was nuts. Most people, however, stopped to listen, as if Primo were actually the real Santa, having now given up chimneys for curbside self-improvement lessons.

And so there he stood, this once-shy Holocaust survivor and memoirist brought back to life on Broadway, adorned in ill-fitting vestments and caught up in an abundance of Yuletide cheer. He shook his bell, recited his script, and listened to the sounds of benevolence and decency at work. Everyone was in a good mood. There were fewer fights now that the Golems had arrived. And more charity—Christian or otherwise. Even though the streets were overcrowded and there were so many reasons for nerves to collide, the air was spiked with civility and kindness and the fellowship of neighbors.

But the sounds of Primo's bell and the shuffling of shoppers were not the only noises traveling along Broadway on that day. There was also the sweet, buoyant music that had become the theme song of Zabar's, amplifying from its front entrance like carolers on Christmas Day. While this was shaping up to be a white Christmas, the music itself was not at all about chestnuts, sleigh bells, flashy reindeer, or frosty snowmen. Ariel's violin was mournful and loud, even during silent nights.

Out of the corner of one eye, the klezmer gypsy girl winked at her new competitor, the costumed Jewish Saint Nick who was stationed across the way, panhandling for his own alms. They were in concert, but it wasn't only the music of a violin and a bell that made it so. Each nodded appreciatively to the tune that a coin makes when dropped into a violin case, and a wishing well.

Not far away, in a playground in Riverside Park, Piotr watched as Nathan and Malka took turns chasing each other around the sandbox, sliding pond, and jungle gym. Other parents and nannies sat on benches, busy drifting or dozing off, reading newspapers, or speaking urgently into cellular phones. Piotr would have none of that. A playground was meant for play, and parents with children had much to celebrate. One never knows when fortunes change, when families come to an end.

There were other children in the park, but Piotr could only hear the laughter of two. They were young again, and of course, even more important than that, alive. Unscarred. Protected. Safe. Their lungs were now smoke-free, as if scrubbed clean. The baby carriage was gone, no longer needed. They had at last outgrown it.

The sounds of their laughter drowned out the traffic on Riverside Drive. They giggled and ran, and Piotr, his face alight, his body rejuvenated, his eyes sharp and joyful, raced after the two children, never letting them out of his sight.

∽∾

Of course none of this actually happened. You must have realized that all along. Ariel never did concoct another secret formula. She made no other visit to the Hudson River to retrieve more of that magic mud. No klezmer lollapalooza; no hocus-pocus kabbalah. Ariel didn't even try. What the Golems most wanted out of life could never be reclaimed. Not even a wizard of a high school freshman could alter those facts in the long-buried ground.

You can't bring people back from the dead, at least not in a way that restores life as it once was. There are other ways for the dead to return, if they have to, if we're willing to receive them. But the idea of a full-circle return with no questions asked, with the furniture still in the same place and the feelings unmoved, as if it had all been a nightmare that would be forgotten in the morning—well, that kind of miracle can only exist in the dreams of the Golems of Gotham.

19

 I WANTED THEM TO SEE THE LITTLE RED LIGHT-house. Not the story that Oliver doesn't read to me anymore, but the place itself. What I didn't know was that they had been there before. Many times, actually. When they were alive but also now, as golems and ghosts. I had no way of knowing that. Who knows where ghosts go? They don't give advance warning; they just show up.

It was like the way they moved into our brownstone; I called for them, but they didn't need my permission. Now I guess they were haunting the lighthouse and the bridge, too. The very place where I found the clay that gave them life. The same place that still haunts their son. But until they brought me there, I didn't know why.

The lighthouse was always on their minds. Our family—what's

left of it, anyway—wasn't finished with it yet. It was coming back into all of our lives, and not as a children's story this time. My grandparents knew that. I guess that's one of the advantages that Holocaust survivors have over the rest of us. They know you can't bury things and run away without expecting the very thing you're trying to hide to come back later, teasing you into settling the score. And the ghosts of Holocaust survivors know this better than the survivors themselves.

"All right, young lady," Lothar said. "Time for bed."

"Lothar, she's not a baby anymore, for God's sake," Rose admonished. "She's too old for this."

"Don't be ridiculous," Lothar answered brusquely. "I have already told you. No one is ever too old to be tucked in and read to at night. The problem with the world is that people go to sleep with their worries from that day, and the next, trapped in their heads. All the past pain. The regrets and the guilt. The fears about tomorrow. That's no way to rest; that's why there are nightmares." He nodded to himself. "It would be much better for all of us if people went to sleep with their minds clear and tuned to the faraway places of their imaginations rather than to the disappointments of their daily lives."

"Yeah, yeah, okay, I know this, but should we at least change the story? I'm tired of the Little Red Lighthouse already," Rose said, holding up a stack of children's books as if she were about to juggle them. The bright book covers dangled in the dark like moonbeams. Some of the books were about dragons and witches; others had princesses and potions. There was even one with a boy wizard— also a prodigy like me, but his sorcery had nothing to do with the kabbalah, or the klezmer violin. Each of these stories took place once upon a time in lands and kingdoms, some without names. None of the tales mentioned Auschwitz. That was good, because you wouldn't want to have to explain that to a kid at night, even a young teenager, right before she goes to sleep. And besides, Auschwitz wasn't a fantasy. My grandparents would want me to know the difference.

"Well, what should we read?" Rose asked again. "Any of these?"

"To the lighthouse we go!" Lothar bellowed, already knowing that I would agree, as if he was even giving me a choice.

"Yes, the lighthouse," I said.

I was already way old enough to read the book by myself. Actually, before I used a kabbalah voodoo doll to bring them all back, I had been putting myself to sleep every night by reading Dickens and Swift, Hawthorne and Poe, Austen and Wharton. When I was through I would turn out the lights by myself. I got good at this self-tuck method, because Oliver wouldn't do it for me. But the ghosts who were my grandparents were insistent. They wanted to do the reading, and the tucking in, as well. Every night they would read the lighthouse story, even though the book was for children and I already knew it by heart. And then they would mold my pillow and batten down the top sheet and comforter, cutting off all air vents. Finally they would turn out the lights.

They were making all the decisions, in all of our lives. Maybe that was good. Ghosts don't care about formalities and etiquette. They do everything out of order. Only the living worry about details. When ghosts are with us, they have their own way of doing things, and reasons for doing them. And we can't change their minds. That's because ghosts always come for a reason of their own, even if we send for them first. My grandparents never knew their granddaughter; now they were making up for lost time.

Rose took me shopping in the East Village. Grandmothers like to do that. They want to spoil their grandkids. Rose and Lothar had already done that with Oliver, but in another way—not spoiled like they gave him too much, but like milk that goes bad, the kind of thing that happens from neglect. We walked down Eighth Street toward St. Marks Place. There were record stores that carried a lot of underground alternative music, and vintage clothing for cool college kids and wasted high school dropouts who wanted to dress up in either army surplus uniforms or Hell's Angels leather.

"You sure you want to be on this street, Grandma?" I asked. "You know, we could go to the Lower East Side if you want. It isn't that far away. There are all kinds of stores down there you might like."

"I want to be with young, wild people," Rose said. "We're not shopping for a menorah or a seder plate today. This is much more interesting. What I want to see is body-piercing and kids in Pearl Jam T-shirts."

Fine, but hanging out with my grandparents was always a little embarrassing, and not for the same reasons you hear other kids say it. I had to be careful about not making it so obvious that I was talking to myself. Even the worst stoners and acid freaks, tripping out all over the East Village, wouldn't have been able to hallucinate my grandparents as ghosts. And no one would believe it if I told them that the ghost of a Holocaust survivor was shopping on this block, and that's who I was talking to. They would want to know what kind of crack I'd been smoking, and where they could get some for themselves.

I bought some bangles and bracelets from a street vendor on Avenue A, and a pair of earrings from a roach-clip shop on St. Marks. Rose was deep into a pair of leather biker pants with a retro raincoat that I think she saw Jerzy wear just the other day.

"Where can we buy a scooter?" Rose wondered as a skinny freshman from NYU made change and put our stuff inside black plastic shopping bags. "You know, the new shiny kind. Maybe we should pick up one for all the boys. Primo and Paul would be afraid to get on one, Jerzy would ride like a child, and Jean would be dangerous, taking his aggression out on the street, but they do look like fun."

"Okay, Grandma. I'll show you where they have them."

There were all sorts of field trips that we went on together. Most of the time Lothar joined us. There was Ellis Island and the Statue of Liberty, and the top of the Empire State Building. We took a Circle Line cruise, and had good seats for a New York Jets football game. One day we rode the Wonder Wheel at Coney Island. We also went to the ABT and the New York Philharmonic.

"You play better than he does," Lothar boasted as we listened to the young, hot Joshua Bell play Brahms.

Whether at Madison Square Garden or Lincoln Center, my grandparents had me buy three tickets for each game or performance, with me sitting in between. The seats by my side were empty but not unoccupied; my arms stretched out like I was giving blood, but actually we were all holding hands. Ushers asked if I would mind scooting over to make it easier for late-arriving patrons. I said no, which sent them scoffing away. Obviously I was a surly, spoiled-rotten kid, they thought. But I learned from my grandparents that ghosts don't care what others think of them. And those seats were not empty.

We went to hear Elie Wiesel speak at the 92nd Street Y. I never heard him before, but everyone around us said that he seemed real nervous, like he was having an off night. Some whispered, wondering why his hair color had gone from dark gray to white so suddenly. The answer was that celebrity ghosts were in the audience. But no one would know that—although Mr. Wiesel somehow sensed it—even with the house lights flooded on.

One day in early January, my grandparents announced that we were going to take a special trip together. They didn't say where to. But I went along, trusting them. I realized that what they wanted from me was to know more.

We rode the subway, the A train, uptown. A homeless man sat next to us in one of the middle cars. His jean jacket was torn, and his shoes were too big for his feet; the laces were untied, looping up and down like a double-Dutch jump rope. He was sitting slouched over and groggy, like he had just woken up from a nap. I wondered whether he had been on this train all morning, riding back and forth, not getting off because he had nowhere else to go. It was warm in the cars, and it was winter on the streets, so there were good reasons to stay on the train. But all that clacking in his ears, the flashes of darkness, the snide stares, and invisible looks couldn't be so good for him either.

I offered him half of a pumpkin muffin, which I got at a health food store on Broadway before we went down into the subway. The homeless man placed it on his lap and looked straight at me. He was bone thin with gray whiskers, watery eyes, cracked skin, and only a few teeth in his mouth. He then looked to my left and right, framing the family picture. "Thank you, sweetheart," he finally said. "And also thank your friends for me, too." He winked at my grandparents, the familiar spooks, who smiled at me. We got off at the next stop while the homeless man stayed on.

We walked over to 181st Street and took a left, up a steep hill, heading west. I knew they were leading me to the lighthouse and the bridge, and it all made me feel strange. I hadn't been back there since I went on that Stuyvesant class trip, the one where I got my hands dirty and cut my finger, all to rescue my father and to start a fire that I didn't know how to put out, or whether I should even want to. My grandparents were taking me to the place where they were born— not Poland, their actual birthplace, but Washington Heights, underneath the Great Gray Bridge where I found the clay that brought them back from the dead.

I sensed we weren't going there to reenact the lighthouse story. This wasn't about the children's story, at all. And yet I felt that the lighthouse, and the surrounding patch of Manhattan marshland, was important in ways I couldn't understand. Were my grandparents going back there for themselves, or me? Did they see the Hudson mud as a place of burial, or as the primordial flesh that made them alive again? They were created out of a quagmire, but the mud and the muck were only part of the story. The other part was the quandary, what I wanted to accomplish in becoming a kabbalist in the first place.

It was all so spooky because I had never been to the Miami graveyard where they were actually buried. Oliver never returned, and so I didn't get to go, either. After the suicides he was done with Miami forever. His parents were buried there, and with them so went the city. Everything associated with that place was closed like a casket covered under dirt. He never visited again—not to pay his respects, or even to work on his tan. He never opened the door to his former home, and his parents' tombstones went unveiled.

That's not supposed to happen in Judaism.

For most people, Miami, so close to Disney World, is thought of as a sunny place. But to Oliver it is a never-never land. For him the Sunshine State is cloudy, dark, and haunted. Writer's block is only one example of the roads that are closed to my father, the doors he has shut himself out of. No wonder the Golems came back, to coax him out of all the places where he's sealed himself in.

So there I was, trading one swamp for another. I had never been to Miami, but I was headed in the direction of that other place where dirt and clay was so important in my grandparents' lives. Buried in the mud of Miami, yet my grandparents became ghosts from the mud of Manhattan.

Ashes to ashes. Dust to dust. Mud to mud.

Were the banks of the Hudson River and the site of the Little Red Lighthouse a place to leave flowers and say Kaddish? Or was it more like an Easter tale, one of rebirth and resurrection? What kind of story was this? All along I thought that the Little Red Lighthouse was a story about rescue—for the boats on the Hudson, and for my father. Now I was starting to see it a little differently, taking the story more personally. This whole area was about me somehow. It was no accident that this is where I found the clay. I somehow knew to come here, like a homing pigeon, coming home. It wasn't the mud that was magic, but the memories and souvenirs that were left back here, the story I didn't know yet, the one that still awaited my father.

We made our way down the sharp hill to the river's edge. The trees that lined the trail were bare, unlike when I was here last, when there was bright fall foliage everywhere. Over two hundred years ago these leaves must have made great camouflage for England's redcoats. On this day it was ice cold, and the wind in this corner of Manhattan didn't have wide, brick buildings to block its way. The Hudson was rough, much more like a rapid river than the quiet stream that usually borders this crazy island. There was a red-and-white buoy hanging on for its life on the Fort Lee side of the water. And snow was sprinkled along the cliffs of the Palisades like a badly frosted cake. The bridge was humming with afternoon traffic, and the lighthouse stood shyly underneath, as if trying to eavesdrop on our conversation.

"So this is where it all happened?" I said, ending the silence.

"Yes, this is the beginning," Lothar said.

"Of how you came to life," I said.

"And some of the memories that made your father dead," Rose joined in.

"What do you mean?" I wondered. "This is where I found the mud, . . . you know, . . . to make the golems. That has nothing to do with Oliver."

"There was more in that mud than the organic ingredients to bring back your dead grandparents," Lothar said.

"And some of their friends, too," Rose added.

"Why, what else can that mud do?"

"It can cut flesh," Lothar explained.

"This river, this place, has meaning beyond the lighthouse, and the mud, Ariel," Rose added. "There is something that is broken here that explains why your father stopped reading that story at night, and why he stopped reading to you at all."

"What's here that I don't know about?"

"The glass," Rose said.

"Glass?"

"Yes, right there, in the water," Lothar pointed beyond the bluff, beside a pathway of rocks that snaked out into the Hudson River.

I had been on those rocks before, I remembered. That's where the mud came from. But something else was obviously out there too.

"It is the broken glass from your parents' wedding," Lothar continued.

"What?"

"That's right, little one," Rose said, stroking my hair. "This is where your parents married. Overlooking the river, right on this point, beside the lighthouse and the bridge. A beautiful view, don't you think?"

"We weren't here, of course," Lothar reminded me. "Only in spirit, I suppose you could say." He chuckled. "But this is where it happened."

"They were married . . . right here?" I asked, talking to myself.

"There was no real family on either side," Rose said, "and your mother wanted something private, away from the noise of the city. She loved nature, and this was such a nice, simple, lovely spot for Manhattan. And of course a red lighthouse is bound to bring good luck."

"And it was also the neighborhood where your father was born. You know we used to live here before we moved to Miami Beach. Oliver was only a boy back then."

"I think I knew that," I said softly. "Were there guests, you know, at the wedding?"

"Not living ones," Lothar replied. "No witnesses, just a young, guitar-playing rabbi with bad teeth who performed the ceremony."

"They said their vows, then they sat quietly by the shore, holding hands, imagining their future together," Rose reminisced, closing her eyes with a smile. "It was a beautiful day. Lots of sun. Brisk autumn wind."

"And when it was over, and they were ready to leave, your father decided to bury the glass," Lothar said.

"What glass?"

"The one that he stepped on and shattered," my grandfather said. "That's what a Jewish groom does, on the day of his wedding, under the huppah, the final act that sanctifies the marriage." Lothar stroked his beard and mused, "Although after the Holocaust, I don't see why they still continue with this ritual. After *Kristallnacht* breaking glass is not something Jews should do—even in celebration."

"Wait a minute," I said slowly, my memory unfogging, "I found that glass."

"When?" Rose asked.

"When I collected the mud," I replied excitedly. "I dug so deep, I cut my hand on a piece of glass. I still have a scar from it. See?" I showed them, taking off a mitten and proving to my grandparents that I had shed blood trying to rescue their son. "I thought it was a beer or a Coke bottle down there, but no . . . now I know for sure, it was the glass that Oliver stepped on when he married my mother and then buried in the Hudson."

I ran out onto the rocks, teetering from side to side as if I were walking along a wire as high as the George Washington Bridge, without a net, or even water, below. Then I plunged my hand into the river.

"Be careful, dear!" Rose shouted.

"She knows what she's doing, Rose. Leave her alone. She'll find what she's looking for."

Splashing around with my hand, I scraped against the glass again, but this time there was no cut. The flesh wound went even deeper. I fished out the glass, which was wrapped in two white, cold yarmulkas.

"I found it!" I shouted back to my pleased grandparents, who were waiting for me at the shore.

"Bring the glass home with you, Ariel," Rose said as I returned with my sunken treasure. "It belongs there now, not buried under water."

"The glass is still broken, like your father, our son," Lothar said, his voice sinking. "The marriage didn't last a lifetime."

"Hardly." Rose sneered. "Barely a day, and with it, a shattered dream."

"He wanted more for himself," Lothar lamented. "He wished for more. He stepped hard on that glass . . . , so hard he stepped, like he wanted to make sure that nothing else in his life could ever be broken like that so easily. Let him have the glass back, even if it's not, and can never be, in one piece ever again. Let's go home, Ariel."

That night I sat on the windowsill of my bedroom with the window wide open, the violin under my chin, and Rose and Lothar perched on the twin set of laughing gargoyles below. And with the bow sliding, as always, with a movement and rhythm of its own—

almost free from my own hand—the violin played a long lullaby of "Invitation to the Dead." For my grandparents, Oliver's wedding to my mother had already happened—a long time ago. And it didn't turn out so well. Maybe it was better that they weren't alive to show up that time. But as their granddaughter, I was now giving them an open invitation—for any family gathering they wanted to attend.

The cold wind flushed out the heat in my room, but I kept on playing. There was not going to be a bedtime story tonight. I had seen the lighthouse in a different light earlier that day, and I couldn't go back to the children's version so soon. And Lothar and Rose were tired. It was now my turn to tuck them in and put them to sleep.

The sounds of a weeping klezmer violin haunted all of Edgar Allan Poe Street that night. Oliver stood by his bedroom window, searching out into the sky as if summoned by the sounds of all that had not been said. And me? Well, I never stopped serenading my grandparents, whose eyes were closed, their arms wrapped around the gargoyles like sleeping lions.

20

THEY GATHERED AS THEY ALWAYS DO, THESE New Yorkers, at Rockefeller Center, for the annual celebratory lighting of the Christmas tree. The sacrifice this year was a mammoth evergreen, chopped down in Canada and brought to the Big Apple like King Kong. Towering behind the gilded statue of Prometheus, the tree stretched toward the clouds beside 40 Rock, reaching nearly five flights and then giving up, as if conceding the sky to manmade wonders. God and nature can never compete with man at his most inventive, when his mind races and runs wild with hubris and passion.

The outdoor skating rink below the tree was empty, except for a manger scene that the owners of Rockefeller Center had erected on the ice as an added attraction for out-of-town tourists. For the few weeks leading up to Christmas, Bethlehem was given honorary status as a temporary borough of New York City. And for reasons having as much to do with satisfying the Chamber of Commerce as the P.C. police, Judaism received equal billing during the holiday season as well. The pagans and the priests were all properly represented this year. So to complement the Nativity set piece, there was a large, freestanding menorah with a substantial wingspan hovering above the Three Wise Men and the baby-doll Jesus wrapped up in swaddling clothes. Yet all religious symbols were positively dwarfed underneath the circus-tent shadows of the tree.

Everyone who was anyone was at Rockefeller Center in attendance, including the mayor, whose job was to pull the switch and bring on the lights that turned the tree into a torch. The Christmas tree was about to blaze each night like a burning, but unconsuming, bush. Except that the evergreen offered no revelation; it was simply a colossal tree being prepped up for a fervid dose of Con Edison shock therapy.

Thousands gathered by the promenade to watch, all pressed together and standing above and around the skating rink. Many young families arrived early. These were the same folks who show up near the Museum of Natural History on Thanksgiving Eve to witness the intravenous feeding of helium into the rubber rectum of a dinosaur. Not those skeletal, Jurassic creatures long past the point of ever becoming airborne, but rather Barney and some of his postprehistoric friends: Cat in the Hat, Garfield, Pokémon, and Arthur.

While there were no balloons and floats at Rockefeller Center to celebrate Christmas, there were various New York luminaries. Builders and bankers, performance and takeover artists, and even some Yankees, still smarting over their vanquished pinstripes, were spotted at the center of the spectacle along with singers, dancers, and chorus gypsies from the Great White Way. Writers and artists, normally too cool to attend such a gauche event, also dropped by, maybe sensing some sort of supernatural occurrence that had become the norm on the Upper West Side. Some had the sixth sense that Rockefeller Center was the place to be on this most mystical and holy of nights, where religion and ritual merged with some black magic and a whiff of the macabre.

Festive Christmas music blasted through the open-air vista, along with some waltzes, polkas, and even Will Smith's "Gettin' Jiggy Wit' It," which pleased the young, privileged white kids who suffered from hip-hop envy and dressed in baggy Mecca jeans and Timberland boots to prove it.

The mayor approached the platform, gave a hearty, jerky wave to the crowd, and said, "Good evening and welcome to one of this city's magic annual moments—the lighting of the Christmas tree at Rockefeller Center."

A deafening swell of untimed drunken cheers traveled through the canyon of Rockefeller Center.

"Once again we have a beautiful tree this year," the mayor continued, not waiting for the applause, or reproach, to settle down. "I'm told that this tree behind me"—he motioned backward as if introducing a guest—"is over one hundred feet tall and has a trunk that is thirty feet around." Looking at his index card as a crib sheet, he squinted and said, "Ah, yes, the tree comes all the way from northern British Columbia. That's in Canada, for those of you who don't already know.

"There are over thirty thousand lights on the tree, and they're connected by ten miles of wire. And as you can see, there is a special angel on top that we have used as a crown. It was sent to us as a gift from the government of Austria and one of its leaders, Jörg Haider."

The audience, many of whom were ethnic minorities, cheered mindlessly. But then, all of a sudden, the crowd grew anxiously restless. They hadn't come all this way, from other countries and states and boroughs, exposing themselves to a crushing mob on such a frigid night, to hear stump speeches and platitudes about "how much bigger our tree is than yours!" The mayor was jabbering on as the goodwill ambassador of an infamous city, speaking to a captive, concentrated audience on this special night when goodwill toward fellow men and women was the whole point of the celebration.

These people wanted lights, and they wanted them now. They were there for the flame. The voltage. The wattage. The juice. The incandescent, swaggering, primitive allure of fire. Fuck all that tinsel! The mob wanted real sparkle. Burn, baby, burn! Not you, Jesus, but those lights, and those branches. It is what makes Fourth of July events so appealing. And bonfires and campfires and the burning of books, draft cards, and bras. And of course there are the traitors burned either in effigy or, better yet, at the stake. Bring on the marshmallows and video camera for the home movie. Man craves the awe and wonderment of a roaring fire, and failing that, there's always the flying-chair circus of professional wrestling.

"This has been a great year for the city," the mayor crowed, oblivious as always to public sentiment. "Crime and murder are way down in New York. The homeless have been removed from the street."

"What about homes? They still don't have any!" a housing advocate shouted from the herd. She was taken away immediately and impounded in a paddy wagon.

The mayor was unfazed. "Yeah, well, as you also well know, the city has recently become more civil. This is all part of my Quality of Life Program," he said, lifting his arms into the air with his fingers spread apart like a dream catcher. "And the subway trains are now running on time."

"But they're usually empty!" an angry, bored straphanger shouted.

Still undistracted, the mayor said, "There is no more smoking or smoke in New York. What other city can claim that? We are completely smoke-free. We now take baths instead of showers. And all barbed-wire fences have been removed. Tattoos are all gone. Con Edison has eliminated gas. Our city is now powered solely by electricity."

Many tourists who hadn't heard or read about any of these

recent developments wondered exactly how these laurels of the mayor's administration could even be considered civic improvements. Wouldn't the successful repair of potholes be a better measure of great statesmanship?

"Turn it on, Mayor. Light the tree, goddammit!" a burly Italian from Canarsie threatened.

"Yo, motherfucker! I want to see the goddamn lights already!" an African American from Red Hook insisted.

"We're freezing out here, you fascist bastard!" an old Jew from Midwood complained.

"I don't see why it is taking so long," an Indian from Jamaica—not the Caribbean but Queens—shouted quickly but shyly.

"I can't believe this mayor, what a windbag," a large-haired woman from Staten Island said, her daggerlike fingernails apparently readying themselves for an assassination attempt.

"Okay, okay, settle down, everyone," the mayor said, suddenly turning avuncular, a disposition that didn't suit him well at all. "I know what you came for. It's not me; it's the tree, right?" A heckler who was not one for words threw a formerly soft, but now stale, pretzel at the mayor to assure him that he was indeed right about that. "So here we go," the mayor said, having recovered from a successful duck. "Let's count down, like we do when we drop the ball in Times Square on New Year's Eve."

This final decree was met with no public dissent. On the contrary, the citizens of Gotham all joined in to make the mayor's job easier. Countdowns are a kind of cultural touchstone in New York. So many of the city's outdoor spectacles resemble a communal aerobics class, with an endless procession of gadgets that either light up or drop from the sky.

The fireworks were all set to begin.

"Ten, nine, eight, seven . . . ," the mayor led his constituents, who numbly parroted his math skills like toddlers watching *Sesame Street* for the first time. "Three, two, one . . . okay, here goes New York!"

The tree did not disappoint; it lit up in line with everyone's expectations. The faces in the crowd were all bathed in holiday greens and reds; the winter lights shining on all of those spellbound expressions. Given the awe and wonder, they could have just as well been staring at an extraterrestrial as a mutant evergreen. A tree was masquerading as an urban lighthouse—a bright, colorful, twinkling beacon bouncing off the concrete and flashing through the streets and avenues of Manhattan.

But then, finally, it was time for the real miracle to begin. Far into the sky, high above Austria's angel—beyond even the Rainbow Room on the top floor of 40 Rock—eight distinct laser beams of light made the gigantic Christmas tree look like a puny birthday candle. The Golems were not going to remain silent on such an auspicious night, particularly not after the mayor had invoked their deeds, without crediting their names, as the cause of all that was good in the city.

With all the focus on the tree, no one had remembered to put any flames on the Hanukkah menorah, which was a shame, since Hanukkah is, after all, the Festival of Lights. No menorah, especially during this time of year, should have to take a backseat to such a pompously inflamed tree. The Golems decided to set the sky on fire, leaving the wicks alone and converging on a much larger horizon. There were eight Golems, eight nights of Hanukkah, and eight bright beams skywriting all over the velvet Manhattan night.

What wasn't placed into the menorah was rocketed into the sky. Shooting stars. Uncracked lightning. Gamma rays from Gomorrah. Roman candles on a Jewish holiday. The miracle of Hanukkah, this time with a twist. No inexplicable oil that burned for eight days. No magic carpets or wands, genies in a bottle, broomsticks, or Promethean piracy. Just eight ghosts with lasting memories of smoke and an acquired flare for fireworks.

Nobody in the stunned, but still-crammed, audience knew what to make of it all. Given everything else that the island had experienced since the Golems' arrival, this perhaps wasn't all that remarkable an occurrence. And yet somehow it was. The eight shadowy, shimmering flames huddled together like a phantom parfait, drawing strength, invigorating the fire as though they had all come together for one final kiss above the mistletoe.

Meanwhile, on Fifth Avenue, the big metal Atlas, standing with the weight of the world on his shoulders, simply shrugged, no longer the color of black onyx, but now, unaccountably and yet par for the course, a lucid shade of snowman white.

21

 HE DIDN'T EXPECT A KNOCK AT THE DOOR, OR the person standing behind it. Nowadays nobody knocked. Everyone who was missing a pulse, whose existence did not depend on oxygen but on something else in the atmosphere, had a standing invitation to enter his home. Visitors merely glided in, seeping through walls and doors like gas.

No ghost in Oliver's universe stood on ceremony. There was easy access to his home, and his mind. He was opening up. Some of that had to do with the unlocking of his physical space, which no longer offered the same sanctuary, and some of it had to do with his head, which was equally trespassable.

Yet when it came to mortal visitors, the house on Edgar Allan

Poe Street was no more inviting than a leper colony. It was, by every-one's estimation, a ghost house. No one came near the place. The *New York Times* no longer delivered.

"Hey, wait!" Oliver yelled down Eighty-fourth Street in the early hours of the morning, his words trailing through the unpeopled street. An echo returning to him, but not in his own voice. "Where's my paper?" he shouted at the delivery man, who was dashing down Broadway.

"Not a chance, mister," the small man in a navy pea coat replied without ever looking back. "There are ghosts in there; it's not safe in that house."

How could Oliver explain that it was actually the other way around, that everything was strangely safer now, even if the feelings, and all that history, no longer benefited from the guard gates of denial.

Oliver wasn't getting any of his mail, either. Or pizza. Or his FedEx or UPS packages. Con Edison stopped reading his meter. Even the menus from neighborhood Chinese restaurants were no longer slipped underneath his front door. No one was taking any chances. Not even the Census Bureau wanted to know whether there were occupants living inside.

It's also fair to say that during Halloween, parents refused to escort their little witches and goblins anywhere near the Levin house. This brownstone had taken the pagan ritual far too seriously, parents thought. Their costumed children, however, knew better, and pleaded to go trick-or-treating in the most authentic haunted house in all of Gotham.

"Come on, Dad," a little masked Zorro cried. "Don't be such a wimp. Nothing will happen, I promise. That's where the baby car-riage goes home every night. Whoever is pushing that carriage isn't going to hurt anyone."

Ah, yes, further proof that children, despite the paternal cautions of society, do have better perceptions about strangers than adults often give them credit for.

The general consensus among the neighborhood and beyond was that the Levin place was haunted. No question about it. Someone had cast a spell on that brownstone, and while the inhabiting ghosts seemed to be friendly, and downright neighborly for that matter, they were ghosts nonetheless. The evidence against Oliver was certainly incriminating. After all, he had written those mystery thrillers, and his daughter had magically taken up the klezmer violin, spooking the streets with dead music. It was time to start regarding the Levins, and their house, with suspicion. If there were going to be phantoms on the Upper West Side, where else would the ghosts go? The Levins were surely at the center of this. The Golems no doubt belonged to them.

Now, nobody, of course, doubted that the ghosts were harmless, and that in fact they had done much good for the community. Yet how could anyone overlook the fact that we were talking about dead people here? Spirits way past the point of autopsies and rigor mortis. Zombies, admittedly with souls and good hearts, but still repatriates from the otherworld. No one had considered inviting them to their home for dinner. The Golems might prove to be dangerous yet. Besides, they were invisible. How does one extend an invitation, or for that matter, put down a place setting?

Given how much this city delights in a self-image of savvy, hard-boiled street smarts—impervious to scam artists, able to tune out all the smooth talkers—it was unsurprising that there were still those who resisted the idea that all these unexplained phenomena were Jewish witchcraft at all.

"Come on!" you'd hear people say in subways and on buses, on park benches, at dinner parties, posted on e-mails and inside Internet chat rooms. "It can't be ghosts. There's no such thing. Somebody is playing a trick on us, and soon we're all going to read about it in *The Observer* or *Mad* magazine."

Among the rationalists, the scientists, the antimystical and aspiritual, there was a strange impulse to indulge in speculative, residual doubt, to seek some other explanation that everyone up until now had somehow overlooked.

This, of course, was futile. The mind always engages in such mind games with itself. Our species is always so guarded and chauvinistic when it comes to strangers and the strange. The Golems didn't look like us or act like us. In fact, except for Levin and his daughter, and that homeless man on the subway and Broadway meridian, no one could see them at all. The proprietary, exclusionary nature of this secret naturally fed into everyone's fear of the unfamiliar. The more people couldn't see, the less they believed and yet the more they feared.

Oliver Levin's home became a landmarked pariah-asylum for spirits. And because of that, nobody dropped by to borrow a cup of sugar, throw salt over their shoulder, wear garlic around their neck, or post a crucifix on the front door. For this reason it was somewhat shocking that Tanya Green, traveling without an escort on what was now a deserted street, showed up at Oliver's door and knocked with no reservations at all. A sign of either unmitigated spunk, or insanity. Or perhaps it was entirely consistent for a woman who already spent so much of her time communing with a lost world.

Oliver came to the door, looked through the funhouse glass, and turned the knob. He couldn't recall the last time he'd had to open the door for anyone other than himself.

"Oh, hi," he said, awkwardly, and at the same time pleased. He was lonely but didn't know it.

"Sorry to intrude without calling first," Tanya said. She was wearing a blue ski parka with the hood drawn up. He was in black jeans and a black denim shirt, the outfit of a Wild West gambler. "I was afraid you wouldn't even pick up the phone."

"Good guess. I usually don't."

Neither spoke for a short while. Oliver forgot his manners. He had no idea what to do or say next. Should he just shut the door in her face, or was she required to say something first?

"Well," Tanya began, nervously, realizing that this was a dance where not only was she expected to lead, but to also drag her partner's feet around like the dreadlocks of a mop. "Can we go play in your attic?"

Oliver would have registered some emotion if he had any. But these were strange times. Aside from the return of his parents, and the invasion of the Golems, he was becoming a new kind of writer, and that was taking up much of his self-awareness. The airlift had arrived. The blockade had finally been penetrated, or maybe it had just surrendered. Writing sentences was now the least of his problems. If there was a problem, it was the frequency of those sentences, and what was in them. Emotional sentences. Uninhibited. Unreserved. He held nothing back. Such were the sentiments that went into his laptop, sparing nothing for the interactive world. The flesh and blood of the outside held little interest for him. Life was lived exclusively on the keyboard, gelling within a suddenly unblank screen. That's where the tears were spilled, the loss felt, the pain managed. Written, achingly arranged words had become his anchors. He lived above and below them. Only there could he find the clarity and freedom that was not accessible on the street.

He had lost weight. His white hair had grown out, thin and stringy, and his face had become ghostly pale, except for the flecks of unshaven stubble, the only sign of life on his skin. His ingrown hairs were prematurely gray as well. The black shirt and black pants hung large from his underfed frame as if he were a punk Raggedy Andy.

"I was just joking," Tanya said. "You don't have to be afraid of me. I won't rape you in your own attic, in front of the Ark, no less. Hey, what's the matter? You know, you don't look so well."

Too much immersion leads to madness. But neither Oliver, nor Ariel, nor Tanya would have known that. The Golems, of course, knew the risks of Oliver's freewheeling, mindspinning adventures in word processing. But their motives in nudging him there were compromised, their interests conflicted, their loyalties both dual, and in a duel.

The Golems had set him on this course, because that's where he needed to travel, and where they wanted him to go. But in marking off this path, they knew that it would result in more than just a traffic jam of unparked emotions. No, what they feared—what they anticipated for certain—was a head-on collision, a game of chicken resulting in a pileup of such gruesome proportion that rubberneckers would have to turn their faces away in horror.

"Well, are you going to let me in?" Tanya wondered, tugging away at a knotted cord on her parka as if trying to release a parachute. "Hello? Are you there?" She waved a hand in front of his face.

A broken spirit is a natural anesthetic. And it's worse when there are other spirits running interference.

Oliver had started to have dreams. That too was different. He never recalled having any before the Golems arrived. Now they came at him furiously, like a pitching machine out of control with him standing there, swinging a flagpole for a bat. There were visions of Lothar and Rose still alive, with Oliver as a young boy in Miami Beach. He had been an athletic prodigy, excelling in all sports. But in his recent dreams, he fumbled all the balls thrown to him, or kicked them with stumbling feet. The basketball he dribbled was filled with helium. When he ran, his shackled legs lifted like bricks.

And there were also dreams of Samantha—the ones shattered and the ones never imagined. In some of them she tried to explain why she had left. But each of her efforts were foiled by faulty audio. Her voice was garbled and scrambled, as though censored by the KGB. At other times her voice was clear, but recorded at too slow a speed, as though the batteries in her larynx were running low. The distortions in all of Oliver's dreams were simply maddening.

And when Oliver spoke to Samantha, encouraging her to hurry up her sentences or raise her voice, nothing exited his mouth, although it was open and he was clearly attempting to sound out something in English. He was voiceless and mute. She was chatty but unintelligible. Foreigners looking for directions, using exaggerated hand gestures to find the Eiffel Tower. A hapless game of charades.

Samantha's desire and intent were there in trying to provide him with answers, yet Oliver's subconscious was bent on sabotage. She wanted to make amends; his dreams were going to keep him as far apart from his wife as he was while awake.

In other nightly episodes they were playing Frisbee, or running around the reservoir in Central Park. Before Ariel was born, they had done that together often. But in Oliver's dreams the Frisbee took flight from Samantha's hand and sailed off into the streaky sky. And, running on the reservoir, Samantha was too far out in front. In both cases, Oliver was left behind—chasing down a Frisbee or sprinting after his wife.

And there were dreams of suicide. His mind offered him a variety of pictures and scenarios: pills, deadly weapons, drownings, free falls, gaseous vapors. But these dreams did not come with mug shots. Many deaths, but no faces. The victims had all succeeded in ending their lives, but their tombstones were blank on biographical data. Perhaps he was one of the casualties, without knowing it.

Maybe the highlight reel was, in actuality, an audition tape for the same human being. One person playing out various death strategies and wishes, all with his own hand. He called the shots and therefore got to rehearse them in his head. Perhaps that's why Oliver woke up so often in cold sweats and hot shouts. It might also have explained why he was having so much trouble sleeping lately, and why, in addition to everything else, he looked so exhausted.

"I'm sorry," he finally answered. "You're standing out here in the cold, and my mind is in a deep freeze. Please come in."

"Thank you."

She removed her coat and took a seat on the sofa in the living room. Oliver surveyed the room to see if they were alone, and noticed no one. He also quickly checked whether the black sofa was free of the tenacious bloodstains of the suddenly undead. Oliver and Ariel had gotten better at scrubbing away the signature rust that the Golems had deposited wherever they went. The room was, fortunately, for the time being, free of Golem hemoglobin.

"Have you been upstairs lately?" Tanya asked.

"You mean to the attic?"

"Yes."

"No. I've decided that the top floor is now Ariel's domain. I don't even want to know what's up there and what any of that stuff is for."

"That's probably a good idea," Tanya said, folding her arms, then returning them to her sides. She was wearing a maroon sweater with Aztec runes stitched between the shoulders and on the sleeves. "Sometimes it's best to leave things as they are. You know, undisturbed, untouched. You open things up, and who knows what kinds of things come out. Some doors are probably shut for a reason. Although"—pivoting her head backward and looking straight up at the ceiling—"it was kind of interesting up there. And that's where Ariel found the violin . . . ," she said, trailing off.

"Look, if you want, I'll show you the way, but I'm not going up there again. You're on your own this time. It may be part of my house, but it's off limits to me."

"Maybe some other time, but thanks anyway. The attic is not the reason I came here today to see you."

"That's good to hear. So, what's up?"

"I need you to sign a permission slip. You know, as Ariel's legal guardian."

"Permission for what? Are the police cracking down on panhandlers outside of Zabar's?"

"No, this isn't about street music but concert music, at Carnegie Hall."

"Carnegie Hall?"

"Yes, they're sponsoring a special holiday concert. They're calling it the World Music Youth Concert, and it's in three weeks. They've been planning it for nearly a year. Somebody just recommended Ariel to them, and although they've already scheduled most of the performers, they want your daughter to do her own klezmer violin solo. They didn't have any other Jewish music—or Central European, for that matter—so when they heard Ariel audition, they flipped out. It's such a great opportunity for her. She's going to be one of the featured soloists. Let's see . . . ," Tanya began to count off, "there's an Irish flautist, a Russian pianist, a boy on a Jamaican steel drum, a South African percussionist, a Chilean guitarist. What do you think about that? Isn't it simply fantastic?"

"Ariel, on stage at Carnegie Hall? The klezmer violinist from the Upper West Side?"

"Yes, playing the violin she found in your attic only a few months ago. I still can't believe it. She mastered the klezmer violin without ever playing it before," Tanya said knowingly. "Imagine that, and music doesn't even run in your family."

"That's true. The only thing that runs in my family is people running away."

Tanya heard what Oliver had just said, but how does a stranger, even a sympathetic one, respond to something like that? "Yeah . . . ," she began haltingly, "so what do you say? You have to agree to allow her to appear, because she's underage and can't legally make these kinds of decisions for herself. The concert promoters require your approval."

Did the concert promoters know that Ariel was apparently old enough to be a black belt in kabbalah? Oliver mused. Playing with fire, showering all this supernatural acid rain down on New York City? Pretty mature kid by most standards. If she can do that without a license, or her father's consent, why demand a permission slip for her to simply, and harmlessly, play the violin. Kabbalist or violinist? Which one did they think might do more damage to Carnegie Hall's acoustical architecture and had they known, which one would they have wanted to show up?

"Sure, where do I sign?"

"This is the form. Sign right there at the bottom."

"Do I get any free tickets?"

"Why . . . sure, . . . I suppose. How many should I ask for?"

"I don't know. How about one for me and eight more, all right up front."

"That's a lot of tickets. Are they all friends or family?"

"Neither really. Just some ghost writers I know."

Tanya smiled and shook her head. "Okay, thanks, Mr. Levin. This is going to be a very exciting night. I can't wait. So many of my friends and former students are going to come hear Ariel play. And there'll be record executives and orchestra managers out in the audience. Even people from Juilliard who have heard about Ariel and may want her to transfer to their music school next year or maybe even attend college there."

"Why would they? Ariel doesn't play any musical instruments," Oliver said, and then let out a laugh. "I mean, come on, not really. Let's face it, we both know the truth: She's exceptionally good at klezmer karaoke."

Tanya wasn't sure if Oliver was joking.

"I better be going, Mr. Levin." She stood up to leave, pirouetted around and said, "By the way, how's the writing coming? Ariel told me you had been experiencing writer's block for some time now. I hope it's okay that I know that."

"It's fine that you know, but it's no longer true. I'm cured, only the cure is even worse than the disease. If you know a way for me to get writer's block back, please tell me."

"I will," she said, her face trying on yet another tentative expression.

As he opened the door for her and she began to climb cautiously down the snow-layered steps, Oliver said, "Hey, listen, before you go, I was kind of wondering. Do you want to take a walk sometime? I haven't been getting out much lately. I could use some air."

"How about now?"

22

IT GOT TO THE POINT WHERE IT WAS ONLY RIGHT that Zabar's would name a sandwich in Ariel's honor—the Ariel Levin Klezmer Combo—whitefish salad, avocado, and provolone cheese on multigrain bread. In short order it was flying out the door as though it had wings, which in this particularly supernatural climate, was a cliché with real wind behind it.

She had, after all, become a main attraction, a bigger lure in reeling in the smoked-fish crowd than any advertised specials or goat cheese cravings. She was community theater, a neighborhood treasure, an essential stop on any visit to Manhattan. The Statue of Liberty and the Empire State Building were now in direct competition with an Upper West Side detour. Tourists piled out of buses that had parked outside of Zabar's, but their destination was not necessarily the food. They came instead for the transporting shtetl music. Nova was no longer a novelty. Cheese and coffee were still staples, but Ariel's music had added new flavor to the experience of eating appetizers.

Rather than snap pictures of the violin prodigy, they held tape recorders up into the air as if they were reporters for the Associated Press, sampling the sounds of this solo symphony. More than anything else, they wanted to bring the music back with them, wherever it was that the music, and the visitors, had come from.

This was one American export that was staying put—unplugged, landlocked on the island of Manhattan.

All the local news shows did features on this latest offbeat New York fad. There was coverage not only in the *New York Times* and the *Daily News*, but also in *New York* magazine, the *New York Free Press*, the *Spirit*, *Good Day New York*, and on *New York 1*. Ariel was invited to be a musical guest on *Saturday Night Live* and *Late Show with David Letterman*. She even made it onto the Top Ten list.

"You really play that thing great," Dave said after Ariel had come off the stage from her solo. When the cheers from the audience died down, he waved her over to take a seat beside him. "How many lessons did you have before you could do all that?"

"I never had a lesson," Ariel said defiantly, "but now I am starting to study with someone." Her heart was pounding; her grin widened as she beamed at Dave and his audience.

"Tell me something," Dave continued. "I read somewhere that one day you just went up into your attic, found that violin over there, picked it up, and found out you could play klezmer music better than anyone else in the world. What else do you got up there in your attic?"

The audience laughed.

"That sounds impossible to me. Paul, don't you think that's impossible?"

"Pretty hard to believe, Dave," Paul mumbled coolly from behind his keyboard.

"Paul, that's not how you learned how to play the piano, is it?"

"No, I took lessons in Canada."

"Now, there's a mystery you don't hear about every day," Dave acknowledged. "But for you folks who are from out of town, there have been some pretty strange things going on around here lately." Dave sneered, not realizing that Jerzy, who had been hiding underneath Dave's desk all along, was now seated on top of it, preening and making stretchy, funny faces, which caused Ariel to giggle uncontrollably.

"Before you go, let me ask you one more thing," Dave began, this time without any trace of sarcasm. "What do you know about this self-propelled baby carriage that's been wheeling around Manhattan? I'd like to book that thing as a guest on the show."

Ariel had become a pop-cultural phenomenon, replacing the macarena, cigar bars, summer shares, Yankee games, spin classes, kick-boxing, Woody Allen movies, and *Cats* as essential New York pastimes. And best of all, the listeners of her music, and those who joined the caravan to Zabar's, were not all Jews. The shtetl, which the world had once reviled, revolted against, ransacked, annihilated, mocked, and sentimentalized, had now become everybody's hometown.

The one person, however, who astoundingly didn't show the slightest curiosity in what the hell was going on some several city blocks from his brownstone was Oliver Levin, the musician's father. Long after Tanya Green had told him about Ariel's afterschool, street-performing activities, he still managed to steer clear of Broadway between Eightieth and Eighty-first Streets, always mindful to head in a different direction, either by way of Amsterdam or West End Avenues. There are places and things to be avoided in life. Not everything must be confronted head-on. Sometimes a detour is the best route, even if it takes longer and displays far less courage.

But this was more than just not showing the kind of nurturing interest that is expected of a parent. Far different from missing a soccer game or a parent-teacher conference. This was strategic neglect. The snub was intentional. It had nothing to do with absent-mindedness, or being overworked. Oliver was acting as if all the fuss about his offspring wasn't happening at all. No matter what Tanya Green had told him, or how much whispering he heard behind his back, to Oliver, Ariel's sudden mastery of the violin was just myth. What one didn't see or hear was ultimately still unknown. And he wanted to keep it that way. If he never actually attended one of his daughter's solo shows, if he never actually heard her play, even though everyone was talking about it, it would all still be in the category of rumor. And a rumor is always less threatening than the unvarnished, intimately experienced truth itself.

How is it possible to have a musical prodigy in your home without even knowing it? How deaf can you be? The talent and specialness should have been apparent in some way. Tanya Green was right: You just can't pick up an instrument like that. This was more than simply being able to play by ear or having perfect pitch. No ear is that good. What Ariel could do with the violin went way beyond the formalism of notes and scales. Her greatness was not in what she could play, but in what she could transmit. She was a medium of medieval magic, the axis of those Central European sounds, the willing rod that lightning struck.

The music within her took command, a possession that was neither hostile nor adverse. Somehow it got planted there, like a squatter who had no immediate or future plans of leaving. And it would have still chosen her as human amplifier even if she had been tone deaf. The relevant genes here were not for music but emotion. That was her greatest qualification for the job. She had been handpicked to bring something back. The courier of a message, delivered in a most unusual key. The way in which she decoded the music was no more an act of free will, talent, and improvisation than the playing of a piano roll.

But no father wants to see a child getting in over her head. Or, more pointedly, fathers—even underprotective ones—always fear that someone or something will gain access into that head, turning it around, brainwashing it, influencing it in misguided, destructive ways. For this very reason, there are justifiable fears of cults and, sometimes, occults. A child can be snatched away without the child ever leaving home, without a ransom note or a demand of any kind. The body is there, but the spirit is elsewhere. A kidnapping without a crime.

What parents most wish for their children are unclouded dreams. But among the many curses of the Levin family was the fact that dreams were never one's own. Borrowed and recycled, repeated and invented. Oliver knew this to be true from his own recent sleeping experiences. For the Levins, dreams were family affairs even though there was no living family to speak of. That's what happens when the events that precede you are larger than anything you can ever accomplish, or dream up, on your own.

Oliver wanted nothing more than to deprogram his daughter. Unplug her from that violin and whatever other outlets there were—protected from surges but from nothing else. Surely he could flip the switch to a new, earthly frequency. Scramble the reception. Cut the wire completely. Tilt the antenna so that these satellites of Holocaust survivors would beam their signals to some other child. But he knew better. These metaphysical forces would not allow him to exercise parental control. He had forfeited his rights. They had taken his daughter because she had called out for them, and he had grossly neglected her. Now they were the surrogates of his own default. His only hope was that she would either succeed or fail quickly in whatever it was she had set out to do by inviting them in.

But on this day Oliver had decided to see for himself. The street, the sounds, the crowds, the tearful melodies radiating from beneath his daughter's chin were something he wanted to witness firsthand. All of a sudden it was all real, even if piped in from some other faraway, unreachable place.

Oliver lurked in the back of the crowd on Broadway, afraid to come forward, even to be seen. He wasn't able to hug his daughter, so instead he directed his affections toward the curb. Uncomfortable as it was to observe her in this way, like a spy, a parent PI, he was fascinated by how Ariel had transformed life on Broadway—all with a bow, a violin, and an answered prayer. The faces watching her were mesmerized. Their bodies swayed. Legs lifted. Heads bobbed. And so many closed their eyes. Nobody was paying much attention to anything else other than this klezmer sideshow. It would have been a pickpocket's dream, had the pickpockets not been equally enraptured. Instead they gave their fingers a rest from everything other than snapping to the sounds of a bygone Transylvania. When Ariel was in concert, everyone put their day jobs on hold.

Soon it was all over. Snow was falling fast, piling up on the pavement. The crowd disbanded, returning home, their faces still flushed, but not from the cold.

Oliver gradually made his way to his daughter, who was counting gratuities and tucking her violin into its case. As the father came closer, the daughter somehow appeared even farther away.

"You put on quite a show, Ariel. I'm . . . I'm stunned, really, really shocked. I didn't expect to feel this way at all."

"Oliver . . . ," Ariel lifted her head and gasped. "Wow . . . you're here! I can't believe it. You actually came."

"It took some time, I know. Clearly I'm not a stage parent or a soccer mom. This is all a little too weird for me. I'm having enough problems with what's happening back on Edgar Allan Poe Street."

"The Golems?"

"And the new novel. Everything around me is now haunted, you know."

"Not more than it was, Oliver. Actually, as I see it, you're much better off now than before they all came."

"You think so?"

"Definitely! Maybe you can't see it yet, but it's true."

He helped gather her things. Oliver swung Ariel's backpack over his shoulder.

"You want to carry the violin case instead?" she asked.

"No thanks. What if it turns out I can play that thing, too?"

"You probably can," Ariel said, sidling up against her father as if docking in at his hip. "I bet we both now have the magic. The music's already in us."

Oliver was about to ask his daughter what she meant, but he was interrupted by onlookers and silent whisperers, pointing at Ariel and smiling, hoping that she would notice them.

"That's her," he could hear them say about his ponytailed daughter, a grunge flannel shirt on her back, slacker painter pants covering her legs, and blue Dr. Martens on her feet.

"Who?"

"The girl with the violin . . . you know, on Broadway. The klezmer kid."

"She's so young and pretty. She doesn't look like Mozart, or Prince, at all."

It was particularly distracting, and distressing, because there had been a time when Oliver was the one singled out on the street, this local writer of bestselling mystery novels, a few of which had been made into major motion pictures. He was once an Upper West Side celebrity, only to be surpassed by his own progeny, who was now an artist in her own right—and a legitimate one, at that. Of course he was still conspicuous, but not in the way that he had been before.

"That's her father," he could hear them say. "Yes, the tall man with the white hair walking next to her. The guy with the ghosts in his house."

"He used to be a writer, didn't he?"

Oliver winced, then continued. "What did you mean back there when you said about us both having the magic?"

Father and daughter turned the corner on Edgar Allan Poe Street. "Well, we both found our true calling," Ariel explained.

"In what way?"

"For one thing, you're not a blocked writer anymore."

"Yes, that's true."

"And as for me, I'm a kabbalist, and a klezmer. I create golems out of Hudson River clay. I make the real thing; golem sculptures that work," she said with the self-confidence of Rodin and Rabbi Loew. "And I can re-create the music of the shtetl."

"True, not everyone can say that. We're certainly an unusually talented family, a real circus act—the flying Levins. I hate to break it to you, Ariel, but before you and I came along, there was no art in our family. This is all new to us."

"Are you kidding, Oliver? We're natural artists. That's what family history is all about. It's true for alcoholics, incest survivors, victims of physical and sexual abuse, and us. There's the Holocaust, and the suicides, and the abandonments. What do we do for an encore? It had to go someplace. Grandma and Grandpa gave us a good head start."

This question Oliver pondered seriously. Perhaps the Levin family did have vast resources in both artistic material and motivation. Father and daughter finally reached the front stoop of their brownstone and were greeted by unthreatening, smiling gargoyles whose stone eyes for a second seemed happy to see them.

"You have a concert coming up at Carnegie Hall. I know about it. Tanya told me."

"You're okay with it, right?"

"Sure, I'll be sitting in the front row, lit up like a lighthouse. After today I think I have a good feel for your repertoire. It will be a big night, Ariel, but we've had plenty of them lately."

"No kidding."

"And your audience, they'll definitely be there in full force—dead and alive."

The snow had added inches to each step that rose up to the parlor floor, cold crystals that left tracks, but not from all the brownstone's inhabitants. Except for parked cars, the street was barren. Garbage was stationed at the curb for the morning's pickup. Twilight was fad-

ing as families settled in for dinner. The winding down of a day with
little anticipation about tomorrow.

Once inside Oliver and Ariel removed their coats, hats, and
scarves. They also shook off their boots, ice shards clinging to the
treads, and placed them on a rubber mat to dry. All around the house
they could hear the voices of ghosts in conversation. What was once
a spacious home for two, comprised of four floors, eight unused rooms,
two dens, several walk-in closets, and enough crevices to have kept
even someone as stealthy as Jerzy occupied, now seemed claustrophobic and airless. With eight invisible guests settling in for the long
winter, if not longer, the square footage had the feel that it was
shrinking indefinitely.

"Let's go upstairs," Ariel suggested.

"Where?" Oliver wondered.

"The attic."

That family precinct of resurrection and return.

Oliver seemed reluctant, but then the noises in his head
reminded him that he had been running extreme deficits in shared
private moments with Ariel. And he also needed to put some distance between the Golems and the one other living member of his
family. If climbing back into that attic was the only available buffer
between the living and the dead on Edgar Allan Poe Street, then to
the attic he was willing to venture as a sacrifice for his child.

The attic remained just as he had last seen it: an exact replica of
the Altneuschul in Prague. This synagogue was where Rabbi Loew
first created and then disassembled the original Golem. Later the
Golem was buried under mounds of prayer books, to be revived if
and only if the Jews of Prague should once again face some future
implacable danger. Oliver noticed the dusty velvet curtains and the
blotched, wood-paneled walls. The richly ornamented and dusky-
scented benches. The empty Ark, except for a few cutouts of Hebrew
letters teetering sideways and toppling over like toy soldiers.

"Ariel, I know I haven't been a low-maintenance father. You
could have done better with a different parent."

"I'm not complaining, Oliver. You're my father, and I didn't have a mother. You're doing fine. I love you."

Oliver's face squirmed and blushed in various shades of unearthly tones. "No, that's not true. As if it weren't enough that you didn't have a mother, in some ways you were orphaned completely. When Sam left, I did too. You've grown up by yourself. And I'm sorry for that. There's no good excuse for what I've done. It was just so hard, Ariel . . . just so hard."

Ariel understood exactly what her father meant. She also lived in this house. The obligation to rescue, mixed with the desire to run away, was something she had long felt. And Oliver had experienced it too with his own parents when they were alive. She reached out and hugged her father, drawing him in, bringing him closer. And she was crying—for herself, for the two of them. She peered up to examine his face, measuring all that mystery, the wild-eyed frenzy and dead-eyed numbness. He had become the sort of person who you fear leaving alone by himself, the kind of human being in whom even a dog would sense the need for a best friend.

"I know what happened at the Little Red Lighthouse, Oliver."

"What do you mean? The children's story? Of course you know what happened there. You've read it a million times."

"No, not the children's story, but your story. The one you and Mom are in."

Oliver didn't answer. He needed more proof that Ariel was actually on to something.

"I know that's where you and Mom were married."

"How did you find out? Who told you?"

"Grandma and Grandpa. They took me there."

"They took you to the lighthouse? Did they use public transportation? No, don't even tell me." A pause. Oliver looked away. "How would they know anything about it?"

Oliver then realized what should already have been obvious: His dead parents had indeed been watching over him long after their double suicide. Theirs was a schizophrenic departure: They had sepa-rated themselves from this world, but they also remained, as though death made it even more impossible for them to leave. Oliver had no way of realizing this. His parents wanted to be present for all the important occasions, and they weren't going to let a little thing like death stand in their way.

Lothar and Rose didn't simply slip away and pass idly into the otherworld. They lingered, and turned back, if to do nothing else then at least to observe. Oliver married, but without parents to give him away. Yet they were there, literally, in spirit. They didn't need to hear "Invitation to the Dead" in order to feel welcome. Human beings always harbor such starry illusions about their dead loved ones. But maybe it's sometimes true. Lothar and Rose were no longer Oliver's legal guardians, but they were still his parents, still guarding, and they wanted to be at his wedding. He stepped on the glass all by himself, but he was not alone. His leg had additional leverage. The sound of the shattered glass sent a soul-tingling jolt into the spirits of proud but wary parents.

"I'd already been to the lighthouse and the bridge," Ariel contin-ued. "We took a class trip there in the fall. I never told you about it, maybe because after you stopped reading the story to me, I figured it was a place you didn't want to think about again; like it had spooked you or something."

"You were right."

"And now I know why. But look, here," she said, walking over to a shelf that stored a cluster of *yortzeit* candles. She removed a crushed-velvet jewel bag that was tied up with a gold string. "I brought you back a souvenir."

What could it be? Oliver wondered. "Are they selling T-shirts and mugs nowadays with pictures of the Little Red Lighthouse?"

"No, it's just glass," Ariel said, and then opened the bag so that her father could peek inside without cutting himself. "I fished it out of the Hudson and . . . I brought it back for you. Here it is."

"What kind of glass is this?"

"Broken glass. Wedding glass. The glass from your wedding."

"The glass from a broken marriage." Oliver understood, and then carefully took possession of the glass he had once shattered with one decisive, hopeful stomp.

Unfocused and fuzzy, he recalled Samantha, shimmering in a long, snugly sheer white dress, her blond hair flaxen in the noonday sun, her hands clasped around the rough stems of wildflowers, her smile wide and reassuring, as she said: "What are you doing, Oliver? You're not putting the glass in the Hudson? Somebody might step on it."

"I'm burying it in the river, and it will stay there forever," he spoke confidently, and guilelessly, to his new bride. The white yarmulka had already sailed off his sandy blond hair and fallen into the water. He picked it up, and retrieved another, and used them both as underwater packaging, forever keeping the top of the glass covered, as if it were a religious Jew. A sidelong stream from the wake of a schooner lapped over his shoes while a strong sun washed his formal, navy blue suit in the half-baked glare of a sailor's dream. "Just like us: We came together from brokenness, but now nothing can break us apart."

So many years later, his optimism humbled by life, a daughter—the only woman in his life—now standing before him, he held the uprooted glass next to his body like a newborn baby. It had finally been returned to him, reclaimed as if he had been looking for it all along. And so he asked his daughter: "What am I supposed to do with it?"

"I don't know. All I know is that it was drowning in the Hudson. It needed some air. Maybe you can find a way to put it back together, and breathe."

"So I can step on it again? I won't do that."

"Maybe just drink out of it this time. Grandpa said that Jews shouldn't break glass anymore. I think he was right."

Oliver stared into the wise, glowing face of his daughter. The outside street lamps poured light through the sharp, splintered remnants of her parents' marriage, which she now cupped in her hands. Glimmering like magic gems, like a crystal ball that had been smashed into clairvoyant spikes of forever divided glass.

"You're getting better, Oliver. That's all I know. You just have to have some faith; you just have to have some faith."

23

THEY WERE ALL CALLED TO THE TORAH, NOT FOR target practice, but this time, to actually say the blessing. In death Lothar had learned many lessons. He had once put a hole in his head in order to end his suffering. But this grand exit was not without consequence. The result was a desecrated Miami Torah and a scarred son. Now he and his friends finally knew that sheepskin was not to be used as a tablecloth for a human sacrifice. You don't bleed on a Torah; you just *daven* before it.

The Golems had become regular congregants at B'nai HaNeshama, a Conservative synagogue on the corner of West End Avenue and Eighty-sixth Street. Strangely, the religious structure on that block, a large stone-white edifice with gargoyle-infested turrets and a thin bell tower, was in actuality a Lutheran church, and not at all a place of Jewish worship. The building that housed B'nai HaNeshama, back up on West Eighty-eighth Street, had suffered through a fire and now a renovation that was proceeding much too slowly. In the meantime, the synagogue elders made an arrangement with the Lutheran minister, whose own congregation was dwindling and who shrewdly realized that he was sitting on prime, underused, holy real estate in Manhattan.

After some heated ecumenical negotiations, the rabbis and the minister reached an agreement that resulted in a brotherly Judeo-Christian sharing of the church—for a fee, but also with some structural compromises.

The Lutheran minister did not stop there, striking similar deals with Alcoholics Anonymous and its long-suffering Al-Anon companions, as well as with the folks from Overeaters Anonymous, Narcotics Anonymous, Sex and Love Anonymous, and those from Debtors Anonymous and Gamblers Anonymous—two groups that should probably keep away from each other—all of whom, in their shared secrets and addictions, shaking and stumbling up the twelve steps, made claims to the basement and the meeting rooms on the upper floors.

But the sanctuary of the church would now have a new cast of worshipers. On Friday nights and Saturday mornings, a curtain was hoisted up, discreetly covering all the crucifixes, Virgin Marys, and baby Jesuses in the sanctuary. An Ark loaded with Torahs would get wheeled in like an ice-cream truck. Old Testaments replaced New ones, and hymnals were concealed and silenced, all so that the Jews of Congregation B'nai HaNeshama could lease a spiritual home until somebody could figure out how to put a roof back over their own synagogue.

In some ways, however, this physical displacement made sense for this particular congregation of Jews. They were an unusual tribe, almost separate from the other twelve, in fact. For one thing, they knew to give themselves a suitable name. Unlike so many American-

Jewish congregations that showed no gumption or imagination in naming their *shuls*, B'nai HaNeshama, Sons of the Souls, was a purposeful christening—no fluke, no random, impulsive choice out of the Doctor Spock synagogue-naming book. They could have chosen Temple Sinai, Temple Torah, or Temple Dreidel, for that matter, but instead they knew their own kind, the allegiance they had for those no longer of this world, the mystical connection to the unspoken and unseen, the interior universe that may have been dark but not without light.

And that's not all. Often, and for no apparent reason, the congregation was given to spontaneous dancing during the services. They welcomed almost any opportunity to get up from their seats, join hands, and form a massive line of hora dancers, spinning through the aisles of the sanctuary, winding through the rows, twirling about like Jewish leprechauns, eyes closed as though being transported to places impossible to get to only by dancing. Their faces were tearful and joyful, their hearts pumping with an uncommonly juiced adrenaline, their spirits filled with Jewish, ecstatic prayer. Martin Luther, had he been alive, would have thrown up at such a spectacle, especially since it was taking place in one of his own churches.

When the Golems settled on the Upper West Side, the congregants of B'nai HaNeshama couldn't have been happier. For one thing, the return to ritual, a phenomenon that the Golems had restored in the neighborhood with no more difficulty than the sprinkling of pixie dust, was nothing really new to the members of this synagogue. They were already well ahead of everyone else, having long ago reconciled and reunited their Jewish and secular lives. Yes, they had embraced the modern, and knew the difference between iMacs and Big Macs, fighter pilots and Palm Pilots. They traded on-line and brought bottled water to their gyms to keep their electrolytes in perfect, harmonic balance. But even all these secular enrichments and distractions were not enough to entice them away from their religion and faith.

Yet theirs was an especially unconventional faith. Mostly because

it was guided by the internal spirit rather than the externally scruti-
nizing world. Frankly, they didn't give a shit what anyone thought.
This was a self-guided congregation. Comfortable with spiritual
experimentation. A place where silence was not threatening, even
on a planet that had long ago surrendered to noise. For them it was
possible to meditate in Manhattan. Here the sound of the breath was
primary, and sacred, even if it registered very few decibels. A *shul*
equally at home with both rational and blind faith.

The service itself was gender neutral in all possible ways. Men
and women sat together, and both sexes, if they wished, wore
yarmulkas and *tallisim*. Such equality also carried over to the Deity.
God was still the most Holy of Holys, the unutterable, the main
Adonai, but such credentials didn't necessarily make God a man. A
female divinity could just as easily have been responsible for fucking
up the planet, and this congregation was wise enough not to get
caught up in that contradiction.

Standing at the *bima* were two rabbis, dressed in long white
gowns and hats the shape and durability of soufflés. Standing next to
them was a long-fingered woman who was communicating the service in sign language for the hearing impaired. There was a pickup
jazz band all plugged in and visible off to the side, with the cantor
stationed at the keyboard. He, too, was in white. The rabbis and the
cantor were all from Brazil, a geographical anomaly no one could
quite account for, but no one seemed to mind, either. The music
always possessed a decidedly South American up-tempo beat, as if
these Jews had somehow convinced themselves that the melodies
of Eastern Europe were democratically danceable, whether one is
standing in a hora or a conga line.

Perhaps because of all its exotic, ethereal, and eccentric features
of Jewish worship, the Golems had decided to attend this *shul* to the
exclusion of all others in the neighborhood. And it wasn't as if B'nai
HaNeshama didn't realize its good fortune. The congregants were
uniformly discreet about the presence and personages of their newest
members. The church was now haunted, which surprisingly didn't

scare these Jews. Religious people are comfortable with accepting what they can't see, to embrace other worlds that are unlived and unknown, to touch the intangible and stomach the ambiguous.

How different was a god from a ghost?

It was clear to everyone at B'nai HaNeshama that whatever metaphysical phenomenon was taking place outside the church was being felt even more intensely inside the building itself. And perhaps for this reason alone, they refused to exploit what they all knew to be true.

"They have come to pray with us," one of the rabbis, a slight man with a thin face and an oval forehead, explained sternly in a Portuguese accent.

"Yes, it is our secret," the other rabbi, heavyset, with a warm face and dark curly hair, added with an equally rough pronunciation.

"Why they are here we do not know," said the first rabbi, "but what is for sure is that we can all feel it, and therefore we must respect it and treat it as a holy."

But neither rabbi chose to actually name it. Because they couldn't. There was no way to know exactly what it was that everyone was feeling. Could it be more than that, or maybe the feeling itself was enough?

"Whatever happens in here stays with us," the heavyset rabbi commanded. "We don't speak about it when we leave this synagogue. The Ark gets closed, and so does our story."

The rabbis were both relatively young men. Perhaps that made them more patient. They didn't have to know right now what had overtaken their *shul*. There would be plenty of time for that later. They were also the kind of men who could tolerate the undefinable and live quite comfortably with the untroubled sense that if they never did actually find out, then that would be okay, too.

So on Saturday mornings the rabbis would reserve the final *aliyah* for the Golems, although they didn't name them, or make a big deal out of it. It seemed to just happen on its own. The Golems acted on cue. Eight ghosts congregated on the *bima*, circling the Torah, the *yad* moving in the air like a dancing scepter, a canopy hovering above. They began the blessing in shrieking, ungodly, ghoulish voices. So piercing and thundering were those sounds that many in the congregation covered their ears tightly, squeezing their hands against their skulls. *Yortzeit* glasses shattered all over the Upper West Side.

The Golems had already made their presence known all throughout this reconstituted shtetl, but until they came to this synagogue, their voices were silent to everyone except Oliver and Ariel. Only here, at B'nai HaNeshama, did the Golems refuse to keep their voices down, and only in this way—reciting the blessings over the parchment, and of course, near the end of the service, the reciting of the Kaddish. Outside the church their voices echoed in the narrow creases and padded chambers of the wind; inside the church the acoustics were more amplified and reverberating—a simultaneous translation from the dead. But even when the Golems spoke, it was not done without internal conflict among themselves.

"This is absurd, crazy, ridiculous," Jean complained each Saturday morning, like a child with a bogus stomachache trying to weasel out of a day at school. "I will not go into a synagogue to pray to a god, especially this God. This is the same God who has all the morals of an advertising executive. A Supreme Being who has successfully been conning Jews for five thousand years that they are the Chosen People. He just never bothered to tell them what they were actually chosen for: the gas chambers and crematoria." Jean tried to reduce his fever but couldn't. "Come on, admit it, all of you: There is no God, only poets."

The others frowned, knowing that when Jean got stridently started in this way, Jerzy was likely to get silly, and they would all once again be late for Saturday-morning services.

Sure enough, Jerzy was cackling and egging Jean on. "Oh, come on, God's a poet, too," he said, dressed in an afghan and a Turkish headdress. "There's great poetry in watching genocide while sitting in a La-Z-Boy throne, eating grapes, listening to a harp, and waiting for the next show-time slaughter to materialize through the clouds."

"If he's a poet," Jean wondered, "what language does he write in? We abandoned Hebrew and Yiddish, and so did he."

"We only abandoned the language, but not the Jewish feelings—the Jewish soul," Paul replied.

"At least the services are in a church." Tadeusz, the lone Catholic of the bunch, returned the conversation to the rituals at B'nai HaNeshama. "These Jews aren't taking any chances. They're playing on both teams. Of course, I hope they don't get too carried away with the Christian symbolism. It would be a mistake for them to start believing in the afterlife. We all know better than to do that."

"Yes, we know better," Primo said, "and that's why we go to *shul* each week. To remind them all of what's most important: not necessarily the commandments of God, but the belief in one. It is only through faith and love that moral courage can exist in the world."

"Primo," Jean scoffed and laughed, levitating himself two feet higher and raising his eyebrow at the same time, "the Nazis loved, too, and they had enormous faith—faith in the Führer, faith in the Reich, and faith that it was morally virtuous to kill Jews. How much moral protection do faith and love actually provide?"

"Faith is everything," Primo insisted. "Without that, there is nothing, no hope, just suicide. Faith is what we lost, and faith is what we must give back."

"Fine, but not in a synagogue, especially one with a church complex," Jean said. "Synagogues are places of sin. That's not where I want to spend my morning."

"I don't care what either of you say," Jerzy said. "I like the dancing at this *shul*. That's why I go. And also because they have young, luscious women dancing around in tight pants. It's like a go-go club for Conservative Jews. Belly dancers covered up in prayer shawls."

The others had already stopped listening to Jerzy. "My fear is that we will give them false hopes," Paul said. "If we keep showing up to their *shul*, they may come to believe that God is responsible for our reappearance, which we all know is not true. We are ghosts, but not emissaries from God. We are not holy creations, but rather kabbalah miracles. To us God may not exist, but Ariel's magic tricks do. But the congregation has no way to understand the difference. They will see in us the miracles of the Bible. That's what they are already saying about Piotr's baby carriage."

Piotr blushed, knowing that these friends who shared his parallel universe did not necessarily appreciate having a Swedish stroller along for the ride.

"Yes," Primo conceded, "there is a difference between hope and false hope. But I would rather they have hope, some kind of hope— even delusional and artificial hope—than nothing at all."

"I'd still rather be at the Central Park carousel right now," Jean steamed, even though he was the only one who didn't so much care for the merry-go-round. "If there is a God, I bet that's where he is, too."

Nevertheless, after the reading of the Torah, the real show began. A most amazing sight took place every Saturday morning at B'nai HaNeshama, the kind of believe-it-or-not event that Fox Television would have loved to capture on tape and air on prime time if they could, sandwiched between natural disasters and UFO sightings. But no camera could have picked up any of these visuals, because this tip was too hot to receive. The otherworld was right here, not playing tricks or hurling fire and brimstone, just doing what you're supposed to do with a Torah.

As is customary in all synagogues, the Torah and each of its vestments and accessories—crowns and breastplates, mantles and *rimonim*—are carried throughout the sanctuary in a processional that winds its way around the congregation, all of whom are standing and given an opportunity to kiss the Torah, using either the fringes of their *tallisim* or the spines of their prayer books. Such are the obsessions that Jews have with words, particularly holy ones inscribed on parchment.

Now, the people responsible for chauffeuring these relics from the Ark are usually the ones who were the last to read from the Torah, as well as others who were being given a special honor, per-

haps the family of a bar- or bat-mitzvah boy or girl, or a couple cele-
brating their impending nuptials. But all such dignitaries had taken a
back seat while the Golems were in town. The parade of the Torah
and its posse of adornments was now theirs alone.

And aloft they all went. Each Golem, including Rose, the one
female in this cabal, wore a *tallis* and a yarmulka—the only physical
evidence that they were actually there at all. Lothar, Primo, and Piotr
each carried a Torah. Jerzy held the crown. Rose the breastplate. Paul
the *rimonim*. Tadeusz the mantle. Jean lingered in the back, not really
wanting to participate, so he grabbed the least imposing trinket of all,
the *yad*, and then followed after the others.

Although they were used to it by now, all the faces of the congregation lit up like those of small children watching the Macy's
Thanksgiving Day Parade for the first time. But these were not balloons passing before them, although the Torah and its adornments
did indeed float. There were no clowns holding lines from below, just
ghosts, covered in prayer shawls and topped off by skullcaps—
wrapped in sheets, just like in the movies. Yet this scene was
painfully, poignantly real, even if see-through. A Hail Mary of talismanic Jewish objects, seemingly unheld, cracked open from the Holy
Ark from which they came and chaperoned all along the perimeter
of the sanctuary with its creaky wooden floors, warped pews, and
windows stained with the symbols of Christian suffering and sacrifice.

The procession of Torahs and *tallisim* made its way around the
church with the festiveness of a pious toga party. The Golems glided
in figure-eight loops underneath the brown, domed ceiling and gangplank buttresses. Gothic chandeliers, shaped like octopi, dangled
from the slimmest of ropes. As they passed through the aisles and
around the white Romanesque columns that supported the balcony,
the Golems left behind a trail of crusted, track-marked, ancient
blood—a reminder of where they had just noiselessly stepped, as if
anyone at B'nai HaNeshama needed any further proof. Everyone
reached out to touch a Torah, or to plunge a hand into the aura of a

ghost. Knowing that the Torahs were being escorted by the dead, the kisses from the lips of the congregation were delivered with the smoldering heat of a Spanish lover rather than the reserved, respectful peck of an Oxford Englishman.

As the caravan of Torah treasures made its way toward the back, Lothar and Rose glanced at their son standing there against the wall, underneath a crucifix bundled up in a sackcloth. This wasn't the baby Jesus in swaddling clothes, but the fully grown, bloodied martyr thrown now into a figurative broom closet to make room for Jews at prayer. And positioned directly underneath where there was once a Messiah, was Oliver, the mystery writer.

And he was not alone. Rose and Lothar noticed their granddaughter standing beside their son. Oliver hadn't been to a synagogue in years, even though he lived a mere two blocks away from this one. No doubt Ariel, that shaman of the souls, had just brought him here, for the first time; perhaps the first of many firsts to come.

"You get to see the Golems in action at the *shul*, Oliver," she coaxed him. "And it's time that you finally go, too, for yourself."

"We have a *shul* upstairs, Ariel. Remember?"

"But you don't go there either," she reasoned. "And besides, the one in the attic doesn't have a *minyan* like this one."

Oliver and Ariel were the only ones in the church who could actually see these dead Holocaust survivors, these ghosts who didn't want to be mistaken for gods—either the benevolent or wrathful kind. Did that make this father and daughter fortunate for having inside information, or were they all the more cursed for it? They did not know, because as the processional neared, they were unable to think of anything other than their eight houseguests who were now making house calls in this house of God—albeit with a Lutheran landlord.

Lothar brought the Torah he was carrying right up to his son, the author, and waited—waited for his offspring to respond in the way that a Jew should when in the presence of the most important book of all. But Oliver was dead—to the custom, and to the life. Maybe he simply didn't know what he was supposed to do. Ariel lifted her father's hand and stroked it against the Torah, then brought it to his lips for a kiss. Oliver's hand went limp, his mouth unpuckered, as if the nerve endings for a kiss had abandoned him, as well. Rose began to cry, nearly dropping the breastplate to the ground.

And then they were all off again, heading in the other direction. But suddenly the solemn march found a new groove. Synthesized music started up, and the congregation joined hands and got swallowed up in the pixilated melodies of the shtetl. The enraptured community chased after their dancing ghosts—true boogiemen, poltergeist golems, spinning like dreidels, that other Jewish creation made from clay.

Oliver had lost his parents in the whirl of this dancing mob. Even his daughter found herself separated from him, now linked to a bouncing chain of galvanized Jews. Everything was a blur. Oliver could no longer connect a specific image to those once-floating artifacts from the Ark. The ghosts had become indistinguishable from the rest of the congregation. His memory was now locked, stuck in flashback, all that backstory now front and center.

21

GOMORRAH. MEDUSA. ORPHEUS AND EURYDICE.
Salt and stone. Looking back has always been
deadly. Even in a car, we are constantly reminded
that objects in the mirror are closer than they
appear. Indeed, they can be right on top of us or,
in the case of the self, inside us all along. Probably all the more reason why it's best not to look
back so much. The risk is too great. You may face a future as a statue
or a pillar—the cold carbon of the periodic table. And nobody would
want that for themselves.

But that's much easier said than done. We are, if nothing else, an
untamable lot, plagued by curiosity and mischief; fragile and yet
adventurous. Always tantalized by the forbidden, if for no other reason than it is so. Breaking curfews. Taking joyrides. Exceeding speed

limits. Ignoring signs. Eve was easily seduced into taking a bite out of that apple. Pandora couldn't live without looking inside her box. We don't do so well with warnings. An entire subgenre of storytelling is devoted to the moral lessons that come from being told not to do something, and yet doing it anyway. Don't go into the woods! Don't drink that potion! Don't leave your post! Don't hit the rock with that staff! Our species has endured a long, feeble history of having to hear "I told you so," but it has brought us no discipline, no moderation. If you don't believe me, go ask the surgeon general.

All we have to hear is that something is behind us to make it, regardless of what it is, all too tempting to ignore. Blinders are for horses; the allure is too irresistible for man. And once the free spirit assumes command over the rational, practical mind, it's already too late. Willpower loses its will. The siren song of sin lurks back there, tantalizing, summoning.

For years you can go without any appetite for such things, as if existing solely on a diet of cold turkey. Better off looking straight ahead. Then, all of a sudden, for no apparent reason, the past becomes something worth revisiting, or at least remembering. A memory returns. A flashback turns into a freeze-frame. A fault-line crack is found in what was once frozen. Everything reminds you of something else. The calendar starts to have meaning as a personal marker, a way to recall all the skid marks, even some of the smooth sailings. You pause, and take a peek.

And that's your first mistake, the path to salt and stone. But perhaps the biblical Jews and the ancient Greeks got it all wrong. Maybe life is all about backtracking, those inexorable glances over the shoulder. Maybe it's the marching forward that is the unnatural human posture; racing too far ahead, the real danger—not because of the speed, but the impertinence, and conceit. If abandoning people is wrong, then leaving memories behind is no less a transgressive act. The past is there for a reason. It lingers and lurches even when the rest of your life is throttling away at full speed. It follows from behind and is bound to catch up—whether you actually peer back and take notice of it or not. And whether it appears as a demon or a dream, a ghost or a nervous breakdown, eventually it will be sitting right beside you, no longer to be avoided.

Ladies and gentlemen, Oliver Levin has now left the building!

I have opened myself up. I am now open. It is as if I were conducting an autopsy on myself for some future coroner's report. I can see right through me—the veins and the arteries, the holes that are anatomically necessary and those that got put there maliciously, or from neglect. It surely would have been better had there not been any holes at all, or had someone graciously come around to fill them up. But that's wishful thinking. Holes are central to human existence. They exist in the atmosphere, and in the heart. You can fall into them and never touch bottom, or you can land on a ledge and wait to be rescued. You can even climb your way out. But at some point some combination of courage, provocation, or internal persuasion insists that you do *something* about that space into which you've fallen. And that's when you have to decide how you feel about salt and stone.

The Golems are drawing me in too deep. That can't possibly be good for me. The same thing is happening with feelings. I am having them—all of them. They are raw and real. And the rediscovery was unrehearsed. I received early admission and advanced placement. Once I started the exercise, I found out I was a true natural at it. There was no need to demo the feelings or to wear a retainer or put on training wheels. I was matriculating all along, but I didn't know it.

Grief. Agony. Loss. Imprisoning rage. Numbing sadness. It had been so long since that last emotional heartbeat. But now it's all there, on the surface, changing the expression of my face, monitoring my mood, all because of an interior world that has come alive. Strange sensations that I thought had died have now been resuscitated—nerve endings given a new beginning, synapses refiring without interference. I am taking baby steps toward life, or perhaps I am going in the other direction, rehearsing the steps of an old person right before death.

If ignorance is bliss and knowledge is sinful, then I am an unholy, born-again sinner. No longer am I ignorant. If anything, I have channeled and downloaded way too much information. Overdosing on a man-made disaster. The circuitry is heating up, about to break, causing a meltdown and a crash. I gave up on lightweight mysteries and directed myself inward, where the real mystery was. The legacy of my family. The losses that can't be counted. The book is not a thriller, not a page-turner, just something you have to sit with, preferably in silence. I am writing it because I have to, and you are reading it for the same reason, although that might not be so obvious to you. The imperative of the bitter pill. It doesn't go down easy, but it does go down, because the soul can't be suckered by a placebo.

You can literally see the world more clearly if you look at it through crying eyes. Humanity comes across in all its dappled complexity. Good and evil are opposites that actually attract. Everything can be observed through a looking glass that is broken, shattered, smashed to the point where it's lost its power to cut—although it could heal. Yet, if you stare too long and never blink, it will eventually take its toll—on the soul, and the sanity. That's when it's time to look away. But you can't. The ghosts won't allow you to. They have set you in front of the screen, captive to endless frames of unwatchable private newsreel, footage that can be neither edited nor ignored.

And when you position yourself that close, when nerves are that raw and exposed, when feelings and emotions rise up with such fury and abandon, you wonder how we can all live with so much loss? How do we do it? Who are we? This species, cursed with feeling too much and not recognizing it as both a contagion and a cure. When will all the ghosts go away?

∽o∾

Before there were ghosts, there was the gun. The one locked in this desk, up here in the study, where I normally conjure up hardened serial killers and cold assassins. I always keep the gun—which I have never pointed or fired—beside me, not for protection or inspiration, but rather good luck. It is a family heirloom, a bequest no doubt intended to remain in the family, and has so remained, whatever is left of it. It is the only household item I took with me from that old apartment in Miami Beach. Thankfully, the police saved the murder weapon. They gave it to me—dusted, examined, and clueless—after having concluded their investigation, successfully eliminating all suspicion. I kept the gun as a souvenir, a memento of my father's farewell. In lieu of a conventional note, this was the message he left behind, for me more than anyone else. A birthright that was both revolver, and silencer.

But some treasures of an estate are clearly meant to be used again. Homburg hats. Cigarette lighters. Pocketknives and watches. Briefcases. If you like the way they feel or fit, you can almost relive the lives of those who once wore them out. The events themselves can get repeated, as if shot out of a revolver. Pop! Pop! But my father's handpiece came with a silencer attachment. Maybe that was the problem all along. A silent gun mutes the ultimate message. A loud bang would have been better.

I am alone with my gun and my broken glass. The central reality of the Holocaust: We are all alone, holding on to some sentimental, sacramental object that we probably don't need but grasp anyway, the illusion of comfort, all the while alone. There is no God who watches over us. Churches and synagogues are not sanctuaries. Families and homes can be lost forever, whether by larceny or atrocity. Governments are surely not saviors, since it is they who supply the unbending rules, the isolating neglect, the uniforms, and the uniformity. The only thing humanity can hope to depend on is the unfailing presence of ghosts—looming and absorbed in our struggles. Because ghosts are no doubt watching, even if their righteous sobs are impotent against the real monsters among us.

We had suspected that this, our inalterable fate, was true all along, but it was hard to face up to until the Holocaust made it finally real. But now there is no reason to doubt or debate the point any further. The optimists have surrendered as sore losers; the cynics, thanks to the Nazis, will forever be hard to dethrone.

And so with the gun tucked away and locked in a box to my right, I examine this mound of broken glass, the size of a small breast, and wonder how its maker could blow life back into it—if that were at all possible. Or maybe what I'm really asking is whether a glassblower would agree to perform mouth-to-mouth on me. The glass that lived under the Hudson for all of those years looks none the worse for it. It has fared better than this author, in fact. Somehow it was preserved even though the marriage for which it had sacrificed itself had long ago become corroded and warped, no more buoyant than a drowning piece of driftwood.

Maybe there is something purifying about those waters that slosh and lap along the clay banks of the Hudson. It can moisten the mud for making a golem, and it can embalm broken glass. Water has always had the capacity to wash away sin and regret, and perhaps in the languid cadences of the sea, hold out the promise of restored life, as well.

Or maybe it's not the water but the Little Red Lighthouse. The world is simply more luminous when the eye can travel through the shafts of its light. Follow the beams and go where the eye will take you. Or perhaps there is something in the bridge itself. The way it connects the cliffs and settles above the currents of busy, unquiet water, inviting cars to cross while it hangs so serenely and majestically high into the air, a marionette of the clouds, the kind of faraway vista that incites a second look.

25

HE WAS NO LONGER BLOCKED, BUT THIS WAS ridiculous. It was as if a former impotent had been allowed to run wild inside an unpatronized cathouse. Perhaps it was better the way it had been before.

Never had Oliver Levin worked this fast on his prior novels, his sentences flowing this freely and feverishly, the story coming together in such an instantaneous explosion of brooding creativity. Normally, when it came to his Gothic mysteries, Oliver could pretty much knock them out as if working from a template. Once he had the plot, the sentences would follow, as if dragged by a leash.

But serious fiction was another animal entirely. Books like these don't get written so quickly. You can't rush them; they come out when they're ready. For Oliver this novel was ready now. Not enough time for a normal delivery. An emergency C-section was required here. The book was in breech. A novel premature in so many ways, even if prodigiously conceived, cut from the placenta and now living on its own.

Here he was, a novice when it came to literary fiction, displaying the output of a one-man publishing house. He wrote *Salt and Stone* in a mere five months, which was no small achievement. Multiple, single-spaced pages got burned into the memory of his hard drive every day; his printer spawned white sheets as if outfitting a Klan rally.

The emotions in the book were relentless, like the whirring lights and bells of a jammed pinball machine. Along the way, he not only stared at the scars, he opened them up wider, peppering salt all over the place, not even bothering to wince from the pain. No internal thought was deemed too personal, no injury too unpleasant to recall. The buried past was now the unself-conscious present. Oliver had become a truth-seeking missile. Like an Oedipus, he wanted to know who had committed the crime, and he wouldn't stop asking even if one day he wound up as the accused. The buttons of his vest were violently snapped and nothing, absolutely nothing, was now kept too close inside.

So, what could make him stop?

That was Evelyn Eisenberg's greatest worry as she sat by her desk, ruminating out the window, occasionally getting up to gaze at the Flatiron Building or look down on Madison Square Park. Yet, no matter how much she changed the scenery, the problem she was having with her most famous client and close friend remained the same. The new novel might actually be brilliant, but its author was in way over his head.

Evelyn's large eyeglass frames dropped down onto the tip of her nose like a face mask. Her hands fidgeted with each other like playful kittens, then reached out to grab some toys of distraction—paperweights, rubber-band balls, rainbow-colored paper clips—that divided the piles of manuscripts on her cluttered desk.

"Why can't he go back to his bread and butter instead of this preposterous, ruinous business with *Salt and Stone*?" she kept repeating, although no one was listening.

She returned to her desk, sat down in the high-backed swivel chair that swung a few degrees clockwise with her in it, and reread the letter, the one she still hadn't faxed over to Oliver yet. There was a basket of similar ones, all with the same discouraging news, that she would have preferred to keep away from him.

March 16, 2000
Evelyn Eisenberg
The Evelyn Eisenberg Literary Agency
15 East 27th Street
Suite 800
New York, New York 10011

Dear Evelyn,

Thank you so much for sending me Oliver Levin's latest novel, *Salt and Stone*. I'm glad you warned me in advance that this wasn't a typical Oliver Levin thriller. But even with the warning, it was not what I had expected.

While I admire Oliver's new sense of direction and all that he is trying to accomplish here, I'm afraid I'm going to have to take a pass on this one. *Salt and Stone* is no doubt an ambitious and worthy book, but in my opinion, it may be too ambitious. The literary, postmodern elements are impressive indeed (who knew he could write this well?), yet I fear that the public will not take to this serious, downbeat although important book, particularly from this author, who has given us so many commercial page-turners over the years. This is a novel essentially about pondering, and not turning pages. How long has it been since readers were interested in that? I just don't see how Levin's audience will respond to this book, and I can't see this book, despite its obvious merits, generating much interest on its own.

Frankly, in my opinion, Holocaust novels don't sell, even a book like this one, which is admittedly a clever, humorous, dark, and heartbreaking post-Holocaust tale. I wish I felt otherwise, but I'm not willing to risk trying to prove myself wrong.

Now, Evelyn, we hope you'll include us in any future submission should Oliver Levin decide to one day return to the genre that made him famous.

And when you do speak to Oliver, please send along my regards, best wishes, and congratulations.

Sincerely,

Murray Dubbin

"So, what's your point?" Oliver asked, having read the letter and now sliding it across Evelyn Eisenberg's desk as if he were playing a game of knock hockey.

"What do you mean, 'what's your point?'" Evelyn responded curtly. "The point is obvious. It's all right there! There is only one point. Everyone I have sent this novel to has rejected it. They are all saying no."

"Every publisher in New York?"

"No, there are other houses, here and elsewhere, but I'm afraid to send it to them. I don't want these rejections to get around town. You are Oliver Levin, after all. You haven't been rejected in years."

"Well, since I'm breaking down, getting rid of old habits, trying out new things, maybe rejection will wind up being good for me, too. I'm sure that's what Ariel would say, anyway."

"So what now, Oliver?"

"Sell the book, Evelyn."

"I don't know if I can."

"Of course you can. You have to."

"Oliver, this is not about you at all. Don't take this personally. It's the material. Nobody wants to read this stuff," she said, pointing at the manuscript with a derisive hand gesture and sour face, as if poison, and not words, were contained between the covers. "It's a new century, and a new millennium. The Holocaust is dead. People want a clean slate. It's over, Oliver. The Nazis won. Nobody wants to read about it, even when it's made into art. They're not buying film rights; no one's writing sequels. The whole subject is too dark and depressing."

"Of course it's too dark and depressing! What do they expect? Happy endings! Mass murder is not for mass markets."

Oliver rose from his chair and moved toward a credenza crowded with pictures. There was one of a New Year's Eve party at the brownstone on Edgar Allan Poe Street. Much happier, mindless, unreflected times. Evelyn was in one of the photos, wearing a top hat painted with gold glitter; a purple noisemaker bursting with confetti was pressed against her lips like a Cuban cigar. Samantha was in the picture, as well, dressed in a man's sport jacket, looking furtive and uncomfortable, like someone who was in the throes of plotting an escape and hated being recognized.

"This is the Holocaust, for Christ's sake!" Oliver ranted. "There's nothing you can do to soften the blow, because the blow was delivered, it happened, and it was a big one. The number-one-ranked atrocity on everybody's list of horribles and achievements. The Holocaust wins hands down. Trumps everything else—Hiroshima, moon landings, polio vaccines, computer chips, Beatlemania. The most lasting memory of the last hundred years, maybe even of all time. You know something about the Holocaust, then you know something about everything."

"Oh, please—"

"It's true Evelyn, no matter what those rejection letters say. The Holocaust is an omnibus curriculum. Manna from the universe. The ultimate tree of knowledge. Food for thought with all the versatility of tofu. It's all there. Psychology, philosophy, theology, chemistry, art, medicine, law. You want to know about life, you want to know about death, you want to know humanity—you want to know inhumanity—you study the Holocaust. You want to know Yiddish; you want to know what happened to Yiddish? It's that simple: The Holocaust is encyclopedic in its vastness and complexity. Breathe in its fumes and you stand a good chance of being a better human being, unlike what happened to those who inhaled the original Zyklon B, and lost everything about what it means to be human altogether."

"So what! Even if you're right, the world doesn't care. People aren't looking for that kind of self-improvement. They're not listening, Oliver, and what's more, they don't want to listen."

"What do you mean? They *have* to listen! I'll make them listen. Evelyn, this story can't just end with me. It has to be told and retold, in many different ways. There have to be more tellers, and many more listeners, because there aren't that many more survivors. . . ."

Oliver's voice was cracking, as if there were a poor line connection somewhere. A few tics had their way with his face. He was perspiring, even though the room was cold. His blue eyes turned momentarily red, severely bloodshot, as if someone had snapped his picture with an inferior flashbulb.

"What's gotten into you?" Evelyn asked with alarmed concern. "This is not normal! I should have left you in the hospital that night after Tavern on the Green for further observation. What's with this Holocaust obsession all of a sudden? A few months ago I swear you didn't even realize you were a child of Holocaust survivors. I think you forgot you were even Jewish. None of it was a big deal. It never came up in your conversation, we never heard a word out of you about concentration camps or smokestacks or barbed wire or train tracks. You never put a Nazi, or even a reference to Nazis, in any of your thrillers. And now look at you. You come in here looking like a ghost, and you bring me this depressing book, filled with all of this Holocaust, suicide, and abandonment imagery. . . . I just don't know what to say." With magnified, worried eyes she stared at her client and yelled, lovingly, "Stop already! It's not healthy."

"I can't stop! Not now. Maybe never. I have to publish this book. They won't let me get away that easy. They'll never let go or leave me alone now that they've found me."

"Who's they? Is there somebody out there who's threatening you? Are you in some kind of trouble with the Russian-Jewish Mafia, those guys from Little Odessa in Brighton Beach? Have they put you up to this? Because if they're the reason this book was written, I'll kill them myself. It's like they've put a hit on your career. I think we should call the DA's office. Don't you have friends there?"

"It's not the mob that's after me, Evelyn."

"Well, then, who?"

"I can't say. You wouldn't believe me if I told you."

Evelyn thought for a moment, and placed her open palm on Oliver's manuscript as if feeling for a pulse, or a premonition. Finally she asked, "This book that you've written here, with all these golems, ghosts, and suicides . . . it's not true, is it?"

"Come on, Evelyn. Even with all that's happening outside in this city, you don't really believe in ghosts, do you?" Oliver rose from his chair, circled around Evelyn's back without her bothering to swivel in his direction, and shrieked, "Boo!"

Oliver's agent didn't flinch.

"Of course you don't believe in ghosts. And neither do I," he reassured her. "The point is, no matter what or who is driving me, the path I'm on, this path," he said, pointing at the stacked pages of his novel, "is the right one, no matter what else happens. I just don't want to be responsible for fighting this battle alone—all by myself. I need help. Most of the really good Holocaust writers are already dead."

"Yeah, I wonder what killed them? I bet it wasn't Auschwitz. More likely it was these manuscripts."

"That's not funny."

"Who's being funny? Oliver, you're playing with fire."

"I know, literally."

Evelyn's voice started to soften. "This all reminds me of what happens on Passover."

"What do you mean?" Oliver seemed startled.

"You know, Passover is all about remembering how the Jews were once slaves in Egypt, building all those pyramids and then finally the Pharaoh sets them free, but not without a fight. There was a little help from the plagues, a temporary drought in the Red Sea, Moses, and of course, God."

"Go on," Oliver urged.

"Okay, here's my point: Every year, in almost every seder I've ever been to, when Jews sit down to read from the Haggadah, more and more of the story gets left out. The Haggadah gets whittled down, digested, like a Cliffs Notes version of the Exodus. I have this theory that most Jews don't know what Passover is about anymore. I mean, other than the most superficial explanation, they can't even begin to tell you what they're doing at the seder. They think it's just another family gathering, like Jewish Thanksgiving, without the corn and the Indians. All they know is some sound bite. Everybody's hungry, they don't have time or interest to listen; they don't know Hebrew, and they want to move on to the latkes and the challah."

"You got it wrong, Evelyn. Latkes are for Hanukkah; and you can't eat challah on Passover."

"Whatever. The point is, this is what happens with history. We sell mattresses in honor of our presidents, we throw barbecues and picnics instead of remembering our workers and veterans—dead and alive. And one day the Holocaust will be just another excuse to sit down with family and have dinner and some disgustingly sweet wine. The best we can hope for is that some Jews will at least have the decency to memorize the sound bite. They'll walk around reciting words and phrases like *Red Sea*, *Mount Sinai*, *Auschwitz*, and *Zyklon B*, but have no idea what any of those things actually mean, because when it comes right down to it, they don't really give a shit."

"I don't believe that."

"Get used to it, Oliver. You already have."

Oliver inhaled a long swallow of air as if breathing for more than one. He searched the room, looking for his imaginary friends—the ones he had concocted for his novel—worried about their feelings, what they would say if they heard what Evelyn had just said. But Evelyn and Oliver were alone. The outside sky grew dark. A full moon had slipped through a crease in the welkin night.

"Latkes and challah," Oliver finally said.

"Yeah, latkes and challah. That should be the name of your next novel. It makes about as much sense as *Salt and Stone*."

26

THE LEVINS WERE NOT ALL THAT KEEN ON FAMILY talks back in the days when they lived in Washington Heights, and later, on Miami Beach. They kept meetings and conversations to a minimum. There were no heart-to-hearts or man-to-mans; no shared secrets or private confessions; nothing that had the formerly umbilical, followed by the occasionally bendable, consistency of a mother-son-father bond. Neither were there any inside family jokes or precious inner-circle moments, the kinds of memories that receive a "you had to be there" smile when repeated years later. In fact, for the Levins, intimacy was so inverted that everything seemed to cling to the extreme margins of outer circles. There was no classified family information, because no actual, pertinent information was revealed among the rank and file. And there was zero risk of blowing anyone's cover, because there wasn't anything other than cover—nothing to contrast with, either in personality or profile. No smokescreens, just smoke.

Oliver's parents had been essentially strangers to him. They were a family that shared physical space but kept their inner lives in solitary confinement. A family that functioned more like roommates, bound by the same surname and a monthly utility bill, and yet divided by an uncommon past and a fierce commitment to remain unclose.

Now that Lothar and Rose had returned to their son as ghosts, they were determined to be a presence in his life, to bond with him in a way that, when he was younger, they would have feared to be disastrous and irresponsible.

"Why should he accept us now, Lothar?" Rose cried, her legs crossed, sitting on top of one of the smiling gargoyles that greeted visitors to the brownstone on Edgar Allan Poe Street. "Who needs dead parents? The time to be a parent is when the child is young, not when he is full grown, has a big house, and a teenage daughter. We can't just knock on his door after all these years and announce that we're ready to do our duty. And certainly not in our present condition."

"We didn't knock, don't you remember, Rose?" Lothar said. "We can walk through walls. That gives us certain advantages over living parents. Besides, we couldn't be parents then. Now we can. Now we know about life. Unfortunately it took a double suicide to teach us all that. We finally have something to offer him other than lessons in death."

But maybe it was too late for that. Ghosts, even those with good intentions, can't change fate. Perhaps they shouldn't be able to. Yes, art offers such redemptive, transformative possibilities. Only in art can the fatally damaged commune with the benevolently dead. But the real world is less amenable to moral lessons. *A Christmas Carol*, for instance, is a fictional story in which ghosts show up and help

Scrooge see his life differently and make amends. But that was a Christian parable. For Jews—a long-suffering people who, biblically speaking, at least, are suspicious of the metaphysics of the afterlife—hands are dealt without dealer interference or divine intervention. The only lessons are life lessons. There are no second acts. No do-overs, mulligans, courtesy shots, or give-me's. Dead people are not allowed to lend a helping hand, even to their own son.

How painful it must have been for Lothar and Rose, brought back by their grandchild but powerless to fix their son. They had finally reached their prime as parents, yet as Lothar had said, it had come too late.

Of course, when they were alive, parenting hadn't been possible. These were people without much confidence in the preservation and continuity of a family. For them the shelf-life of a seed was predictably short. The Nazis could come back. Or there might be new Nazis, or Nazis known by another name but with the same unoriginal, murderous agenda. No reason to get too close to a son who might eventually be taken away. And wouldn't it be reckless and selfish to give him the false sense that parents are forever, that a home is always safe, that there is no such thing as betrayal among friends? What kind of parents would do that to a child? Parents, of course, who lived in a fairy tale, where good witches conquer the bad, where bad apples go uneaten, where magic potions cure everything, where people who sleep forever awaken to find everything just as they had been, or better yet, remarkably improved.

The Levins were of the opinion that the real child abusers were the adults who make believe that this is a once-upon-a-time world of happy endings. Such parents are guilty of inadequate, delusional, lackadaisical preparation. Their children should be removed from their care. The security blankets taken away, the rose-colored glasses surrendered, pitch black accepted as the most primary of colors.

The Levins wanted Oliver to know the truth. Not the Hollywood, candy-coated, feel-good Sunday punch. But the mess, mire, and disarray of all these upended lives. The certainty of random misfortune.

This was the message the Levins wanted their son to understand viscerally in lieu of a suicide note. All that nuanced snubbing and neglect was their way of showing him. And weren't they ultimately vindicated? After all, Oliver did carry on after their deaths. He didn't wilt or melt. In fact, in many ways he thrived.

And even more impressively, if not curiously, he didn't miss them very much either. He just picked up and moved on. Never lost a beat. No tardys or demerits. Unstruck by grief. And isn't that what the world wants from its orphans, its widows and widowers, its shut-ins and hermits, its old maids and cranky old men, and all those who simply can't, or won't, reconcile themselves to what they no longer have, what was cruelly taken away or simply left on its own?

What we all want, what we expect, in fact, are people who can adjust to hardship and heartbreak without complaint or social disruption. Those with the mettle to keep moving, who can reorder their priorities, the kind of borderline type A personalities whose game face is always a stiff upper lip. The celebration of puritanical rectitude; the staid, stoic, self-contained, always-preferred coping strategy for personal crisis. After all, wounded people—the physical cripples, the emotional head cases—make us all feel so uncomfortable. The sad encounters we have with them interfere with our day, leaving us less focused and productive, unable even to eat our lunch. We find ourselves in a bad mood, and they are to blame. And who are they to do that to us? Better they should remain apart, in a ghetto, perhaps, or, even more appropriately, a sanatorium. Let them work out their problems on their own, restore some measure of equanimity before we allow them back among us. Above all, they must be able to function without despair. Is that so much to ask?

Before the arrival of the Golems, Oliver had been a model citizen. He had made a seamless recovery. His troubles were his own. He never showed his scars, didn't even think he had any. Judged by conventional standards, how could anyone not help but admire the job

Lothar and Rose had done with their son? At their funeral he didn't drop even a single tear. There were no better candidates for Parents of the Year.

"Look at him, Lothar, just look at him," Rose pointed from the doorway outside of Oliver's study, on the top floor of the brownstone, right below the attic. He was tapping away at the keyboard of his laptop, oblivious to the whispering of his parents, who were checking up on him from behind.

They were new at this. When Oliver was a boy, there were no rules of the house, no curfews or chores, no parental supervision whatsoever. Now he was too old for them to lay down the law. They couldn't very well ground him (as ghosts, they couldn't even ground themselves) or send him to his room without dinner.

"He is losing himself in that book," Rose whined. "What have we done?"

"He was lost before he started to write that book." Lothar tried to calm his wife. "It's just that now he's lost in a different way, maybe a better way. You can be lost while standing in one place, you can be lost in running away from something, and you can also be lost when you return too soon. He's not lost, Rose," Lothar assured her. "Actually, he is more at home than he's ever been before, even though I agree that he may be overdoing it. He's disoriented because he doesn't recognize what he is now seeing. Our son never thought about where he came from, or looked at the world in this way before. It's going to take some time for his eyes to get adjusted to these new surroundings."

"We should make him stop writing," Rose pleaded. "I am afraid of what this will all come to. The other writers who live here are not good role models for him. We must protect our son."

"Come on, Rose," Lothar said ruefully, "we both know better than that. Parents can't protect their children. Nobody can. The Nazis made that a proven fact."

"Ariel brought us back to rescue her father, our son. Why are we here if that's not what we're going to do?"

"To watch over him. That's all. Everyone needs that, even if in the end it does them no good. We can't save our son. We can only stand by him, which is more than we did when we were alive."

The keyboard on Oliver's laptop was clicking away like an overheated secretarial pool. His fingers seemed to grow large and stubby with each pistonlike stroke. His eyes were dilated like a night owl shining up a forest. His glands released sweat feverishly.

"This family is broken, Rose. We can't fix it. We can only pay better attention this time. And we can hope"—Lothar choked—"we can hope that the next time there is a sunrise, Oliver won't miss it. Because for his entire life, all he's noticed are the blackouts."

Rain was falling outside on Edgar Allan Poe Street, beading up on the windows and then slipping as if it had lost its suction. There were dogs barking at both ends of the block, a canine conversation, spreading neighborhood rumors.

"Should we tell him we are here?" Rose wondered. "I want to try to reach him, to at least push him to take a vacation from that machine."

"Now that he is finally unblocked, I don't think he wants to pause."

"We should invite him to walk over with us to Amsterdam Avenue. We'll have pizza at Freddy's. Tadeusz loves that place. Piotr goes there with the baby carriage."

Lothar rolled his eyes. "How many slices does the stroller order? Besides, it's pouring outside."

"Why do you care? We don't need umbrellas. The water just passes right through us."

"But he's going to get wet!" Lothar pointed pathetically at his son.

"We'll make sure he brings a coat and a hat." Rose laughed. "Isn't that what you mean by watching over him?"

Oliver's parents glided into his study. They moved within inches and each laid a hand on his shoulder, a stealth touch, often hard to know whether they were there at all. Indeed, recognizing their presence required its own talent, a sense more than anything else—but not one of the conventional five.

It didn't matter because Oliver was no longer capable of being startled.

"Oh, hi," he said. "I didn't know you were here. Have you been standing there long?"

"No," Rose said.

"Were you reading over my shoulder?"

"Absolutely not," Lothar said. "What's in that machine is none of our concern."

"I wouldn't say that." Oliver laughed. "You definitely have something to do with this. You live in this book, and in my head. I just can't figure out how you and your friends wound up becoming so real to me." He then pushed the F12 button to save.

"Are we disturbing you?" Rose asked.

"No, I can take a break."

"Good," Rose said, smugly staring at Lothar.

"Would you like to go out with us for some pizza?" Lothar asked. "Just down the corner."

"The three of us?" Oliver asked.

"Of course, like a family," Rose said, "except Ariel is not home. She's at the violin teacher's house. What's her name, Oliver?"

"Tanya. Tanya Green."

"Yes, Tanya Green. She is such a nice girl. Don't you think so, Lothar?"

"Yes, yes, very nice. But what about the pizza? It's time for a nosh."

A family outing, without Ariel. Oliver couldn't recall ever taking many of those when they were in Miami. Back then the Levin version of a nuclear family was missing a nucleus, and yet much could be said of its destructive, subatomic, imploding impermanence. The very center of the family was entirely undemanding and noncommital, so vacuous it could vanish into thin air without anyone giving it a moment's notice.

And yet here he was, going out for pizza with his parents, who were only slightly more substantial than rarefied air. Lothar and Rose

suited up their son, making sure that he wouldn't drown in the tor-
rential pellets of the night's wet weather.

They walked down Broadway. Rusted mesh garbage cans had
overflowed from the day's steady surge of people eating on the run, or
emptying their pockets of flotsam that they had forgotten to discard at
home. Bouncing open umbrellas were moving about, grinding against
one another like go-carts. Standing inside a newspaper kiosk a man
with dark skin the color and grain of dried figs was hauling in the day's
unread *Times*, *Post*, and *Daily News*, not wanting the newsprint to
stream down Broadway like wildcat crude oil. Elsewhere a woman
was struggling with an old Sony Walkman, the tape unraveling like the
libelous loops of a lie detector test. As Oliver and his parents continued
another block downtown, a stray mutt of a dog sniffed away at Oliver's
pant leg, then made whimpering noises as if it understood all the sadness that was attached to that leg. Lothar and Rose reached down to
pet the dog as they all waited for the light to change from red to green.

At the pizza shop Oliver ordered for his parents, despite not
knowing their topping preferences in pizza.

"One spinach with goat cheese," Oliver recited his order, "two
eggplants . . . how about one garlic pesto and . . . one broccoli with
ricotta."

"Ah, you must be hungry, no?" the proprietor, a heavyset man
with a thin black beard and a tenor's stomach, wondered. "That's a
lot of slices for one."

"Yeah, still eating solo."

"Where is little girl?" he asked while scattering toppings on top of
baked, already tomato-, and some white-sauced, dough. "She no
come tonight? She still making music on the street?"

"I don't know about tonight, but yeah, she's still appearing live
outside of Zabar's. You can catch her act almost every afternoon of
the week. You want her to start playing at this venue? Maybe we can
arrange a booking."

Things had changed enormously in pizza cuisine since the days
when the Levins used to order from Sunshine Pizza back in Miami

Beach. Pizza was not a familiar food for Eastern Europeans, so it never did quite become a staple at the Levins' dinner table. But now they sat there, hovering an inch above their seats, eating a couple of slices, seemingly without any worries, unaffected by how much more complicated a simple pizza had become. All those exotic refinements and tony toppings. Pizza triangles floated like paper airplanes, chewed up by invisible, toothless mouths. The slices disappeared without leaving a stain. Merely shadows pointing fingers at each other. The pizzeria owner cradled a telephone against his chin, whispering to someone who probably wasn't his wife. He never did notice that Oliver wasn't eating alone after all. There were deep tomato-red blood blotches collecting on the table right beside the grated Parmesan cheese and the powdered garlic.

Watching his parents eat, Oliver's mind was trapped in a forgotten memory, like an afterthought that comes from having stared too long into a microwave oven. As rare as it was to see his parents eat pizza, it was even stranger to imagine them eating without a knife and fork. Stringy cheese stretching out of a mouth was not how a dignified European wanted to be seen in a restaurant. But there they were, chomping on slices of pizza like a couple of beer-slugging Steeler fans.

Finally Rose spoke. "Oliver, now that you've eaten, there is something we would like to say to you."

"Go ahead."

"Well, we're worried . . . about you."

"What about me? I've never been better."

"You can't live with this pain for the rest of your life."

"The hell I can't! Now that I've found this pain, you want me to give it up? I'm finally willing and able to touch, feel, and sit with all this pain and sadness. I'm reimagining Samantha and why she left. I'm reimagining and re-creating you, and the reasons why you left. You're not really here; I invented you," he babbled while the pizza pie maker glanced over at his customer, who was always strange, but somehow stranger now. "I even invented Ariel's violin. This pain is a gold mine.

What are you here for if not so that I can experience this gift? For the first time I have feelings. I can feel! Do you hear me?" he asked his parents triumphantly.

"Feel!" Lothar retaliated. "What are you talking about? These feelings aren't yours; they don't belong to you. You've taken on the trauma of the gassed and murdered ones, and the survivors, too. You've stolen their feelings. That's all this pain has brought—theft. And what good is that? Go find your own feelings!"

"What your father is trying to say is—"

"What I'm trying to say is that book you're writing can't heal the world, or you. No book can. Not even the two Bibles. Not the Torah or the Koran or the Tibetan Book of the Dead. It's all just words on paper. The enemy of mankind is much larger, and it can't read."

"Tell that to our roommates," Oliver said. "They have more optimism about words."

"If that's what they think, then they're wrong, too. The world has been broken a long time. It can't be fixed, and certainly not with literature. I don't mean to say that the world is coming to an end. I don't believe that at all, no matter how much anger, pollution, and corruption we spill out into the universe. We are a resourceful species, and so is the planet. We adapt. We compromise. We overlook. Our bedrock is solid. But as long as the planet continues to spin and stumble, it's important that those who walk on it keep their balance, that we not try to accomplish too much, otherwise we'll end up disappointed. The world has not been kind to saviors, Oliver. Maybe because in the end, we know that messiahs and magicians offer us nothing but wishful thinking. So don't sacrifice yourself for that book."

"This is what we want you to know," Rose said. "We are proud of what you are writing. We're just not sure why you are writing it, and where it is taking you. Human beings don't need more books. What they need is more humanity."

"Now that you have found us," Lothar said, "you must not hold on too tight. No matter what Ariel wanted, we can't save you. We are a death raft, not lifesavers. No life comes from where we have been."

"But you are here now," Oliver said, "and you have been for many months. Why be so cynical? It is a miracle that you are even here."

"Soul is the stuff you think you can't see but ultimately blinds you the most," Lothar said. "Your daughter may be a real *tzadik* with the kabbalah, but rest assured, those shadows on the wall over there are not ours. There is life for us only in your books. We are not really here, and we are also soon going back."

"I don't understand. What are you saying?"

"That's what you should be writing about, Oliver," Lothar said sagely. "That's the mystery you should be seeking to discover. One day we hope you'll learn this for yourself."

Oliver shook his head as if being slowly slapped around, which the pizzeria owner took to mean that he didn't want any more slices.

Lothar continued, "For you, Oliver, all that trauma of your life is alive in time. It is immediate. It doesn't take much for you to be able to conjure them. Nothing about it is past; it's entirely present. It is so easy to access your flashbacks. Just reach out and recall them. But they're not really there. They're just demons without masks. Unfortunately they are too familiar, and addicting, but you have to try to make them go away."

"It's all too painful."

"We know. It must be," Rose said. "You were born with terror in your blood."

"Medical laboratories don't test for that kind of thing," Lothar said. "We gave you this disease, after the Nazis gave it to us. But it is not part of our family's genetic code. It is not like eye color or finger-prints. This you can change."

"I don't know," Oliver said, his hands making fists around two cans of seltzer. "Too much has happened, and . . . not happened."

"Yes, this is true," Lothar said.

"Salt and stone," Oliver murmured to himself.

"You should not look back so much," Lothar said. "It will only make you feel worse. It's good to do sometimes, but not always. That book may have put you on the right path, but you are now traveling on it too fast and far in an extreme direction. You are playing with fire, just like your daughter, the kabbalist."

"I thought you weren't reading over my shoulder?"

"Maybe just a peek," Lothar said.

"Put the book down, Oliver, and then put it away for a while. You need to do it for Ariel," Rose said. "She deserves a better future, not one clouded by all that European smoke. Give her some fresh air. There is still time—for both of you."

"There is so much I can't give her," Oliver acknowledged. "That's why she called for you. This family is grossly undermanned. I know what it means to not have grandparents around. I didn't have any either. Surviving the Holocaust must be only a Pyrrhic victory. You live on, but without relatives. I don't know how you did it."

"We didn't," Lothar said. "The synagogue suicide was our way of saying, *Enough. We give up, too. We now join those whom we once loved.*"

"But we gave up our son in order to do it," Rose said tearfully. "Shame on us! Oliver, you are wrong about Ariel. You are very wrong. She didn't do this for herself. She did it for you. Yes, she wants grandparents, but she wants a father more. Listen to what I am saying."

But Oliver couldn't. For so many reasons he just couldn't. And then, adding to all the interior static that interfered with what his mother had just said, came yet another sound, that of a klezmer violin, coursing down the avenue, tracking down and shadowing the father of the neighborhood's resident streetside soloist.

27

 IF YOU CAN MAKE A GOLEM IN YOUR ATTIC, THEN why not at Carnegie Hall? That's what I was thinking on the night I made my debut as a soloist—this time indoors on a stage rather than on the street in front of a fish shop. Even while playing solo, I was far from alone. Carnegie Hall was packed with a full house, as if it were a Yo-Yo Ma premiere. But I had plenty of my own backup, although none were musicians.

The whole thing was so cool and crazy. I mean, just a few months ago I couldn't even play the violin, or maybe I always could, but I never tried, so I never knew about this talent I had. They called me this pied piper with strings, but they didn't know the half of it. It wasn't kids who were following me around, but ghosts. And they were coming to the concert, too.

The next thing I know, I was booked at Carnegie Hall as part of this World Music Youth Concert. Not only that, I was the last performer on the program; the one who closed out the show. The final act. The main attraction. The last sounds the audience would hear that night would come from my violin—or so I thought.

This wasn't Zabar's anymore. This was a real music hall, not some street corner where I serenaded customers who were counting their change after buying bags of freshly ground coffee, blueberry farmer cheese, and rugelach. I was playing in one of the finest concert halls in the world. The same place where Dvořák's Symphony No. 9 had its debut, where Mark Twain, Winston Churchill, Albert Einstein, and Amelia Earhart once spoke, where Rachmaninoff, Caruso, Prokofiev, Toscanini, Stravinsky, Gershwin, Duke Ellington, Isaac Stern, Billie Holiday, Frank Sinatra, Bob Dylan, the Beatles, and the Rolling Stones all performed.

I don't know who most of those people even are. I read their names off one of the signs in the lobby. All right, I know about the Beatles and the Stones, but still, what was I doing appearing in the same place?

Big things could happen at Carnegie Hall. I wasn't thinking musically, as a way to advance my career, but kabbalistically, to bring her back, to make us whole again. In such a famous setting, where so many legendary singers and musicians have played, where all sorts of amazing sounds once bounced off these walls and soared up into the balconies, maybe in a place of such magic and majesty you can bring back the dead, or the missing.

From backstage I could see where Oliver was sitting. He was in the third row, dressed in a shiny tuxedo without a cummerbund, but still looking uncomfortable. There were eight seats right next to him, a "reserved" sign on each chair in case anyone thought they were vacant. When the show started, the signs remained on the red velvet, even though the seats were taken—but not by full-bodied members of the audience. The seats were down, and I could see the Golems, with their programs on their laps, staring up at the stage, all beaming like proud grandparents, even though only two of them actually were.

They had all dressed up for this special night: each in smoothly pressed tuxedos, with stiff, ruffle-fronted shirts, top hats that they never took off their heads, and patent leather shoes. The people sitting behind them could see right through the hats, and the heads, so it didn't matter. Jerzy had a long tail attached to his jacket, and his bow tie was red, whereas the other Golems all wore basic black. There was also a breastplate over his shirt, as if he were a tenor in some Italian opera, and a red feather taped on to the side of his top hat. As for Rose, she wore a long black gown with silver studs and costume jewelry that clung to her body like jellyfish.

I had made them all promise that there would be no fireworks on this night, nothing like what happened at Rockefeller Center, the way they were skywriting high above the Christmas tree, or at B'nai HaNeshama, with the levitating Torahs, or at other places around Manhattan where they made their presence so magically known.

I even asked Piotr to leave the stroller back at the brownstone.

"But I take it everywhere I go." He whined a bit before finally giving in.

This was supposed to be my night; that's how I explained it to them all. They've had their fun with Manhattan—bringing order; doing away with tattoos, cigarettes, and smoke; clearing the air, inspiring people to be nicer to each other, making it possible for everyone to believe in God again, or at least something higher than the World Trade Center. But I didn't want them, or any of their high-jinks, to mess with my latest experiment.

I had plans, and they weren't just about playing the violin. But to do it right I needed to be able to concentrate, not just on the notes and chords, but also the numbers, the incantations—that's what it took the last time. The clay sculpture was not going to be enough. I needed an extra boost from someplace. Luck wouldn't hurt either.

There was so much to remember that night that I had to remind myself that I was giving a concert, too. Everyone else had come to hear the music—music from all over the world. Played by kids my age. As far as I knew, or from what I read on the wall in the lobby, there never had been any science experiments at Carnegie Hall. That's not what Einstein did there. But I was a versatile double threat as a performer, like a dancing bear who could also play the kazoo at the same time.

The good thing was that my playing of the klezmer violin was completely based on instinct, or something like that, and it wasn't like I had to think about it so much. I just got up there and slid the bow back and forth, up and down, my fingers pressing down on strings and scaling the frets as if I was reading braille, my body bent forward, and music pouring out on random play. I tried to explain to Ms. Green that her lessons were pointless. The more I thought about what she was teaching me, the more confused I became. The music was inside me. It was all ready to come out; I just needed to hold on to the violin, not let go, and start stroking. It was best for me to just play the violin my way—or whose ever way it was.

But as for my other talent, as a golem performance artist, there I could have used real lessons. Hebrew school is not enough of an education. You can't learn how to make this kind of thing over the Web. Nobody can walk you through it. And you're supposed to be a lot older before you can dabble in the kabbalah. I was lucky the first time. But maybe the odds were running against me now. Maybe I should have quit while I was still ahead.

The Peruvian *queña* panpipe player was amazing. So was the kid from Greece who was strumming this fretted, lutelike instrument called a bouzouki, which made the sound of Turkish melodies with Near Eastern church chords. There was a young African boy from Zambia who was thumbing away on his *kalimba*, a piano slab on wood with metal slats that you ping with your thumb. One of my favorite performers was the Australian Aborigine kid who was blowing on a didgeridoo, a long tube that made a deep, low, overtone sound, a lot like a rain forest. A Chinese girl was playing a *sheng*, which is a cylindrical mouth organ. And there was a dark-skinned boy playing an *oud*, an Arabic fretless lute with a round back and short neck. A tall blond-haired boy from Norway was strumming on a Hardanger fiddle, which had double sets of strings, one on top of the other, with strange meters and melodies that they use for Scandinavian dancing. A girl with red hair and about my age was playing a Hungarian *gardon*, which is a folk cello carved out of wood with only one string, in a duet with a boy hitting away on a cembalom, which is a harp played on its side and struck with tiny padded hammers. There was a girl from China on an *er-hu*, a one-string fiddle played on the lap like a tiny cello. There was a steel drummer from Trinidad. And a girl playing an Indonesian gamelan. And a prodigy on the Indian tabla.

The audience was in love with all of these unusual but beautiful sounds from all over the world. Act after act I waited, until it was my turn on stage. I wasn't really nervous at all. Maybe because I had faith in the music. It was only the mystical portion of my performance that I was a little worried about.

"You're on after this young girl from Malaysia, Ariel," Tanya Green said. We were each allowed to have one adult backstage with us, and I knew that Ms. Green would want to be the one standing beside me. She was dressed in a sleek, tight black jumper with sapphire-studded earrings. She looked like she was going out to an East Village punk bar after the concert. Her hair was combed out straight and long, as if the curls had been teased right out of their coils. "You're not nervous, are you?"

"No."

"Piece of cake," Ms. Green said. "Just like Zabar's, right? Except here, I'm sorry to say, at Carnegie Hall, nobody is going to drop coins inside your violin case."

"That's not the only difference," I predicted, and then said nothing further.

With my head in the clouds high above the acoustically friendly roof of Carnegie Hall, I heard my name called and made my way out onstage.

"Our final performer this evening," began the master of cere-
monies, a silver-haired man with the kind of stuttering body language and grandfatherly face that sells aspirin on television, "is
someone who has become very special to us all who live right here in
New York. In fact, she is the only performer this evening from the
United States, but those of us who have heard her play before know
that she is even more local than that. She normally plays her violin
on the streets of the Upper West Side of Manhattan. It is the music of
the Jewish shtetl, and even though most New Yorkers are not
Jewish, we have all, through this young lady's violin, been taken
back to a place, a home, that seems familiar to each of us."

The New Yorkers in the audience all closed their eyes, then
returned for a reassuring sneak peek before the actual music began.

"So, on behalf of Carnegie Hall and the producers of the World
Music Youth Concert, I am very proud to present to you the klezmer
violin stylings of Ariel Levin."

With the violin and bow in my hands, I walked to the center of
the stage, freaked out at the standing ovation, curtsied like someone
who had never done that move before, which I hadn't, and waved at
Oliver, who was already standing, clapping, and waving back. My
grandparents, along with Primo, Paul, Jerzy, Tadeusz, Piotr, and Jean,
were all flying through the air like a meteoric trapeze act. Carnegie
Hall has three balconies and a really high ceiling, so there was a lot of
legroom for ghosts to air it out and show their appreciation. After a
few minutes the audience settled down. While they were still cheer-
ing, I rushed backstage to get my props.

"What are you doing?" Ms. Green said, shocked and annoyed.
"They're still applauding. Go back out there and get ready to play."

"I forgot something."

"What did you forget? You're only playing one instrument. Wait,
don't tell me you're a prodigy with others, too. I won't be able to
take any more surprises."

I scooped up what I came looking for and then walked back
onstage. The audience was now quiet, and so I began to put together

my backup group. I took twelve small glass jars filled with *yortzeit* candles out of a box and arranged them in a large circle with me in the center of it. Then I lit each one, making a ring of fire—like a stage within a stage. The audience was curious, since this was supposed to be a musical performance and I hadn't started playing yet, although I seemed to be pretty busy anyway. Then I took a clay doll dressed up in old baby clothes and a white floppy hat, seated it in a tiny Adirondack chair, and also placed it inside the circle of *yortzeit* flames.

I still wasn't done setting up the scene. I ran back offstage with everyone still seated, craning their necks, and looking at me like I was crazy. The stage manager, the MC, and the concert's producers all waved at me to get back out there and start playing like they were some Formula One pit crew on the final lap. But I wasn't going anywhere until I found the box, which I dragged out onto the stage. From inside it I removed a bunch of pictures and scattered them all around the circle, along with a Frisbee and a piñata in the shape of a dragon that I made myself (copied from what it looked like in a picture) and hand-painted green with a red heart on its chest. Finally, I reached in and carefully took out a big glass bowl. Inside the bowl was a gleaming mound of broken glass.

The whole sight—me, the *yortzeit*s, the golem doll, the dragon, the photos, the broken glass, and of course the unplayed violin and bow—must have made for an unusual presentation for this, or any other, concert at Carnegie Hall. I was trying to create a mood for my music. Not so much for a klezmer concert, but a performance séance—all with the goal of bringing on a resurrection.

Surrounded by a ring of *yortzeit* lights and my latest Hudson River mud sculpture, along with personal mementos that I hoped would lure her back, I wanted her to hear me and to recognize me, if only she knew how much we needed her. But there was one other missing link, probably the most important part of the experiment. The music. And so I began to play "Invitation to the Dead"—over and over, changing the tempo, tapping my feet, whispering her name out loud, leaning my body toward the stage floor, crying on the shoulder of my already warped violin. The audience applauded, the *yortzeit* flames danced, the golem doll shook on its chair as if it had been jolted by electricity, which it very well might have. Because even inside the cavernous tomb of Carnegie Hall, we could hear what was pounding outside. The thunder sounded as if it was coming more from within the building than out, booming much louder than all the percussion instruments had managed to produce on stage that night combined. And the crushing noise was all followed by blankets of lightning that looked like it was going to split the ceiling and reach down to carry me and my show up to some other, more celestial house of music.

Carnegie Hall was quaking, the large hanging flags outside the building were being whipped around like underwear on a clothesline during a hurricane. All the while I kept playing "Invitation to the Dead." And it was received loud and clear. And then, finally, the house, stage, and interior lights in Carnegie Hall all went dark, except for the twelve *yortzeit* flames that were still burning bright. The audience gasped; I kept playing. Maybe there was a short in the wires, or in the heavens. No one knew, or ever bothered to tell me. The blackout was probably caused by the thunder, but who brought that on? They say that the heavy-metal thunderstorm was heard and felt nowhere else in Manhattan other than on West Fifty-seventh Street, directly above Carnegie Hall. Everywhere else the skies were clear.

And while technicians were searching for fuse boxes and the audience was busy catching its breath, I never stopped playing my music. The *yortzeit* candles put a shine on the golem, and on the pictures of my mother, and cut right through the broken glass from my parents' wedding.

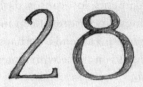

28

OLIVER BEGAN TO SEE THAT HE HAD WRITTEN
the Golems into a horror to end all horror stories. What's worse, to have seen it all and survived, or surviving only to see it all happening
again? Not an exact replica, but a second-tier
substitute, the condescending, degrading spectacle of trampled memory.

The Golems started to look more closely at the world—the one
they were now inhabiting, the one they had hoped to improve.
There were some undeniable measures of success, but after a while
they didn't like what they began to see. Ghosts are by nature fussy,
honest, and self-aware. Death does that to you. It brings about a clarity and an integrity that the living only pretend to have. And so with
candor and resignation, the Golems conceded there was a limit to

what they could accomplish on the Upper West Side and beyond. It was all much too much. There were only eight of them, and billions of problems, unjust judgments, lost causes, dashed hopes, permanent insults, wounded feelings, open sores, deep indignities, and slapped faces for which there were no amends. Perhaps it was all a lost cause from the very beginning. Even those with a messiah complex are also waiting for the Messiah.

But it was more than that. Human beings were now living in a new century, and millennium, but some of the outrage that once caused the Golems to take their own lives decades earlier was still very much present. Of course, the degree and manner of the effrontery had changed. It was less violent, and lethal, but dehumanizing and destructive nonetheless. The crime here was one of disrespect. And the list had lengthened, as if it had been replenished and fortified, as if everyone was dying to see the new and improved model. The world was without shame or decency, and for that the Golems had no cure.

It was all about reduction. Turning the sacred into the trivial. Chopping down awe until it was rendered meaningless, finally descending into sacrilege. The language became one of indifference; the vocabulary was supplied by neglect.

There was still Holocaust denial. That would never go away. Slavery, disease, hurricanes, earthquakes, race riots, murder, political and sexual revolutions, drug overdoses, poverty, corruption, scandal, assassinations (of both body and character)—all of those tragedies, calamities, and upheavals have taken place at one time or another on this planet, but the genocide of six million Jews continued to be a debatable bone of contention. Surely no one doubted that the Armenians, Cambodians, Rwandans, Bosnians, and Kosovars all were casualties of genocide in this century, but the Jews . . . well . . . they made it all up. It didn't happen to them. And if it did happen, then it wasn't as bad as they say. And if it was as bad as they say, then they must have deserved it somehow, otherwise why would anyone have unleashed such savage fury against innocent people?

This is what the world began to say about what had once been a singular, sacrosanct, epochal event. The number wasn't six million, but something far less. Any number less than six million proves that the Jews were lying all along. Nobody died in the camps, but only, if at all, in the ghettos. And if they died—which they didn't—but if they did, it wasn't from murder, but rather from starvation. Oh, and one more thing: There were no camps. And there were certainly no such things as gas, or ovens, or smoke. The Germans didn't intend to kill anyone; it was all a mistake. And if it wasn't a mistake, then it was a left-wing, socialist Zionist illusion. Nobody gave an order; everyone gave orders. Everyone was in charge; everyone followed orders. People acted on their own, but most didn't act at all. There was no one to blame because everyone was involved, but everyone was also completely innocent. Such are the consequences of living in a time of chaos. There are going to be accidents, and everyone is given undiplomatic immunity, which comes with either a license to kill or free admission to watch. No one did anything morally wrong, because there was no morality. Right and wrong had traded places, a shell game with empty shells, three-card monte without faces or suits, a bait-and-switch where it was impossible to know which was which.

Who could really judge anyway?

They used to call it revisionism, with a dash of moral relativism, but those were far too fancy words to describe simple hate. What these people wanted was not a different way of looking at the same thing, but rather erasing the thing itself, pretending that it never existed, that it was all a conspiratorial dream, without truth, without living texture, without coffins or Kaddish. You could bring the deniers to trial, have them unmasked and bankrupted, but, like locusts, their numbers and their hate were limitless even if their finances were not. They would keep coming back, printing mimeographed neo-Nazi books held together by staples and Scotch tape; their sentences written in red, the words misspelled.

And what they couldn't accomplish with crayon and coloring

books, or through the hard-porn virus that crept onto the World Wide Web, there was always the marching boot and the robotic, impulsive, reflexive, reverse-lever salute—an indispensable gesture for people who can't go a single day without trying to *heil* somebody. Impossible as it was for the Golems to imagine, there were still people in the Western world who wore their hearts on their sleeves in the shape of a swastika. Wouldn't you just know it, the Jews and the blacks, the Asians and the Slavs, all the subhumans were still responsible for all that was wrong in the world. They had to be stopped, resettled, eliminated, and gassed. Could someone please finally come up with a foolproof final solution guaranteed to work this time?

In the United States, there had been middle and high school curricula devoted to the study of the Holocaust. Whether it was for an entire semester or a short unit, young people were getting some classroom exposure to the single biggest atrocity of the past century. There were readings of Elie's *Night* and Primo's *Survival in Auschwitz*. And of course Anne Frank's diary was always a trusted classroom staple, like recess after lunch. *Schindler's List*, the movie, had become required viewing, with all its good-guy-triumphs-over-bad-guy sanctimony, its ultimate feel-good imperatives, its insulting inversion of contrasting truths. The Holocaust isn't about the fortuitous rescue of twelve hundred Jews at the hands of a repentant, benevolent German. That story line has mass appeal, but the Holocaust is about mass death. It may not do as well with test audiences, but it is the unsentimental grand narrative of why there is a severe shortage of Jews on the European continent. Some stories are morally entitled to be told in a certain way or not at all—even if unappealing, even if the world won't buy it.

In time the students and teachers, the principals and the parents, grew weary of all these genocidal statistics and images. It had become too depressing to digest as a steady diet, even in its diluted, sanitized, sugar-coated recipe. No one had been treated to the real thing, and yet everyone somehow found the low-cal substitute to be too filling.

Schools stopped teaching it and discussing it, or even mentioning it during passing conversations on the way to something else. In colleges throughout the country, classes on the Holocaust were removed from the course catalogs. And in towns and municipalities, hate-speech laws were expunged from the books. Holocaust resource and documentation centers disappeared nearly as fast as they had been erected, no sturdier than foreclosures on a Monopoly board. So too did all of those nicely landscaped, architecturally ambitious Holocaust memorials. Cities argued passionately, and civically, that they needed the public space for parking lots and condos. There were all sorts of budget cuts and shifts in public opinion, changed fashions and retooled political agendas. Everyone began to concede that morals and memory can't be mandated. You can't legislate people into being more virtuous. And nothing should interfere with progress.

But progress is all about marching forward, that undeviating, unconflicted, headlong, and mindless forward thrust, while memory, and its moral imperatives, are only concerned with looking back. Forgetting is the easiest and most tempting of human enterprises; no one needs to be reminded to forget. It can be done at one's leisure; the couch potato's guide to conscience and morality. The Holocaust, which had once been front and center, slid out of sight into the upper-deck margins of cultural obscurity.

And this is what replaced it. Swastikas spray-painted on synagogue walls. Jewish cemeteries treated to fresh coats of graffiti. Desecration was everywhere, an infectious, untreatable disease, but they didn't call it that. Deniers got good seats right next to Jerry Springer, Sally Jesse, and Leeza, while survivor testimonies rotted away in dusty, airless archives—unseen, unread, unheard. The propaganda of hate became unchallenged, common knowledge.

Hollywood, and all of its bar-mitzvah-boy moguls, decided that the Holocaust was less sacred, and more profitable, than they had once originally thought. A movie made by an Italian clown in which Auschwitz was depicted as no more threatening than a circus became popcorn for emotionally desensitized audiences. Such a brilliant marketing ploy to suck in audiences with the promise of sentimentality that could rot your teeth, comedic sight gags that require absolutely no intelligence, and of course, an absurd feel-good ending. From now on the two greatest false advertisements about the Holocaust are *Arbeit Macht Frei* and *Life Is Beautiful*. When it came to the camps, neither was true.

The Holocaust was now a legitimate, moneymaking commodity, even though almost everyone had lost interest in it as a subject for serious study. The Holocaust Memorial Museum in Washington, D.C., had become a popular tourist attraction on the strength of its high-tech visual gadgetry and flawless air conditioning. It wasn't clear whether anyone was learning anything useful to take back home with them to Kansas.

"Hey, Mom," a little boy could be heard saying. "I think that's a picture of Himmler on that wall over there."

"That's nice," the mother replied, "but we're late for the pandas at the National Zoo. Let's just go and buy a hat or a key chain in the gift shop and then we can leave. It's too depressing, and we've seen enough. I think I understand the Holocaust now."

"But I want to play with the computer upstairs!" the child whined. "I think there are video games on it. And there's a real cattle car up there, too!"

"Stop crying this instant!" the mother scolded. "And don't let go of my hand. I don't want you to get lost in a place like this!"

When did indifference and amnesia begin to rule the world, or was it always this way?

There is such contempt for silence even in the presence of what should otherwise produce awe. The Holocaust is still the greatest secret of all, but the time would come when no one would be searching any longer for the clues. Maybe that's because the human impulse to claim that all mysteries have been solved is quite strong. It doesn't take much: A visit to a museum, the reading of one book, sitting through a single film, one dinnertime conversation, and it has all been digested, mastered, and taken in—and then we're on to the next thing. Humanity is all about rebuilding, all in the process of evolving—one seamless march forward, no matter who gets trampled underneath. And yet the most consistent but detested movement of them all is the unsurrendered retreat, the chastened doubling back to the unsolved crime scene.

Wasn't there supposed to be some kind of new covenant? Not between God and Abraham, but this time between the Jews themselves? And this was the deal: As long as there were survivors, there would be memory. The world would not, could not, forget. Continuity and renewal depended on it; decency demanded it even more. But instead this new covenant was ultimately breached, just like the old one. The sky continued to cast long shadows of broken promises, all from a horizon that gave up on offering even a glimpse of faith and trust. The whitewashing of history, the distortions of truth, the disacknowledging of pain. It is a crime that ruptures the heavens and sends the gods into an even more remote hiding spot.

Maybe this all would have happened sooner or later, but it would have happened eventually. It's just that for the Golems, newly arrived and naive, it was all happening now. Their patience had worn out just like everything else on them. They simply couldn't tolerate any more. After all, it had all taken place on their watch. And for this there was no forgiveness, no good reason to look the other way.

29

THE WORLD YOUTH MUSIC CONCERT AT CARNEGIE Hall had been an electrifying event, power outage and all. Most people in the audience, in fact, believed that the lightning, thunder, and blackout were all part of the act, purposely choreographed in some grand, show-stopping finale typical of a New York premiere. World music, no matter how scaled down at its inception, requires lavish, expensive, production numbers to impress a New York audience. Every dramatic or musical performance on a New York stage has to be an interactive triple threat, combining special effects, metafireworks, and fancy production values. Spectacle is everything. The surrounding noise—the bells and whistles of Broadway—is generally more important than the music itself.

As it turned out, the most exotic music of the evening came from an electrical charge fired out of Ariel Levin's klezmer violin—the kind of music you can both hear and see.

This is how the *Daily News* reported it the next day in a tabloid headline no one could miss on an eye chart: KLEZMER PRODIGY LIGHTS UP, THEN BLACKENS, CARNEGIE HALL.

The story mentioned how the concert had gone smoothly but then the local klezmer sensation, the final act of the evening, armed with alien accoutrements, commanded the stage and brought the house, and the lights, down.

Other media reported the story, as well, capturing the spirit and talent of the performances and the freakishness of the night's conclusion. Yet all of them had missed the real story. The true highlight of the evening was what had occurred in the dark when almost everyone had already lost sight of what was on stage. Ariel's performance didn't stop simply because she couldn't see, or because no one was watching her anymore. The most spectacular part of the show wasn't a musical experience at all but rather a nocturnal, mystical, metaphysical one. The fiddle, and the surrounding fire, had given life to yet another member of the family who had long been dead. Such a revelation would have been too much for a mortal audience to grasp, even one that had gotten pretty used to having golems around.

Ariel's father wasn't the only one of her parents in the audience that night. Samantha, Ariel's mother—materializing, shaping, breathing in her daughter's wishes and supernatural air supply—was there, too.

The next evening Ariel, Lothar, and Rose approached Oliver carefully. They had spent all day rehearsing what they were going to say. In some ways he should have been prepared for the news. After all, these past few months should have warmed him up to the idea that the spiritual world is much nearer than you think. And yet Oliver's parents and his daughter realized that the return of an AWOL wife would produce even a greater shock than the homecoming of his dead parents and their similarly once-suicidal friends.

"Oliver," Rose began, "we need to talk to you. We have something important to say."

"Another family meeting?" Oliver wondered apathetically. "Whatever it is, why don't you just let me find out on my own this time?"

Oliver was in the kitchen, clanging pots and pans, upending bottles and jars, searching for some kind of frosted breakfast cereal. His head was plunged thoroughly inside a cabinet. The freedom he had been experiencing at the keyboard had emancipated his appetite, as well. Most days his body worked up a sugar rush that couldn't be appeased by candy bars alone.

"Actually, yes," Lothar said. "The family is getting even bigger."

"Why's that?"

"Dad," Ariel said, slowly, emphatically, knowing that if she addressed him as Dad rather than as Oliver, he might pay more attention, "we really need to speak to you."

"What is it, Ariel?"

"Mom's home."

"Funny. Real funny. Let's get something straight around here: You're the klezmer violinist and kabbalist, and I'm the fiction writer in this house. If there're going to be any make-believe stories, then I'll be the one dreaming them up."

"It's true, Oliver," Rose said.

"What can we say?" Lothar laughed. "It is yet another kabbalah miracle. Lightning has struck twice with your daughter."

"Samantha? Here? In this house?"

"Where else but in this house?" Rose replied.

"What do you mean?" Oliver asked.

"This is the house of the dead," Rose said.

"And she is one of us, son," Lothar said.

"Where is she? How did she get here?"

"She didn't arrive by taxi or car service," Rose said. "That's for sure."

"She's a ghost, Oliver," Ariel said. "Mom's a golem, too."

"What? How could that be?"

"I brought her back the same way. That night at Carnegie Hall. When I was playing, the whole time, that's what I was thinking of. I thought about it for weeks. That's one of the reasons I even did the show. That's why I had all of those props up on stage with me— *yortzeit* candles, pictures of Mom, and a golem doll that I dressed up in my old baby clothes, because I knew Mom would remember me that way, because that was when she was still my mother. And that song I was playing, "Invitation to the Dead." That's how I did it up in the attic the first time. I made a different golem sculpture, and I used different props, and I said different incantations, and I got new *yortzeit* candles, but the music and the feelings were the same. I wanted to make it happen all over again."

"She's alive again," Lothar said, "but only in the same way that we are."

"I didn't know she was dead." Oliver panted.

"We did," Rose confessed. "We know such things about our kind. We just didn't know how to tell you."

"And you knew?" Oliver asked Ariel.

"No, I just wanted to bring her back—in any way I could. I found out the same way you did."

"Where is she? I want to see her."

"Maybe you should wait a little, Oliver," Rose said. "Give it more time to sink in."

"That's a good idea," Lothar added.

"No, right now. Ariel, where's your mother?"

Ariel sought her grandparents' counsel, searching their worrisome eyes, then made her own decision. "Up in the attic."

Oliver pushed through the swinging kitchen doors and bounded the stairs two steps at a time. On the top floor he pulled down the ladder, climbed up, poked his head through the square portal, and, in the dark, like a periscope, circled the room to find his wife.

"Samantha? Are you up here?"

The only light in the attic came from a moon a few notches short of full, aided by a cloudless sky and some slippery, furtive beams from a corner street lamp. The red velvet blackout curtains and blinds were undrawn above the window.

"Sam?" Oliver said, his voice breaking, the beats of his heart clattering against his chest.

"I'm here, Oliver," a voice came from the Ark. "I'm home."

Oliver aimed himself at the Ark that was empty of Torah yet not without treasures. With each step, he felt as if he had been caught in some vortex of golem gravity, yanking him toward whatever was in the Ark, as if he could stop walking altogether and still make up the distance. He didn't know whether what he was being drawn to was actually his wife, and yet although he couldn't see her, he felt no fear, and he couldn't resist her, either.

"Don't be afraid," Samantha reassured him.

Oliver then realized that it was unmistakably her voice, the same tone and intonation—soft, unassuming, retiring, almost withdrawn, the kind of voice that needs to conserve itself before attempting that very next syllable, a voice with no aspirations for the final word. Not all voices are capable of returning from the dead, but maybe Samantha's voice, so inactive in life, had that kind of EverReady ambition. A long-distance voice. Patient. Persevering. Assertive when it has to be. Perhaps that's how voices from the dead find their way back to their loved ones. Gradually, without much fanfare, a walkie-talkie for the family who can't get past the grief and the silence.

Oliver considered the possibility that what he was hearing was nothing more than a voice in his head. Maybe there was nothing behind that curtain after all. As much as he wanted to see Samantha, the sound of her voice was already proving too much. Everything lately was all too much.

"Almost there, Oliver. A few more steps."

As he neared, she floated from behind the Ark and appeared before him, caught in the shadowy beam of an urban nightlight— Oliver's missing dead wife.

"Samantha—it's you."

Oliver shuddered, his breath reversing itself, going backwards, choking on the exhale like swallowed pride. The shock that registered in him was not from having seen a ghost. It was the fact that she had reappeared in any form—dead or alive, body or soul, ghost or golem. It had been more than a decade since he had last seen her in the flesh. But now he didn't need flesh—the spirit was plenty on its own.

Samantha had not aged. The Golems were all cryogenic creatures—preserved, not in ice, but in time. Yet since the visions were seen through Oliver's eyes and imagination, his memory wouldn't yield the remote control, restoring and rearranging the images as he perhaps wanted to see them. Maybe Ariel, in the way she looked at Samantha, was seeing something else altogether: the vision of her mother fixed in the mind of a toddler.

Her hair was still long and blond. Unmarked, unlined face; the skin translucent, yet with color, as if the soul's inner glow overcame the cadaverous exterior, lighting up the body in its own way. Her pale blue eyes were gemstones in the darkness. Roving eyebrows. Her movements had a levitating bounce to them, a jerky, desperate need for some kind of horizontal hold.

"You're here," Oliver said, his face mostly in silhouette. "I don't get it. . . . What's going on?" •

"Ariel brought me back."

"I know that. But from where?"

"You know where, Oliver. Don't make me say it."

"Where did you go? What happened to you? You left this place, and it's been so empty ever since."

"I know that. But I've brought something back for you. I should have never taken it in the first place."

"Tell me what happened. Please."

Fearless but tentative, Oliver edged closer to his wife. He hadn't yet reached out for her or tried to bring her near. Embracing the dead had its limitations. There is nothing to latch onto, just the wrapping of arms around luminescent air.

"I had to leave you. I couldn't stay here anymore."

"Why?"

"This house was haunted."

"Not then! Maybe now . . . , definitely now, but not then."

"No, it was haunted then," Samantha said knowingly. "Now, after all these years, it's finally unhaunted. You just can't tell the difference yet."

"What are you talking about? There was nothing wrong with this house back then when you lived in it."

"Oliver, that's not true, of both the house and me. This was a broken family long before I came along and made it worse. It was a house built on the ruins. Millions of dead Jews, a silent childhood, and two parents who ended their lives by suicide. No matter how many murder mysteries you wrote, you couldn't solve the big, unsolvable one that we lived in."

"We were happy here. I was happy. We started a family. There was a future for us in this house."

"No, you were just painting over a bad, corroded foundation. It was all bound to eat away at you one day. You can't move forward until you get a good look at where you come from. And you never did that. For you the Holocaust, the way your parents died, the reasons why they might have done it, was something to be buried. The deeper the better. But that just doesn't work. What you buried was still very much alive. This brownstone was like 'The Telltale Heart.' The walls were beating with the sounds and memories of the undead long before the Golems arrived. At least now it's all out in the open."

"That's not why you left, Samantha. That can't be it!" Oliver's voice rose. "You denied Ariel a mother, and me a wife and family, because I never gave the Holocaust a second thought? You have to be kidding! Are you saying you would have rather had an obsessed husband, someone who was a rage-filled avenger, a Frankenstein monster bent on revenge, who lived with death on his mind all day long? Who would want a life like that?"

"That's not what I'm saying, but at least that would have been more emotionally honest than what we had here—feelings papered over with the words from mystery novels. You never dealt with any of the losses in your life, and by the time I showed up, it was all too late—backed up, clogged like a big bottleneck without any opening for this terrible family history to release itself. You were constipated with all the shit that happened to you and the Jews of Europe, and you weren't taking any laxatives. You said you were happy, but there was deep pain inside you, and I couldn't fix it. No one could."

"And that's why you left?"

"Not entirely." Samantha paused and stared into the frightened face of her husband. "Oliver, I was never the right woman to marry into this family. I didn't have enough emotional resources of my own. There was a long history of pain in my past, too, stuff I never told you about, but I came to this house with my own set of demons, and yours were too big to manage on their own, making mine seem trivial by comparison. I couldn't live here. I had to run away. But I couldn't take with me the only family you had left, the only pure survivor of the Holocaust. This family was morally entitled to a third generation. That's why I never dreamed of taking Ariel with me. It would have been too cruel and self-ish if I had done that. And of course," Samantha continued haltingly, "I also knew that I was sick, and I didn't trust myself."

"What do you mean? Where did you go?"

"It doesn't matter; it makes no difference anyway. All that matters is that within six months, I was dead."

"How? An accident?"

"No, it was no accident. I killed myself, Oliver. I have a lot in common with the other Golems who live in this house. It's not just the Holocaust we share in some loose way; it's also the way we made ourselves free—not through *Arbeit,* but through death."

Oliver was silent, although his mouth was open just in case.

"I know it's awful to hear, especially after all these years," she continued. "But you shouldn't be too surprised. I married into the Holocaust, and brought in my own scarred history, which I added, like salt, to this family's true legacy."

"What legacy?" Oliver sounded totally perplexed.

"Suicide. That's the way the Levins die, you know. Not from Hitler, or from cancer, but from their own hands. We do it to ourselves."

"Sam . . . why you? This didn't have to be your way out. You married into the family, but you didn't have to take on all of our customs."

"Wrong, Oliver. The Holocaust isn't like alcoholism or bowling. It's not a hobby or a habit you either pick up or reject. You never realized that, did you? What did you think, I was marrying some ordinary Jewish boy? You might have closed yourself off from the burdens of your legacy, but I didn't. I was very much aware of it. I felt it for the both of us. There was no block on my end. If you marry into a family that survived genocide, keeping your maiden name isn't enough to insulate you from the tragedy. It's impossible to maintain your distance; it will find you, because the reach of the Holocaust is relentless. I followed the family script—abandonment and suicide. Maybe I thought that by doing everything I was supposed to, you wouldn't follow me. I wanted the Levins to break the pattern somehow, so maybe our daughter would one day have a chance at a different future."

"So you sacrificed yourself to rescue us?"

"No, I was just saving myself from all the pain."

"What happened to forever?" Oliver, his arms thrown up into the air, asked anyone, and everyone, who would listen. "When you promise to hold someone's soul, that means that you can't let go."

Samantha chose not to answer, because the answer was obvious, and Oliver had already heard enough. There was no reason to force-feed the bitter pill his family had swallowed a long time ago.

Suddenly all he felt was fear. Not because of all the ghosts in his house, but because of the sum total of metaphysical activity it had taken for them to arrive at his doorstep. It was overwhelming. They had arrived at a crucible of time and place in the shape of a brownstone. Oliver simply could not fathom what all this reappearance and resurrection symbolized in the universe. This was no casual return; the Golems were not merely passing through, reinserting themselves into the narrowest zones where light meets twilight. These were golems moonlighting as oracles. Nightmares with friendly faces but prophetic messages.

Oliver began to feel alone in the darkness of his own home. He wanted to hug his wife. He wanted a hug from his wife. He reached out for her and grabbed nothing but an armful of air. A cold wind stroked his face. He opened his eyes and searched the attic for Samantha.

"Where did you go, Sam? I need you now."

There was no reply. He pulled on a lamp's chain, which interrupted the darkness with a small bubble of light. There was still no sign of the ghost to whom he had been betrothed, to whom vows were spoken and glass shattered underneath his foot. But hanging from a thin cord attached to a medieval Czech chandelier that anchored the center of the attic was the green papier-mâché dragon with the flaming tongue and flamingo pink heart. Not Ariel's substitute, but the genuine arts-and-crafts article. The stolen piñata had finally been restored. It now dangled in the garret of a brownstone, in the Altneuschul on Edgar Allan Poe Street. A dragon that was not truly fire breathing, but perhaps it could breathe some fire back into Oliver Levin's frozen home.

30

"THIS IS WRONG OF US. WE CANNOT DO THIS! IT IS a sin. Why did we come back if this is how we are going to be remembered?"

Piotr was always the softie in the group. That made sense, because he saw his resurrection first and foremost as an opportunity to experience, as if for the first time, fatherhood, even one as pointless and pathetic as the empty stroller he wheeled around the Upper West Side. For him the return was entirely a gift. He knew the urgency of the mission—what Ariel wanted for her father, what the Golems wanted for humanity—and accepted it without complaint, but most of all he just wanted to push a baby carriage, to engage in the most joyous of all jobs, and remind the world of what had been lost.

Now the others had different agendas. Jerzy was partying too hard, infiltrating the guileless nightclubs of New York as one party animal who could neither be seen nor smelled. And even if seen, he would have been unrecognizable anyway, appearing each night in a different guise. Tadeusz sat in on as much music as he could listen to on any given day, sampling New York's urban variety of clashing concerts—from Chopin to Kid Rock. Primo and Lothar spent time in the libraries and bookstores of New York. Rose strolled Central Park, observing people during their lunch hours, all robotically anticipating the next shift. One day she rode the bus to Atlantic City and played the slots, the lever of the one-arm bandit cranking feverishly without any human assistance, as if in desperate need of maintenance. Paul showed up at poetry slams in the East Village. And of course, when they ventured out as a group, they could often be found sitting on the heads of stone gargoyles, or whirling in circles on wooden horses, smiling into the faces of all those flashing rainbow lights at the Central Park carousel in the dead middle of the night.

Jean was perpetually angry and indignant. That was his main extracurricular activity, how he chose to spend his free time. He had no hobbies and participated in little that was offered on the island. So no one was particularly surprised that the rampage was his idea all along. A riot is a fine way to get some exercise. He would be the one who would insist that the Golems do their duty. Yet, at the same time, on this overly sensitive subject, surprisingly no one, other than Piotr, registered much dissent when it came to aborting their original mission in favor of a new plan that would wreak havoc on New York City and beyond.

"The decision is final. We begin tomorrow," Jean said determinedly.

The official meeting place for such encounters was always the island that separated traffic on the avenue at Eighty-seventh Street and Broadway. That's where matters of official business and vital importance were conducted. Everyone was in attendance, along with the same homeless man, who functioned as a living witness, a recording secretary who had sat in with these ghosts before. He was mostly silent, his shopping cart by his side, next to Piotr's stroller. The cart, unlike the baby carriage, was occupied, full of both charitable and discarded items that had been left out on neighborhood curbs or tossed into trash bins: old shoes, a smashed computer keyboard, recyclable bottles, a Hawaiian shirt, the ball bearings of an office swivel chair, the fishnet of a tennis racquet, old cans of hardened Play-Doh, a stack of stained, hardcover self-help books.

"Are we sure this is the right thing to do?" Rose wondered.

"The discussion is over! We have seen enough of what they have done," Jean snapped.

"I'm afraid Jean is right," Jerzy said. This time he was dressed up as a toll booth collector who worked on the Tappan Zee Bridge. "They have broken the contract. We trusted them with the story, and they have trivialized and corrupted it to the point that no one will now ever know what really happened to the Six Million."

"And they have plagiarized it, too," Piotr said.

"That is not amusing," Jerzy said.

"We don't want to see obsession in their hearts," Paul said, "but we also don't want sacrilege—the debasement of all that we lived through and ultimately died from. We can't survive that, even as ghosts."

"If they have no respect for the dead, then we must teach it to them," Primo said ambivalently.

"But why this way?" Piotr pleaded.

"There is no other way," Jean said. "The human species only knows how to listen to rage, and outrage. They don't pay attention unless they are faced with violence, irrational acts, property damage."

"Like in Watts, Liberty City, and in Crown Heights," the homeless man said, flashing a gummy smile. The analogy was duly noted.

"Yes," Paul conceded, "that's the only time when man seems to listen."

"How do we start? And how do we know when to stop?" Piotr

asked, gently rocking the baby carriage, not wishing to disturb the innocence of a symbolically sleeping child, who would otherwise have been woken up by these quarreling adults.

"We don't stop!" Jean said. "We're golems. We can't be stopped once we get started. We are machines of destruction and retribution. That's the whole point of our existence: to exact revenge, to teach the vile and ignorant important lessons about compassion, fairness, and respect, so they will be decent the next time."

"No, that's not what Ariel created," Lothar, the creator's grandfather, reminded his friends. "She didn't bring us here to start a riot. Her motives were both more selfish, and pure."

"We are a different breed of golem," Rose said. "We are not here to punish anti-Semites, but to save our son."

"And to free the world from the pain of the last century," Primo added.

"It does not matter what the original plan was," Jean said, leaving no room for negotiation. "This is what we found when we arrived. We wanted it to be different, but it is what it is. And now we have no choice, because if we don't do this, who will?"

"They have trampled on our memories," Tadeusz said.

"And it will only get worse," Jerzy said. "They think if they see a movie, if they can name a few Nazis, pull them out of a lineup, identify them from a picture, then they have figured out the whole thing. 'There's Eichmann, and over there, that's Mengele, and next to him, Heydrich, the Blond Beast.' What do they think, this is an All-Star Nazi rotisserie league?"

"This is what happens with the passage of time," Primo said somberly. "It mocks history and makes it harder to be gentle with our memories. With each year there are fewer moral imperatives to be respectful of our fellow human beings."

"What wasn't funny all of a sudden gets a laugh," Jerzy said.

"And people then move on to the next thing," Paul said. "History falls out of fashion. Human atrocity becomes commonplace. Tragedy becomes boring. That's what happens when CNN and the digital world bring horror and excitement into the living room every night. School shootings, carpet bombings, moon landings—everyone feels as though they've seen it all before. Nothing leaves an impression on anyone."

"People are no longer shocked," Primo said. "That's what it is. We have lost our capacity to be shocked. The victims are dehumanized. And everyone else is simply desensitized. Hooked on the drug of indifference."

"They need a wake-up call, something that will frighten them," Jean said, now feeling even more emboldened. "And who is better equipped for that task than a pack of ghosts?"

"Can we do it without leaving behind shattered glass?" Lothar wondered. "That's what happens during a riot, you know. It would be wrong if we, of all people, left behind broken glass."

"Lothar is right," Rose said.

"I still say no," Piotr said. "I don't want any part of this."

"Don't come," Jean growled, getting within inches of Piotr's face. "Push that stupid baby carriage around Manhattan if you must, instead. You think they know why you do it? You think they understand? They don't even care about their own children. How do you expect them to remember the ones you lost, and the millions of others who lived on only as smoke, lampshades, and soap? You are wasting your time doing it your way."

The sky was now filled with a rain envious of snow, an in-between flaky moisture, cold but unwhite. No matter, it still managed to cool Jean off. Slush cascaded over the meridian like a tsunami as buses and taxis barreled up and down Broadway on their way to various rush-hour destinations.

Primo put a wedge between Piotr and Jean, then said to Piotr, "We understand what you are feeling. Nobody wants this, not even Jean. But we must. We once all killed ourselves because the world had forgotten, or never remembered, what we had seen. And now, after all we have tried to accomplish, in some ways it has gotten even worse."

"There must be another way," Piotr sobbed. "We are not monsters. The original Golem was created to protect and defend against an external enemy. But we came not because of the outside world, but because of the broken world inside of Oliver—the enemy within. That was our target."

The meeting was over. The decision finally made, and unanimously—except for Piotr—so. Even the homeless man cast a vote. This community on the Upper West Side of Manhattan that had grown fondly accustomed to the meddlings of these happy spirits had no idea of what was now awaiting them. How could they? They had been suckered in by a false sense of security, the tempting illusion that they were being watched by angels.

But they were unaware of the sordid history of their saviors. That was the main problem right there: not knowing the difference between an angel and a golem. And for this reason, and because of other delusions, and of course omissions that had made the Golems angry in the first place, they would be caught off guard. A disaster was in their future, a calamity for the ages, and they were no more prepared for it than had been the ashen human sculptures of a bygone Pompeii, or the Jews of Babi Yar. An assault that would rival the plagues of Egypt, the wooden horse of Troy, the raid on Entebbe, the Golem of Prague. A rampage of massive scale and epic upheaval. The Golems of Gotham were now lying in wait, soon to strike, with no remorse, all because civilization had gone too far in not going far enough.

31

THE DAUGHTER HAD PLANNED IT ALL. RIGHT from the very beginning. The experiment itself, and the way it would ultimately play itself out.

She had never seen her parents together, or perhaps she was too young to remember them as they once were—as an intact family. And so the desire to reunite what had long ago been broken was overwhelming for a young girl who was otherwise riding an impressive streak of creative improvisation.

The next afternoon, ghosts and mortals walked guardedly about the brownstone, aware of the sharp edges of everyone's feelings. Ariel set a scuffed white Frisbee on the kitchen table, hoping to scare up a game—not for herself, but between her parents. She wondered whether they could be enticed by this once-familiar aerodynamic disk. And she was right. They fell for the bait. Oliver blinked when he first saw the Frisbee, which had been hidden upstairs in some forgotten closet. Samantha entered the kitchen, saw her husband poised over the Frisbee as if it were a dead bird. They stared at each other, smiled, then laughed shyly. The shared intimacies of couples, the hidden messages, inside jokes, and special mating dances that only they know.

Perhaps this was a good way to reacquaint themselves. After all, the game of Frisbee required that the parties keep their respectful distance. At the same time, the players had to rely on each other for sure, gentle hands. Showboating and recklessness were ultimately a self-defeating strategy. The object was to keep the pairing in play, not to drop the disk, but to grasp and keep its journey within sight.

Oliver once told Ariel that he and her mother used to play this game together, before she was even born. During many late-spring and early-fall days, just before sunset, they would head off into Central Park, in a section known as the Pinetum, where a narrow patch of pine trees gave off rich, foresty smells. Fallen, crunching pine cones gathered underneath Oliver's and Samantha's feet as they chased after the soaring disk, circling under it, judging its descent, anticipating new pockets of wind, reaching for a memorable acrobatic catch. In shorts, tank tops, and running shoes, they were young and hopeful. Racing like the wind. Running without missteps or hesitations. Together they were as light as the air that propelled their Frisbee. That's how Ariel wanted to remember it, even though it wasn't her memory to remember. A daughter's aching imagination filtered through the prism of internal longing.

It was mid-March, a warm day for what was still a winter month. The sun was holding the horizon in the west, staying out longer than usual, blanketing the island with an amber light that filled in the cramped spaces between buildings and avenues. The sky was clear. The air somehow felt cleaner, lighter, the ideal conditions for a Frisbee to take charge of its own flight pattern.

They walked up Edgar Allan Poe Street, which turned back into

Eighty-fourth Street east of Broadway. Oliver and Samantha had the preposterous impulse to hold hands, as they had always done years earlier. But too much time had passed, and not enough had yet been said between them. Feelings of tenderness are difficult to restore and even harder to put into action. And after all, a touch between a ghost and a mortal was an empty one anyway. So instead they shared the Frisbee as a circuit breaker, something to stand between their stalled intimacy, like a marriage counselor that would ground them, buffering their touch until it was safe to remove the braces from their broken marriage.

For several blocks not a word was spoken. Finally, as they cut through Central Park at Eighty-fifth Street, heading toward the Pinetum, Samantha said, "I can't believe Piotr is getting all that use out of Ariel's old baby carriage."

"Are you kidding?" Oliver replied, loosening up. "That old Swedish thing has become a big hit on the Upper West Side. It's now a neighborhood mascot. Even if we wanted to take it back, the community wouldn't let us. They're about to designate it as a landmark. The baby carriage now has a life and history all its own."

Husband and wife continued walking toward the Pinetum. Spider web shadows from the chain-link fence that surrounded the Central Park reservoir looked like graffiti art on the soft dirt ground. There were signs of an early spring as a momentary burst of wind created a rainstorm of pollen, which got dusted from unsuspecting buds. A woodpecker was buzzing away at a hollow tree. And there were sightings of other migratory creatures, breathless in the beauty of what nature had dreamed for them.

A small child was sitting in a rubber basket attached to an overhanging swing. The basket wasn't swinging at all, yet the child didn't seem to mind. Her Jamaican nanny was off getting a Good Humor ice-cream bar from a nearby hot-dog vendor, and the swing had run out of momentum. It was now just an elevated chair with a good view. Off to the side, a seesaw leaned against the earth like an unparallel plank empty of passengers; the opposite end pointed skyward.

Ariel had followed her parents to the Pinetum. They hadn't noticed her trailing a half block from behind. She was determined not to miss what she had set in motion and longed for: her parents back together again, even in such a physically imbalanced, improbable state. The family reunited in the way it was even before they were a family. She wanted to commit every second of it to memory, so that it would be real, forever exhilarating, if only in her mind.

"Can we do this?" Samantha asked, pulling the Frisbee and releasing Oliver's hold on his half.

"Why not? It's what Ariel wants to see most."

"Let's give her a show."

"I should tell you, Sam, that I haven't played since you left."

"Don't worry, Oliver, I haven't either. They don't have these things where I come from. It's the spirits that fly, not the toys. At least I know a lot more about air than I used to—the way it helps you breathe and how it can carry you away."

She hesitated to say anything further. Oliver simply stared into the pale blue eyes that had once held his attention so infinitely and bracingly.

"Come on," Samantha said. "It's just like riding a bicycle. You never forget."

"Never forget. Never again," Oliver mumbled. "Can't keep them straight."

Oliver and Samantha strolled through the Pinetum, counting off paces, deciding how far away to stand from each other. Ariel crouched down and hid behind a pine tree that was wide enough, and willing enough, to not blow her cover while she observed her parents at play. Since that night at Carnegie Hall, she was no longer merely a klezmer impresario, or a kabbalah wizard, but a playful Puck and Cupid as well.

Except for the Levin family, the Pinetum was deserted. The nanny had retrieved her charge and taken the child home for dinner. The hot-dog vendor had been scooped up by a flatbed truck that came to load the cart, along with all those unsold franks, buns, soda cans, pretzels, and sauerkraut. It was now certain that no one other than Ariel and Oliver would see a Frisbee sail off in one direction and stop in midflight, caught by a tall, blond-haired ghost who could fly as well, if not better, than the Frisbee itself.

Who should throw first? What would be polite or appropriate under these odd circumstances? Surely the rules of the game, as set forth by the Frisbee's designer, could not have anticipated such questions of complicated etiquette, compounded by this particular pairing of players—the living and the dead, the broken husband and his departing wife. Should the damn thing even be thrown at all?

Standing thirty yards from Oliver, Samantha sent the Frisbee airborne with a firm backhanded toss. A nice first strike. It sailed sweetly into the sky, cutting through air without much arc or bounce, the pine trees nothing but a blur of background and bark as the disk smacked against Oliver's palm. He then brought the Frisbee closer to his chest, as if cradling a newborn.

"Good catch!" Samantha cried.

"Nice throw!" Oliver returned the compliment.

"Yes!" Ariel whispered to herself as a small tear left her eye, skied off her face, and dropped like rain through the rough grooves of a parched pine cone.

Each took a few steps backward, increasing the degree of difficulty. Husband and wife rose to the challenge. The Frisbee flew in both directions—sailing back and forth between body and ghost—unerringly. The tosses were sure and swift. No hesitations. No misplays. Ultimate Frisbee champions. Ironically they had never played this well in the past. There were no hanging, jackknife tosses that came crashing down like dead quails. Or low-lying bullets that skidded on the ground like a lawnmower, digging up pine cones and hurtling them end over end. The throws were so accurate that Samantha and Oliver didn't have to run too far to chase them down. But when they did, they moved with the grace of gazelles. Samantha glided with the familiar moonwalk swiftness of a Golem;

Oliver's long, nimble stride had the footwork, if not the swagger, of a flanker.

Even the wind cooperated. There were no unexpected flurries that carried the Frisbee off into jetstream oblivion. The unpredictability of flight had somehow been harnessed. The fading sun didn't get in the way, either. There was no collision with trees, or tangled-up feet from the mosh-pit of pine cones. Oliver and Samantha even managed to flick the disk with their forehands, a talent that neither had exhibited when they were both younger, and alive.

"Fantastic grab, Oliver. Way to go! Wa-hoo!"

"This is so great!" Oliver screamed.

Ariel couldn't contain her happiness, but she had to, because she didn't want them to know how much this meant to her, how much she wished that her magic could bring about an even bigger miracle, the one that could make this game even more real, somehow carrying over into the rest of their lives. Wasn't there a procedure in the kabbalah manual to reunite flesh and blood with an overachieving spirit?

Years ago, during a talk when her father drifted into a rare moment of sentimental longing, Oliver had told Ariel how he and Samantha used to finish off these games of Frisbee in the Pinetum. First they would decide how many more throws to complete.

"Three more!" one of them would call out.

"Okay! But they better be good ones, otherwise we'll throw some more!" the other would reply.

Then, after the third toss, provided that the final throw was sizzling and assured, followed by an equally balletic catch, they would triumphantly race toward each other, embrace, kiss, and then, still in each other's arms, bounce up and down, moving counterclockwise.

"That's funny and cute." Ariel had giggled when she was much younger, after hearing the story for the first time.

Now, sitting on the damp earth moments before twilight, that's what Ariel was waiting to see—the postgame celebration, the way

Oliver had described it and his daughter had reimagined it. But would her parents remember it? For now Ariel only wondered whether this game would ever end, given how much fun her parents were having.

Ariel never got her ultimate wish, because the game never actually concluded. It was prematurely called on account of a more pressing, timeless matter. With dusk surrendering to night, Oliver, overcome by renewed life, hurled his final toss of the day with such force and emotion, that the Frisbee left his hands and did not return. It was taken by the wind, traveling through the night, sailing away without any thought of ever touching ground, reversing course, or finding its way back into Oliver's arms. Neither the Frisbee, nor love, is a boomerang.

Samantha gave chase, keeping the disk within her sights, flying through the forest, out into the open of the Great Lawn and up high above the turrets of the Belvedere Castle. Now that she had finally come back, she refused to let go—but only of the Frisbee.

"Sam!" Oliver yelled with a smile on his face, thinking that his wife was playing a joke on him. Surely she could retrieve the Frisbee no matter where it landed. Neither of them had yet to drop a toss. She would snag it and return. After all these years, she had come back for good, he believed. Ghosts are notoriously playful, he thought. No doubt she was baiting him with a game of hide-and-go-seek. He sloughed off a nervous laugh, as if all this time she had been hiding behind a tree or on one of its branches.

"Sam!" This time he screamed more seriously. "Where are you, baby?"

Ariel was crying fiercely, her face awash in tears as though caught behind a running fountain. She got up and ran to her father, hugging him around his waist and bouncing up and down, counterclockwise, trying to bring the afternoon to a satisfying end. Once again she volunteered for the thankless role of the unwanted, futile, and undersize substitute spouse.

"It's going to be okay, Oliver," she cried.

"Samantha!" he screamed, a sound that echoed through the wind tunnel of the empty Pinetum.

And off in the distance, too far away for father and daughter to see, a blur of refracted light tore deep into the horizon, racing underneath a white dot of an unidentified flying saucer. Ariel squinted for her mother. But Samantha was gone, all over again.

32

KRISTALLNACHT HAS COME TO THE BIG APPLE There would be broken glass after all—everywhere, in fact. Lothar's advice and warnings had gone unheeded. The Golems no longer cared about civic pride, decorum, and safety. They had once been friendly ghosts, do-gooder golems, the unearthly manifestation of saintly survivors. But that was an unusual predisposition given who they were, and what the kabbalah expects of its monsters.

As should have been anticipated, they had finally reverted to the ancient myth, conformed to the stereotype. The legend of the Golem is not a particularly happy tale. It climaxes in a full-scale riot, and in the center of the maelstrom lies the monster. The Prague Golem was a mythical fighting machine. Why should the ones from Manhattan be any different? They are not agents of peace or angels of compassion. They are monsters without a soul, man-made creatures hell-bent on rage and retribution. Golems, even the Gotham variety, have no reason to stray too far from their medieval raison d'être.

It was all doomed from the start, really. Yes, the Golems—save perhaps Jean—had hopes for this new century, one with an abiding respect for the bloodiness of the past. And they also had equal faith that the big leap forward required the dissipation of fury and the desire to heal. Obsession had its place, but the Golems believed that it was time for that place to take a backseat to new possibilities. Human beings would be better served by taking a cue from these Golems, who knew that vengeance is best stored far beneath the surface, always under lock and key, opened only as a last resort—and even then, with extreme caution.

The very same Golems who had helped bring so much new music to the Upper West Side had now changed their tune. They would have preferred that it be otherwise, but how could we expect more of them than we demand of ourselves? The human race, after all, has had a long screaming, sometimes latent, relationship with violence and self-sabotage. It lurks even in moments when we appear to be in love.

Who are we kidding? We don't want to surrender our rage under any circumstances, so why should our monsters be any different? Indeed, what is a golem if not a surrogate for our own trigger-happy, smoldering, but suppressed anger? We need our golems to pacify our hatred just long enough before the next round begins. Because we can't be trusted. The violence from our own hands makes our monsters look meek by comparison. What can't be settled in a boxing ring usually gets taken outside, to the back alleys, parking lots, street corners, town squares, and courthouse steps. All that violence to the body and spirit spills out, where the mobs are, where anger breathes best. And some things are easier to get angry about than others, although human beings don't need much help in that regard.

The Holocaust was always way too hot, which is why the Nazis were right to make fire the defining symbol of the Final Solution. It was a crime that could not be appeased; largely because the original insult was too great. And its potential to evoke even further disgust would forever go untempered and unabated. The Shoah would always remain a revolting enigma, no more comprehensible than the madness and hatred from which it sprang. If only the world had undergone more sensitivity training, perhaps the Golems would have been more tolerant and been able to look the other way.

The Golems had alas come too late, and without enough fire-power of their own. The plan had backfired. In coming to rescue Oliver, they never imagined that the world from which they had once unplugged themselves would one day get worse—on their watch, no less. And now the Golems were pissed. They had accomplished some things, but they soon realized that their work would forever be undone. It was no better than crumbling Sheetrock, a condom with a hole in it, a Band-Aid applied to a decapitation, a drop of dehydrated spit falling into an active volcano. Their well-meaning efforts were ultimately meaningless, headed in reverse. The world was not merely cruel and forgetful; the world was ungrateful, and for that more than anything else, the Golems would insist on exacting their own brand of medieval revenge.

That's when Alejandro reentered the picture. Since the Golems had showed up, Alejandro had essentially been out of a job at Oliver Levin's brownstone on Edgar Allan Poe Street. Oliver left himself without a building superintendent. Those tasks were now in the capable hands of the Golems themselves.

According to the original legend of the Golem, when the monster wasn't off fighting anti-Semitic crimes or avenging injustice against the Jews of Prague, he was left back at the Altneuschul, performing custodial duties for the synagogue. And until the Golems left the brownstone, marching off to rampage the very community they had once blessed and protected, these former Holocaust survivors had done a fine job taking care of Oliver's home—except for the testy streaks of red blood they left behind wherever they went, an eerie incontinence that could not be helped.

Fortunately Alejandro arrived back just when Oliver and Ariel needed him most.

"Mr. Levin, I don't know why you told me to stay away, but I'll tell you this: Now that I'm here, I don't think I'm ever going to leave," he said as he entered the foyer and removed his coat, tool belt, and tape measure. He brushed some loose soot off his sleeve, then cricked his neck to the left. "Have you seen what's going on outside? The sky is blacker than night, but it's still the middle of the day. Are we having some kind of eclipse? And the clouds, they look like they're filled with cinder and ash, like every cloud has its own private boiler room and smokestack. And the wind is making strange noises. And the streets are whistling—no, not whistling, more like screeching."

Oliver didn't respond. Ariel looked away. Alejandro continued reporting on the outside weather.

"It sounds like there are ghosts out there running around like wild animals. But they don't seem like the same kind of ghosts we've been having lately. Are they?" Alejandro wondered out loud to his favorite landlord, because there was much talk around the neighborhood, fueled somewhat by Alejandro's own inside suspicions, that the ghosts had indeed originated right here, in the brownstone that he once supervised, the one owned by the Gothic mystery writer and his Jewish sorceress of a daughter. He looked to Oliver for answers and received none. Ariel merely shrugged, smiled, then dropped her chin.

"Well, if it's all the same with you," he continued bashfully, "I wouldn't mind riding out the storm in here for a while before I start getting back to work. What do you say?"

The Levins did not object. Oliver had, as of late, with *Salt and Stone* completed and his wife's reappearance once more in reverse, become even more noticeably depressed and distracted. His tall, lean frame now seemed shrunken and tilted forward. His face lost weight, which the rest of his body could ill afford. His cheeks were hollow, his lips became thinner, his hair was inexplicably whiter than before. Only his blue eyes took on a larger presence on his face. He spoke little, wandered much, but walked slowly, keeping his hands clasped behind the small of his back, a posture that was familiar to him, even though not his own. This had once been Lothar's self-targeted handshake, when he was still jailed by life, when he popped nitroglycerin pills under his tongue. Now the movement had been inherited, and adopted, by his son.

Alejandro noticed how much Oliver had changed since he had stopped making regular visits to the brownstone. But he wisely understood that the effects were far too dramatic, and Oliver too far gone, to assume that he could fix his landlord. After all, Oliver was not a broken fuse box or a clogged drainpipe. Alejandro had special tools to make those kinds of repairs. But human breakdown is different from routine building maintenance. Even humans who are experts at such matters fail all the time.

Alejandro limped into the kitchen; his hump appeared to have atrophied over these past few months, as if it had benefited from the time off. He stepped over a red skid mark that would have yielded a fine DNA sample, and got himself something to drink as if readying himself for the outside show.

He was right to settle in, because the Upper West Side was soon to be swallowed up in a primal scream. The rooftops shouted through the mouths of awakening, roaring gargoyles. And the gargoyles themselves, thousands of them from all over Manhattan—stationed upon large buildings, small brownstones, and town houses, as well as on ledges and in corridors—suddenly came alive. Their menacing stares were no longer mere expressions. There were the added features of growling breaths and foaming mouths. They came out to stretch their legs after a century or more of being encased in stone. Even the gargoyles that were attached to Oliver's brownstone became unhinged, and their faces—which had gone from forbidding to embracing—now reverted back to their originally mounted poses.

The carousel horses in Central Park turned from colorful wood to snarling beasts. They galloped away from their posts, roaming the island in a fierce trot that didn't quite match the Viennese waltzing sounds of a merry-go-round. Rather, this was a gait that was more death march than anything else, like the pace of horses that carry coffins off to cemeteries.

Manhattan and the four other boroughs of New York were undergoing a monstrous makeover. The Golems were determined to teach everyone a lesson by way of an old-fashioned riot. Everything was being upended. The ornate crowns and lightning-rod spires of various Manhattan skyscrapers blasted off into outer space, never to be seen again, leaving unsightly stumps as new symbols of New York architecture. The Wonder Wheel disengaged from its bearings and rolled toward Manhattan via the Brooklyn Bridge. The House that Ruth Built collapsed without any wrecking ball in sight, burying Monument Park under mounds of Yankee stone and lore.

Tourists took off for the airports. Penn and Grand Central Stations were overrun with passengers willing to go anywhere but here. There was a bonfire in Bryant Park where books that had once been shelved at the main branch of the New York Public Library, and that had anything and everything to do with the Holocaust, were being burned. Works of history and philosophy, psychology and theology, drama and poetry, and of course fiction, all went up in smoke. Even words once written by the Golems themselves were added to the blaze.

Con Edison lost all power, which the Golems immediately usurped—the new utility in town that preferred blackout dark. They desecrated tombstones—both Jewish and gentile. When it came to hate crimes, the Golems did not discriminate. Gargoyles dressed up as Nazis were seen goose-stepping down Fifth Avenue, *heiling* Trump Tower with a lefthand salute. All German-made vehicles that existed in Manhattan—from Mercedes-Benzes and BMWs to Volkswagens, sedans, SUVs, and convertibles—whether in parking garages, showrooms, or out on the road, got compressed like miniaccordions until they compacted into tin cans.

There were confirmed reports of bombings of neo-Nazi paramilitary installations in Montana, Washington, Idaho, and Nebraska. Oddly enough these bombs emerged from below, raised from the ground up, imploding without impact. The Polish pope, invisible hands squeezing his wrists and turning back his fingers, finally, finally apologized—this time at last with more sincerity and passion—for the sins of his native people and his Catholic followers.

In Hollywood and New York, film studios watched in horror as the final director's cut of nearly every Holocaust-related feature film and documentary seared like wildfire, going from celluloid to smoke faster than it took to get on cable. When the ersatz embers cooled, they left behind a vaguely flesh-scented smell. Video rental stores experienced the same phenomenon. From here on *Life Is Beautiful*—thank God for little things—was nowhere to be found.

Storefront windows were smashed. Madison and Fifth Avenues, and West Thirty-fourth and Fifty-seventh Streets, had become a carpet of shimmering, lethal crystals. Showers throughout the five boroughs hissed and dripped blood. The theater district was dark, and not because it was a Monday. This was a new version of Black Monday, one that had nothing to do with a stock market crash (which did in fact crash, as well). There would never be another show like it; the end of all future matinees. The Golems had brought their own entertainment, and they didn't even need a spotlight to flash the night sky with the announcement of a premiere. Live theater was taken off the stage and presented right on the street in the form of an unscripted, ad-libbed, unchoreographed, sold-out riot.

Men wearing beards had them snipped off. Longhaired citizens found themselves with shaved heads. Women in their twenties lost their periods, as if menstrual cycles could be pickpocketed. All children's toys were taken away, along with strollers and baby carriages, which ultimately joined the parade along Fifth Avenue, falling in right behind the gargoyles. Gold teeth popped out of undentured mouths like BB pellets. Torah scrolls flew through the air on the wings of unanswered prayers.

This rampage also had its playful side. The Golems pillaged Manhattan of all its lox and smoked fish. Zabar's was ransacked of its foremost appetizers. No one had any excuse to come hear Ariel play her violin anymore. The same thing had happened at Dean & DeLuca, Balducci's, Grace's, Jefferson Market, Eli's, and the Vinegar Factory—everyone was out of stock indefinitely. From now on—if there even was to *be* a now on—brunch and business meetings would be conducted loxless.

Moreover, all the bagel stores on the island stopped production, their ovens permanently immobilized and shut down. Corned-beef and pastrami shops were robbed of their main meats. The city was brought to its knees. All the broken glass along Madison Avenue didn't compare with the deprivation that was felt from the piracy of these particular New York delicacies. The Golems obviously knew how to play dirty, how to hit hard and below the belt.

It was right smack during the middle of this siege that the mayor of New York City, his honor himself, cowering alongside a stymied and paralyzed police commissioner, decided to telephone Oliver Levin to see if he could render some assistance on behalf of the Big Apple. The mayor would have paid Oliver a personal visit, but frankly he was afraid to travel over to Edgar Allan Poe Street at this particular moment in the city's history—even by limousine, and with a police escort.

Alejandro answered the phone. He and Ariel had been watching live television coverage with up-to-the-minute bulletins on the Golem uprising while Oliver rambled around the house, muttering to himself, his face fixed downward, following the blood trail on the floorboards.

"Mr. Levin!" Alejandro announced like an excitable butler. "Where are you? The mayor is on the phone! He wants to speak with you!"

"The mayor?" Ariel asked, a quick glance at Alejandro, her face showing signs of bafflement, too.

The two of them shrugged at each other while Oliver shuffled over slowly, indifferently, and retrieved the phone.

"Yes?" Oliver said, almost inaudibly.

"Mr. Levin, I'm glad you're home. This is the mayor here."

"Hello." Oliver registered no surprise at the mayor's call.

"Yes, well . . . you may have noticed that we are having a city-wide emergency."

The mayor waited for Oliver Levin to acknowledge that he at least had some minimal awareness of current events. Hearing nothing, the mayor continued. "Before we call in the National Guard and the Guardian Angels, I'm about to ask you a favor on behalf of the decent, hardworking citizens of New York. Are you listening?"

"Yes."

"Mr. Levin, for the good of this city and the future of our children and my political career, please, please, I beseech you, give up your Golems. Put a stop to this madness now. Call them off. Do something!"

Oliver shook his head as if struck by a tuning fork. Then he said, "Your Honor, honestly, I have no idea what you're talking about. There are no Golems—"

"Cut the crap, Levin. Stop right there. What do you take me for, some kind of moron?" The police commissioner nodded his head approvingly, like a dyspeptic lapdog stuffed with bone biscuits. "I'm the mayor of this city—the biggest, most important city in the world, need I remind you? I didn't get this far for nothing. You think it's easy to pull something off on me? Look"—his voice calming a bit—"I haven't said anything up until now because the Golems of Gotham were good for the city. But I know about you and your kind. You fiction writers are all so full of shit. Living in your heads all the time, ignoring what's happening in the real world, playing make-believe with your bullshit imaginations!"

Oliver moved the receiver away from his head, mellowing the mayor's treble and bass.

"And that kid of yours, with her unlicensed serenades outside of Zabar's! We should have arrested her and impounded that violin ages ago before this thing got too far out of hand. There's been some strange goings-on over there in your neighborhood, but I kept my mouth shut. I could have called in my special SWAT units, sealed the place off, hauled you and your daughter in for questioning. That's what my police commissioner recommended, but I told him to lay back for a while and see how things played themselves out. That was probably a mistake. So now I'm calling in my debt and calling on you to do your duty, to finally do something right with your life. Put an end to this, Levin! You must know what to do. For heaven's sake, Gotham needs your ghosts to stop."

Oliver slowly and gently laid the receiver down, hanging up on the mayor without giving him an answer or even saying good-bye. He peered down at Ariel, then up, not toward the heavens, but the attic, where there was an ancient Ark inside which slumbered the Hebrew letters *aleph* and *shin*, and the words *emet* and *met*. The *aleph* or the *emet*, slapped on a golem's forehead, spells life; the *shin* under the tongue or the *met* on the forehead brings on the golem's death.

But the mayor was right in one respect. Oliver was indeed a fiction writer. Perhaps it was finally time that he rely on his own words to free the city, and himself.

33

THE GREAT IRONY ABOUT THE GHOSTS WHO ARE my houseguests (and some of you, the readers of *Salt and Stone*, have probably already considered this on your own) is how is it that men of such literary virtue and accomplishment would one day choose to kill themselves without writing down so much as even a few original words of explanation? A totally absurd paradox. In the end, with this book as proof, they may have cured me of writer's block. But as I see it, in their own most crucial test as writers, they completely failed.

After all, these were not mute men, protective of their vulnerabilities, reserved in their emotions, inhibited about sharing their feelings or interior lives. They were novelists, poets, and writers of the finest literary caliber, men whose emotional complexity had already been revealed to the world through their art. They had lived extraordinary adventures and yet were unafraid to dream up new possibilities—places where none of us had been, could never have traveled on our own, or would ever have wished to wind up. And yet, when these writers arrived at the ultimate decisions of their lives—the premature, unnatural demise, the one that was screaming for reflection, self-doubt, confession, and acknowledgment—what happened to their gifts for language and expression? Were they now suddenly overcome with writer's block? Couldn't locate pen or paper? Weren't able to find the right words, so instead they chose to say nothing at all? As a grand finale, these men who had already survived one of the world's greatest mysteries decided to leave behind an even greater one.

I mean, we could all understand if they were writers of crass, tawdry, cheap thrillers, the type of fiction I had been known for—sphinxlike artistic expression, sentences that just get you to the next one but never get you inside the soul of the author, words without passion, poetry, emotion, or anguish. On the contrary, these were writers with thoughts on their minds and who had something to say, men of letters who knew how to use them—the vowels and the consonants and all the attendant sensations of tenderness and treachery that artfully chosen words can evoke. They were writers who wanted their readers to feel.

Maybe the answer is that an author with ambition, someone who has attained a certain literary stature, can't kill himself and leave behind a simple suicide note. That would be far too trite and pedestrian an exercise for someone used to telling larger, more complicated tales. For a novelist a note would never do. The gesture must be grander.

What am I then to leave behind, knowing that these men exited without saying even the bare minimum, checking out without so much as a chicken-scratched farewell, scribblings on a napkin, code-words smeared on toilet paper? I could depart in the same way, using them as my models and mentors in suicide, or I could strive for

something more ambitious, if not long-winded. Given the fact that I
am no longer blocked, this may be my best opportunity to prove it—
with the final chapter of this book—to set myself apart from my
elders with whom I was never equal, except when it came to this,
where I had the courage to explain myself in ways they could not.

But their situations were admittedly much more complex than
mine. Look at it this way. There they were, having already displayed
such great natural resources and instincts for survival, and yet, years
later, they wind up choosing a course of finality that is its irreconcil-
able opposite. Rather than perfect their survival, they instead die in
the most willful, vile, and deliberate of ways. Their impulses must
have been warring at their polar extremes, a critical mass of joie de
vivre and self-negation.

Fortunately I won't have to deal with such glaring contradictions.
There will be no paradox of me having survived only one day to
choose suicide. The main reason is that children of Holocaust survivors are not survivors of the Holocaust. They may have survived
something, but not that. All that is certain is that they lived with
damaged parents. Yes, they were indeed witnesses to an uncompro-
mising trauma that held the parents hostage—the penitentiaries of
memory, the labyrinths of loss. But that didn't make them survivors
themselves. And yes, their insight into the aftermath of mass death—
the absurdity of trying to begin again when what came before ended
so mercilessly and radically—is greater than it is for the average pop-
ulation. There is an innate and practiced feel for how fragile the psyche can be, how locked in we all are to our nightmares, how little it
takes to return us to the scene of those unpunished but forever pun-
ishing crimes. The secrets are deep, and the confessions don't come
easy.

All that is true, and there is more.

Despite there being children of Holocaust survivors who have
demonstrated a passion for social justice and activism, traveled to
Germany to protest Reagan's moronic, degrading gravesite gesture at
Bitburg, confronted Arab terrorists, fought for equality and against

discrimination, committed themselves to healing patients and in some cases, the world—in short, highly functioning men and women of moral conscience—the fact is, these children are unlike other adults of their generation.

Undeniably they register deeper sensations and sensitivities to parental pain and silence. There is also the burden of vicarious living, knowing that your life is a replacement for some other child, cousin, aunt, or uncle, and that you may actually be an unsuitable, unsatisfying, unworthy replacement. The nonnegotiable pressure to protect the parents, to somehow end their grief by filling their lives with artificially inseminated joy. And yes, perhaps there is some psychological validity to the idea that living in the same household as people who had survived genocide and witnessed atrocity at such close range— breathing beside them, observing their every movements—invariably exposes children of Holocaust survivors to second hand smoke, plaguing them with cattle-car complexes, and that these symptoms and pathologies are more than mere metaphors.

Yet regardless of this legacy of contamination that would, even in the best of circumstances, interfere with a healthy, normal childhood, these children are still not survivors. And that includes me.

But we can still be poets, and that's why in addition to this note by way of final chapter, this unfinished matter with the gun is also something I wanted to discuss and leave behind.

It all started back at the synagogue, Temple Beth Am, in Miami Beach. The *tallis* bag didn't interest me, nor did the *tallis* itself. There was a much more poignant souvenir. Almost everything in my parents' apartment I placed in storage; other things I just gave away to Goodwill, and some small items I brought with me back to school. Nothing sentimental, except for that gun.

The police first took it in as evidence. When they were finished learning absolutely nothing, they returned it to Rabbi Vered, who then passed it on to me. It was, after all, part of my legacy, the most curious and alluring object of my parents' estate. It didn't belong to the people of Miami Beach or to the members of the synagogue. The gun was legally and morally mine, an asset and heirloom of my family, the last thing my father touched, the final noise he heard, the last message he delivered in lieu of a suicide note.

More than anything else, the gun was to be my most intimate, personal, and metaphoric possession. I've always kept it near me ever since his suicide. It was in my dorm room back at college. And in the top desk drawer of my first few apartments. When I married Samantha and moved into this brownstone, it was the first item that crossed the threshold. Now it rests in a blue-velvet-lined gun case by my desk, right beside the shattered glass from my wedding day, which, thanks to Ariel, I only recently reclaimed. I am grateful that I possess these two precious artifacts. So rich in meaning. So profoundly symbolic of the red-letter dates, the sunken treasures, the blood on the tracts.

I had the gun checked out. Lothar wasn't firing just any old handpiece. This was a special pistol. German made. Manufactured by the Walther family before the war. It was a PPK *(Polizei Pistole Kriminal)*, a small, elegant handgun, blue in color before they made them in shiny stainless steel, and firing 7.65 mm caliber bullets. Not the type of shells you normally see in the United States. The gun shop in New York, down on Houston Street, told me that the PPK was an officer's gun, the kind of concealed but stylish pistol that would have been carried by members of the SS brass. And this one came with a special silencer attachment. How Lothar had gotten his hands on such a gun while living in Miami Beach I never knew. And even though his spirit had recently moved back into my home, I had forgotten to ask him. My mind was too busy processing the vast list of other questions that his return had prompted, and which I still never asked.

But now there is clarity: What to do? How to do it? I have all that I require. I have lived as long as I need to. I have finally seen too much—through my own eyes and the eyes of others. It is the privilege of excavation, of interior digging, of self-knowledge, and of immolation. Like Icarus, I too have now flown too close to the sun and shuddered in the gaze of its smile. The wings are melting. The heat is too much to bear. I now see things that I had been afraid to even acknowledge in my dreams. I ignored the warning labels, the buyer bewares, the hazardous-to-your-health and no-trespass signs. My pupils are now wide open, and I have been a good student. Too good, in fact. I discovered that I have a photographic memory for moments of my past, and the pasts of others, that would have been far better had they all remained forgotten. A voracious appetite for certain kinds of forbidden knowledge. A death wish for doors that were meant to stay closed.

I have traveled too far in too short a time, and now I am dizzy from it all. The awakening of my once-slumbering sentences, the reinventing of my dead relatives, the Frisbee that is no doubt still soaring, orbiting through other galaxies, stratospheres, and time zones with my dead wife streaking after it. And now there are golems who no longer haunt this home and draw breath from my attic and this laptop, but who have set off on their own, terrorizing my neighbors and threatening to sink this already overweighted island with the second coming of a biblical flood.

Just as you think you can't break into any more pieces, there goes another snap.

I only wish I could save Ariel from all this. Were I only the kind of father who could rescue his daughter, that would be reason enough to remain, to stick it out, see it through to its conclusion, and in the end, perhaps with faith, and some soul, it will be all right after all.

But I can't. And it won't. So good-bye.

34

HE RETURNED TO THE VERY SAME POSITION THAT preceded his birth—a fatal, fetal position. At that time, hooked up umbilically and with placenta in tow, such a curled-in, thumb-sucking, blissfully ignorant pose would have suggested nothing other than the promise and possibility of life. But his destiny was different. There was simply too much death imprinted on his DNA for a fetus to get too comfortable. When it came to the matter of genocide and suicide, his genetic code wasn't all that hard to crack.

So now, in crisis and desperation, it only made sense that he would return. He would have gone all the way down to Miami Beach if he had to, but that wasn't going to be necessary. There was an even more fitting and reminiscent altar right here in Manhattan. Splendid views of the island. A complicated but panoramic setting.

Oliver was returning to the beginning, not the very beginning, but close enough. It was where everything had all started, and then ended too soon, leaving him with a true sense of insecurity, which, given his origins, was the kind of defensive position he should have adopted all along.

Fortunately he would have an audience for this swan dive as swan song. There would be spectators; the only question was whether they would be mere bystanders. A small army of liberators, rescuers, and lighthouse operators had come to the scene of this somehow preordained killing.

Ariel, her grandparents, and the other Golems ambushed Oliver. They headed him off at the pass, sensing that the rocky cliffs of the Hudson River, the wide expanse of the George Washington Bridge, and the grit and gumption of the Little Red Lighthouse would be his ultimate destination. He knew the perfect setting for his final act. The unblocked mystery writer had developed the romantic impulses of a poet. Too bad he would never get to use them for anything other than his own scripted suicide. As Oliver came to learn, atmosphere and mood mattered. Death making has a lot in common with love-making. Both have elements of fantasy to them. And unfulfilled wishes. But one allows for repeat performances, while the other must be done right the first time.

It was the middle of the night. The weather on the northern part of the island wasn't particularly accommodating—so much potential for an inadvertent slip and fall. A cold, black rain dropped in chutes from a thundering sky, and the wind was slashing from all directions. The shorelines of New York and New Jersey were under siege, and for the time being their interstate rivalry was suspended by a bridge that hosted an even more urgent show. The knotted, swooping steel cables, which from a distance resembled the plunging neckline of a Gucci gown, rattled like the loose strings of a harp. Girders swayed like the floor of a funhouse. The toll booth had blown its roof. The Port Authority no longer had any.

There were no cars on the bridge at that time of night. Some of this was due to the late hour and the treacherous weather. But perhaps the main reason was that the Golems were rampaging, bending back the needle on the Empire State Building and turning it into a cheap set of rabbit-ear antennas, fusing the World Trade Center together like Siamese-twin towers. And of course there was more. The Golems reversed the direction of the torch on the Statue of Liberty, set free the animals in the Bronx Zoo, and sank a few of the ferries shuttling commuters to Staten Island. All of a sudden the five boroughs of New York City no longer seemed like such a happening place to be—day or night.

The only vehicle on the bridge was Piotr's baby carriage, which was parked along the interior sidewalk of the bridge itself, having ignored E-Z Pass altogether. As for Piotr and the other Golems, they had each climbed upon the bridge, clasping the cables, their feet balancing on rivets, their bodies like cylinders of refracted light, catching the falling rain.

All were waiting for Oliver, even though he still hadn't noticed that he wasn't alone. The Golems didn't take their stations on the bridge until Ariel's first beam put him inside the womb of his own spotlight. They were ready for his close-up, but was he ready for them? Against the black undertow of the river and inky mist of the Manhattan night, the lighthouse beam was a celestial ray, a slice of heaven both blinding and revealing, showing Oliver decked in all his white-and-gray-striped infamy.

He shrieked and shuddered as if he had been caught in the act, which he had. There he was, standing red-handed on the skeletal pilings of the bridge even though his hands hadn't yet gotten the chance to swim in their own blood. Ariel manned the lighthouse, a structure that had been dormant for years. In truth, unlike the more sanguine version offered up in the children's story, the George Washington Bridge, so much a larger presence on the Hudson and a more gleaming producer of light, had in fact made the little red lighthouse obsolete. There was no longer any reason for it to turn its beams back on.

Until that night. Ordinarily the tugboats, cruise ships, kayaks, barges, and steamers could navigate the Hudson quite well, even during dense fog, drawn by the luminous architecture of the bridge. But Oliver was in desperate need of light, far more light than this bridge was ever equipped or designed to handle. Oliver required his own private beam to show him the way, because the path had never been certain, and now that was truer than ever before.

He squinted and brought his hands to his face in shame. The beam cut right through him and flashed into the night, creating an alternate moon, a Batman signal without wings. It was only then that Oliver saw that he had company: The Golems had followed him. His orchestrated farewell had distracted them from their still-unfinished riot. All because of him they were forced to take a break. He had brought them together once more, reminded of why they had originally come and rethinking what they had been doing. Their task was never intended to be the same as that of the Prague Golem: Their manner and method of rescue was all about inner transformation, not outward violence. Maybe it was time for them to stop, after all.

The light revealed something about him that neither the Golems nor his daughter would have expected. Oliver wasn't merely planning on jumping. That would have been bad enough, though the fall might have been survivable. He could swim, and the Golems could have been a lifeline out of the water. Oliver obviously wanted to make an even bigger splash.

One of his hands was holding a gun—Lothar's gun; its blue metal barrel drew the lighthouse ray into its shaft. And hanging from his waist like a hillbilly belt clip was a bag of shattered glass tied up with a string. The contents of the bag would have remained a simple drinking chalice had he not gotten married fifteen years earlier, below where he was now standing, on muddy land at the nearby shore where the Hudson River meets Manhattan Island. At the time he did what he was told. And that's what he wanted to do. He followed the tradition with the firmness of a bootstrap, stepping on the glass for good luck. And when that display was over and the ceremony ended, in a stroke of spontaneous creativity he drowned the splintered shards in the Hudson River. Now he had the even more dramatic, deathly conceit to return the glass, and its luckless seeker, back to where they both belonged.

With the wind and rain crisscrossing mercilessly like a fire hose, making it hard for Oliver to keep his balance, the Golems decided it was time to take Ariel's wish for the rescue of her father onto the next level.

"Oliver, it is me, your father," Lothar began, not with the voice of a father from the dead, but rather with the calm, placating tone of a police hostage negotiator.

"Stay away!" Oliver yelled, taking a roll call of the Golems who were staked out at various points along the bridge. "You can't stop me! I know what I'm doing. I've learned my lessons well, and I owe it all to you—my teachers, my parents! Heil Hitler!"

Jean and Jerzy were sitting on the swooping bell curve of the longest support cable as if waiting for someone to give them a push on a swing. Appropriately Jerzy was dressed as a merchant marine. Jean was smoking a Gitane, which admittedly was against the rules, but the events of the past few days had made even him fitfully nervous. They glanced at each other knowingly, as if Oliver's response, while demented, was in fact predictable.

"We have made a terrible mistake," Lothar continued. "We pushed you too far. You needed to see some things, but not everything. The truth is not for everyone, even small truths, and you have seen too much of both kinds."

"It is like the kabbalah," Piotr joined in. He was standing right beside Oliver now, like a guardian angel. "You have to be a certain age before delving into it, unless of course, you are a *tzadik*. With the Holocaust, no matter how old you are, no matter how much you prepare, you can study it, but you can't actually visit it, or even pretend to visit, or finally master it. It is forbidden, and it is dangerous."

"They are right, Oliver," Primo said, taxiing in the air in front of Oliver's face. "The Holocaust is another universe. No matter how many planets NASA lands on, they'll never get there. Only the survivors understand what it means, can ever imagine what it was like, can share the intimate details of death. Only we know the secret language. And you know what that secret is?"

Oliver shook his head, because even with the imagination of a former mystery writer, he didn't.

"It is no language at all. It hasn't been invented yet, because there is no justification to create words that describe such pain. It's more like a feeling that we all know in our bones, an ache and emptiness that is immediate, reflexive, and always accessible. That's what we share, but not with you. The world has too often degraded the survivors, cheapening and trivializing our experience, telling us how we were supposed to feel and act. How to move on. Many others simply wanted to be us. But that is not possible. There is no disguise. There is no pretend. If you were not there, then you do not know, nor will you ever. We have seen a black death that is not for you. And you have been looking too closely at something that requires a special license, and you don't have one."

"You have overdosed on the most addictive drug of them all—human atrocity," Tadeusz said, standing behind Oliver on the ledge. Oliver gasped when he heard his voice, which was delivered almost in a whisper, but yet came at him with the pulsing, jarring, fading frequency of surround-sound stereo. Dolby for the dead. "It causes everyone to slow down in their cars and peek at the accident. The worst accidents are always the ones that bring out the most bystanders."

"It is important that you know where you come from," Paul said, the rain slicing through his head and pouring down his long, thin nose. "That was missing in your life. You have to feel responsible. The whole world does; children of survivors, too, children of Nazis even more so. But there isn't any more for you to see or do."

"You have taken on too much," Rose said, "and what you are now carrying is too big, even for the entire world."

"The living have always been better off with ignorance," Jerzy reasoned.

"Salt and stone! Salt and stone! Salt and stone!" Oliver, dissembling further, chanted like a howling madman searching for a full moon.

"Put the gun down, Oliver," Lothar said. "Give it to me now, and then give me your hand."

"No! It was your gun, and now it is mine." Oliver seethed. "It is our family's secret weapon. Remember? We don't fire it often, but when we do, we make sure it is our last time. It doesn't make much noise, but it is a final shot. And now it is my turn."

Such a strange, eerie setting for the first-ever attempt at Levin grief counseling.

"You should not be using that gun," Lothar continued. "It is a sin. I know why you think you have picked the right poison for what you want to accomplish, but you don't know the full story. I was wrong back then, and now you are wrong, too."

"Tell him, Lothar," Rose said.

"Yes, tell him," Primo urged.

And Lothar began his short, horrific tale of how sometimes souvenirs—from either paradise or hell—shouldn't travel along with the tourists who claim them. "That gun in your hand, the one I turned on myself, it is the same gun that killed my parents and two of my sisters. The gun has too much of our family's blood on it. Let mine be the last."

Oliver's grip suddenly loosened, but the PPK remained in his palm.

"Yes, it is not my gun. I never owned or fired a gun before the war. It is German made, and German executed. It belonged to a young SS officer in the ghetto of Radom. I watched him murder my family. At the time, I was already in hiding with a band of partisans. And when the war was almost over and the Germans were retreating, a miracle happened. Only then did I believe there was a God. I saw him again—the officer, the butcher. We came out of the forest, and I couldn't believe my eyes. My family I knew I would never see again, but I assumed that was also true about him. He would blend back into the world, and I would never find him and never get my revenge. Or maybe someone would get to him first—finishing him off and depriving me of my satisfaction. But I was wrong, on both accounts. He was still alive, and even with his death, there would be no satisfaction.

"The young assassin had gotten older and had probably killed more along the way. But this time I was the one who used his gun, and I used it on him. It was a small pistol, but I knew where it was on his body. He had already been captured, but I expedited the death sentence. That gun in your hand has been busy throughout its life. It is time for it to finally retire. Give it to me."

"Yes, surrender, Oliver," Rose said. "Please—"

"I can't give up!" Oliver cried. "I got a late start, but now I'm too close and too far gone. I'm hooked into this tragedy, and there's no escape, no rescue."

The lighthouse continued flashing its searing, solitary beam with Ariel guiding the light, keeping track of her father. The Golems remained perched on the crossbeams and gray trestles like fearless black crows sitting pretty on a straw man. The rocks of the Palisades hummed from the combined kiss of wind and cold night air. The Hudson below lapped itself with the unsteady flux of a channeling river.

"Don't cry, Oliver." Rose stroked her son, but he couldn't feel her touch at all. "We plugged you back into life, but now it's time for you to live it."

"No," he stammered, "it's my time to end it."

"Oliver, you haven't even started to live yet," Lothar said.

"And you have this young daughter," Piotr said with a wistfulness everyone understood. "And there is so much light in her, and life ahead of you."

"And you are finally writing something important," Primo said.

Oliver's body began to quake as if shivering from the cold. But this was a shudder unrelated to the weather. It came from the temperature inside, not out. "There is so much that is missing and has been lost forever," he said.

"Nothing and nobody is forever, Oliver. And that discovery, which is a sad truth about humanity, is not terrible," Lothar said. "The secret of survival is that many things can be survived. Men and women have always been adaptive creatures. Life is precious, even with all that's missing. If we have taught you anything, that is what it should be."

"There is pain, Oliver," Jerzy said as a late-night 747 roared overhead, "but there is also a party. You have to be able to cope with one, and show up at the other."

"I am alone."

"There is someone behind that light who you haven't let in," Rose said, her arms parallel with the beam. "Samantha didn't come back to you forever, and you wouldn't have wanted her as a ghost. The same is true with us. But that young girl who is over there in the lighthouse, your daughter, is real, and very much alive."

"Our passport is expiring soon," Lothar said. "We too will shortly fly away."

"But we're not going anywhere if this is what you want for yourself," Primo said. "The ancient Golem lived as long as the Jews of Prague were in danger. And you are still a danger to yourself. We cannot leave you like this."

With his daughter shadowing his every facial move, Oliver's face took on the battle-weary, spastic fatigue of someone who hadn't slept in months, which was largely true. He had been too busy typing and recalling memories—some his own, the rest on loan—to sleep. Now he looked back at the lighthouse, staring down its beam, searching through the cylinder of light for his brave daughter, the projectionist at the other end. Not far from the lighthouse, he locked in on the place where he and Samantha had committed themselves to spending their lives together. It was now a black, barren patch of damp grass and submerged rock in the high tide of midnight.

Shrieking voices called out from the ebony horizon; a mournful echo that didn't belong to any of the Golems who were hovering around him, whose mouths were closed and eyes wide open, luminous dips and shadows on their drawn faces. The cables on the bridge appeared to him as electric barbed wire. The mist that settled over New Jersey became the remains of human smoke. The water towers that commanded the rooftops of Manhattan were watchtowers—empty of water, overflowing with hate.

"The gun, Oliver," the parents said.

"The gun, Oliver," the Golems repeated in unison.

Then came the plunge. There was no way to prevent it; anything would have slipped through the Golems' arms. But this fall from grace was necessary in order for Oliver Levin to live. The gun and the broken glass dropped into the Hudson River, one after the other, each sending up its own tiny cascade, sinking beyond any hope of future rescue, out of range of any lighthouse beam.

35

IT WAS THEIR LAST SUPPER—NOW AND FOREVER. That was also true of the first Passover of Christianity, a dinnertime meal shared by Jesus and his disciples. They would never dine all together like that again.

The same thing happened at Oliver Levin's brownstone on Edgar Allan Poe Street—without the duplicity and crucifixion interlude. There were eight Golems and a father and a daughter sitting down for a Passover seder. Next year Oliver and Ariel would perhaps invite other guests, human ones, to the seder—Evelyn Eisenberg, Tanya Green, and maybe even Alejandro, who wasn't Jewish but who would work his way back into the lives of this family, as caretaker and friend.

Oliver hadn't hosted many seders before. In fact, since Samantha left—the first time—he hadn't attended any Passover meals, neither for the first night nor the second. Ariel would head off to the home of one of her friends, where there would be tables overflowing with food and family. The Levins were always outnumbered in this regard, and that's why Ariel never turned down any invitation and loved sitting next to somebody's grandfather or grandmother, a cranky uncle, an old aunt, a crotchety, black-sheep cousin. There was simply no real family in her life. During Passovers and Thanksgivings she couldn't get enough of borrowed, makeshift ones.

Oliver, of course, was invited to these homes as well, but he graciously declined. He chose instead to stay home or go off by himself to chow on Chinese noodles at Ollie's or thin-crusted pizza at Ray's.

But this year, and particularly this night, was somehow different from all the other nights of Jewish neglect in his past. This was a time to celebrate and commemorate. A time to think about the Exodus and emancipation—for his forebears and himself. An evening of reflection about the once-enslaved Jews of Egypt, those bronzed, lashed followers of Joseph who ended up as unrequited pyramid builders. And by contrast and transitivity, and also sheer proximity to the dead writers who haunted his home, tonight was to be an early observance of Yom HaShoah—Holocaust Remembrance Day. The Golems wouldn't be here in Gotham for that much longer. And the Haggadah only tells one Jewish tragedy, and by all reckonings, not the worst one by a long shot.

Oliver reasoned that there ought to be a ritual meal and a designated book that properly honored and commemorated the murder of the Six Million. The unwritten tombstones, monuments, and artifacts were not suitable to tell the story on their own.

"The camps were worse than the pyramids," he said. "And Zyklon B was far more poisonous than any plague."

The Golems, writers all, lived as long as they did in order to tell their stories. And when they no longer could, or when the story began to take on intolerably less tragic dimensions, there was no longer any reason to live. For this reason, beside the traditional

Haggadah, Oliver made sure that the place settings also included each author's body of work. The seder table had been transformed into a lending library, ensuring that on this night, slavery and genocide were given equal billing. And on the seder plate itself, in place of the traditional bitter herbs and mortar recipes, Oliver had substituted potato peels, watery soups, an old onion, and tasteless, leavened bread that had all the density of clay sculptures fresh out of the kiln. The true fruits of their *Arbeit*.

Oliver also arranged to have an especially long table brought into his home for the seder. He sat at one end, next to his mother. Lothar was at the other end, with Ariel right beside him. The Golems filled in both sides. There were yarmulkas, kiddush cups, and stacks of matzos. A large, gold-plated chalice with curious Grecian engravings served as the Elijah cup. It was filled to the top to quench the thirst of yet another ghost, who was expected to drop in toward the end of the evening. There was a white, crushed-velvet matzo bag that would eventually be used to hide the *afikomen*. Jerzy, who came dressed as a butler, wanted that job. Oliver decided that he would let Lothar lead the seder, to honor the way it was when Oliver was a boy. Passover had been meaningful to him back then. Lothar and Rose Levin's home, so underrepresented by family, was nonetheless overpopulated by local Floridians, strangers without seders of their own.

"To honor the Exodus," Lothar would say, "you have to make a home for those who are still wandering in the desert."

Oliver didn't exactly know what that meant when he was younger. All he knew, even back then—long before Ariel came to the same conclusion—was how much the Levins were cursed with insufficient numbers. There were simply not enough bodies around to call family. Instead they recruited from the outside, bringing in Jews who were even more deprived, all bottom-fishing for family, selecting from the taxi squad, the bench sitters without their own benches.

Now, as the head of his own household, Oliver reflected on how his parents, then only recently removed from the concentration camps and the bloody forests, had understood the moral imperatives of caring for strangers. They could have been selfish, but they weren't. And they had all the entitlement in the world to be angry, and they were not that, either.

Despite everything that had happened, Lothar and Rose still had hope for the future—just not theirs. They wanted better for Oliver; they just didn't know how to make it so, recognizing their own limitations. They believed that if they influenced him too much, he would only know their world, which had nothing in common with the new one he had been born into. There was no way to filter out the toxic effects of what they had witnessed. Yet, by ignoring him for his own good, they were also abandoning him—even as they all lived in the same house. And, even worse than that, he would know nothing of his birthright, the legacy he was morally obligated at least to remember and pass on to his own children.

As parents they wanted him somehow to know, and at the same time, to also never know. Parents always want it both ways. To screen out the unpleasant thread of family history, and make a tapestry out of the rest. But true stories rebel against such attempts at beautification and redaction. All of it has to come out—the nasty and the chaste—no matter how much silence and pressure are placed on keeping it short and light.

Lothar and Rose were acutely aware of this contradiction: wanting their son spared and yet knowing that too much separation from the story would be a sin. And that paradox, in spite of all their own improbable courage and hope, ultimately planted the seeds of suicide, adding yet another tragic chapter to the story they would have wished had come out differently.

And so, in keeping with the family tradition, Oliver, for the first time, opened his home to family and strangers. And he was pleased at how simple and natural it felt. By filling his home, even with those who existed only in air, there was a comfort in numbers, and a new sense of self.

It was springtime in New York. It took a while to restore order in Manhattan and beyond. The Golems showed themselves to be quite effective and resourceful maintenance men. Magic often works both ways—in the upheaval, and in the cleanup. Even Elie's hair returned to its natural color.

Central Park was blooming with seasonal flowers and shade that had returned to the trees. There were cherry blossoms growing in Riverside Park, bright purple leaves popping with buds but not with actual cherries. All along the curbs, shrubs were now present where there had been slush. Edgar Allan Poe Street welcomed back some of its foliage, as well. Daylight monopolized more of each day. The bloodshot amber sunset over the Hudson, with its streaky mists of clouds, gave Manhattan the gloss of an island paradise, temporarily relieving the city of its codependency on Gothic grime. Oliver's Levin's brownstone received regular and very much welcomed beams of golden sunlight.

Perhaps it was the time of the year, or this special occasion, but Lothar finally decided to assert himself in his son's home. For the last several months he had taken many humbling backseats to his more famous Golem brethren. He admired them all—always had, in fact—and wanted some of their literary genius to rub off on his son. But tonight he was fully in charge. His reclining position at the head of the table symbolized that this was his seder. And he couldn't have had a more distinguished array of guests—dead or alive.

"All right," he said removing his eyeglasses and peering officiously down the length of the table like a benevolent chairman of the board. "It is now time for the four questions. Ariel, you are the youngest, and this should be your job, but I have a better idea. This is, after all, a special seder. In no other house in Manhattan—or anywhere, for that matter—will there be one quite like it. So we should let the other homes ask the standard, unoriginal questions. The guests at this table have better, smarter ones on our minds, because we have spent our lives, and even some of our deaths, asking the most difficult and unanswerable questions of all. Maybe it's time for us to ask them again."

"Sorry for the change in the program, Ariel," Rose said. "But we do have another part for you to play."

Ariel's face brightened.

"Yes, we do indeed," her grandfather said. And from behind his chair he pulled out the coarsely blue, unshellacked violin. "Please, play for us," he asked, holding the violin up like a seder plate. "Maestro, bring music to our questions. Give us the proper sound track, create the right mood for what we want to know."

Ariel stood up, retrieved the instrument, crouched forward, and began her dramatic, melancholy strokes. And as the music once more settled and soothed this home, the Golems asked these questions, without stopping after only four. There were indeed so many questions, and this was a singular and different night. And these questions would never be asked by this assembled group again, because after this night, and this seder, these guests would themselves be just another question.

"How is it that mankind continues on when there are so many reasons not to?" Lothar began.

"How can hate and love spring from the same parts of the soul, while one is a cancer and the other is a cure?" Paul asked.

"Why is the world so impatient, indifferent, and arrogant when it comes to someone else's suffering?" Primo wondered.

"Why must we treat people with such hostility and neglect that it becomes necessary for them to hide from others, and themselves, with such boiling rage?" Jerzy asked.

"Why would a God who is all-powerful not intervene to save his children unless he was a monster of a parent?" Jean sneered.

"How is it possible for a parent to outlive a child?" Piotr asked.

"Why do we have to create so much noise that it becomes impossible for us to hear life's music?" Tadeusz wondered, then nodded at Ariel, who was serenading them all with repeated bars of "Invitation to the Dead."

"Why does science continue to invent toys that have no purpose other than to kill everyone, including our children?" Primo asked.

"Why do we repeat our mistakes so easily, yet forget how to love and care for each other as if we never knew how?" Rose asked.

The questions, unrehearsed and innumerable, poured out one after another. Oliver tried to remember them all—for some future occasion. Perhaps, like the spruced-up seder plate, these addenda to the Haggadah would become a tradition in his home, which the Levins would from now on recite faithfully each year.

As the evening proceeded the Golems, deprived of their bodies, had difficulty holding their liquor. The fourth cup of wine ended up provoking all sorts of immoderate conversation.

Piotr started it off with a reasonable question, given the credentials and constitution of this gathered crowd. "Do you think Elijah will come? That sure is a big cup of wine over there for just one ghost to drink all by himself." Piotr giggled and covered his mouth, but his hiccup could not be corralled.

"I predict he'll never show his face around here," Jean said. "After all, he knows who's in this house. He'll pass right over us and instead go to all the other homes where they don't know him personally."

Oliver and Ariel glanced at each other with surprised faces.

"You know Elijah?" Ariel asked, nearly gasping. "*The* Elijah?"

"No, Elijah Muhammad. Of course, that Elijah," Jerzy said. "He's one of us, just a ghost—no different—although he's a terrible writer."

"That's true," Jean said. "Not a poet, just a prophet."

"Come on," Paul scoffed. "He's not at all like us."

"Sure, he's a big-shot prophet, and none of us are that," Tadeusz said. "We're just former writers who are all now dead."

"Honestly, I think he is so overrated," Jean said dismissively. "I don't see why he was given such an important job."

"He'll never work out as an advance man for the Messiah," Jerzy predicted. "I'll tell you that."

"You're right, you're right," Jean agreed. "Not him. He's a nobody. No special talents. Why God picked him is a mystery to me."

"He had very good connections," Piotr said. "That's what I hear."

"He can't make the peace, or he'll never be able to keep the peace," Jean exclaimed. "That's why the Messiah will never come. It's all Elijah's fault."

Tadeusz and Jerzy nodded their heads in agreement. Oliver tried to follow the conversation, moving from voice to voice as though kindling a row of candles.

"This is so cool," Ariel yelled across the table to her father. "They know Elijah!"

"You realize we're going mad, don't you?" Oliver shouted back. "That's what this is all about these past few months. Father and daughter bonding together by way of insanity."

Ariel didn't agree. "Do you really not think he'll come?" Ariel asked them all.

"The Messiah?" Primo replied.

"No, Elijah, tonight," Ariel said somberly. "Will he not show up here tonight, in this house, for Passover?"

"Sure he'll come, dear, maybe for a short visit," Rose replied. "At least to say hello."

Just then there was a knock at the door, which isn't even an approved stage entrance for Elijah, anyway. Nowhere in the tradition is there supposed to be any knocking. The visit all depends on faith— good faith and blind faith. The household opens the door for Elijah at the appointed time of the seder—whether he's ready or not, whether he's out there or not. Children then stand before the brimming cup and imagine that an imperceptible sip has just taken place before their eyes. But perhaps on this night, in this home, Elijah would make an exception. Here, at this seder, he would actually knock and announce his ghostly arrival. They had all traveled from the same otherworld. This was the one home where it was safe to demystify and just be himself.

"Who could that be?" Ariel wondered out loud.

"Answer the door, Ariel," Lothar, the leader of the seder, instructed his granddaughter.

Ariel rushed to the door without fear, and also without asking who was standing on the other side. She didn't even glance through the semi-opaque, funhouse glass. Acting on instinct and faith alone, she simply turned the knob and pulled the creaking door open. The Golems, now standing by their chairs, got a good look and smiled.

"I told you so!" Jean boasted.

Yes, Elijah had indeed missed this house as well, in the same way that he probably skips a good many of the rest. So powerful is the impulse to believe in miracles and higher powers. The human eye willfully deceives itself by accepting as true what it simply can't see.

There was another guest that night, and he too was indeed a ghost.

Rabbi Vered, that old kook of a cleric from Miami Beach, entered the parlor floor and stood before the Levins and the specters of their dead friends.

"Sheldon Vered," Lothar said, "what are you doing here?"

Oliver hugged his daughter, whispered in her ear, and explained who it was she had just allowed in.

"What happened to you?" Rose asked. "You are like us?"

"More so than you could ever imagine," the rabbi replied.

"What do you mean?" Lothar said. "You are a ghost; we can see that."

"Not just a ghost, but a ghost with your same history."

"The camps?" Rose said.

"And the suicide," the rabbi replied.

"You too, Rabbi?" Oliver asked. He then turned to Ariel and wondered, half accusingly, "Are you responsible for him coming back, too?"

"No way!" Ariel swore. "This wasn't me. I don't know how he got here."

"Yes, me too," the rabbi said, with resigned sadness in his voice. When he was alive, Rabbi Vered had been nothing but a tennis-playing rabbinical joker. His ghost was apparently more thoughtful and serious. "One day, after hitting some tennis balls in a game of doubles at South Shore Park, I impaled myself on the chain-link fence that surrounded the court. I took a running start, climbed up as if I was trying to escape or electrocute myself, and then fell on the barbed-wire spikes as if they were daggers."

"Why?" Rose asked. "You weren't a writer like most of the Golems in this house."

"True, but I was a rabbi, which may have been even a worse job for a survivor to have in the post-Holocaust age. Much worse than an artist, to my mind. How could I have been expected to teach about God and his ways, his bad moods, his often vengeful and irrational acts? Me, a survivor of a death camp, leading a congregation that reads the papers and already knows how cruel and indifferent this God can be. How do you sell God to a world that has heard of Auschwitz?"

"I like this rabbi," Jean glowed. "Now, *his* services I would gladly attend."

Rabbi Vered continued. "An least an artist has the freedom—the responsibility, in fact—to become a conscientious objector, to practice religious disobedience. The artist can function as the disloyal opposition to God. But what outlet for dissent does a rabbi have?"

"I think you did okay for yourself, Vered," Rose reminded him. "No shiksa or shellfish was safe when you were around."

"Yes, but God still wasn't listening to my protest, and perhaps that's why I joined you, after all. Why did any of us end our own lives? I could ask the same question of each of you. And you would each return the same blank stare. There are so many reasons to say good-bye, and not enough to remain. I heard you ask this question before, Lothar. To answer you, in the end I wasn't going to be outdone by the two of you. After I killed myself with that dramatic tennis stigmata, Miami Beach forgot about you altogether."

"That's okay with us, Rabbi," Lothar said. "We didn't want to be canonized; we just wanted to end our pain. We're happy for you, I guess. The tennis court was always your true pulpit, anyway."

Rose and Oliver laughed, the sounds mixing in their heads with the giggling of a mother and son decades before. There was a brief time, when Oliver was very young, when the raw material of life had seemed lighter to Rose. Only later did she decide that shared maternal moments of laughter were dangerous for her son, because they would bind him to his parents in ways that life would eventually undo.

"Are we finished yet with the seder?" Rabbi Vered asked breathlessly. "Am I too late? Who found the *afikomen*? I love that part."

"No, you're not late, Rabbi," Oliver said, welcoming his old rabbi inside his brownstone and escorting him over to the table.

"Yes, come," Primo offered. "But when we are finished here, we will have a favor to ask of you, Rabbi."

"What is it? Anything for you guys," he said, clapping his hands together. "I'm honored to be in this company."

"Yes, a favor, Rabbi," Paul said. "It is a proper rabbinical role for you. The kind of task God himself would have given to Moses."

The rabbi's outsize ego was inflating like an airbag that had just been triggered by a head-on collision.

"Tell me," he urged. "What can I do?"

And his old congregant who was now leading this paranormal seder said, "Take us out of Gotham, Rabbi, and lead us back to Miami." Lothar looked not at Rabbi Vered but directly at his son and granddaughter. "Yes, lead us back to Miami."

36

OLIVER AND I TOOK THE PLANE. THE GOLEMS arranged for their own transportation. And we all, in our own way, wound up in Miami Beach.

It was the scene of the crime—not the Holocaust, but what came after for my family. If not for the suicides, everything else about Oliver's life, and the way he responded to the world—what he brought to it and what he walked away from when his dreams became broken—would have been different, too. That's probably why we were all meeting in Miami: because Oliver couldn't go forward—with or without the Golems—unless we retraced the steps of how he got lost in the first place.

The Golems wandered around the South Beach Art Deco District like old Jews complaining about the service at Wolfie's. There was a time, Oliver told me, when many of the people who lived in South Beach were Jewish refugees and survivors of the Holocaust. But that's not true anymore, which is why the Golems, aside from being invisible, didn't blend in so well on this trip. They had the right accents, and wore gold-crested cabana clothing with white fishermen's hats—all except for Jerzy, who was attired like a *Baywatch* lifeguard. And for cadaverous people, they somehow managed to tan.

Yet they still stood out from this crowd. It wasn't just because they were dead, but because Jewish grandparents didn't live in Miami Beach anymore. The accents had died out a long time ago, like the final gasp of a fading echo. Today when you hear broken English in South Florida, it usually comes from Cubans, and not Jews.

There is still a Jewish community, of course, but most live farther north, in Broward and West Palm Beach Counties. South Beach, where the Jewish refugees used to be, is now the home of partying homosexuals, fashion models, and German photographers, and—for the short while that we were in town—golems who used to live in Gotham.

"I can't stand this place," Jean said.

"I know. The humidity is murder," Tadeusz said. "It's like an oven in this city. How could so many Holocaust survivors have once lived in a place this hot? It makes no sense to me. You'd think they would have wanted to stay away from ovens."

"It's not the weather that makes me sick," Jean explained. "It's the sound of all those Nazis."

"They're not Nazis," Paul scolded. "You know better than that! Just because a man has a German accent and a fancy Leica camera and his name is Helmut doesn't mean he's SS. I wrote poetry in this language, after all."

"The models are luscious, that's all I have to say," Jerzy said, wearing yet another outfit of white tennis shorts, white cotton polo shirt, and white zinc oxide ointment smeared all over his nose. "And the beaches are topless. I hear Twelfth Street is where all the tops come off," he said.

"I think yours came off a long time ago," Jean said.

The material world of Miami Beach had come up against the spirits of refugees past. But the Golems were now officially out of the rescue business. They couldn't be tempted back. Like the Jews who once lived here, these ghosts were now retired. It would be more likely for them to be found on the golf courses and tennis courts, or in the card rooms and jai-alai frontons, than haunting Miami Beach with their miracles, makeovers, and spiritual largess.

It's not that the Golems didn't see anything wrong with Miami Beach that needed fixing, because they did complain about almost everything they saw.

"Everyone is too thin," my grandfather said.

"And too tall," my grandmother added.

"And they smoke too much," Tadeusz observed.

"Where are the synagogues?" Primo wondered.

"And the kosher butchers?" Paul asked.

"And where are the small children?" Piotr asked. "You don't see young families."

"There is too much neon and not enough books." Primo shook his head.

"There were never any books," Lothar muttered.

"The only thing that they have better is the sunscreen, and the women," Jerzy conceded.

The Golems would have loved to do for South Beach what they had already done for the Upper West Side of Manhattan. They could have brought the shtetl back to the Art Deco District and made it look the way it did before anyone even noticed that these buildings were art deco, back when the district was just called Washington Avenue on Miami Beach. The Golems could have fixed it so that the hot sounds could be tuned to klezmer instead of house, reggae, conga, or salsa. And they would have replaced some of those Thai and Vietnamese restaurants with Jewish delis. Where there were now locations for modeling shoots they could have rebuilt synagogues. And they might even have brought back some golem version of

Jackie Gleason and gotten rid of all those all-night, velvet-roped, beautiful-peopled hangouts.

But instead the Golems spent their time in Miami as tourists, acting like they had no special powers at all. They were winding down. Getting ready to go back to wherever it had been they were before I sent for them. Miami might need help, but the Golems weren't taking on any new projects. The cigarettes and tattoos would still burn, and the Torahs would never get to fly around inside any of Miami's synagogues.

Oliver and I still didn't know why they had brought us down here. If the Golems were going to leave, why couldn't they just do it from Manhattan? Was Miami Beach some kind of special portal? A magic meeting place for visitors from the otherworld? A convention center for the dead, as opposed to schoolteachers or teamsters?

They didn't tell us. While we were waiting to find out, Oliver dragged me around to all the places he used to go when he was a kid, when he was my age and even younger, when my grandparents were still alive. He had never taken me to Miami before, so it was pretty cool to see all these things. The parks he played in. The schools he went to. The beaches. The playgrounds and ball fields. The canals where he fished and water-skied. The old high-rise building that he and my grandparents lived in. All the neighborhood hangouts.

"And over there, that's where we used to play tackle football," he said, pointing out a thin patch of mixed dirt and concrete, sprinkler heads sticking out from the ground like aquatic mushrooms.

It's strange visiting places where your parents lived as kids, because it's hard to imagine them not as your parents, but as children with parents of their own. It makes it even harder when you never knew your grandparents, like me, and when your father couldn't father. I can't picture Oliver any other way than the way I have known him. Kids need to be able to slip their hands into the larger hands of their parents without having to look up to make sure they are still there. The contact should be made on instinct alone.

That wasn't true with me and Oliver. At least not before now.

Hand holding never led to a safe feeling. And it was the same way with Oliver and his parents. Every time Oliver held my hand and squeezed, I could feel him crying, even though his eyes were dry. That's why I conjured the Golems. To stop his crying.

But here he was, taking me around Miami Beach, holding my hand with self-assurance, his face bright not from the Miami sun, but its memories. For some reason everything about his childhood was now finally okay. He had come back, not to shout, but to listen. He was able to look around without the blinders and blackout goggles of the Holocaust. He could step more freely, look ahead, and not only down. The sky wasn't falling, and it wasn't full of human smoke, either. He could hear what was being said, and all that was unspoken, just by listening to the silences. And if he heard nothing at all, that was okay, too.

It took his parents coming back to make it possible to finally know them—not as they are now, but as they were back then. The Golems were like a mirror image of themselves when they were alive—the same, yet inverted, upside down, imperfect clones, the left side was not exactly the same as the right. The whole purpose of ghosts being around is to remind you of what you've done wrong. But sometimes they also give you a way out. Oliver was doing his best to make sure that he didn't miss any of the signs.

The world of my grandparents was always mysterious, but not any more so than a world where there are actual golems—the ones who both rescue and leave behind moral lessons. Because golems do live in each of us, whether we bring them on with the help of the kabbalah, or in some other way. Each of us has private golems; dybbuks from the dead. They are always there, even if we don't know why, or what they want. You don't have to live on Edgar Allan Poe Street to have an Altneuschul of your very own—an attic where the Ark is empty but the magic is always full of surprise.

The interior world is always more interesting and exciting, anyway. It's where the best dreams get played out, where the most important messages are delivered, and where our special talents sink into our soul until it's time for a live, solo performance. Maybe I was always supposed to be a klezmer violinist—whether the Golems had showed up or not. Maybe that's the gift they left for me instead of real grandparents. The violin is my legacy, just as the story belongs to my father.

The last stop on Oliver's Miami tour was the gravesites where Lothar and Rose were buried. He had never said Kaddish, not even the first time. He never did his duty as a son. And it never bothered him, either, until now.

Somehow he felt that there was no going forward unless he stood before their graves and remembered them. Their spirits may have been portable, but their bones were not. They had come to him as ghosts. But he still owed them a visit of his own.

At Lakeview Memorial—the flat, open cemetery where my grandparents were buried—we stood in front of their graves. A brass plaque marked where their bodies rested. Nearby was a small tree that threw a tiny shadow of shade over their graves—pretty lame protection from the scalding sun, like the tree in *A Charlie Brown Christmas*. A puff of a breeze brushed against our faces and then never came back, as if a door had opened for a second and then closed immediately.

"You okay, Oliver?"

"Yes. Nice spot, don't you think?" he said, keeping, as always, his true feelings inside, as if he was simply commenting on the weather instead of admitting that we were in Miami, standing on special ground.

I started to cry. I was fourteen, and I was here with my father after all that had happened to our family. And how could I not cry, since he wasn't, or couldn't? Somebody had to. But then I heard the sounds of other tears dropping from behind us like light rain, and I realized that my grandparents were back there—crying for their son, and saying Kaddish for themselves, because he never got around to it, and probably never would.

As Oliver and I headed back to the car, he said, "We should probably see about getting a plot for Samantha. What do you say?" I took out my violin and played "Invitation to the Dead" one more time. Oliver wasn't getting married, at least not yet, and I wasn't inviting Lothar and Rose to any wedding of any family they knew. But maybe Oliver was being born all over again. This piece of music might also substitute as an invitation to a *pidyon haben*—the redemption of the firstborn. Their son was getting a second chance, and that was something to celebrate, too. They should be there to see it, if they weren't there already.

The next day, late in the afternoon, shortly before it got dark, Oliver and I met the Golems on the bronzed, crystal sand of Miami Beach. The beach looked cold and hard as it got ready for each returning wave. There was only one other person on the beach: A tourist who had fallen asleep suddenly awoke with sand all over his body like a piece of breaded veal. At first he was bewildered; then he realized that he was late for something and ran off, dragging his towel behind him like a tail he couldn't control.

The sky was dark with fast-moving clouds along a horizon that hung low and didn't seem to stretch too far. The wind, which couldn't decide on a direction, was kicking up a sandstorm of beach. The clouds were swollen with gathering rain and thunder that for now was only grumbling but soon would have more to say. There were so many noisy clouds, with dark, purple shapes, that Piotr couldn't stop himself from looking up to see the faces, and hear the tears, of the children.

For a while none of us had anything to say. The first to speak would be the one to start this game of good-bye, which nobody wanted to play. Finally Oliver began. "You're all leaving now, aren't you?"

He was speaking to them all, but he was looking directly at his parents.

"Yes," my grandfather replied. "This is now our time to go."

"Our work is finished," Primo said. "All along you had nothing to fear from anyone but yourself. There is no danger anymore."

"Yes, you are finally safe," Paul said.

"The same was true with the original Golem," Piotr explained. "Only when Prague was safe and there was no further danger did Rabbi Loew return the monster to lifeless clay."

"The golems inside you now need to die, Oliver," Primo said. "We gave them life by pushing you to search for truth, to know yourself and where you come from, and how to live, *really* live, for tomorrow. Now the truth is a little better understood by you, and so it is time for the golems to leave this world, and face death yet again. All of life starts with an *aleph* on the forehead and ends with a *shin* in the mouth."

"Let go of us, son," Lothar said. "And then we can let go of you."

"It's now time to finally move on," Jerzy said. "For all of us, but most especially you."

"I hate that advice," Jean steamed softly, "but it is true."

"But moving on is the enemy of remembering," Oliver said, his hair blowing fiercely, standing nearly straight up, as if propped by a sand dune.

"And not moving on is the enemy of life," Primo said.

"Then why did you come?" Oliver pleaded. "You rescued me, but what did you want in return?"

"To be remembered," my grandfather answered, "by you, and by the world."

"Now go on and live your life, Oliver," my grandmother said. "Please be gentle with yourself."

"And remember to never forget," Jean warned, "which isn't the same thing as shouting, Never Again!"

My grandparents then swallowed up their son in a spiral of floating stardust, the kind of hug that wasn't possible when they were alive, when they didn't know how to hug—even though that's when Oliver needed it the most. After they were finished, they gave me a bath in the same swirl of untouchable, ambient love.

And when the Levins were through, the Golems lifted themselves up into the Miami night like mist sucked into the vacuum of twilight. A vapor trail disappearing inside a tropical sky. They were fiery comets streaking over spotted clouds, splitting the heavens like an injection from a syringe—an antidote for the unforgivable, and for the unforgiven. Black clouds turned into dangling white beards; sunshine leering, looming; and Piotr's baby carriage, like the tail of a kite, struggled to keep pace from behind.

Oliver and I felt so small standing below on the sand. Within seconds the Golems drifted away. The two of us still stood there, waving good-bye.

∽∘∾

After all these years Oliver was rusty reading out loud. But I wasn't too old to listen. I had missed having my father read to me at night, and now that he was ready, I was more than happy to lie there and have him sing me to sleep with a bedtime story. Sometimes his voice would crack, because in so many ways, the story about the Golems of Gotham, and the lighthouse, and the bridge, was so sad. And its ending, which was very cool, still wasn't a happy one. There is so much in life that we can't ever know, and while books can end, the stories inside them always leave questions—right from the very beginning, and without obvious answers.

Maybe that's what happens when twilight worlds collide, souls bump into one another like crossing stars, and the supernatural begins to look pretty ordinary. The sky folds into itself, a window opens, and that's the cue for all the angels, dybbuks, and golems from the otherworld to reenter ours, turning the longing into something real.

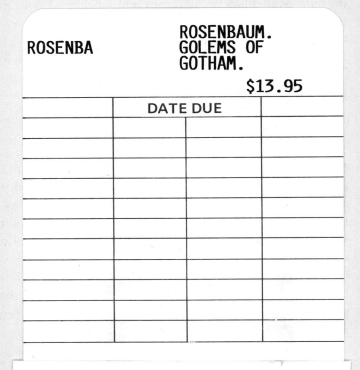